"Ye won't be sa... me clean out of...

Harris traded her glare for glare.

Then, unexpectedly, one corner of his wide, mobile mouth curved into an irresistible grin. "Since we're each bent on driving the other mad, maybe we ought to find a nice cozy lunatic asylum and settle down."

"This is nothing to joke about." The unbidden chuckle that burst out of Jenny belied her words. "We're at each other all the time. Ye and I never would have made a happy match, even with all the money in the world."

"Don't ye believe it, lass," Harris replied in quiet earnest. A stray ray of rising sun pierced the foliage, burnishing his hair like new copper and lighting the rich warmth of his hazel eyes.

It cost Jenny every crumb of her self-control to keep from bolting straight into his arms....

Dear Reader,

In *The Bonny Bride* by award-winning author Deborah Hale, a poor young woman sets sail for Nova Scotia from England as a mail-order bride to a wealthy man, yet meets her true soul mate on board the ship. Will she choose love or money? Margaret Moore, who also writes mainstream historicals for Avon Books, returns with *A Warrior's Kiss,* a passionate marriage-of-convenience story and the next in her ongoing medieval WARRIOR series. Theresa Michaels's new Western, *Once a Hero,* is a gripping and emotion-filled story about a cowboy who rescues a female fugitive and unexpectedly falls in love with her as they go in search of a lost treasure. For readers who enjoy discovering new writers, *The Virgin Spring* by Golden Heart winner Debra Lee Brown is for you. Here, a Scottish laird finds an amnesiac woman beside a spring and must resist his desire for her, as he believes she is forbidden to him.

For the next two months we are going to be asking readers to let us know what you are looking for from Harlequin Historicals. We hope you'll participate by sending your ideas to us at:

Harlequin Historicals
300 E. 42nd St.
New York, NY 10017

Q. What do you like about Harlequin Historicals?
_____
_____

Q. What *don't* you like about Harlequin Historicals?
_____
_____

Whatever your tastes in reading, you'll be sure to find a romantic journey back to the past between the covers of a Harlequin Historicals novel. We hope you'll join us next month, too!

Sincerely,

Tracy Farrell,
Senior Editor

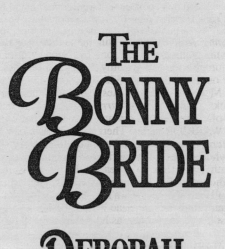

THE BONNY BRIDE

DEBORAH HALE

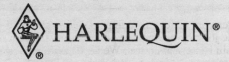

HARLEQUIN®

TORONTO • NEW YORK • LONDON
AMSTERDAM • PARIS • SYDNEY • HAMBURG
STOCKHOLM • ATHENS • TOKYO • MILAN • MADRID
PRAGUE • WARSAW • BUDAPEST • AUCKLAND

ISBN 0-373-29103-5

THE BONNY BRIDE

This edition published by arrangement with Harlequin Books S.A.

® and TM are trademarks of the publisher. Trademarks indicated with
® are registered in the United States Patent and Trademark Office, the
Canadian Trade Marks Office and in other countries.

Visit us at www.romance.net

Printed in U.S.A.

Please address questions and book requests to:
Harlequin Reader Service
U.S.: 3010 Walden Ave., P.O. Box 1325, Buffalo, NY 14269
Canadian: P.O. Box 609, Fort Erie, Ont. L2A 5X3

In memory of my great-great-great-grandparents, John and Ann Graham, who also fell in love on their way to the Miramichi. And my grandfather, Edwin Graham, who told me their story and many others, igniting my enduring passion for the past.

Chapter One

"Where can they be? They should be here by now."
For the tenth time in half an hour, Jenny Lennox turned
from the quay of Kirkcudbright's small harbor. Her anxious eye scanned the slate-roofed buildings of the town,
searching for some sign of her traveling companions.

"Wist, wist ye now." Jenny tried to calm herself. "I
ken they'll be here soon enough. Mr. Walker never believed in getting anywhere too soon, and his wife isn't a
hustler, either."

Indeed, it was a running joke in Dalbeattie that the family should change their surname to Plodder. Still, on this
of all days, couldn't they have come a few minutes early?

"They should be here by now," she insisted yet again,
as though her words were an incantation to conjure the
tardy Walkers out of thin air. "The tide's coming in fast.
We'll have to board before long."

Salty Atlantic waters swelled into the mouth of the River
Nith, covering Kirkcudbright's muddy tidal flats. A hundred and fifty years earlier, Covenanter girls no older than
Jenny had been tied to stakes and drowned by the inexorable Solway tides as punishment for their religious beliefs.
To this day the gulls grieved those martyred souls, wheel-

ing and diving in the clear June sky. Their shrill keening struck a mournful counterpoint to the bass dirge of the sea.

Not I, thought Jenny, as she watched a boom of timber being floated ashore from one of the ships moored out in the channel. *I'll not be martyred—tied to some bleak upland croft and slowly drowned by a life of drudgery.* From the time she could hold a broom, Jenny had taken on the work of a grown woman. Toiling side by side with her mother, she'd cooked, cleaned, spun, churned, washed and mended. Not to mention minding the ever-increasing tribe of boys her parents had bred in their high box bed. Since her mother's death, full responsibility for the Lennox household had fallen on Jenny's slight shoulders. Today might be her only chance to escape.

The lighter barges were already beginning to ferry cargo out to the barque *St. Bride.* Word had come ashore that her master meant to weigh anchor when the tide shifted, roughly two hours hence. In two hours Jenny would be on her way to the New Brunswick colony and a new, better life. If only the Walkers would hurry up and get here!

She peered up the street again. Where could they be? A huge knot clenched in Jenny's stomach, as indigestible as her stepmother's oatmeal porritch. It had been many hours since she'd worried down a bowlful and taken tearful leave of her brothers. The older ones had masked their moist eyes with manly gruffness. Warning her not to fall into the ocean during the crossing, they'd begged her to write often—forgetting she didn't know how.

Wee Malcolm had clung to her skirts wailing fit to wake the dead, until manhandled into the cottage by their stepmother. If only she could have taken him with her, the babby she'd cared for like a mother ever since her own mother's death. Sinking down onto her new brass-bound cedar trunk, Jenny bit her lips together hard between her teeth. If the Walkers didn't soon come, she feared she might start bawling herself, pleading with her father to take her home again.

Unwelcome tears were just forming in Jenny's eyes when she spotted a familiar figure among the Kirkcudbright townsfolk. It was not Mag Walker, a big sowdy woman who outweighed her husband by nearly two stone. Rather a slender girl, wearing a gay bonnet and fashionable traveling outfit.

"Kirstie!" Jenny hailed her friend as she dodged through the crowd on the quayside. "Ye're a sight for sore eyes," she exclaimed. "Don't tell me ye've come all the way from Dalbeattie just to see me off?"

Kirsten Robertson was as close a friend as Jenny had made during her hardworking, restricted youth. Though her prosperous father owned Dalbeattie's granite quarry, Kirstie was not one to put on fine airs. One day, many years back, the Robertsons' housekeeper had brought the child along on her routine visit to buy eggs from Jenny's mother. After the two little girls struck up an acquaintance, Kirstie insisted on coming every time. When she got older, she took over the chore herself. Jenny had always looked forward to Kirstie's visits. They were practically her only chance to hear about school and town and the wide world beyond the Lennox farm.

"Jenny! Is it today ye're off?" Kirstie looked pleasantly astonished to meet her friend this far from home and so dressed up. "I've been the fortnight with my auntie in Dumfries. I didn't reckon ye were away for a while yet. What a bit of luck I got here to see ye off."

"What are ye doing in Kirkcudbright, then?" Jenny asked.

Blue as the day's clear sky, Kirstie Robertson's eyes twinkled with mirth. "Papa drove Harris Chisholm over to catch his boat, and he made me come along. It fretted Papa something fierce when Mr. Chisholm took it into his head to emigrate. He doesn't suppose he'll ever find as good a manager again.''

Hearing the name Harris Chisholm made Jenny's mouth pucker as though she'd just bitten into a crab apple. She'd often encountered Dalbeattie's most notorious misogynist at kirk. On those occasions, he'd acknowledged her with a frosty bow and thinly veiled contempt.

''Maybe yer pa was hoping ye'd make a match with Mr. Chisholm so he wouldn't go away,'' Jenny teased her friend. A rich man's daughter, and a very pretty one, Kirstie had her pick of suitors. However, she showed no interest in settling down anytime soon.

''Harris Chisholm!'' Kirstie gave an exasperated chuckle. ''Oh, he'd not be so bad if he didn't always fix me with that lairdly stare of his. It's plain he thinks I'm a fickle wee dolt.''

Jenny joined in her friend's laughter. She felt strangely lightened by the knowledge that Harris Chisholm was equally uncivil to lassies far richer and better educated than she.

''Did ye happen to pass Lowell and Mag Walker on the road?'' Jenny asked. ''I'm to travel with them and I'm getting a mite worried they'll not make it in time.''

Kirstie Robertson's blithe little face took on an unwontedly sober cast. ''The Lowell Walkers. Haven't ye heard? Lowell was harnessing that foul-tempered bay of his this morning when the wretched beast up and kicked him in the leg. Broke it in three places below the knee, I heard. Poor Mag is fretted he might lose it. They'll not be sailing today, if ever.''

''Oh.'' Jenny could feel the blood draining from her face. There was no hope of persuading her father to let her make the Atlantic crossing on her own. Her brother, Ross, was second mate on the brig *Bunessan*. He frequently wrote home lurid tales of the shiftless degenerates who made up his crew. Before Alexander Lennox would suffer his daughter to board the *St. Bride,* unchaperoned, he would sell himself into indentured servitude to repay her passage money.

She should have known this was too good to be true, Jenny chided herself. It had all worked out far too easily and smoothly—until now. When Roderick Douglas had written home for a bride, the other eligible lassies in Dalbeattie had been reluctant to accept. Some felt nervous of crossing the cold, wide ocean. Others could not abide the notion of parting with their families. Jenny had jumped at the chance to wed a man she'd once adored from afar. A man who was now a prosperous shipbuilder, able to give her the refined, affluent life she craved. Why had she let herself hope for something so miraculous, only to see her dream wreck on the shoals of reality?

Setting her mouth in a resolute line, Jenny squared her shoulders. It would take more than Lowell Walker's bad-tempered horse and her father's strict Presbyterian propriety to keep her from her bright destiny. She would find her way to Roderick Douglas even if it meant swimming the North Atlantic!

Kirstie slipped a comforting arm around Jenny's shoulder. "There must be someone else who'd offer to keep an eye on ye. Folks are awful good about that kind of thing. Let's go find the agent who booked yer passage and ask him to point out the other passengers to us. There might be a family going who'd be glad of some help with their wee ones."

Letting Kirstie lead her toward the agent, Jenny barely heard her friend's optimistic chatter. The man shook his head regretfully when Kirstie asked about other female passengers. Mag Walker and Jenny Lennox were the only women booked aboard the *St. Bride.*

The agent read off the names of the other half-dozen passengers. "Gregor McKinnon, Donald Beattie, Lowell

Walker, George Irving, Gavin Tweedie and Harris Chisholm.''

Fairly dancing at Jenny's elbow, Kirstie thanked the man
for his time.

''That's a mercy,'' she whispered. ''For a minute I
feared we were out of luck. I'll ask Mr. Chisholm to keep
an eye on ye during the crossing. Then we can just present
it to yer pa like it's all settled. Mr. Chisholm may be a
man and he does have a queer way about him. Still, when
all's said and done he's Dalbeattie born and goes to kirk
every Sunday. I ken he's the best ye can do at short notice.''

As though summoned by the deprecating remarks of his
employer's daughter, Harris Chisholm suddenly appeared,
head and shoulders towering above the harborside throng.
Jenny would have recognized him anywhere by his shock
of auburn hair. His long, lean face might have been handsome but for the striation of scars along his jawline and
his perpetual expression of cool disdain. Evidently on the
lookout for Kirsten, he strode toward the girls.

Giving her friend's hand a reassuring squeeze, Kirstie
muttered out of the corner of her mouth, ''Let me do the
asking. I've yet to meet the man I couldn't talk 'round.''

''Thank ye, Kirstie, but I'll speak to Mr. Chisholm myself.'' Jenny held her head high and tried to swallow the
lump of dismay in her throat. Wasn't it just like life, to
play this kind of cruel joke? Placing the power over her
whole future into the hands of a man who despised her.

It took Harris a moment to recognize the well-dressed
young lady standing beside his employer's daughter. He
wished Old Mr. Robertson hadn't insisted on bringing
Kirsten along. Harris had the uncomfortable conviction
that, behind her twinkling blue eyes, the irrepressible creature was laughing at him.

As he steeled himself to speak to the ladies, Miss Robertson's companion looked up at him. It was a gaze of singular scrutiny, as though he, Harris Chisholm, was the only man of consequence in the world. Never had he beheld or imagined a woman as lovely as Jenny Lennox looked at that moment.

He'd only ever seen her in a work dress and apron, or in her severe Presbyterian Sunday best. Today she wore a traveling gown and a matching pelisse of royal-blue. Trimmed with paler blue ribbons, her deep-brimmed straw bonnet served to focus his eyes upon her face.

The classic regularity of her features put him in mind of several white marble sculptures he'd seen in Edinburgh. How much more alluring such a visage looked in living color. Her skin had a luminous quality compounded of roses and cream. The pert delicacy of her upper lip contrasted bewitchingly with her full, almost pouty, lower lip. The warm red of ripe strawberries, together they made an eminently kissable combination. It was her gaze that held Harris transfixed, though. Whether by some fortunate reflection from her blue dress or the azure sky, her wide gray eyes had taken on a striking violet cast.

"Might I have a word with ye, Mr. Chisholm?" Her voice held more than a hint of asperity. Harris realized that, while he'd been gaping at her with such blatant admiration, Jenny Lennox had been speaking to him. Lost in the contemplation of her beauty, he hadn't heard a word.

"What's that?" Harris strove to compose his expression into proper gravity. "Ye're a ways from home today, Miss Lennox."

"I am," she replied, "and mean to go farther. I have a great favor to ask of ye, Mr. Chisholm."

So that was it. She wanted something. Why else would such a bonny lass look at him with anything less than aversion? He should be accustomed to it by now. Women always brought out the worst in him. Pretty young women like Jenny Lennox in particular. He'd grown up on a lonely hill croft north of Dalbeattie, with no one but his father and grandfather for company. Women were as foreign to him as creatures from another star. The only females of his intimate acquaintance lived in the pages of Walter Scott's novels—Flora MacIvor, Diana Vernon, and Ivanhoe's Rowena.

In dreams nurtured by Scott's epic romances, Harris had often imagined how sweet it might be to have a woman look at him tenderly, speak to him lovingly. When instead the lassies drew back in fright—or worse, pity—it hurt him. Out of his pain and anger he spoke coldly, or sharply.

That only made matters worse. He'd be much better off living in a place with as few women as possible, and those few safely married to other men. New Brunswick, a northern frontier colony across the Atlantic, would fill the bill perfectly. Without the distraction of pretty girls to fuel his hopeless fantasies, he could channel his abilities into the quest to make something of himself.

Harris felt his brows draw together and his face harden into a stern, intractable mask. Jenny Lennox appeared to sense his antagonism. Staring deep into his eyes, she willed him to look at her, to hear her out, and to grant whatever she might ask.

"It's like this, Mr. Chisholm—I'm going to Miramichi, New Brunswick, on the *St. Bride,* same as ye are. Have ye heard I'm to wed Roderick Douglas?"

Refusing to let her draw him into a two-way conversation, Harris gave a stony nod.

"I meant to travel with the Lowell Walkers. Now I hear tell Mr. Walker has suffered an accident and they won't be sailing with us after all. My father will never let me board that boat if I don't have somebody he trusts to look out for me. There're no other women passengers on the *St. Bride* and ye're the only man aboard I've any acquaintance with. I need ye to promise my pa ye'll see me safe to Miramichi."

She paused to gulp down a breath. Harris detected a slight tremor in the ribbons of her bonnet.

"I..." The word came out in an adolescent squeak. Clearing his throat, Harris tried again, consciously modulating his voice to its accustomed deep baritone register. "It wouldn't be fitting."

Privately he bristled at the insult. What was he—some eunuch to be entrusted with protecting a woman from the lascivious attentions of the real men on board the *St. Bride?* Because Miss Lennox wanted as little as possible to do with him didn't make him immune to her charms.

"Why not just wait and take a later boat?"

"Because..." A husky note in her voice portended tears.

Harris wanted to throw back his head and howl with vexation. As if women hadn't enough other advantages in the age-old struggle between the sexes! The creatures could dissolve into tears at the drop of a hat, reducing a man to quivering mush.

"Because I've paid my passage money already," she said. "I don't expect the agent will want to hand it back again, just because Pa objects to my traveling alone."

"Surely yer...intended, Mr. Douglas, can spare a few coins more for another passage." A somewhat less positive note crept into Harris's voice.

"Even if he would pay again, by the time I send word, I'll have lost three months. I ken Mr. Douglas would like to wed soon. It'll be less trouble to find himself another lass."

Harris stood there grim and silent. Roderick Douglas would be a fool not to wait for a rare bride like this one.

"So that's how it stands, Mr. Chisholm." She summed up her case. "Either I sail on the *St. Bride* today, to be the wife of a rich man, or I go off to London to be a scullery maid in some rich man's kitchen."

Having uttered so dire an ultimatum, her lips unexpectedly twitched into a teasing grin. "Did ye ever fancy yerself as a fairy godfather?"

Part of Harris wanted very much to oblige her, but another part protested. Jenny Lennox embodied everything he hoped to flee. It made no sense to take him with her. "Well…"

Perhaps sensing his indecision, she brought all her powers of persuasion to bear. "Roderick Douglas is a man of influence in Miramichi. I expect he'll be grateful to ye for helping me out. Whatever ye want—money, a job… anything. Ye'll have only to ask and I swear I'll do all in my power to grant it."

She cast him a look of desperate sincerity, as though making a pact with the devil. Stung by the implied comparison, Harris opened his mouth to refuse once and for all. Then Jenny Lennox reached out and took his hand.

"Please?"

Her touch was so soft and warm. Harris could not find it in his heart to deny Roderick Douglas the chance to feel it. Perhaps he'd follow Douglas's lead, Harris thought— make his fortune in the colonies, then send home for a bride.

"Aye. I'll do it," he agreed at last, with a marked lack of enthusiasm. "I'll see ye safe to Miramichi."

Jenny swayed slightly on her feet. For a moment Harris feared she might faint from surprise and relief. He gripped her hand to steady her. Returning his firm hold, she pumped his hand in a vigorous shake to seal their agreement.

"It's a bargain, then. I swear I'll be no bother to ye."

For an instant Harris did fancy the role of fairy godfather. How often in a lifetime was one given the power to grant another person's dearest wish? There was something rather edifying about the prospect.

"If I live to be a hundred, I'll never be able to thank ye enough." With those words, she lavished upon Harris a smile of such sweet esteem that he felt entirely repaid for whatever the undertaking might cost him.

The *St. Bride* eased out of Kirkcudbright Bay on the ebbing tide. Her passengers clustered at the taffrail to catch a final glimpse of the homeland they never expected to see again. Acutely aware of being the only woman on board, Jenny stood apart from the male passengers. She waved her handkerchief in a last farewell to her father and Kirstie.

The barque's timbers creaked. Pulleys squealed as sailors adjusted the rigging. When the wind began to fill them, the sails flapped like giant sheets on a clothesline. Above all these noises rose the deep voice of the first mate. He bellowed instructions to his crew for the disposition of various booms, spars and sails. Several inexperienced sailors looked as puzzled as Jenny by this nautical cant. Others might have understood the orders, but appeared too overcome with the aftereffects of drink to accomplish much.

Remembering the bold, speculative stares that had greeted her arrival on the *St. Bride,* Jenny suddenly appreciated her father's concern for her safety. Aware of the substantial presence of Harris Chisholm looming protectively behind her, she moved closer to him. God bless his perpetual scowl and the facial scars that gave him such an air of danger. With her fierce-looking escort, Jenny knew she was safe from anything worse than a few impudent stares.

After the barque rounded Little Ross, most of the passengers abandoned the top deck to the fresh winds off Solway Firth. Harris and Jenny lingered at the taffrail after the others had gone below decks.

"Are ye wishing ye'd waited for another boat, after all?" Harris squinted in the direction of the western horizon.

The question came a little too close to reading her mind for Jenny's comfort. She replied with more conviction than she felt. "That was not an option, if ye'll recall. I'm glad to be on my way to New Brunswick, and I thank ye again for making that possible. I trust ye'll be able to look out for me."

Her words made Harris abruptly aware of the grave responsibility he'd undertaken. "I want to make certain we're clear on terms," he growled. "Ye'll not leave yer cabin for any reason unless I'm with ye. Ye're not to let anyone in. Is that understood?"

Jenny nodded readily.

"Good." He headed for the companionway that led to the lower decks. "We ought to find our cabins, settle in and get a bite of supper. I don't like the looks of that sky. Unless I miss my guess, we're in for heavy weather before we clear Ireland."

"Just give me a minute, will ye?" Jenny begged. "Before today I've never been more than twenty miles from home. This is my first time on a boat."

"Very well." Harris tried not to let it come out as a sigh. "One minute."

Some intuition told him to keep his eyes off her, but they refused to obey.

Untying the ribbons of her bonnet, Jenny slipped it off. Deftly she extracted several pins from her hair. It fell to her waist in rippling chestnut waves, while shorter wisps curled softly around her face. Turning into the wind, she closed her eyes as the fresh breeze billowed her hair out behind her. She looked like the carved figurehead of *St. Bride* on the prow of the barque—magically, gloriously come to life.

Harris did not doubt his ability to protect Jenny Lennox from any other man aboard. But was he capable of protecting his own heart from being painfully ravished by her?

Chapter Two

"Miss Lennox?" Harris called. Getting no answer, he pounded on her cabin door more insistently. "Jenny!"

As he'd predicted, a nasty gale had blown up when the *St. Bride* rounded the treacherous north coast of Ulster. If she'd been crossing the Atlantic in the other direction, with holds full of heavy New Brunswick timber, it would not have been so bad. As it was, running against the wind, lightly laden with mercantile goods, the barque bobbed helplessly in the heavy seas.

Beneath Harris's feet, the deck gave a sudden violent roll, sending him crashing against the door of Jenny's cabin. The flimsy deal boards gave way before him. He lurched into the cabin, barking his shin on something sharp and solid before sprawling onto the floor. Behind him, the cabin door banged open and shut in time to the shifting pitch of the vessel, admitting fleeting flashes of lamplight from the passage. Between those flickers, the small chamber was impenetrably dark.

Where could Jenny Lennox have gone? Harris wondered as he rubbed his smarting shin. She had agreed not to leave her cabin without him. *Women,* he grumbled under his breath. Making all sorts of glib promises to get their way.

Then they went ahead and did as they pleased, without so much as a by-your-leave.

A low, anguished moan sounded near Harris's right ear. Flailing out in the direction of the sound, his hand made solid contact with the clammy flesh of Jenny's face.

"Miss Lennox, what are ye doing lying here in the dark?"

"Dying," came a weak, raspy reply.

Beneath the pervading odors of salt water and wet wood, Harris smelled the sour stench of vomit. Masked by the darkness, he allowed himself a wry smile at Jenny's expense. Apparently, beauty was not proof against the mundane rigors of seasickness.

He let his hand linger on her cheek. "Ye're not going to die."

"I want to." The words came up on her rising gorge.

Harris dodged out of the way as Jenny leaned over the edge of her berth. For several seconds she gagged agonizingly, but with little result. When she sank back onto the pillow again, Harris bent over her. He had to lean close, to make himself heard above the thunder of waves crashing against the hull and the high, fitful whine of the wind.

"If ye can feel that bad and still make a joke, I expect ye'll pull through," he said gently. "Rest, now. I'll go fetch Dr. Chisholm's cure for ocean belly."

"I don't care," Jenny whimpered. "Do what ye like with me."

Harris almost laughed. *Ye've no idea what I'd like to do with ye, lass,* he thought to himself. *If ye did, ye'd never have made me such a tempting offer, no matter how poorly ye felt.* Leaning so close to Jenny, he could feel the warmth emanating from her body.

He must be daft to even entertain such fancies, Harris rebuked himself as he reluctantly pulled away from her. Minding his tender shin, he felt his way toward the door with ginger steps. Once the gale subsided, he'd have to do something about that broken latch. In the meantime, the damp air below decks had swollen the wood enough to make the door stick shut when he pulled it to.

He staggered back down the companionway a while later, lantern in hand and a book under his arm. A firm nudge from his shoulder was all it took to push Jenny's door open again. Harris held the lantern high as he entered the cabin. He was not anxious to injure himself further, nor to pitch face-first onto the slimy floorboards.

Jenny shrank from the light, pulling a blanket over her head. "Put it out. It's not so bad when I can't see everything in the cabin rocking and swaying."

Harris took his bearings. Somehow, Jenny's brass-bound trunk had worked itself out from under her berth. It must have been the culprit responsible for his bruised shin. He cast the trunk a baleful glare and pushed it up beside the head of the berth.

"I need the light for a minute," he told Jenny. "Then I'll put it out."

Her head still covered with the blanket, she did not respond. Harris hung the lantern from a hook driven into one of the ceiling beams. He found a heavy stoneware jug of water and tipped a splash of it onto his handkerchief. Securing an enamel basin against future need, he extinguished the lamp. Then he felt his way back to Jenny's trunk, and sat down on it.

"Why don't ye go away and leave me to die in peace?" Jenny moaned. She must have thrown off the blanket, for her words were no longer muffled.

"All part of the bargain." Harris found her face and swiped his wet handkerchief across her forehead. "I promised yer father I'd see ye safe to Miramichi."

Fumbling in his coat pocket, he produced a small flask. Supporting Jenny's shoulders with one arm, he held it to her lips. "Take a sip of this. If ye can keep a bit of it down, it'll help ye sleep. I ken that's as much as we can do for ye tonight—let ye sleep until the storm's past.''

She sat bolt upright, spitting a fine spray of whisky into his face. "What is that stuff? It tastes foul!"

"Fouler than what's in yer mouth already?" Harris growled, mopping his face with the handkerchief. "For yer information, this is the finest single malt whisky—good for a variety of medicinal purposes, including the treatment of seasickness. Now drink it!"

Reluctantly she obliged. Harris could almost hear her grimace at the taste of the liquor.

"Lie back, and let that settle a minute before we try another drop."

"I'll never keep it down. It's burning all the way!"

"Aye," he replied dryly. "It'll light a fire in yer belly, too. Now, while we're waiting for the whisky to do its work, ye need something to keep yer mind off how miserable ye feel. If ye'd let me light the lantern again, I brought a book I could read to ye."

"What's the book?" she asked.

Harris thought he heard a note of longing in her voice.

"One of my favorites—Walter Scott's *Rob Roy*."

"Oh."

Never had he heard so wistful a sound as that brief word.

"It's no use," Jenny said finally. "I couldn't bear the light. *Rob Roy*—it sounds a brave story. What's it about?"

"Take another drink of the whisky first."

She submitted with a sigh of resignation. Though she gasped as the whisky went down, she did not spew it back up again. Harris took it as a sign his prescription was working after all.

Hunching forward, he brought his mouth close to Jenny's ear so he would not have to shout above the storm. Harris began to relate the story of Frank Osbaldistone and his adventures with the outlawed Rob Roy McGregor. Now and then, he lapsed into Scott's dramatic prose, reciting whole passages from memory. At regular intervals, he paused to prop Jenny up and administer another dose of whisky.

"Feel any better?" he asked after an hour had passed without further bouts of vomiting.

"I feel queer," she replied in a thick, drowsy voice, "but not so bad as before."

"I'll go away and let ye sleep then."

She groped for his hand. "Stay. Yer story keeps my mind off my stomach. It must be grand to be able to read books like that."

"I'd be happy to lend ye anything I have," Harris offered. "I expect ye haven't had much money for books."

Sinking back on her pillow, Jenny gave an oddly bitter laugh. "No money. No time. No learning." She sniffled. "I fear I'll be a right disappointment to Roderick Douglas—an ignorant farm girl who can't read a word or write her ain name." Her words trailed off into quiet sobs.

That would be the whisky at work, Harris decided. It often had the unfortunate side effect of making the drinker wax maudlin.

"There, there." He wiped her face with his handkerchief. "Wist, now. Ye'll upset yerself and end up sick to yer stomach again. It's a daft chap who'd complain of a bonny bride like ye, Jenny Lennox."

"What are ye doing here anyway, Harris Chisholm?" She pushed his handkerchief away. "I ken ye reckon I'm stupid and common. I've seen ye look down yer long nose at me often enough. Go 'way, now. I don't need yer drink, nor yer stories, nor yer pity, neither."

Harris could hear her moving about in the narrow berth—turning her back on him, most likely. For a moment he sat, not knowing what to say or do. He'd always thought of pretty girls as heartless, impervious creatures. It had never occurred to him that they might have easily bruised feelings or entertain the same kinds of self-doubt that plagued him. It came as an unpleasant revelation that his bristling demeanor, intended as a purely defensive measure, might have wounded one of their number.

If the light had been shining and Jenny not addled and half-asleep from the whisky, Harris would never have said what he said next. "I reckon nothing of the kind. Ye oughtn't mind me, anyhow. I ken well enough there's no lass'll want anything to do with me. It saves my pride a mite to pretend I don't care. I'd no notion to offend ye, and I beg yer pardon if I have."

He felt a sudden need to make amends. "We've a good five or six weeks more at sea…"

Jenny groaned at the very thought.

"It'll not all be as bad as this, I hope," Harris continued. "Once this squall passes and ye find yer sea legs, I could teach ye to read, if ye've a mind to learn."

The bedclothes rustled again as she turned toward him. "I'd love to. It's something I've always wanted. I used to envy my brothers when they went off to school. Since I was the only girl, Ma couldn't spare me. One winter I pestered Ian to teach me, but we didn't make much headway. I was always that worn-out at night, I'd fall asleep over my books before I could learn anything."

Harris wondered whether she realized he was still listening, or whether she had fallen to reminiscing aloud. He heard the plaintive, hungry edge in her voice.

Apparently she had not forgotten him, for suddenly she asked, "Why do ye want to put yerself to all the bother?"

"We fairy godfathers like to do a thorough job." Harris chuckled. "It's a point of professional pride, ye ken. Any other wishes ye'd like me to grant while I'm about it? Straw spun into gold? Pumpkin turned into a fine coach?"

"If ye can teach me to read, and see me safe wed to Roderick Douglas, ye'll have made me the happiest lass in the world. I only hope ye don't plan to ask for my firstborn as payment."

"Would that be a problem, then?" Harris asked face-tiously. "I recollect ye promised me anything in yer power to grant, with no provision exempting yer firstborn. I can amend the contract, but it'll mean charging an added penalty."

Jenny did not reply immediately. Harris wondered if he had strayed into uncomfortably familiar territory with his jest about her future offspring. The wind had audibly lessened, he noticed in that moment of silence. The pitch and roll of the barque had also slackened to a gentler undulation.

"I'll pay yer penalty with a wee spell of my ain," Jenny said at last. "I'll turn ye into the kind of charming gentleman who can have his pick of the lassies."

Harris laughed outright. "If ye can perform that kind of magic, ye'd better mind they don't burn ye for a witch, lass."

"I'll give ye yer first lesson right now," she murmured. "The next time ye speak to a woman, pretend ye're in the dark and she's a mite tipsy with her first taste of strong drink. Then ye talk to her just like ye've talked to me tonight—soft and kindly. After five minutes, I wager she'll not even notice those scars on yer face."

Jenny woke to the sound of footsteps and voices in the companionway. Fine shafts of sunshine squeezed into the cabin through chinks in the deadlight. Morning had dawned, and the gale had passed. Her stomach still felt queasy, but infinitely better than it had the previous night. This relief was offset by the dull pain that throbbed in her forehead.

Quite nearby, she heard a man snoring. The walls between the cabins must be as thin as paper, she grumbled to herself. Rolling over in the tight quarters of her berth, she came nose to nose with Harris Chisholm, snoring serenely with his head resting on her pillow.

"Mr. Chisholm, what are ye still doing here?" Jenny shrank back into the corner of the berth, gathering the blankets protectively over her chest.

Harris sat up on her trunk, pulling his head and torso off their resting place on the berth. "Where? What?" He peered around the cabin through half-closed eyes. When they focused on Jenny, he gave a visible start.

"I must've fallen asleep telling ye the last of *Rob Roy*." He yawned and stretched his long arms.

"Do ye know what this means? If word gets out that I've been entertaining ye in my cabin all night, my reputation'll be ruined. Roderick Dhu will never have me for a wife! How could ye let this happen?"

"I?" Harris drew himself up indignantly. "Ye were the one who begged me to stay. 'Do what ye like with me,' ye said. 'Stay and tell me more of the story,' ye said. Ye reckoned ye were going to die of the seasickness but I nursed ye through it. And this is the thanks I get. Bawling at me like a fishwife. Making it sound as though I forced my way into yer cabin and attacked ye in the night!"

"Ye did bust down my door!" Jenny accused him.

"That was an accident, and well ye know it. Now keep yer voice down, woman, or ye'll have the whole crew onto us. We both know nothing happened last night to sully yer fair reputation—unless ye count puking on my shoes and spitting whisky into my face." Harris started to laugh at the thought.

In spite of herself, so did Jenny.

"I'll keep mum about my being here if ye will, and no one the wiser," Harris assured her. "Besides, if it does get back to Roderick Dhu and he jilts ye over it, I promise to make an honest woman of ye."

Jenny seized her pillow and fetched Harris a solid clout on the ear. "If ye do anything to queer my wedding with Roderick Dhu, Harris Chisholm, I won't marry ye supposing ye're the last he-creature in North America!"

*   *   *

Fortunately, Harris was able to steal out of Jenny's cabin that morning without being caught. The crew was too busy assessing storm damage, while the other passengers were dealing with their own seasickness in varying degrees. Later that day, in a show of innocent concern, he helped the ship's carpenter repair Jenny's broken door latch.

Jenny kept to her cabin all that day, with the excuse of recovering from her bilious attack. When she finally emerged the following morning, she treated Harris with the frosty politeness reserved for particularly odious strangers. To his surprise and amusement, Harris found himself unable to take offense. When one had nursed a woman through a bout of seasickness, Harris discovered, the lady in question—no matter how attractive—permanently lost her ability to intimidate a fellow.

It might also have been partly due to Jenny's admission of her own inadequacies. Perhaps it owed to his status as her protector. Whatever the reason, Jenny Lennox had pitched headfirst off her pedestal. Harris found it an odd and rather heady experience, being on equal footing with a woman. As he might never enjoy such a novelty again, he decided to make the most of it while it lasted.

He gave Jenny precisely forty-eight hours to grow tired of her own company. Then he made his overture.

"Do ye plan to give over snubbing me before we get to Miramichi?" he asked with good-natured disinterest, as he escorted her back from breakfast.

She appeared to have trouble preserving a straight face. "Ye ken my snubbing ye for two days squares yer snubbing me for years?" Her eyebrow cocked in an expression of bewitching arrogance.

"No." His mouth twitched with the effort to suppress a smile. "But I ken feeding ye all my good whisky, and resisting the urge to brag of spending the night in yer company, does weigh heavy on the balance."

"Keep yer voice down!" Jenny glanced nervously around to see if anyone had overheard. She must have decided there was no one within earshot, for her expression grudgingly softened.

"I ken there's some truth to what ye say." She held out her hand. "I'm willing to make peace if ye are."

Harris grinned. "It's a bargain."

He shook her hand. It was not soft or dainty, but roughened by years of work. More eloquently than any spoken plea, it told Harris of the life she longed to leave behind.

"It'll be a relief to have someone to talk to." She looked genuinely relieved. "Who'd have thought after twenty years of slaving away from dawn till dusk, I'd get sick of idleness after only two days. Time hangs heavy on yer hands when ye've nothing to do."

"I stand behind my offer to teach ye to read," said Harris. "A good book's the best antidote for boredom I can recommend. While we're about it, ye can instruct me in the gentle art of charming the ladies, like ye promised."

"We'd better get busy." An amethyst twinkle gleamed in Jenny's gray eyes. "If I'm to teach ye some manners before we land in Chatham, there's not a moment to lose!"

Chapter Three

"The...con-dit-ion..." Jenny sounded out the unfamiliar arrangement of letters.

"Condition," Harris prompted.

"Oh, aye." Her eyebrows drew together in a grimace of intense concentration as she attacked the passage once more. "The condition of the English nation was at this time...suf...suf..."

"Sufficiently miserable." Harris helpfully supplied the last two words of the sentence.

"It's no use." Jenny blew out an exasperated sigh, which stirred the lock of hair curling over her brow. "I'll never be able to read like ye can, Harris. I fear I'm an awful dunce."

"Nonsense," he protested. "It took me years to read as well as ye can after only a fortnight. Ye're a clever lass, Jenny."

The compliment warmed her more than she cared to admit. She pretended to dismiss it with a derisive wave of her hand. "Get away with ye!"

Tutor and scholar nestled in their usual perch—a short flight of wide, shallow steps leading up to the poop deck. These seldom-used side steps made a convenient retreat for Jenny's reading lessons, out from underfoot of the crew. They had the added advantage of receiving shade from the spanker in the morning, and from the mainsail for the rest of the day.

Of late, shade had become a rare commodity on the *St. Bride*. Ever since that inauspicious gale at the outset of their journey, the North Atlantic weather had turned unusually clement. The wind had died to a light, fitful breeze, while the lazy waves rocked the barque as gently as a baby's cradle. Day after day, the sun beamed down from a canopy of deep, tranquil blue. Filmy clouds floated high in what the master of the *St. Bride* called a "mackerel sky."

"Ye'd likely have learned quicker with an easier book." Harris leaned back from his seat two steps below Jenny. He cast an apologetic glance at the fat volume of *Ivanhoe* lying open on her lap. "Other than the Bible, I fear Mr. Scott's books are all I could afford to bring with me."

"Don't fret yerself." Jenny felt her natural optimism rebounding. "I know the Bible well enough already. I like these stories. I'd far rather read a book that's hard but interesting, than one that's easy but dull."

Harris grinned. "Aye, there's sense in that."

They had finished *Rob Roy* a few days ago. First, Jenny struggled through the opening pages of each chapter, then Harris rewarded her efforts by reading the rest aloud to her. Between chapters, they discussed the story and the characters. Harris would explain any pertinent historical background.

The high adventure and heroic romance of the stories intrigued Jenny no end. At night they figured in her dreams, the heroes all looking and sounding strangely like Harris.

Every morning, Jenny hurriedly dressed and bolted her breakfast, eager to tackle another chapter. Thanks to Walter Scott and Harris Chisholm, whole new vistas of thought and experience were opening before her. Never in her life had she felt so completely alive.

"Hallo!" called a voice from aloft. "How goes the lessons, Miss Lennox?"

Jenny waved up at Thomas Nicholson, the apprentice boy who was nimbly scaling the ratlines on the mizzenmast.

"Oh, it's coming, Thomas," she called. "Not fast, but it's coming."

"Don't listen to her, Thomas," Harris countered. "Miss Lennox has brains to match her beauty. Why, I could make an Edinburgh lawyer out of her in six months."

With a cheery salute, the boy returned to his work. Captain Glendenning kept men aloft all hours of the day, adjusting the sails continually to catch the faint, fitful winds. As the unpromising weather had improved since the early days of the voyage, so had the crew of the *St. Bride*.

A rigorous stickler for discipline, the master had taken a hard line with slackers and insubordinates. Any sailor who failed to pull his weight soon found himself scouring the deck with salt water and holystone, under the blazing sun. Diligent sailors found the *St. Bride* a soft billet. They ate better than the usual forecastle diet of hardtack and salt beef, and the captain used a liberal hand doling out their daily rum ration.

Discovering Jenny had a champion in the tall, menacing person of Harris Chisholm, the sailors had quickly come to treat her with respectful deference. It helped matters further when word got around that she was on her way to wed a rich shipbuilder in the port of their destination. Any sailor who planned to jump ship and look for work in Miramichi might hope for a good reference from Miss Lennox.

Returning to the text of the novel, Harris searched out more obscure words that might present a problem for Jenny's novice reading skills.

"Brains to match my beauty?" she scoffed.

Though Harris continued to stare at the book, his ears reddened. "Should I not practice my lessons, too?" he asked innocently.

"Lessons? Ah, yer charm lessons." It was on the tip of her tongue to tell Harris he was already a mite too charming for his own good—or hers. Instead she spoke tartly. "The most important lesson I can teach ye about flattery is don't lay it on too thick."

"'He lived long and happily with Rowena,'" Jenny read about Wilfred of Ivanhoe, "'for they were attached to each other by bonds of early affection and they loved each other the more from recollection of the obstacles which had impeded their union.'"

The evening light was quickly fading and Jenny wanted to finish the book before she went to bed. Harris had promised they could start *Waverley* the next day.

"'Yet it would be inquiring too curiously to ask whether the recollection of Rebecca's beauty and magna...magnan...'"

"Magnanimity."

"'Magna-nimity,'" Jenny repeated, "'did not recur to his mind more frequently than the fair des-cendant of Alfred might altogether have approved.'"

She read the final paragraph without further prompting from Harris. Then Jenny closed the cover with a thud of triumph.

"It was a bonny story," she said. "Except that Ivanhoe should have married Rebecca."

Harris cast her a sidelong glance, one brow arched expressively.

"He should," she insisted. "There was more between Sir Wilfred and Rebecca. Mind how she nursed him after Ashby and how he fought the Templar to save her from burning at the stake?"

The lilt of music and laughter drifted back from the foredeck. Off watch, the crewmen often gathered there in the evenings to tell stories, sing and drink their watered-down rum.

Harris nodded in the direction of the forecastle. "Care to go up and join in the festivities?"

Flushed with the exhilaration of finishing her second book, Jenny accepted the invitation eagerly. She and Harris made their way forward and hovered on the fringes of the gathering. The sailors sat or stood in a rough circle, a few lounging against the rails, some perched in the rigging.

The air throbbed with an infectious, rollicking beat. Callused palms clapped together. Bare feet slapped against the planks of the deck. Wooden spoons drummed a tattoo on the lids of the bilge barrels. Above the chorus of deep male voices piped the spritely trill of a tin whistle. Jenny recognized the tune but not the words, which recounted the charms of the women in various ports of call. She soon found herself clapping in time to the music. The singing ended with a loud, joyous whoop.

"Chisholm! Miss Lennox! Come join us," called the burly boatswain. With a flick of his thumb, he motioned a young seaman to vacate his seat on a sawed-off cask so Jenny could sit down. "We'll mind our language, ma'am," he assured her.

"Pay me no mind." She waved away all worries of propriety. "I've seven brothers, so I'm used to the way men go on."

As if taking Jenny's reply as his cue, Tom Nicholson raised the tin whistle to his lips and began to blow another rousing tune. One of the many Irish fighting songs, it gradually picked up a lusty chorus. Several similar songs followed. Then someone called for a jig. The apprentice boy obliged by piping up a lively air. Two young crewmen were pushed into the midst of the circle. After an awkward start, they soon picked up the rhythm and broke into a nimble step.

One of the dancers reached down and caught Jenny by the hand. Hauling her to her feet, he began to spin her about the deck in time to the exuberant music. She'd only danced once before—a few tentative steps at a cousin's wedding. This was altogether different. Her feet moved over the gently swaying deck with an impetuous ease all their own. The sweet, vibrant music pulsed in her veins. Her partner whirled her off into another pair of arms.

A hectic flush crept into Jenny's cheeks. She spun away to a third partner and a fourth. Strands of her hair escaped their confining pins, as though anxious to take part in the revelry. She could only toss her wayward curls and laugh, delighting in the wild joy of the moment as the music built towards its feverish climax. The crewmen greeted her performance with noisy approval, clapping and whistling.

Laughing with what little breath she had left, Jenny subsided dizzily against her partner.

"Roderick Douglas won't care how well ye read, when ye can dance like that, lass." Warm with admiration, Harris's deep voice murmured in her ear.

Something told Jenny she should pull away, with a sharp rebuke to Harris Chisholm for holding her in so familiar a fashion. But she dared not let go. She was off balance. It would be too easy to fall. So she lingered in his arms longer than was seemly, anchored by his strength. Clinging to him for the few steps it took to reach her seat, she collapsed onto her improvised stool.

Some remnant of giddiness left from the dancing must have possessed her, for she slid over, patting the lid of the barrel. "There's room for two," she said in a breathless rush.

Without a word, Harris dropped down beside her.

High spirits exhausted, the crew's music slowed and softened. Tom Nicholson gave his tin whistle a rest. One of the men sang a mournful, meandering ballad about an ill-fated cattle raid. Then three of the lads joined in close harmony on "Annie Laurie." Until that night, Harris had given the extravagant love protestations of Robert Burns a rather cynical reception. The pleasant recollection of hours spent with Jenny and the unsettling awareness of her hip pressing against his gave him a new perspective.

"'For bonnie Annie Laurie, I'll lay me down and die.'"

Suddenly Harris could imagine what it must be like to feel that way about a woman. He wasn't sure he cared for the idea, though. It was tantamount to putting a loaded musket into a woman's hands and offering his heart for target practice. What if the fickle, perfidious creature pulled the trigger?

"Will you give us a song, Miss Lennox?" one of the men asked at the conclusion of "Annie Laurie." "There's some just don't sound right unless they're sung by a woman."

"Aye, like 'Barbrie Allen,'" another crewman piped up.

"Nah, not that one." The boatswain pretended to blubber into his handkerchief. "It always sets me bawlin'. Boo-hoo-hoo!"

"I'll go easy on yer tender heart," Jenny assured the boatswain. Laughter bubbled musically beneath her words. "How about 'Lizzie Lindsay'? That one ends happily enough."

"Aye, it's a sweet tune," agreed Tom Nicholson. He raised his tin whistle and began to play.

Harris had to agree with the boy's assessment. The music floated on the night breeze, softly melodic. It had a haunting quality that warned Harris he'd be hearing it in his dreams and humming it for days to come. Beside him, Jenny began to sing.

"'Will ye gang tae the hielands, Lizzie Lindsay?
Will ye gang tae the hielands wi' me?
Will ye gang tae the hielands, Lizzie Lindsay,
My bride and my darlin' tae be?'"

In the next verses, Lizzie's mother and sister told how they'd eagerly elope with the handsome stranger, if only they were the right age. Miss Lizzie proved a lass of more practical bent. She had no intention of being swept off her feet by a man she knew nothing about.

Harris sat there drinking in the music of Jenny's high, clear voice. Every note rang with a sweet purity, as though pealed by a golden bell. Each one set echoes resonating in his heart.

In the next-to-last verse, Lizzie's suitor revealed himself as the powerful Highland laird, Ranald MacDonald. Discovering his identity had a marked effect on the young lady's scruples.

> "'Lizzie kilted up her coats of green satin,
> She kilted them up to her knee.
> Now she's off with Lord Ranald MacDonald,
> His darlin' and his bride to be.'"

As the last golden note died away, the crew broke into a warm round of applause, calling for Jenny to sing again.

"Another time, gentlemen." She stood and executed a dainty curtsy. "For now, I must beg ye to excuse me. If I don't soon get to my bed, I fear I'll fall asleep sitting here."

When Harris rose to accompany her, Jenny motioned him back good-naturedly. "Ye needn't leave on my account. Stay and enjoy yerself. I can find my cabin well enough by now."

He followed her anyway, after a parting wave to the sailors of the *St. Bride*. When he caught up with Jenny, Harris found her leaning against the afterdeck railing. Silhouetted by the bright moonlight, her loose tendrils of hair wafted on the sea wind in a most bewitching fashion. He stood mute, watching her commune with the ocean, with the night, and with her future.

At last he spoke up. "Yer singing sounded pretty." He could not keep himself from humming part of the tune.

Though she'd given no sign of knowing he was there, Jenny did not startle at his words. She replied matter-of-factly. "Kirstie taught me that song." Her voice took on a note of private remembrance. "We used to argue over it all the time."

"Argue over a song?"

"Aye. Kirstie said it wasn't very romantic for Lizzie to quiz her beau about his prospects. She said the lass should've accepted Lord Ranald before she found out who he was."

Perhaps Kirsten Robertson had a crumb of sense in her pampered golden pate, after all.

"Ye disagreed?"

Jenny gave a derisive sniff. "I should say so. Lizzie Lindsay was a wise lass. It's as easy to love a rich man as a poor one. A sight easier to stay in love with him after the courting and the wedding, too."

"Do I hear the voice of experience?" Harris asked quietly. He had the feeling Jenny was talking more to herself than to him.

"Aye." It was a small word to hold so much bitterness. "There's nothing romantic about working yerself to death to make ends meet. Worrying how ye'll scrape together a few bawbies to pay the doctor bill. Flowery dreams are well enough, but they wither fast in a cold wind."

"Ye do love this Roderick Douglas, though. It's not just his money?"

"I used to sit in kirk and watch him," murmured Jenny. "He was that handsome, with his dark hair and dark eyes. He had such a fine, confident way of moving and speaking. Ye just knew he'd go places and do grand things. Wedding him will be my dream of a lifetime come true."

Harris listened as Jenny recounted the merits of her future husband. With a pang of regret, he realized that he could never measure up to her ideal.

"Ye ought to get some sleep." He didn't mean them to, but the words came out as a gruff command.

"Aye." Her reply floated on the wind like a sigh. Turning from the rail, Jenny picked a cautious path to the companionway. Harris dogged her footsteps like a morose shadow.

At the door to her cabin, she turned to him. "We'll start reading *Waverley* tomorrow. Good night, Harris. I had a fine time this evening."

Before he could turn away, she raised herself on the tips of her toes and planted an impulsive kiss on his cheek. It landed a little low of the mark, brushing against the scars on his jawline. Harris opened his mouth to say something. Before he could get anything out, Jenny bolted into her cabin and firmly closed the door in his face.

Chapter Four

"Where are we now?" Jenny peered around Harris, toward a distant smudge of land perched on the horizon.

After six weeks at sea, she felt as though she'd always lived on a boat, instinctively adjusting her walk to the roll and pitch of the deck. For the longest time there had been no tangible evidence they were getting closer to their destination. Captain Glendenning had his chronometer, of course, and something he called "dead reckoning." As far as Jenny could tell, they might have been sailing in circles around the Atlantic.

Then, suddenly, there it was. Land. It beckoned Jenny with promises of her new life.

"Ye've asked me that same question every hour since yesterday when we hailed that Nantucket whaler," Harris snapped, without even bothering to look at her. "We're an hour closer than we were the last time ye asked."

Abruptly he pulled back from the bow railing and stalked off without a further word. Jenny, who'd been leaning against him, lurched forward, barking her shin in the process.

"Now what's got into him?" she grumbled, rubbing her injured leg. "Much good it's done, my trying to teach him some manners."

In the past twenty-four hours, Harris Chisholm had reverted to his old sullen self. Brusque, unapproachable...downright rude at times, Jenny would have been quite happy to leave *that* Harris Chisholm back home in Scotland. Harris, the patient teacher. Harris, the enthralling storyteller. Harris, the endlessly stimulating companion. Where had he gone?

"We're offshore of Nova Scotia, Miss Lennox." The master of the *St. Bride* appeared at Jenny's elbow. He pointed westward, at a slight indentation in the irregular strip of coastline. "We're making for a wee channel that cuts between the mainland and the Island of Cape Breton. It'll take a day or more off our journey, not having to sail all the way around Cape Breton."

"Do all the ships from Miramichi go that way?" Jenny asked, Harris Chisholm temporarily forgotten. She was eager to learn as much as possible about shipbuilding and seafaring, so she could discuss those subjects knowledgeably with her betrothed.

Captain Glendenning shook his head. "Canso's a treacherous passage in foul weather or with an inexperienced crew. We'll get through her fine today, though. I can smell a squall brewing in the sou'west, but we'll be well through Canso afore she hits. With any luck she'll hold off until we make harbour at Richibucto. The shoals and sandbars at the mouth of the river are dangerous enough in fine weather. More than one ship I've lost..."

"Richibucto?" Jenny asked, with a mixture of annoyance and alarm. "I thought we were destined for the Miramichi."

"So we are, lass. So we are," the master reassured her. "We only stop in Richibucto a day or two—more's the pity."

Jenny cast him a questioning look.

"It's my home port," Captain Glendenning explained. "Got a little farm near there, where my wife and family live. I won't get much chance for a visit with them this time. Though I may be able to help my brother-in-law get some hay in.''

''It must be hard for yer wife, having ye away from home so much,'' said Jenny.

The captain shrugged, but she detected a slight flinch in his craggy, weathered features. ''It costs money to build up a good farm. Money for seed, tools and stock. A man can make good pay with his master's papers. Besides,'' he owned, somewhat sheepishly, ''I'm one of those bootless fellows with salt water for blood. Every winter I say I'm done with it, going to settle down on the farm for good. Then come spring, when all the wee shipyards on the river launch their new crop of barques and brigantines, I get bitten by the sea bug again, and I'm off.''

Jenny had to admit the attractions of the life Captain Glendenning described. In six short weeks, she'd come to feel quite at home on the *St. Bride*. She loved the clean tang of the ocean breeze, and the rhythmic slap of the waves against the hull that lulled her to sleep each night. When a freak easterly filled the barque's sails and sent her bousing along with her rigging taut and straining, something in Jenny's soul stirred with a sense of expectancy and adventure.

''If you'll excuse me, Miss Lennox.'' The captain touched the peak of his cap. ''There's a few things I must see to, before we make Canso.''

Jenny excused Captain Glendenning with a cheery smile. At the moment her heart brimmed with goodwill toward the whole human race. By nightfall they'd be through the Strait of Canso, heading for a short stopover at Richibucto and then on to the Miramichi. Impossible as it had once seemed, her dream was coming true. Thinking of her dream made Jenny remember the man who had made it a reality.

''Thomas,'' she called up to the apprentice boy scaling

the rigging. "Any sign of Mr. Chisholm?" If Harris was
on deck at all, Thomas Nicholson could easily spot him
from aloft.

"Back by the poop deck, Miss Lennox," the boy yelled
down.

So Harris was waiting for her in their outdoor school.
That was it, Jenny decided in a flash of insight. Preoccu-
pation with the end of their journey had made her forget
her reading lessons. That was why Harris had spoken to
her so impatiently. She'd sensed his enjoyment of their
studies together. It must be a marvelous feeling to open
another person's mind to the world of books and knowledge. One day she would pass along the precious gift Harris had given her, by teaching others to read.

She must settle down and concentrate on her lessons,
Jenny chided herself as she went in search of Harris. For
one thing, it would help make these last anxious days pass
more quickly. Besides, she should enjoy it while she could.
Soon there would be no more lessons. No more stimulating
discussions. No more good-natured arguments. Somehow,
that thought cast a dark cloud over Jenny's dream of a
sunny future.

Harris sprawled on the steps of the poop deck, gazing
blindly at the pages of Scott's *The Heart of Midlothian,*
open before him. He knew enough anatomy to realize that
the human heart was merely a muscle pumping blood
through the body. Yet he could understand why people had
once believed it to be the seat of emotion. Love, in particular. For when love went awry, as it invariably did, it left
a heavy weight pressing down on one's chest. With every
beat came a twinge of pain.

Harris heaved a sigh that started somewhere in the region of his toes. He'd been right, back in Dalbeattie, to
avoid women. The creatures were nothing but trouble. Not
knowing what he might be missing, he'd felt a certain rest-

lessness, a vague sense of discontent. Now his longing had a focus—Jenny. That focus served to concentrate and hone the feeling, until it was heavy enough and sharp enough to lance his heart.

Day after day he'd sat beside her, their hands sometimes brushing or their eyes meeting over the pages of a book. She had a way of looking at him, with those immense heather-colored eyes, that made Harris feel he was the font of all received wisdom. A sage. A hero. Capable of any daring exploit. Her soft, musical voice had wrapped itself around his heart and invaded his dreams.

Jenny Lennox was everything a woman should be—an amalgam of the best of Scott's romantic heroines. As beautiful as Rowena, as tender as Rebecca, as spirited as Flora MacIvor. And Harris had promised to deliver her to another man. With the date of delivery rapidly approaching, Jenny was eager for it to come. Only one other time in his life had Harris felt so abjectly miserable.

He had no one to blame but himself. He should have known better than to fall in with Jenny's plan. Six weeks spent with any lass in the close quarters of this barque— had she been half as bonny as Jenny and one-tenth as good-natured—a man would still likely have developed feelings for her. How could he have been so daft?

Well, the time had come to cut his losses. Bandage up his poor mauled heart and buffer it against any worse abuse at the deft, gentle, deadly hands of Jenny Lennox. Harris felt his features freeze into his old intractable mask.

"Harris?" Jenny offered him a conciliatory smile. She was graciously willing to overlook his recent churlish behavior. "Am I late for lessons?"

He didn't move aside to offer her her accustomed seat. Glancing up absently, Harris looked as though he'd been thinking of something else and had scarcely heard her.

"Captain Glendenning says we'll be through the Strait

of Canso by nightfall," Jenny informed him. "If I promise to concentrate and not go tearing off to the railing every five minutes, do ye think we stand a chance of getting through this next book before we reach the Miramichi?"

"There's nothing more I can teach ye." He thrust the book at her. "All ye need now is practice. It's a sight quicker to read it yerself than to read aloud. If ye keep at it, I've no doubt ye'll get it finished in time."

Jenny just stood and stared at him. She could not have been more taken aback if Harris had hurled the heavy volume at her head.

"I...I ken ye're probably right," she finally managed to say. "It's just, I enjoy talking the story over with ye, Harris. Ye're a dab hand at explaining all the parts I don't understand."

"Aye, well..." His expressive brows drew together and his lip curled in a frown of distaste. "I fear I won't have time, Miss Lennox. As ye've pointed out quite frequently in the past twenty-four hours, we'll soon be reaching our destination. I have plans to make." He waved a hand airily. "Important considerations to review."

Miss Lennox, was it now? A wonder she didn't get frostbitten by *Mr.* Chisholm's chilly politeness. Jenny composed her face into a mirror image of his haughty expression. She felt a little sick flutter in her stomach. Curse these choppy offshore waters. Her eyes were beginning to sting as well. Blast this briny wind!

"I'd hate to be responsible for taking up yer valuable time, sir. Not when ye have grand plans to make and important decisions to consider." She snatched the book from his hand. "I'll remind ye, though...this business of teaching me to read was yer idea, not mine. So ye can quit acting like I've imposed on ye."

Harris refused to meet her challenging stare. "I only thought it was time for ye to get used to reading on yer own. Ye soon won't have me around to read with."

Contemplating that prospect made Jenny's knees tremble. This whole upset, this sudden unexplained hostility between them, provoked a battery of strange and unwelcome emotions in her. Damn Harris Chisholm for getting her all riled up!

"No doubt ye're looking forward to having me off yer hands," she said coldly.

"Now, Jenny, I didn't mean to imply that."

"Oh didn't ye, indeed? I'm sure ye're too polite to come right out and say so. All the same, ye must be relieved I'll soon trouble ye no further."

"Now see here…"

"I'm willing to absolve ye of all responsibility here and now," Jenny pressed on, proud that she'd been able to marshal a couple of impressive words from her growing vocabulary. "I've nothing to fear from any man on this vessel. My father's a thousand miles away. He'll never know the difference. Consider yer duty honorably discharged and we can go our separate ways."

A battalion of gulls careened in the sky above the barque's mainmast, screeching shrilly at one another. Before Harris had a chance to reply, Jenny spun about on her toe and flounced off. She clutched the weighty tome of Walter Scott's prose to her heart like a protective shield.

In her dark, cramped little cabin, Jenny made a stubborn effort to read by the wildly swaying beam of her lantern. Her lips moved as she scanned each line of print, clamping together angrily when she came upon an unfamiliar word.

Blast Harris Chisholm straight to Hades! Jenny's strong, slim fingers tightened around the pages of the book. She'd felt a connection with him, a friendship even sweeter than the one she'd enjoyed with Kirstie Robertson. It hurt to discover he'd only been suffering her company, gritting his teeth, biding his time until they reached North America.

Then he'd drop her at the feet of Roderick Douglas, like some odious parcel he was glad to be rid of.

Suddenly she noticed the tempo of footsteps quickening on the deck above. How long had she been shut in her cabin? Jenny wondered. Perhaps they had reached that Canso place already. Closing the thick book, Jenny laid it on her berth. She smoothed her skirts and pinned a wayward lock of her hair severely back in place. She'd go up and catch a closer glimpse of North America as the *St. Bride* sailed through the narrow strait. She'd show a *certain person* she was quite capable of looking after herself, and that she didn't care a whit for his regard.

As she emerged onto the deck, squinting against the bright sunlight of late afternoon, Jenny collided with the tall, substantial person of Harris Chisholm.

"Jenny." He grasped her by the shoulders. "Ye've got to get below at once."

Drawing back from him, she fixed Harris with a stare of chilly severity. "I'll thank ye to move out of my way, sir."

In spite of her stiff retort, Jenny's heart gave a traitorous leap, for Harris had called her by her first name in a tone that had lost its cold, clipped edge.

"I've no time to stand here arguing with ye, Jenny. Ye're going below." With that, he grasped her around the waist and hoisted her effortlessly over his shoulder.

"Put me down, Harris Chisholm!" Jenny flailed her feet and pounded in vain on his back. Her cries filled the narrow companionway. "Let me go this minute, ye great ruffian!"

To restrain her squirming, Harris adjusted his hold on Jenny, bringing one hand to rest on the swell of her backside. The pressure of his hand set a tight, tingly sensation quivering deep in the pit of her belly. It fueled her anger and outrage. "Let me go, or I'll have Captain Glendenning throw ye in the brig!"

Pushing open her cabin door, Harris tossed Jenny unceremoniously onto her berth. "The captain has worse ruffians than me to contend with just now."

"What blather are ye talking, Harris Chisholm?"

"It's no blather. There's pirates in the gut and they want to board us. I have to go above and do what I can to support the captain."

"Pirates?" Jenny felt her insides twist in reef knots.

"When I shut yer door," Harris ordered, "push yer trunk against it. Douse yer light. Don't make a noise and don't come out till I tell ye it's safe."

He had the door half-shut when Jenny called out. "Harris, for God's sake, be careful!"

Turning back for a moment, he fixed her with a fervent look. "I'll protect ye to my last drop of blood, Jenny." The flimsy deal boards slammed shut behind him.

With trembling hands, Jenny pushed her trunk against the cabin door. She doubted it would hinder anyone really determined to enter. Following Harris's instructions, she put out the cabin light and felt her way back to her berth. Crouching there in the dark, she concentrated on the noises filtering down from the deck, trying to piece together what might be happening.

She heard angry shouts but could not make out the words. Then a musket shot rang out. Jenny whimpered a desperate prayer for Harris and the crew of the *St. Bride*. Some heavy object rolled across the deck. More gunfire. Someone cried out in pain. Suddenly a noise like a hundred claps of thunder exploded above Jenny's head. With a shriek, she pulled the bedclothes over her head. Her imagination boiled with lurid images of what pirates might do to a defenceless young woman.

"I can't let them corner me here," she muttered to herself. Better to meet her fate out in the open, where she could run—throw herself into the sea if it came to that. Nothing could be worse than cowering in the bowels of the ship—trapped.

Jenny was well down the companionway when she heard a loud cheer ring out from the deck. She emerged just in time to see a pair of small sloops making for the northern shore. Pretty pitiful pirates. Jenny gave a derisive laugh, giddy with relief. Then she caught sight of several crewmen, huddled in a knot. It took her a moment to realize they were ministering to a wounded comrade. The only visible part of the victim was one booted foot, limp and prostrate.

"Harris!" Jenny shrieked, elbowing her way through the press of sailors in a most unladylike manner. Harris lay there, motionless on the deck. His eyes were closed. His mouth hung slack. Blood soaked one arm of his shirt.

Casting herself down on the deck beside him, Jenny wrested his head into her lap. With trembling fingers, she stroked his face.

"Ye can wake up now, Harris," she coaxed. "The pirates are gone. We're all safe and sound. Open yer eyes for me, like a good fellow. Ye're giving me a rare fright."

Desperately Jenny searched the crowding faces until she found Captain Glendenning's.

"What happened to him, Captain? He's not dead—" her voice broke "—is he?"

Chapter Five

"Dead?" The captain gave a scratchy chuckle. "Whatever gave ye a daft idea like that, lass?"

Suspecting an unconscious, blood-covered man to be dead hardly qualified as daft, Jenny wanted to snap. Too overcome with relief to get the words out, she settled for casting Captain Glendenning a black look. She continued to stroke Harris's face in hopes of reviving him. His skin felt cool beneath her fingers—the chill spread to Jenny's heart.

"What happened?" she finally mastered her voice to ask.

"It was them swill-sucking bottom feeders." The first mate jerked his head in the direction of the rapidly retreating pirate sloops. "Had the gall to open fire on us when the captain wouldn't give 'em leave to board."

Captain Glendenning pressed a bloodstained wad of canvas to Harris's upper arm. "A ball winged young Chisholm here. Bleeding bad, but not serious. Just grazed the flesh, so we won't have to cut the ball out. Cauterize it with hot pitch and—"

Jenny winced. "Must ye?"

"Aye, miss." The first mate bared one brawny forearm

to reveal a wicked-looking scar. ''The pitch hurts some, but it beats letting the wound go putrid.''

''That's enough out of ye, matie,' the captain barked. ''Can't ye see Miss Lennox is getting a mite green around the gills.''

''If the wound isn't serious, what's he doing laid out cold on the deck?'' Jenny demanded.

''Oh, that…''

''Will this help, Miss Lennox, ma'am?'' Thomas Nicholson appeared with a small bucket of water and a cloth.

''Thanks, Thomas.'' Jenny lavished upon him her warmest smile of gratitude. ''Could ye hunt me up a drop of spirits, as well? It might help to bring Mr. Chisholm around.''

The boy looked doubtfully at Captain Glendenning.

''Don't just stand there, lad.'' The captain fished in his pocket and tossed the boy a heavy ring of keys. ''Do as the lady says.''

''I thought the garrison from Halifax had routed out this nest of vipers,'' grunted the master when young Nicholson had scurried off. ''Either they made a bollocks of the job, or there's a new crowd moved in. Lucky for us, I brought along a wee surprise for our friends.''

He nodded toward a squat little cannon lashed to the port railing. ''Picked her up cheap at a foundry in Glasgow. Only a wee four-pounder, but handy enough against barracuda like that lot. Chisholm was helping haul her into place when he got hit by the musket fire. Took a clout on the head when he fell.''

Jenny pressed a wet cloth to Harris's face. His grayish pallor alarmed her. ''Shouldn't he be waking up by now?'' she asked no one in particular.

''He'll come to when he comes to.'' The captain shrugged far too casually for Jenny's liking. ''This may be as good a time as any to apply the pitch,'' he added.

''While he can't feel it. That'll bring him around, if anything will.''

It seemed to take an eternity for the cook, of all people, to prepare the hot pitch. In the meantime, Captain Glendenning ordered his men to look lively and see the barque safely through Canso before sundown. Jenny was left to keep her solitary vigil over Harris, kneeling on the hard deck with his head pillowed in her lap. Thomas Nicholson had brought her a small jug of rum, but Jenny couldn't make up her mind to use it. Much as she wanted to satisfy herself that Harris was all right, by seeing him conscious, she shrank from the prospect of waking him in time for Captain Glendenning to cauterize his wound.

Hadn't the poor man enough scars? Jenny mused as she ran gentle fingers over the puckered pink stripes on his firm jawline. She wondered how he had come by them. From her earliest memory of him, Harris had borne these. Only recently had she come to realize they had marred his character as much as his appearance. A warm tear rose unbidden in her eye and fell onto his cheek. Harris gave a slight twitch but did not wake.

Sailing toward the setting sun, the *St. Bride* edged out of Canso's tight passage into a wider waterway. Jenny suddenly realized she'd been too preoccupied to take a good look at her new homeland.

A low moan escaped Harris's lips, but his eyes never flickered.

''We're through to the Northumberland.'' Captain Glendenning rubbed his hands together in a gesture of self-satisfaction. ''Nova Scotia behind us, Prince Edward Island to the nor'east, and New Brunswick to the sou'west. With fair winds we'll make harbor in Richibucto by first light tomorrow morning.''

''That's fine, Captain,'' Jenny said tightly. This morning she would have been enthralled by news of their nearness to the Miramichi. At the moment she could think of noth-

ing beyond Harris. He'd been hurt trying to keep her from
harm, and he'd feel more pain before the captain was
through doctoring him. The last thing she wanted to do
was cause Harris pain.

"Can we get this over with?" she asked from between
clenched teeth.

"May as well, while we've a bit of light," the captain
agreed. "Matie, hold his bad arm. Bosun, take the other,
and Blair, his legs. Thomas, hold his head."

"I'll hold his head," said Jenny in a tone that brooked
no refusal.

"Have it yer way, lass." The captain shrugged. "He
may thrash around a bit when I apply the pitch."

"I'm strong. I can hold him."

The captain lifted the improvised bandage from Harris's
arm. With a thin slat of wood, he drew a generous gob of
thick, black resin from the cook's cauldron. Ominous tendrils of steam rose from it. Jenny couldn't bring herself to
watch. She turned her head and clamped her eyes tightly
shut.

Harris returned to life with a mad bellow of pain. His
head jerked up, catching Jenny in the chest and knocking
the wind out of her.

"What the...?" A torrent of curses issued from his lips,
the gist of which was—what had happened, where was he,
and why had they seen fit to torture him?

Beneath the acrid stink of pitch, Jenny smelled Harris's
burning flesh. Her stomach seethed.

"Hush, now." She bent close over him, touching her
cheek to his as if hoping to leech some of his pain. "Ye
were struck with a musket ball from the pirate guns. Ye
fell and hit yer head. Ye've been out for ever so long,
Harris. I worried for ye. The captain said he had to doctor
yer wound with hot pitch to keep it from going bad."

Her explanation must have satisfied him somewhat, for
Harris quit cursing. He clenched his lips in a tight, rigid

line. A sheen of sweat blossomed on his forehead. Then Jenny remembered the jug of rum.

"Have a drink of this," she coaxed. "It'll dull the pain."

He swallowed the modest measure Jenny had dribbled into his mouth, gasping at the potency of the raw spirits. Before he could object, she poured more rum into him. Nodding over his work with approval, Captain Glendenning bound Harris's arm with a fresh strip of canvas. Once Jenny had dispensed several more doses of rum, the captain signaled his crewmen to release their hold on the patient's limbs. Harris struggled to his feet. With the hand of his sound arm, he snatched the rum jar from Jenny.

Tendering a clumsy bow that almost sent him sprawling back down on the deck, Harris addressed the captain. "Thank ye for the medical attention. If ye'll all excuse me, I'll retire to my cabin to recover from the day's adventures."

Jenny detected a twitch in the captain's lips. A quick glance at the crewmen told her they were also hiding smiles. She could cheerfully have throttled the lot of them.

"I'll help ye down the companionway, Harris." She cast the men a furious look that dared them to make anything of it. That look had often quelled her brothers, and it worked equally well on the crew of the *St. Bride*. A few began to talk noisily among themselves, while others grew suddenly busy with any little chore that might remove them from Jenny's sphere.

Whether still dizzy from the blow to his head, or already feeling the effects of the captain's rum, Harris weaved and tottered dangerously as he moved away. Jenny overtook him easily, sliding his good arm around her shoulder for support.

"I'm feeling a mite faint from all the excitement, myself." She spoke loudly, that the crew and other passengers might hear. "Since ye're going below yerself, perhaps ye might see me to my cabin, Mr. Chisholm."

"Oh, aye," Harris muttered. The taut set of his mouth suggested he was keeping to his feet, however unsteadily, by will alone.

They managed to stagger to his cabin, where Harris promptly collapsed on his berth. Jenny began wrestling with the knot of his stock. He batted her hands away.

"What are ye trying to do, strangle me?"

"I'm trying to undress ye for bed, so ye'll rest more comfortably," Jenny snapped. In truth, her nerves were more than a little frayed by the events of this afternoon. She half wished she'd taken a swig from Captain Glendenning's rum jar. "If ye'll just cooperate, it'll go easier for both of us."

"Ye can undo my neck linen, I suppose, and haul off my boots. Leave the rest be, do ye hear?"

"Fine. Fine." Jenny was prepared to humor him. The removal of his stock and boots would go some way toward making Harris more comfortable. She wasn't anxious to manhandle him out of his shirt, while trying to spare his wounded arm. As for his trousers, she had no intention of meddling with those.

With some difficulty, she managed to pry off his boots. Setting them neatly by the foot of his berth, she drew the blankets up over him. Spotting a short, three-legged stool in the corner, she pulled it nearer the bed, wilting onto the seat with a deep sigh.

Harris opened his eyes a slit. "What are ye about, now?"

"What does it look like? I'm settling myself down to stay the night and tend ye if ye need anything."

"What about yer fair reputation?" Harris's voice was heavy with sarcasm. "How will ye explain it to yer fiancé, Mr. Douglas, when he gets word that ye spent the night in *my* cabin?"

Casting that up to her after all these weeks, was he?

"I'll tell him the truth, of course. That ye were sore hurt and I was taking care of ye." Jenny could feel her cheeks smarting with an angry blush. "I'll also tell him ye weren't in any condition to make advances."

"What about ye, Jenny Lennox?" Harris asked. "Is my virtue safe from yer advances?"

"I'll make every effort to restrain myself." Jenny tried to match his mocking tone.

Harris gave an arid, joyless laugh. "That's what I was afraid of."

What on earth did he mean by that? Jenny wondered.

His eyes fell shut again. "Go away, Jenny. Leave me in peace."

If Harris Chisholm thought she was going anywhere, he had another think coming. "Isn't that what it's supposed to say on yer tombstone—*Rest in Peace?*"

"I haven't any intention of dying on ye, lass. I may not look it, but I'm made of sterner stuff than that. I just want to be left alone."

"Why?"

Harris struggled to sit up. "Why?" he echoed her question. "Because my arm hurts like hell, and my head hurts like hell, and I feel queer—like I don't know what I might say or do next. I want to rest, without ye gawking at me and fretting every time I feel a twinge."

Contrary, stubborn fool of a man! Jenny could feel herself shaking with the effort to contain her vexation. No one had ever made her feel with the intensity Harris Chisholm did. Whether it was rage or pity or...anything else, he always provoked such explosive emotions in her. She hated it.

"Ye're too proud to give in to yer pain before a woman? Is that it? Well, go right ahead, for I don't care. Moan. Groan. Bawl like a wee babby if ye want to. I swear I won't think any the less of ye for it."

"Because ye couldn't think less of me than ye do already?"

Jenny hesitated a moment before replying. The words that came out surprised her. "No," she said softly. "Because I think the world of ye, and nothing'll ever change that. First ye made my dreams possible, by letting me come on the *St. Bride*."

Though she knew she should speak of Roderick Douglas at this point, Jenny's lips refused to form his name. "Then ye taught me how to read. Ye've no idea what a gift that's been to me. I owe ye so much. Let me do this one wee thing by sitting with ye tonight."

He collapsed back onto his pillow so abruptly, Jenny started toward him in alarm. "What is it, Harris? Are ye all right?"

She leaned over him, relieved to hear his breath coming rapid but even. Then, before she knew what was happening, Jenny found herself encircled by Harris's sound arm, and being pulled down to him. She didn't struggle, for it might reopen his wound. At least that was what she told herself. His lips blundered over her lower face until they found hers.

Her first true kiss from a man.

Jenny and Kirstie had discussed this vital subject often in recent years. On those rare occasions when she'd lingered awake for a moment before falling into an exhausted sleep, she'd imagined herself being kissed by Roderick Douglas. This was nothing like the gallant, tentative salute she'd dreamed of. Harris kissed her deeply, voraciously, the way a man dying of thirst would consume cool, fresh water.

His mouth tasted of rum. It felt hot. So hot, that when his lips touched hers, Jenny half expected to hear them sizzle. His kiss, his arm tight around her, and the oddly pleasurable feel of her bosom mashed against his chest, made her body tingle with strange, intoxicating sensations.

Then, as unexpectedly as it had begun, it ended. Harris wrenched his lips from hers and pushed Jenny back. She staggered away from his berth, breathless and disoriented. Fortunately, she managed to light on the stool. Her body throbbed with frustration and the stirring of a slumbering hunger.

All was quiet in the cabin, save for their ragged breathing.

At last Harris spoke, in a voice hardly above a whisper. Raw. Bitter. And dead weary. "That's the only payment I want from ye, Jenny. I know ye'd never give it to me, so I've gone ahead and taken it. Yer debt's square now. No need to hang around here any longer smothering me with yer pity."

"Pity?" Jenny fairly shrieked. Anger was the only safe outlet for the combustible mix of emotions she barely understood. "Of all the things I feel for ye at this minute, Harris Chisholm—and I don't recognize half of them myself—I can assure ye there is not a scrap of pity in the lot."

"Oh?" He sounded surprised, and more than a little curious. "What all do ye feel for me, at this minute. The bits ye recognize, I mean."

"Rage," Jenny spat, "and in-dig-nation, for a start."

"That's all?" he asked, his tone bleak and hollow.

No. There was more, much more, and Jenny longed to tell him so. After that kiss, she did not dare. No matter what her intense, confused feelings for Harris Chisholm, it made no difference. She meant to marry Roderick Douglas and nothing was going to stand in her way. It would be cruel to encourage Harris to think otherwise.

"I'm grateful to ye, of course." Safe enough to admit that much. She'd be a hard-hearted little wretch to feel less. And maybe that's what it was, after all. A profound sense of gratitude and the habit of spending day after day in close company. Jenny could almost make herself believe it.

"Gratitude." Harris sighed. "That's almost as dry a crust as pity." His voice grew hard. "Stay then, if ye won't go, Jenny Lennox. But mind ye leave me be or I won't be responsible for my actions. If ye come near this bed again, like as not I'll kiss ye again. And I might not stop there."

Stubbornly Jenny held her place. He only meant to frighten her away with his talk, she was certain. Still, the notion of him kissing her again, and following it with even more intimate liberties, made her cheeks smart.

Her heart raced in time to the brisk bounce of the ship. Evidently that sou'wester the captain smelled on the morning breeze had blown up.

Time passed. Jenny did not know how much.

Wind screeched through a hundred tiny chinks in the upper hull. The timbers creaked in chorus, as though each sought to part violently from the others. On the deck above Jenny's head, footsteps fell in a heavy, lurching rhythm. It took her back to that first night on the *St. Bride,* when she'd cowered in her berth, certain she'd never survive the night's storm.

Perhaps she wouldn't have without Harris. She recalled the gentle dispatch of his touch. The soothing timbre of his voice so close to her ear. The comforting fact of his presence.

"I'm sorry, Harris," she murmured to herself. "I never meant to lead ye on, I swear it. I'd not hurt ye for the world."

"Don't fret yerself, lass."

She nearly jumped a foot when his words of reassurance pierced the din of the storm. She'd assumed he was asleep.

"I've a heart of shoe leather," he continued. "Like as not, I only fooled myself about how I feel. Ye're the first lass who's been more than civil to me. What with all the love talk in Mr. Scott's books and ye being such a bonny wee thing…"

"Aye, that's likely all it is," Jenny hastened to agree.

"The next lass who passes the time of day with ye will make ye forget all about me."

Somehow, that thought did not sit well with her, though she could not puzzle why.

Just as Jenny had decided to put the whole matter from her mind, the rapidly moving ship came to an abrupt, shuddering halt.

She plowed across the narrow cabin and onto the berth with Harris. He gave a sharp hiss of pain as she landed on top of him. The lamp went crashing to the floor, where it sputtered for a moment before going out.

"Damn!" cried Harris. "We've run aground." Pushing Jenny off him, he groped for the floor. "Where've ye put my boots?"

With a muffled report of rending wood, the barque lurched forward again.

Reaching down into the darkness, Jenny retrieved one of Harris's boots.

"I have the other." She heard him call as though from a great distance.

She sensed his contortions, trying to pull on the tight boots with an injured arm.

"We've got to get on deck," said Harris.

Before they could scramble out of the berth, the *St. Bride* once again fetched up against something solid. This time Harris fell on Jenny. As the breath burst from her lungs, she felt the soft scratch of his unshaven cheek against her forehead. One of his knees pinned her legs apart. When she raised her hand, it brushed the warm flesh of his chest through his open shirtfront. Some lunatic impulse within her wished they had hours to roll around on this narrow berth.

As the barque strained between the force of the storm wind in her sails and the pressure of the sandbar on her hull, Harris clambered up and hoisted Jenny to her feet. She gasped to feel water soaking into her shoes. There must be a good three inches of it already seeped through the floorboards, and rising fast.

"This way." Harris grasped her right hand and latched it to the waistband of his trousers. "Don't let go, ye hear? No matter what happens."

They staggered toward the cabin door. Jenny hoped that was where they were headed, at any rate. It was impossible to make out anything in the dense darkness of the barque's hold. Jenny fought to master her mounting panic at the thought of being trapped below decks. At least she had Harris with her this time.

She would trust him with her life.

As Harris pulled the cabin door open, someone fell through from the companionway.

"Have a care what ye're doing!" cried a voice. Jenny recognized the gruff, bass rumble of Mr. Tweedie, the cobbler from Wigtown. With a splash, the man regained his feet and fought his way out into the passage once more.

Harris followed, towing Jenny along behind him.

The tight companionway boiled with frantic shouts and grunts and the press of bodies anxious to escape the seawater flooding the lower decks. Jenny clutched Harris for all she was worth as he plunged ahead. They stumbled up the steep stairs, bursting onto the deck at last.

After the suffocating squeeze of the companionway, Jenny gulped in deep drafts of the briny wind, grateful to be out in the open at last.

"We must get to a lifeboat!" Harris bellowed.

His words barely penetrated the howl of the wind and the frantic babble of voices around them.

After a few faltering steps, Jenny felt the solid bulk of the ship's railing. Clinging to Harris with her right hand, she closed around the railing with her left and followed him.

"It's just up ahead!" Harris called back to her as a great billow hit the barque and doused them both with seawater.

Coughing and sputtering to catch her breath, Jenny lost her hold on the railing.

Another breaker followed, driving the *St. Bride* against another treacherous sandbar. Jenny's feet slid on the slick boards of the deck. She felt herself tumble against the rail and over into a black void.

At the last instant, she loosed her hold on Harris. She owed him better than a watery grave with her.

Chapter Six

"Jenny!"

Harris felt her pull on him cease abruptly. He heard the retreating sound of her scream as she fell overboard.

He knew he had not a second to lose. The *St. Bride* might pull free of the bar at any moment and be driven far from where Jenny'd gone over. Some flicker of logical self-interest pleaded with him that it was useless to go after her. In a storm like this, Jenny was surely lost.

Even as his heart acknowledged the futility of it, Harris dove into the sea.

Into the roiling waves he slammed. The salty, silty sea forced its way into his nose and mouth. It stung his eyes. Retching the water from his lungs, he fought his way to the surface, letting the breakers carry him where they would. Struggling for every precious breath, he vaguely sensed the *St. Bride*'s looming shadow moving away from him.

"Jenny!" he hollered again, straining to catch her reply no matter how feeble. "Jenny, where are ye, lass?"

He called and called, scarcely mindful of the swells that washed over him. Even after his rational self had abandoned hope, he continued to cry out her name like some plaintive last lament.

"Harris?"

It was scarcely more than a sigh on the wind, and he wondered if his drowning mind was playing tricks on him. Or perhaps her departing soul coaxed him to a final voyage with her.

He did not care.

She had called his name and he must answer.

"Here, Jenny! I'm here. Can ye come to me, lass?"

"Harris!" It was louder this time and definitely closer. A human voice, choked with fear and exhaustion. No flying angel or echo in his mind, but a lass of flesh and blood struggling to stay afloat.

Battling the opposing billows, he struck out toward the sound, desperately roaring her name whenever he could catch breath enough.

Then, suddenly, she was there. The only other living being in an endless storm-tossed night. Forgetting the need to stay afloat, forgetting his own name in the dizzying relief of finding her again, Harris clasped Jenny to him. She did not even struggle as they subsided beneath the waves and into the relative tranquility below.

And so they might have ended, had not Harris felt his foot strike solid firmament. Surely, it could not be...

With the last ebb of his strength, he anchored his feet to the sand and straightened up. To his amazement, his head and shoulders cleared the surface of the water—at least in the troughs between waves. His wounded arm blessedly numb, he pulled Jenny's head free of the water, too.

Together they sputtered and strained for air until Harris was able to gasp, "I can touch bottom, Jenny! We must be near the shore."

"Shore? Then we're saved!" Clinging to him as though she never meant to let go, Jenny began to laugh. And sob.

Harris held her tight—marveling at how natural it felt

to have her in his arms, wishing the moment would never end.

But like all sweet things, its time was finite.

As Jenny's weeping calmed, Harris sensed her shivering. Until then, he'd been too preoccupied with staying afloat to notice the temperature of the water. It was surprisingly warm. Warmer than the rain that continued to lash them. For all that, it was cooler than their bodies and slowly it was leeching the life from them. They needed to reach land and find shelter.

"We have to get out of the water before ye get any colder." Harris took a tentative step or two in each direction, trying to figure which way led to shallower water, and eventually to shore.

"What I wouldn't give for a bit of light," he muttered. His own teeth began to chatter.

Cautiously he made his way forward, heartened to feel more and more of his chest and back exposed to the air. Bared to the howling wind, the parts of him above the surface felt more chilled than those beneath.

"There, I can touch bottom, too!" cried Jenny. "Come on Harris, the beach can't be much farther."

They wallowed several steps more before Harris realized what was happening.

"Hold on, Jenny. Come back this way, lass. The water's getting deeper again."

"No, it isn't." she protested. "It can't be." A plaintive note of exhaustion in her voice told Harris she recognized the truth even as she denied it.

"This must be one of those sandbars the ship fetched up on," he said. "God knows how far it is to shore, or which way."

"What can we do?" wailed Jenny. "We have to find land."

"So we will," replied Harris with far greater assurance

than he felt. "We just have to hang on here until we've enough light to see the way to shore."

"How l-long do ye k-ken that'll be?"

"I haven't a notion, lass. It feels as though this night's lasted a thousand years, already. There's two things we need to do if we're to last till sunrise. We've got to keep as warm as we can and we've got to keep awake."

"How *c-can* we k-keep warm? It's not like we can light a fire or pull a blanket around us."

Harris tugged her toward him, wrapping his arms around her once more. "This is the only warmth we have, Jenny. Now rub yer hands on my back, like I'm doing to ye. As for keeping awake, we'll have to help each other there, as well. We'll talk. Do ye mind how fast the hours went by when we got to work arguing over something in one of Walter Scott's books?"

"Aye." Jenny didn't sound entirely convinced. "Ye're right about keeping warm, though. I feel a mite warmer already."

So did Harris.

Not just warm, but positively hot. In one part of his anatomy at least. He felt a rush of exasperation with his carnal nature, almost as intense as the rush of straining pleasure in his loins. Here he stood, poised on the brink of doom, yet his body perversely yearned to procreate. He prayed that Jenny, in her innocence, would not grasp the import of the eager bulge in his trousers.

"What will we talk about, then?"

Her question brought Harris back to himself with a start. What were they to speak of? Not the situation in which they found themselves, surely. Not their slim chances of surviving the night. Not this awkward but necessary embrace and the sensations it provoked…in him at least. They needed to occupy their thoughts with something far removed from this storm-swept strand. Preferably something warm.

"I don't know," he admitted, "but I'm willing to entertain suggestions."

Jenny did not immediately reply.

Harris grasped desperately for something to fill the silence and hopefully prime the conversational pump. It seemed absurd to be making small talk when, at any moment, they might die in each other's arms.

"I think the rain has eased." He tossed his head to twitch back the sodden hank of hair that clung to his brow. At the same time he chided himself for being the most unoriginal creature on the planet—commenting on the weather at such a time.

"I wonder if this is how folk in the Old Testament felt when God sent the flood?" mused Jenny. "I mind Pa reading the story of Noah to us. *All in whose nostrils was the breath of life, of all that was in dry land, died.*"

She shuddered, and Harris knew it was not entirely due to the cold.

"I ken even God took pity on those drowning sinners in the end," Jenny added. "Didn't he promise Noah never again to destroy mankind by flood?"

"Better flood than fire." The words were out of his mouth before Harris could recall them.

For an instant he hoped Jenny had not recognized the significance of what he'd said. Then he felt the back of her fingers slide along his jawline in the most tentative caress.

"Is that how ye came by yer scars? In a fire?"

"Aye. When I was a wee lad."

"Do ye mind how it came about?"

Harris hesitated. He had never spoken of the fire or its aftermath to another living soul. Under any other circumstances, he might not have divulged anything to Jenny, either. But this second brush with mortality had dredged up long-buried memories of his first. Besides, there was something about the blind physical contact between them that inspired confession.

"I don't recollect much about it," he admitted. "At least not when I'm awake. I have dreams though, of the smoke and the burning. I wake up drenched in sweat with my heart pounding like I've run a mile."

"Did yer ma die in the fire?"

Somehow, Harris sensed she had not meant to ask this impossibly painful question. Yet, for reasons he could not fathom, he felt compelled to answer.

"Die? No. For all I ken, she may be living yet."

"I don't understand, Harris. How can ye not ken whether yer ain ma is dead or alive? Whereabouts is she?"

"I haven't a notion. She ran away after the fire, so Father said. We never heard from her again."

"I'm sorry, Harris."

She was, too. He could feel it emanating from her fingertips and soaking into him. He could feel as she turned her face and pressed her cheek over his heart. He could feel it in the subtly different way she held on to him. Almost as though she wanted to cradle his lanky frame in her arms.

"Do ye mind anything of her at all?"

"No." That was not quite true, and though he could not think why, it was suddenly very important to him that Jenny know the truth. "At least, I never tried to. There are one or two memories that come to me now and again, though, when I least expect them."

"Aye?" It was a question, and a prompt for him to continue.

"I can hardly remember what she looked like, yet I sometimes get a flash of the way her chin tilted when she laughed. And sometimes, when I'm half-asleep, I can smell her scent and feel the brush of her kiss on my forehead..."

His voice choked off. Lifting his face to the night sky, he let the rain scour it like a torrent of tears.

"Harris?" There was cold fear in her voice. "The water's getting deeper again, isn't it?"

She was right. Even in the troughs between waves, the water level was higher than it had been.

"The tide must be rising." He strove to keep the disquiet from his own voice—without success.

"I can't die now, Harris. I've never lived until these past six weeks."

Harris fought to quench the flicker of hope her words engendered. She must mean her anticipation of wedding Roderick Douglas. "You're not going to die, Jenny. You've too much pluck. Mind about Mr. Douglas. He's waiting for you in Chatham and ye don't strike me as the kind of lass who'd disappoint her bridegroom."

He expected her to launch into a litany of Roderick's virtues. Harris braced himself to bear it. At least it would distract her from the peril of their situation.

"What made yer ma run off, Harris?" she asked instead, with quiet gravity. Her question took him so much by surprise he fairly staggered.

"That's the one other thing I mind about her, Jenny. Her eyes whenever she looked at me after the fire. She left because she couldn't bear the sight of me."

What made him think anything had changed? He still bore the marks of the fire, and once again a woman he cared for was about to walk out of his life. Without a backward glance. Leaving behind nothing but sweetly taunting memories and wounds upon his heart that would scar him all over again. It made him long to give up the struggle and simply lapse beneath the waves with Jenny in his arms.

"I don't believe it." Her words stirred Harris from his painful reflections. He struggled to grasp what she meant.

"No mother would do such a thing. She may have had other reasons a child would never ken."

"Such as...?"

Jenny fought to put it into words. How could a man understand the ceaseless drudgery and soul-consuming isolation? Perhaps the fire that scarred Harris had also wrought destruction on the Chisholm croft, making his mother's lot harder than ever. But enough to leave her son behind? Jenny found that hard to credit.

"Ye don't mind how it is for a woman, Harris. I ken well enough what it's like to crave something different. Something better. It could be yer ma felt that way, too."

Her words met with silence at first.

Then came a low, thoughtful murmur. "Aye, lass. I reckon it could be."

She couldn't bear the thought of Harris dwelling on such bitter memories in what might well be his last hours. Jenny berated herself for raising the subject in the first place. Recklessly she cast about for any diversion.

"Do ye mind what I wish, Harris?"

"Aye, lass." He sighed. "I'm yer fairy godfather, after all. Ye wish to wed Mr. Douglas and live prosperously ever after."

"Besides that."

"Aren't ye being a mite greedy to wish for more besides?"

"It's not *that* kind of wish, anyhow. More a…regret."

"Ah, regret." His voice lingered over the word. "There's something I know about. What do ye regret, Jenny? Besides setting foot aboard an unlucky vessel like the *St. Bride.*"

"I regret…" Her whole consciousness suddenly fixed upon the two warm spots on her body. Her bosom, which nestled against his belly, and the shifting spirals on her back described by the caress of his hands. "I regret that I never got to know ye better while we lived in Dalbeattie. Who knows but we mightn't have made a match?"

She felt the quiver in his belly before she heard his laugh. It was a queer sound—at this time and in this place.

"Can you just picture it, lass? If some old crone with the second sight had accosted us outside the kirk and told us we'd end up like this. Do ye ken we'd have stalked off in high dudgeon or laughed ourselves hoarse?''

''Ye'd have stalked off. I'd have laughed.''

Her quip made Harris laugh harder still. It was so irresistible a sound, Jenny could not help joining in. For a time, the warmth of that shared laughter and the contact between them held the cold, and the wind, and the darkness at bay.

Like a candle burning fitfully in its last puddle of wax, this tiny pocket of light also guttered and failed. Somehow, the cold black void oppressed Jenny even more after that sweet moment of relief. She began to shiver again and a deep weariness threatened to engulf her.

''I don't reckon I c-c-can last much longer, Harris.''

''Ye mustn't give up, lass. Mind about Mr. Douglas and yer wedding.''

This was the second time he'd urged her to think about Roderick, and for some reason it irked Jenny. She knew perfectly well she should be thinking about her future husband and the life that awaited her in Miramichi—if only she could hold on until daybreak. If they were not her greatest motive for living, what else could be?

Hard as she tried to focus on thoughts of her wedding, every notion in her head turned obstinately back to Harris Chisholm. From all she had learned of him in the past six weeks, Jenny knew with utter certainty that her death would haunt him. Unmerited feelings of responsibility and guilt would consume him. That was no fit way to repay the enormous debt she owed him.

''Aye,'' she murmured drowsily. ''I'll do my best to hang on, Harris. For ye.''

Fighting the deadly lassitude that grew heavier and more strength-sapping with each passing moment, Harris held Jenny closer. In a futile effort to stanch the ebb of her energy, he rubbed her back and arms with increasing vigor.

All the while, two brief, whispered words echoed in his thoughts and fired his desperate effort to save her.

"For ye."

It was no dream of handsome, wealthy, powerful Roderick Douglas that stirred Jenny and roused her failing will to live. It was her feelings for him. Scarred, poor and insignificant, he still had the power to lure her back from the siren song of peaceful oblivion.

"For me, Jenny. That's right. Hang on for me. I can't lose ye, Jenny. Not now. I've been waiting all my life for ye, though I never knew it. Stay with me, lass. Jenny? Jenny!"

The pull of death was too strong. Harris could almost feel it sucking her life away. Like a giant whirlpool, dragging her into the depths of eternity. Grasping helplessly for anything that might rouse her, he lifted Jenny as high as his waning strength would allow.

And he kissed her.

Not the way he'd kissed her in his cabin on the *St. Bride,* a lifetime ago. Then he had *taken* a kiss from her. Wresting by force what he knew she would never surrender willingly. Taking some perverse satisfaction from her reluctance, for it made him the master.

This time he *gave* Jenny a kiss, buoyed by the improbable hope that she might want it after all. At first her lips felt cool and slack to the touch, but Harris paid no mind. He molded his mouth to hers, making it an instrument of supplication and enticement. Nuzzling, caressing, satiating, he used his lips and tongue to beseech and beguile her back to life.

What effect it had on Jenny, Harris could not tell at first. But the embers of his own strength rekindled. His heart beat faster, sending feverish blood pulsing through his veins with renewed potency.

Then he felt it.

The gentlest flutter of her tongue. A subtle movement

of her lips. The pressure of his kiss, oh so delicately reciprocated. Somehow he had changed roles from the fairy godfather to the prince, with vistas of "happily ever after" opening before him.

So intent was he upon Jenny, and nursing this flicker of life within her, that Harris scarcely heard oars rhythmically hitting the water. The muted sound of voices did rouse him, however, though he could not understand the words.

Wrenching his attention from Jenny, he glanced around to find that dawn had stolen upon them. The rain had eased to little more than a drizzle, and the wind had died. Though it was still not fully light, Harris could make out the shoreline, no more than a hundred yards away. Then he saw the boat—a long canoe, approaching from the distant opposite shore.

Mustering the last crumbs of his strength, he held Jenny with his good arm and raised the wounded one in the air.

"Here! Help!" he called in a voice so weak and raspy he hardly recognized it.

A voice from the boat exclaimed, but Harris could not make out what. Confident they'd been spotted, he let his arm fall.

As the canoe drew close, Harris saw two rugged men wielding the paddles.

"Lord-a-mercy," cried one. "These must be the folks that washed overboard of the wreck."

With what little grasp of consciousness he still possessed, Harris wondered how they could ever haul him and Jenny aboard without upsetting their precariously balanced craft. It proved no easy feat, their efforts hampered by Harris's ebbing strength and Jenny's deadweight. The men were obviously masters of their strange vessel, for in time they prevailed.

"Lay down with your missus and hang on to her," advised the older-looking of the two men.

Too weary to explain that Jenny was not his wife, Harris

followed the order. The boatmen doffed their coats and laid them over the supine pair. Taking up their paddles again, they struck out for the far shore with urgent speed.

They spared breath for speech only once.

The boat had been making swift progress for some time when Harris heard one of the men gasp "Think they'll make it?"

They must have thought he'd lost consciousness, as well. In truth, Harris was losing his tenuous grip on it.

The last sound he heard was the laconic reply "Him, maybe."

Chapter Seven

The last thing Jenny remembered—or had she only dreamed it?—was the taste of Harris's kiss. It lingered in her mouth, when she finally regained consciousness, hours later.

She did not waken all at once, but rose to full awareness by stages, as if climbing from a deep pit. Her body felt chilled to the very marrow, and by times an uncontrollable palsy shook her. Yet, in some vague way, Jenny knew she was no longer in the water. She lay wrapped in a strange cocoon that was soft and warm. She breathed air faintly pungent of sheep and new-mown hay. She heard the muted but familiar sounds of farm life—the splash of wash water, cows lowing in the distance, the chink of crockery, voices old and young.

How many hours she had lain here Jenny could not guess. She might have been content to lie for several more, her mind drifting drowsily. Except for the thought of Harris.

Through the long, cold night he'd held her, standing like a guardian angel between her and death. Long after she'd been willing to surrender, he had fought for her. She was certain Harris would have grappled for her soul with the devil himself. Now he was gone, and Jenny ached for him.

Her eyelids felt heavier than a pair of overflowing milk pails, but she managed to lift them open. At first she squinted against the bright daylight, but gradually her eyes grew accustomed to it and she was able to take in her surroundings. She found herself lying on a pile of straw in a small structure of roughly hewn wood. Sandwiched between a pair of crude blankets pieced from raw fleeces, Jenny suddenly realized that she was mother-naked.

The sound of a stifled giggle drew her gaze to the entry of the shed. The top half of a child's head peeked around the door, rapidly disappearing again when its eyes met hers.

"Hullo?" Jenny strained to croak the word. Once it erupted from her parched throat, the rest came a little easier. "It's all right. I'm awake."

At first her only answer was a hesitant shuffling just outside the doorway. Then the towhead appeared again.

Jenny smiled encouragingly. Since she hadn't the strength to rise, this child was her only possible source of news about Harris. "Ye can come in," she called softly. "I don't bite."

The giggle burst forth again and soon an entire wee girl materialized. Eyes wide as saucers, she took a cautious step nearer Jenny. "Are ye the lady that drowned?"

The unexpected question made Jenny laugh. Yet tears also sprang to her eyes. "Aye," she replied. "I came close to it at least. The last I mind, I was still in the water. I don't ken how I got here or where this is. Can ye tell me?"

The child gave a broad grin, proudly missing a front tooth. She was a skinny little mite—her bare feet, face and forearms deeply tanned from the sun. Showing below her much-mended dress and apron, her calves were criss-crossed with angry red scratches that made Jenny wince.

"This is Richibucto," the child announced eagerly. "Leastways, it's Jardine's Yard. Pa's boat ran aground last night in the storm."

"You're Captain Glendenning's daughter." Jenny hesitated over the question that immediately leapt to mind. "Is he...? That is—did he...?"

"Aye, I'm Nellie. Pa's fine. Just provoked about his boat being wrecked. Everyone else got to shore safely in the lifeboats, but nobody knew what had happened to ye and that man."

"We fell overboard," said Jenny. "At least I did." Harris hadn't fallen, he'd jumped in after her. "What's become of the man who was with me?"

Her heart clenched in her chest as she awaited Nellie Glendenning's reply.

"They took him somewhere else. Jardine's, maybe."

"Was he...alive?"

"Aye, but in a bad way, like ye were."

The tension ebbed from Jenny's body. If she had survived, surely Harris must have, too.

"Shall I run over and see if he died?" asked Nellie.

Before Jenny could find the courage to answer, a loud whisper hissed from outside the shed. "Come out of there, Nellie. You'll wake the lass with yer jabbering."

The child spun around. "I didn't wake her," she called. "Her eyes were open and she told me to come in. Ask her for yerself."

Brisk footsteps drew nearer. Stooping to pass through the sawed-off hole that served for a door, a woman entered. She was a slight creature, as ill fed as her child. Her face had a pinched, weary look Jenny knew all too well. Furrows of worry etched deep in her forehead and exhaustion had left dark smudges beneath her eyes. Jenny felt a pang of guilt for adding another burden to this woman's obvious load.

"So ye are going to live, lass." Mrs. Glendenning sounded surprised, but her thin face blossomed into a warm smile. Like her daughter's, it was marred by the absence of several teeth. "I'm glad. My Angus would have taken it hard if ye hadn't."

"Thank ye for taking me in, ma'am." Jenny longed to ask the woman about Harris. Mrs. Glendenning might know more than her daughter. Before she could form the words, however, everything in the shed began to spin. Letting her eyes fall shut, Jenny groaned.

"Go easy now, lass. It'll take you a few days to get your strength back. Nellie, come with me and we'll get Miss Lennox a bit of hot broth. Rest, lass. Time enough to talk later. If I was ye, I'd say my prayers, though, and thank the good Lord for sparing ye."

Jenny murmured her agreement. She could not even open her eyes to watch them go. Heeding Mrs. Glendenning's advice, she surrendered to the inexorable tug of sleep. As she sank back into the peaceful depths of unconsciousness, Jenny also followed the woman's admonition to pray.

It was not a prayer of thanksgiving she addressed wordlessly to heaven, but an urgent petition.

"Please, God. Let Harris be all right."

Surprised by his own resiliency, Harris had recovered enough strength that evening to venture a short walk with his host. He'd rather have gone to Glendennings' to check on Jenny. However, the captain had assured him she was well on the road to recovery and spent most of her time sleeping.

Instead, Harris stood on the wharf at Jardine's Yard, watching the battered *St. Bride* limp into harbor. A crew of workers winched the barque up on dry dock for repairs.

"She has a few rents in her hull," said the grave, quiet man beside him. "I'll wager the keel's sound, though. Patched up, she'll do well enough for coastal runs."

Harris looked at Robert Jardine, builder of the *St. Bride*. "How long do ye ken before she's fit to sail again?"

Jardine ran a hand over his bald pate, pondering the question. "If we had a full crew to work, we could have her seaworthy again in jig time. The trouble is, it's hay season. There's scarcely a pair of hands to spare in the whole county. I ken the folks in Chatham will just have to wait for this load of goods—at least what cargo isn't waterlogged. I can't see the *St. Bride* making that run for a good six weeks or better."

"Six weeks." Harris tried to keep the eagerness from his voice. He failed miserably.

Robert Jardine cast him a sidelong, questioning look. "So ye're in no hurry to be on yer way? I reckoned ye might want to get where ye're going and settle in before winter hits."

Harris shrugged. "I didn't have a special destination in mind, so one place is as good as another." Somewhere he might not be an outsider, as he had been in Dalbeattie. He'd enjoyed the enforced camaraderie of the ocean voyage. If only he could find a similar sense of belonging somewhere in the New World.

He relished the thought of six more weeks with Jenny. Six weeks of late summer. No longer confined aboard ship, but free to wander this strange new land. From what he'd seen, Harris knew it was expansive enough to afford them stolen moments of privacy.

Just then, he was tempted to bless all storms and sandbars, for they had conspired to grant him the gift of time. Time to win Jenny's heart.

"If ye've no place else in mind," said the shipbuilder, "ye could do worse than bide here. It's a land of opportunity for a man like ye, Chisholm. Right now, there's but two kinds of folk in the colony. Ones like me and my brother, who have a bit of capital and a notion to make our fortunes."

He nodded toward the crew straining on ropes to pull the barque free of the water. "Then there are the fellows with strong backs, no education to speak of, and not a penny to their names. They only want a bit of land to farm and call their own.''

''Aye?'' Harris didn't quite see where the conversation was headed.

''What we don't have on the Richibucto are men like ye—who've an education and some experience in business. If this settlement's to thrive, we're going to need managers and justices of the peace.'' He grimaced. ''Even a politician or two.''

''I don't fancy myself in politics.'' Harris chuckled. ''But running a business—aye, I can do that.''

''Say the word and ye can have a place with Jardine Brothers.''

''That's a generous offer, sir.'' Harris shook the hand of his prospective employer. ''I'll think on it and let you know in a day or so.''

''Ye may not think me so generous when ye see the state our ledgers are in,'' Robert Jardine replied.

As the two men laughed over this, Harris also shook his head in wonder. Clearly this was a land where opportunities flourished like the endless expanse of forest. He drew a deep breath of air in which were mingled the briny tang of the sea and the spicy resin of pine and spruce.

It smelled like optimism.

The warm scent of fresh milk rose from the churn as Jenny worked the dasher. Like the sharp pungency of lye soap and the fermenting aroma of bread dough, it was one of the many odors of drudgery. Her arms ached and waves of dizziness still took her by times, but she could not lay about being waited on. Not while there was so much work to do and Mrs. Glendenning already worn to a shadow trying to do it.

A pair of black pigs rooted under a nearby oak tree for fallen acorns. In the distance, Jenny could hear the children squealing with glee as they harvested wild raspberries. From the house came the thin wail of the baby. A frail, fitful infant, Jenny doubted he would survive the winter.

With a shiver of apprehension, she wondered if she had made a grave mistake by coming to this wild, alien land. In such primitive conditions, a woman's lot became harder than ever.

Jenny gazed around her at the Glendenning grant. It was one of the more prosperous, since Captain Glendenning plied a comparatively profitable trade as shipmaster for half the year. Yet it made her father's modest upland croft look luxurious by comparison.

The family dwelling was a meanly proportioned cabin built from overlapping logs. Cracks between the logs were stuffed with moss to keep out the wind. A few rough out-buildings, like the one where Jenny had slept, housed the livestock in winter. For now they ranged at will, the oxen and milch cows grazing a bit of marshland on the creek bank.

From what Jenny could tell, the Glendennings' weekday clothes were sewn from heavy sailcloth that made her own plain, serviceable gingham look positively decadent. There was plenty to eat—fish, game and newly ripened vegetables. Imported foodstuffs, like flour and sugar were more strictly rationed. Jenny suspected the early spring must be a hungry season, when stored root crops began to run low and ships from abroad had not yet come.

And what of the winter?

She shivered to think of it. The long, cold, dark days without a scrap of society or cheer. The vast, impenetrable forest looming oppressively around, watchful and hungry.

"Have ye got that butter churned yet, lass?" Mrs. Glendenning appeared, toting two heavy buckets of water from the creek. "The men'll want it for their dinner."

"Aye, I ken it's done." Jenny felt the flush that had

crept into her cheeks. She had taken out her worries on the hapless container of cream, dashing it with frantic vigor.

"Ye can pour off the skim into the pigs' trough." Mrs. Glendenning rested for a moment, her thin bosom heaving.

"The baby was crying." Jenny struggled to keep her balance as the pigs shoved their way to the trough.

After hoisting her pails again, Mrs. Glendenning made for the cabin. "When does he stop?" she muttered, more to herself than to Jenny. "I ken he's hungry, but he'll just have to wait till I get the dinner made."

"Sit down and feed him," said Jenny. "I'll see to dinner, or at least get it started."

"The stew's on and the bread's baked." Mrs. Glendenning made her way into the windowless cabin, with Jenny on her heels. "Ye can cut the bread and set the greens to boil, though. I wish the children would get back from picking berries. I promised Angus a pudding while he's home."

She wilted into a low chair that had obviously emigrated from Scotland with the family. Though not a fancy or expensive piece of furniture by any means, it stood out from the cabin's other rough-hewn appointments. Clearly what was commonplace—even poor—by Galloway standards, passed for elegance in this pioneer settlement.

As Jenny lifted the whimpering infant from his cradle and set him in his mother's arms, a sudden wave of doubt engulfed her. What of Roderick's claims of prosperity? Was he as rich as his letter had made him sound—or only rich on the meager scale of his neighbors?

Gathering the crockery for the midday meal from a high shelf, she mused, "Does everyone in the colony live like this?"

Only when Mrs. Glendenning answered did Jenny realize she'd spoken aloud.

"Nay, lass." The woman's voice held no resentment— at least not of the question. "Mrs. Jardine has a fine big house and all the hired help she needs to keep it. I hear tell there's folk in Chatham with proper houses built of stone. I've been after Angus for us to have a stone house by and by. He says it's daft to build with stone when wood's so plentiful."

As she set the table, Jenny glanced toward the open cabin door. "Aye," she breathed. "Wood's plentiful enough."

And strange it seemed. The Scottish lowlands and border counties had long been denuded of any great tracts of forest. In this new land, forests hovered around the tiny communities that had been carved out on their fringes. Greedy to reclaim the land and push the invading immigrants back into the sea. How could anything tender hope to survive, much less thrive, in such a place?

Jenny followed the smell of meat and onions to the Glendennings' summer kitchen. In the cramped lean-to, she hoisted a heavy iron kettle off the fire and replaced it with another, half-full of water and assorted greens.

Pondering Mrs. Glendenning's words about servants and stone houses, she knew she should be awash with relief. That did not describe the seething stew of emotions that curdled in her belly. It felt more like uncertainty and fear, seasoned with a dash of some nameless longing.

The distant whoops and shrieks of the children reminded Jenny that their mother wanted the berries for a pudding. She picked her way through the dense brush, drawn by their exuberant noise. At last, she found them, clustered around a patch of raspberry nettles—Nellie, her two older brothers and small sister. The red stains around their mouths told tales of many berries that had never made it into their baskets of woven bark.

"What's all the racket?" she asked. "They'll be able to hear your noise clear to Chatham."

"There was a squirrel up that tree." Nellie pointed toward a towering old pine. "John was pelting him with acorns, and one bounced off and hit me on the head."

"It was an accident!" young John protested. "No call for her to throw stones at me, the wee telltale."

For a moment, Jenny had the welcome sensation of being back home again in the midst of her brothers' squabbles. Evidently some aspects of life didn't change, no matter how many oceans a body crossed.

"I'm no justice of the peace," she said. "Ye'll have to settle this yerselves—without letting more missiles fly, I hope. In the meantime, do ye ken ye've left any room in yer stomachs for dinner? Yer ma's looking to have those berries for a pudding."

"Hurrah! Bang-belly!" Forgetting their quarrel, the Glendenning fry snatched up their baskets and headed for home at top speed.

With an indulgent chuckle, Jenny set off after them.

She nearly jolted a foot in the air when a warm whisper sounded directly in her ear.

"Ye've quite a way with young ones. Ye'll make a fine mother someday."

The innocent remark struck at Jenny's deepest fears. Part of her longed for motherhood. Yet, how could she properly nurture children under conditions like these?

When she spun about to deliver a stinging retort, Jenny landed in the waiting arms of Harris Chisholm. Part of her meant to struggle and pull away from him. Another part, powerful beyond all proportion to its size, longed to lose herself in his eager embrace. Conflicting emotions grappled onto her heart and waged a fierce tug-of-war. Thank heaven, she'd soon be in Chatham, rediscovering her love for Roderick Douglas!

"I was none too certain I'd see ye again, this side of heaven, lass." Heedless of all propriety, Harris held her close. "Ye gave me quite a turn, at the last. Should ye be up and bossing the wee Glendennings about so soon?"

Reason reasserted itself. Harris had saved her life. He'd come to mean a great deal to her. That didn't alter the fact that she'd journeyed to New Brunswick to marry Roderick Douglas. After what she'd seen and heard of pioneer life, that marriage was more imperative than ever.

Fighting her inclination to linger against him, Jenny drew back from Harris and tried to answer coolly. "I couldn't loll in bed all day when poor Mrs. Glendenning has so much to do. Ye don't look any the worse for our shipwreck adventure. What brings ye here?"

Harris jerked his thumb back toward the homestead. "I brought yer trunk. I can't vouch for the condition of the contents."

"My trunk!" exclaimed Jenny. "I reckoned it'd be at the bottom of the channel along with the wreck of the *St. Bride*."

"Did the captain not tell ye? The wreck's in dry dock. She may not be up to crossing the Atlantic again, but Mr. Jardine figures she'll fare well enough with a Caribbean run."

"Captain Glendenning's been busy getting his hay in for winter," explained Jenny as they ambled back to the cabin. "He's never said a word about the *St. Bride*. How soon will it be fit to sail to Chatham?"

"Mr. Jardine says she ought to be ready in six weeks." Harris made it sound like a marvel of speed.

To Jenny the time stretched ahead indefinitely. "Six weeks!" she wailed. "I can't cool my heels here for six weeks when Roderick Douglas is expecting me in Chatham. Isn't there another boat I can take?"

Even as she asked, her neck pricked with gooseflesh at the thought of another sea voyage, however brief. One intimate experience with the dangers of seafaring was quite enough to last her a lifetime. Yet, with a curious flash of insight, Jenny recognized that a greater danger to her life-long dream lay in the seemingly benign prospect of six more weeks with Harris Chisholm.

"There may be." Harris shrugged. "And there may not. Mr. Jardine says we oughtn't count on one. What's yer hurry anyhow? After what ye said the other night, I minded ye might be having second thoughts about the wedding."

Jenny rounded on him. "I said nothing of the kind Harris Chisholm and I'll thank ye not to go putting words in my mouth. If I did say something, it was only because I was off my head with cold and fear we were going to die."

So fiercely was she concentrating on her vehement protest, Jenny did not see the tree root snaked out on the path before her. She pitched forward, arms swinging wildly, trying in vain to regain her balance. Harris dove to catch her but only succeeded in softening her fall. Together they sprawled onto a bed of moss and ferns.

The vital fragrance of the forest overwhelmed Jenny, as did her body's vexing reaction to Harris. Her heart galloped almost painfully and her breath came in short, sharp spasms. She felt light-headed and giddy. An alarming, though not unpleasant, warmth spread through her.

It emanated from every point where his person touched hers. His upper arm wedged tight against her bosom. The gentler, but no less intoxicating, pressure of his thigh on hers. The momentary brush of his cheek against her ear. They made her long for all sorts of things she had no business wanting. Least of all from this man, when she was promised to another.

Though her body yearned to lie there, pressing against Harris in even more intimate ways, Jenny's deep-seated practicality won out.

For this time.

"Get off me now, ye great oaf!" Like a scalded cat, she sprang to her feet and began to pick stray fronds of greenery from her hair.

His face a furious red, Harris got to his feet. "I tried to

save ye from braining yerself on the ground, and this is the thanks I get?'' Brushing off his vest and breeches, he kept his back turned to her.

I tried to save ye. The words sliced through Jenny like a saber of ice. How often had Harris come to her aid, only to be repaid with insults and ingratitude? He'd saved her life the night of the wreck and she hadn't so much as acknowledged it. Though he might assume it was because she cared nothing for him, Jenny knew it was because she cared far too much. And feared to care still more.

''Oh, Harris, I'm sorry.'' Though she recognized the inherent danger, Jenny could not resist reaching for him. ''Ye saved me from far worse than a wee fall, and I haven't said a word about it. Ye must think me a proper shrew.''

When her hand came to rest on his arm, Harris jerked away, as if her touch burned him. ''Think nothing of it,'' he muttered. ''I gave my word I'd see ye safe to Miramichi.''

''And ye're a man of yer word.'' That and so much more.

Perhaps thinking her comment merited no reply, Harris stalked off toward the Glendenning farm, where the raucous clang of a dinner bell summoned the family to their midday meal.

Jenny hesitated for a moment to wipe the unaccountable tears that had sprung to her eyes. Why did it gall her so, to learn that Harris's concern sprang from nothing more than a compulsion to honor his word? Surely she didn't want him motivated by more tender feelings.

Or did she?

Chapter Eight

Gritting his teeth and drawing his brows into a stern frown, Harris strove to concentrate on the column of figures before him. Robert Jardine hadn't exaggerated when he claimed the firm's ledgers were a mess. Though Harris hadn't formally committed to a position with Jardine Brothers, he'd agreed to look over their accounts. It was the least he could do to repay their generosity in taking him in.

The hopeless muddle of the company ledger was not what made Harris scowl, however. It was the contradictory behavior of a certain bewitching damsel, and his own daft persistence in caring. After that endless, terrifying night in the river, he'd deluded himself into believing feelings had changed between him and Jenny. The way they'd held each other. The confidences they'd shared. How could it all have meant so much to him, without making a dent in her mercenary little heart?

If nothing else, he'd hoped it would make her have second thoughts about marrying Roderick Douglas. Instead, she appeared more determined than ever to get to Chatham and the waiting arms of her intended. Not for the life of him could he understand her hurry. Richibucto was a pleasant enough place, albeit somewhat unpolished. The town reminded Harris of an awkward but eager boy who would soon mature into his bright prospects. A fellow might do worse than settle here.

Except that Jenny would be forty miles up the coast in Chatham. Could he reconcile himself to the separation? Heaving a sigh of impatience with himself, Harris slammed the heavy ledger shut. Jardine Brothers' tiny countinghouse at least boasted the amenity of a glazed window. Rising from the stool and stretching his long limbs, Harris wandered over to it.

The August sun blazed down on the harbor as it had every day since the storm that had wrecked the *St. Bride*. Gulls wheeled and dove in a cloudless sky, blue as cornflowers. Their shrill cries sounded like a chorus of derisive laughter.

Can you stay here and see her seldom? they seemed to shriek. *Or go to Chatham and see her day after day with another man?*

"Aye," Harris muttered bitterly. "Ye have a point there."

The songbirds seemed to warble a bittersweet love ballad in counterpoint to the baby's sharp, fitful squalling, as Jenny watched Harris approach Glendennings'. Confident he hadn't noticed her lingering on the fringe of the forest, she gazed at him to her heart's content. Rationally she knew his looks had changed little from the day they'd departed Kirkcudbright.

He'd picked up a bit of a tan, which complemented the warm hues of his hair and eyes. And his face had lost its old haughty aspect, relaxing into an air of wry humor that was most becoming. His scars remained, though of late Jenny scarcely noticed them. Possibly because Harris himself seemed less self-conscious.

These subtle differences hardly accounted for the change in her response to him. Lately, whenever he came near, a pulse of warmth went through her, as though her entire body blushed. Her heart skipped from its steady, monotonous beat into a skittish dance. Often, some deft motion of his hands, or some quirk of his smile made her breath catch in her throat.

She'd begun to fancy him.

Though she hadn't fully articulated the notion when they'd arrived in Richibucto a fortnight ago, Jenny had feared this would happen. She'd fought against every sign of it, but to no avail. It was as though the more she resisted her attraction for Harris, the stronger it grew. How long could she hold out against it? Another month?

Not likely.

Harris emerged from the cabin, squinting in her direction. Roderick Douglas's intended bride wanted to turn and bound off into the woods, like the deer she had surprised one morning at dawn. Some irresistible force rooted her to the spot as Harris approached.

"Another fine day." He glanced up, surveying the wide expanse of azure sky unmarred by a single cloud. "Say what ye will about this place, ye can't find fault with the weather."

The raging tempest of conflicting passions within her made Jenny reply sharply. "Easy enough for a man to say. Ye don't have to lug water from the creek to keep the garden from dying."

Harris looked at her as though she had slapped him.

"I ken it's better than rain every day." She softened her tone and smiled her apology. "At least a body can water the crops when it's dry. There's not much ye can do to keep them from rotting in the wet. What brings ye this way?"

He brightened at her question. "Mrs. Jardine sent me with an invitation. Would ye care to dine with us tonight?"

Jenny hesitated for only an instant. "Aye, I would. If

I'm to wed a prosperous man and live in a fine house, I'll need to polish my manners."

"That's fine then," replied Harris. Something in his tone and look suggested disappointment with her answer. "I'll come and fetch ye around seven."

"Seven? That's almost bedtime."

"Folk of quality eat later," Harris informed her. With a sour edge in his voice, he added, "Ye'd better get used to it."

After he'd gone, Jenny hurried to finish as many of the chores as she could for Maizie Glendenning.

"Ye've been a godsend for me, Jenny, and no mistake. The chores'll be there for us when we get to them. Right now, I'm going to dress yer hair. Ye might not think it, but back in the auld country, I was quite the gadabout. Now, what have ye got to wear for yer visit tonight?"

Jenny rummaged through her trunk, which had remained miraculously dry in spite of the shipwreck. As she pulled out each piece of her trousseau, purchased with gold sent by Roderick Douglas, Maizie reacted with raptures of admiration.

"Look at the color of it."

"Just feel the weight of the cloth."

When Jenny unearthed the last garment, her hostess was dumbstruck. "Will ye look at that now," she managed to whisper.

With a self-conscious grin, Jenny held her badly wrinkled wedding dress in front of her. Silk, the color of heather, made up in the latest fashion. For as long as Jenny could recall, women's dresses had fallen straight from beneath the bosom, but she'd seen pictures of older-style gowns. Gowns with tightly cinched waists and voluminous skirts—provocatively beautiful.

The mode of her wedding dress harkened back to those fashions, with a wide band of ribbon below the bust and a flared skirt supported by a rustle of laced petticoats. As she ran her hand wonderingly over the fine, smooth fabric, Jenny fought the urge to wear this gown to her dinner with the Jardines. She had several other good dresses, well suited to the occasion, though none quite so stylish as this. Besides, she felt a superstitious misgiving about wearing her wedding gown before the wedding. She'd spent Roderick's gold on this special garment. She owed it to him to save it for their nuptials.

Yet, when she weighed all this in the balance against the look on Harris's face when he first beheld her in this swath of heather silk, somehow it did not weigh as heavily as it ought.

Quashing her foolish inclination, Jenny briskly stuffed her wedding gown back into the trunk. With forced animation, she asked Maizie Glendenning how they should dress her hair.

By the time Harris arrived to escort her to Jardines', Jenny felt certain she'd swallowed a colony of butterflies. Their delicate wings fluttered urgently within her stomach. She had to clasp her hands hard together to still the trembling that threatened to overtake them.

"Will ye look at that now?" The reverent catch in Harris's breath and the admiration that glowed in his eyes threatened to intoxicate Jenny.

She couldn't help wondering how he might have reacted if she'd worn the silk.

"I didn't want ye ashamed to be seen with me." She tried to sound matter-of-fact, but her voice came out high-pitched and breathless.

With courtly formality, he held out his arm to her. "Any man with sense would be proud to squire such a fine lady."

Jenny placed her hand in the crook of his elbow. Her demure smile twitched into a teasing grin. "So ye were paying me some mind when I tried to teach ye manners?"

Harris laughed heartily. "Aye, lass. Now and again. But

let's not dawdle here while the food gets cold. The Jardines set a good table.''

His recommendation proved true enough, but to Jenny the evening was as much a feast for the spirit as for the palate.

As they sat in the parlor awaiting dinner, Mrs. Jardine remarked, ''Mr. Chisholm tells me ye admire the works of Walter Scott, Miss Lennox.''

''I've only read three,'' admitted Jenny, failing to confess that Harris had done most of the reading. ''I liked them fine, though. Mr. Scott tells a bonny tale.''

Their hostess nodded. ''Mr. Chisholm was kind enough to lend me his copy of *Ivanhoe*. I'm enjoying it very much.''

Her husband added, ''Quite a stroke of luck that yer books weren't ruined in the wreck, Chisholm. I wish I could say the same for the rest of the *St. Bride*'s cargo.''

They enjoyed a congenial meal together, accompanied by the sparkling wine of good conversation. The discussion ranged widely, and thanks to her tutelage from Harris, Jenny was able to bear her part. After dinner, Mrs. Jardine played on the pianoforte. When Harris told their hosts about the impromptu concert on the forecastle of the *St. Bride,* they insisted Jenny favor them with a song.

As they strolled back to Glendennings' in the warm twilight of that August eve, Jenny breathed a sigh of mingled contentment and yearning. ''That's the way I've always dreamed of living. Everything so polite and elegant. Folks so agreeable.''

Harris slowed the pace of his walk even further. As an owl hooted in the distance, he raised his left hand and covered Jenny's, where it rested on his right arm. The euphoria of the evening swept all his misgivings before it.

''I had a grand time, too, Jenny. But it wasn't on account of the food, or Mrs. Jardine's china, or even the music. I've been to dine in Edinburgh and with the Robertsons in

Dalbeattie, but I never enjoyed myself like I did tonight. Having ye there—that's what made it special.''

She turned toward him, gulping a wee breath to speak. Harris knew what she meant to say, but he would not listen until she had heard him out. Swiftly, but with infinite gentleness, he pressed his fingers to her lips. His senses reeled as he felt their soft warmth and the featherlight caress of her breath.

''Rail at me later,'' he whispered. ''For now, just let me speak what's in my heart. Ye make any time of the day or night special to me, lass. Even if it's just reading a book together or wandering down a path in the woods at sunset.''

She stared up at him with those eyes, so full of dreams. Harris could scarcely find his voice to continue.

But continue he did, for he knew this might be his best and only chance. ''Things like that cost nothing. It's having ye to share them that gilds every minute of my day, Jenny.''

Her lip quivered beneath his touch and crystal tears quenched the dreams in her eyes. Was it a good sign, or bad? Harris wasn't sure. Either way, a great choking lump rose in his own throat. Unable to restrain himself further, he gathered Jenny into his arms and clasped her to him as though he never meant to let go.

''Must ye go to Chatham, Jenny? Must ye wed Roderick Douglas? Couldn't ye stay here with me? Mr. Jardine wants to take me on as his manager. I know we'd be starting with nothing, but I swear to ye I'd work hard and make a good life for us.''

Was his imagination playing tricks on him, or was Jenny burrowing deeper into his embrace? He could barely discern the words she murmured.

''Ye mustn't say such things, Harris. Ye've no notion of how much I... Ye don't understand. I've given my word. Besides, Mr. Douglas paid for my passage and my new clothes. How would I ever repay him?''

Was *that* all that stood in their way? Harris threw back his head and began to laugh in a hearty gust of relief. ''*I'd* repay him, Jenny. I'd repay Mr. Douglas every penny of what he spent, supposing he wanted to charge a hundred percent interest.''

Fearing his voice might break, he dropped it to a hoarse whisper. ''And I'd still think it the best bargain I ever struck in my life, lass.''

''There's more to it than that, Harris.'' Jenny tried to push out of his embrace, but only feebly. He sensed she didn't really want him to release her.

So he didn't.

''Don't fret yerself, lass. I'm not asking ye to decide tonight. I only want ye to think on it for a while. Once the *St. Bride*'s ready to sail again, ye can give me yer answer then. If ye choose to marry Mr. Douglas, I'll go with ye to Chatham like I promised, and we won't speak of it again.''

The thought chilled him, even in the lazy warmth of a midsummer night. Resting his cheek against Jenny's hair, he murmured, ''I give ye fair warning, though. I'm going to spend every waking moment between now and then trying to tip the scales in my favor.''

Before Jenny could reply, Harris heard a rustling on the path ahead, and the rapid slap of bare feet hitting the ground. An instant later, a small form barreled into them. In the gathering darkness, Harris could not make out the child's features.

''There now, lad. Who are ye and where are ye tearing off to at this time of night?''

''Mr. Chisholm?'' the child gasped. ''Miss Lennox? It's me. John. Father sent me to fetch Grannie Girvan. The baby's in a bad way.''

"I'll go along with ye to Girvan's, lad," said Harris. "Ye shouldn't be out on yer own this time of night."

"Thank ye, Harris." Jenny fumbled for his hand in the darkness and squeezed it. "I'll go to Maizie and see if I can help."

As Harris and the boy set off toward the river, Jenny found herself perversely grateful for this distraction. The feel of his arms about her and the siren song of his entreaty had been almost too powerful an enchantment to resist. Worst of all, she could not decide for certain if she wanted to resist.

Remembering the Glendennings' sick baby, she chided herself for welcoming the diversion. True, she wanted time to collect her wits, but not at this cost. Willing herself to concentrate on the situation at hand, Jenny hurried along the path to Glendennings.

She found the cottage in an uproar.

Tears streaming down her face, eyes wide with panic, Maizie held the baby as its tiny body jerked in alarming spasms. In the throes of its fit, the infant appeared to have no breath to cry.

The other children made up for that.

From their beds in the loft at one end of the cabin, they stared down, howling in distress at what was taking place below. Captain Glendenning paced the floor helplessly, his face drawn with worry. The stoic calm with which he'd braved the pirates and the wreck had evaporated in the face of this domestic crisis.

"It'll be all right, Maizie." Jenny tried to sound convinced of it. "Harris has gone with John for Grannie Girvan. They'll be here directly."

Mrs. Glendenning seemed scarcely to hear her. Gazing anxiously at the twitching baby, she spoke by dull rote. "He was no worse than usual, today. Then, when I went to feed him after supper, he was burning up."

Jenny had nursed her younger brothers through a number

of fevers and fluxes, but she'd seen nothing like this. Better to leave doctoring the child to Mrs. Girvan. Yet, she could not bring herself to stand about idle.

"Is the baby going to die?" Nellie wailed from the loft. The other children.

It was a small thing, but worthwhile, to quiet them. Maizie might take heart without their plaintive keening in her ears. And Mrs. Girvan would surely work better without the distraction of a racket. Giving the frantic mother an encouraging pat on the arm, Jenny moved to the ladder and began to climb.

"Grannie Girvan's on her way," she told the children in a soft, soothing voice. She could not bring herself to assure them their brother would live, for she had grave doubts. "Now come back here and lie down. Here's my handkerchief to wipe yer eyes, Nellie. Ye must help yer ma by being as quiet as wee mice. If ye'll hush, I'll tell ye a story to put ye to sleep. Things'll look better in the morning, ye'll see."

Sniffling and wiping noses on the sleeves of their nightshirts, the children drew back from the lip of the loft and crowded around Jenny. Anxious thoughts and grim foreboding tightened her throat, but she fought down her own feelings to concentrate on calming the wee ones.

"What good lads and lassies ye are." She smoothed back a lock of hair on one, patted another on the shoulder and smiled sympathetic encouragement to a third.

Keeping her voice low and comforting, she began to spin them a tale borrowed from Walter Scott. "Once upon a time, there was a brave knight, named Wilfred of Ivanhoe. Now Ivanhoe was in love with his father's ward, the fair lady Rowena, but…"

The story proved a potent diversion for the children, who seemed to forget what was happening in the rest of the house. Even the sound of the door opening and the muted urgency of voices below failed to rouse their interest.

While she concentrated on lulling the children with her story, Jenny kept an ear cocked to hear what was going on. She overheard Maizie sigh. "At least he's still now."

Old Mrs. Girvan clucked her tongue with the sound of hollow pessimism.

From the foot of the ladder, Jenny heard Harris quietly advise young John, "Why don't ye get off to yer rest, lad? Ye've done a man's work tonight."

The sound of his voice made Jenny long to scramble down the ladder and throw herself into his arms. Suddenly aware of the children's expectant gazes, she cleared her throat and continued with the story. When John joined them, his brother and sisters allowed as how Jenny might begin it again for his benefit.

None of them managed to stay awake until the end of the tale. Jenny was hoarse and stiff by the time the last one nodded off. She still picked up the sound of hushed voices and faint movement below. While there was activity, there must be hope.

A while later, the hiccup of a sob wakened her from a light doze. She heard Mrs. Girvan's weary voice. "I'm sorry, lass. There was naught I could do for the poor wee thing. Get yer rest now. The other children'll be needing you."

Jenny shivered. Even a decent interval to grieve was a luxury in this unforgiving land.

"I'm sorry for yer loss, Angus," said Harris. Jenny had not realized he was still there. "Is there anything I can do?"

"Nothing to do now but build a coffin and dig a grave," replied the captain in a tight, husky voice. "Ye can see Mrs. Girvan home, Harris, if ye'd be so good. Thanks for yer help tonight."

"I wish I could have done more. I'll be by in the morning with some wood from the yard."

After a soft shuffling of footsteps, the cabin door opened and closed.

Captain Glendenning cleared his throat.

Jenny wished to heaven she was asleep. Or a thousand miles away.

"Don't fret yerself, Maizie. There'll be others."

The reply was a quiet sound, something like a chuckle, but entirely devoid of mirth. It sounded more like a rasp biting against a knot of hard wood.

"Don't expect me to take comfort in that, Angus. I never wanted this one."

"Now, now lass. Ye don't mean that. Ye're worn-out."

"Aye, I'm all of that. But I mean it just the same." Maizie Glendenning sniffled loudly. "It's indecent for a mother not to grieve her child. All I can think is how glad I am to be clear of his caterwauling from noon to night."

The captain did not reply for a while. Then he said, "I won't be able to sleep. I'll go make the box."

"Ye do that. And while ye're at it, make one for me. I envy the dead their rest."

Her stomach seething, Jenny glanced around at the children to make sure they were all asleep and had not overheard. Captain Glendenning might dismiss his wife's words on the grounds of her exhaustion and grief. The children might not understand.

Or perhaps they might understand too well.

The way fourteen-year-old Jenny had understood her mother's dying whisper. *"Don't fret for me, Jenny. I'll be glad for a rest. Light out of here the minute ye get a chance, lass. But mind ye wed well, or not at all."*

Looking back, Jenny could now imagine Mother at her age. Starry-eyed because Alec Lennox had asked leave to walk her home from kirk. Full of romantic daydreams of the life they might share. She had seen a hint of it in Maizie Glendenning that very afternoon as she'd exclaimed over the dresses and plaited Jenny's hair. Once upon a time,

Maizie had primped and prettied herself for a call from a ruggedly handsome sailor. Felt her heart beat faster and her knees wobble like jelly.

And what did it come to in the end?

Exhaustion overcame Jenny again, and for a time she slept. The children began to stir when cock crowed.

"I didn't hear the last of yer story, Jenny."

"Is the baby going to get better?"

Jenny yawned and stretched out her kinks. Better to let the children hear the news from their parents. "Hush, now. I ken yer ma's asleep and she needs her rest. Let's see who can be the quietest getting yer clothes on and sneaking out of the house? If ye don't make a sound, I promise I'll boil ye up some porritch and finish telling ye what happened to Ivanhoe."

Her offer proved a powerful inducement, for the children pulled on their clothes and stole out of the cabin with scarcely a sound. Maizie had gone to bed at last. Despite the bitter words Jenny had heard her speak in the night, she'd taken the baby with her, cradling the small, still form in her arms. The sight brought a queer ache to Jenny's stomach.

There was no sign of Captain Glendenning outside, but from off in the forest, Jenny could hear the bleak sound of a plane shaving wood smooth. As she prepared the children's breakfast and finished the story of Ivanhoe for them, her thoughts churned.

After what had happened last night, there could be no question of her remaining in Richibucto and sharing the fate of Mrs. Glendenning and her mother. However, she remembered the magical feel of Harris's arms about her, and the compelling sorcery of his words. Could she risk staying here another month? Was her resolve strong enough to withstand his subtle blandishments day after day? Even when she knew he was casting a spell that would hold her captive and ultimately bring them both nothing but disillusionment and heartbreak?

"So Sir Wilfred regained his father's favor and wed the lady Rowena and they lived happily ever after," she concluded hastily. "John, do ye know how far it is to Chatham, by land?"

"But what happened to Rebecca?" the children demanded.

"Oh, she left the country with her father." Seeing this did not satisfy her audience, Jenny added her own postscript to the story. "Later she married a rich merchant of her own faith and lived like a queen."

"Chatham?" said John, as if her question had just registered with him. "I've heard Pa say it's forty mile or more. Ye take the road to Aldouane and go on from there. Nobody much goes overland, Miss Lennox. It's much quicker and easier by boat."

"I see," said Jenny. "Thank ye for telling me."

Forty miles. After the hundreds and hundreds she'd come, it seemed like so trifling a distance. Only twice the way from Dalbeattie to Kirkcudbright, and she had walked that before in less than a day. If she needed to take lodging at an inn or a house, no matter. She still had several coins left over from what Roderick Douglas had sent.

Dispatching the children to pick more berries, Jenny marched resolutely to the shed where her trunk sat. Quickly she changed into a plain, serviceable dress for walking and put on a pair of stout shoes. When the *St. Bride* finally weighed anchor for Chatham, surely Captain Glendenning would think to bring her trunk. The only items she really needed to take along were her wedding dress and slippers and her money.

Securing the former into a fat but light parcel, she tucked the coins into her apron pocket and tied on her bonnet. She hoped Harris would not be too upset when he learned that she'd gone. With a qualm of guilt she recalled the painful story of his mother's desertion.

How could she make him understand? She was doing this as much for his future happiness as for her own.

Chapter Nine

Harris did not miss Jenny until early that afternoon, when the Glendennings and their neighbors came together at Kirk Point to bury the baby. As the minister intoned the familiar words of the service, Harris scanned the small crowd for any sign of her. By the time they reached the committal, his panic had risen to an unbearable pitch.

"Earth to earth. Ashes to ashes. Dust to dust."

As the women of the community gathered around Mrs. Glendenning, Harris approached the captain. "Angus, did Miss Lennox get back to yer place last night? When we met John on the path, she told me to go with him. She said she'd go on by herself. I never should have let her alone in the woods at that time of—"

Captain Glendenning stopped his runaway rush of words. "Don't fret yerself, Harris. She came a while before ye and John got back with Grannie Girvan. She's a capable lass, that one. There was naught any of us could do for wee Donald, but she went up to the loft and quieted the others, and that was worth a good deal."

Harris's initial breath of relief strangled again as he looked over the crowd one last time. "Do ye know where she's gone? Have ye seen her at all today?"

The captain thought for a moment. Then, slowly, he began to shake his head. "My mind was that set on other things, I didn't notice. Now that ye mention it, I haven't seen hide nor hair of the lass since last night. Maybe ye ought to ask the children."

Those final words followed Harris, who'd already decided on that very course of action. Approaching the clutch of doleful little figures, he sank to his knees before them. "I'm sorry about yer wee brother. Ye were good lads and lassies last night when yer ma and pa needed the place quiet."

As he took his next breath to ask about Jenny, the oldest girl piped up, "We cried at first b'cause we were scared, but Miss Lennox came and told us a fine story."

"Aye, that was good of her." Harris could not keep from smiling at the children. He could picture Jenny and him with a smart, willing brood like this. "Was she still there when ye woke up this morning?"

The children nodded with varying degrees of vigor.

"She made us porritch," lisped the youngest.

"And finished telling the story of Ivanhoe," said John. "Then she sent us off to pick berries."

"After a while," chimed in the younger boy, whose name eluded Harris, "Father came and told us the baby had gone to heaven. Then we had to go home and dress for kirk."

"Did ye see Miss Lennox after ye got home?"

The four exchanged wary glances with one another.

"I can't remember," said John.

"She was gone," declared the youngest in a tone that brooked no gainsaying.

"Aye," agree the others. "She wasn't about then."

"Did she say anything before she left, about where she might be going?"

The boys shook their heads, but Nellie cried, "Aye, she did. Don't ye mind, John? Just as she was finishing up the story, she asked ye how far and which way to Chatham."

Chatham. The word sent a chill through Harris.

"Aye. So she did." At the look on Harris's face, the boy hastened to add, "I told her it was a long way and nobody ever walked it if they could sail instead."

Coming to his feet, Harris gave the anxious lad a manly pat on the shoulder. "I appreciate yer telling her that, John. Ye may as well learn young, though. A woman who's made up her mind won't be swayed by the best warning in the world."

John Glendenning didn't appear to understand that he was in jest—if only partially. However, the boy relaxed visibly at the bantering tone of his remark.

A coiled spring tightened within Harris.

"Thank ye for telling me what ye know." He nodded to the children. "I'll go find Miss Lennox to see if I can bring her back to tell ye more stories."

He tried to keep the urgency from his stride until he was out of their sight. No sense in frightening them, or making them feel responsible for Jenny's disappearance.

"Robert." Harris fell into step beside the shipbuilder. "Can I borrow a few supplies? Jenny's gone and I fear she may have set off for Chatham overland."

"Take what ye need, Harris." Robert Jardine surveyed the descending arc of the sun. "Be quick about it though. If she has any kind of a head start on ye, she could walk quite a piece the first day. That's no fit trek for a woman, especially one alone. Most of the Indians hereabouts are peaceful, but there are a few I wouldn't care to meet alone in the woods. That goes for some of the settlers and sailors, too. There are rivers to ford—six, at least, and wild animals—"

Harris loped on ahead, spurred by these dire warnings. As he gathered together a blanket, a knife, a flint, wire, a water skin and a little food, he tried to guess what had made Jenny take to her heels.

Had it been the things he'd said to her last night? Had

his unwelcome ardor made Jenny leave town? He could think of no other reason, though part of him protested that she'd seemed far more frightened of her own feelings than of his. In any case, she had made her choice. She wanted Roderick Douglas for a husband. Wanted him so fiercely and so surely that she'd been willing to brave a forty-mile trek in the wilderness just to reach him that much sooner.

Harris had always sworn he'd never make a fool of himself over a woman, but with Jenny he couldn't help himself. Time and again she'd rebuffed him and still he'd gone back for more. Did that make him a fool in her eyes? Probably. Would he seem a greater fool still by following her to Chatham? No doubt.

None of that mattered.

He would never be able to live with himself if anything happened to her. Besides, he had given his word that he would see her safely to Chatham. And he meant to keep his promise.

Even though it might break his heart.

Sweaty and footsore, Jenny wondered if it was her imagination, or if the road was becoming narrower and more overgrown with each mile she walked. The porritch she'd shared with the children at breakfast was a long way down and her belly felt achingly hollow. Perhaps she should have stopped at that little shop in Richibucto and bought herself some provisions. She hadn't wanted to take the chance of meeting Harris, in case he should convince her not to leave town.

A wave of relief engulfed her when she rounded a bend and entered a clearing in the forest.

A cabin even tinier than the Glendennings' squatted in the midst of a partially cleared lot. Fishing nets hung behind the house, waiting to be mended. On the bank of a narrow creek, an overturned canoe lay beached. Two barefoot children frolicked among the tree stumps. Half-a-dozen chickens pecked at the packed earth in front of the cabin door. A thin plume of smoke rose from a hole in the roof.

Jenny's mouth watered at the savory aroma of frying pork fat.

"Hello," she called softly to the children.

They scampered toward the open door of the cabin, screeching "Mama! Mama!"

As Jenny approached the little house, a girl roughly her own age appeared in the doorway. She carried one baby in her arms. Another was due to make an appearance soon, if Jenny correctly interpreted the bulge beneath the young woman's apron. The children who'd been playing in the clearing now peered out from behind their mother's skirts. Fear and curiosity flickered in their round dark eyes.

The woman also eyed Jenny warily. *"Qu'est-ce que vous?"* she asked. *"Qu'est-ce que vous désirez?"*

Jenny shrugged. "I beg yer pardon? Is that French ye're talking?"

"Ou est vous arrivez?" the woman demanded.

"I'm Jenny Lennox." Jenny pointed to herself. "If that's what ye want to know. I'm on my way to the Miramichi…"

"Miramichi?" the woman repeated. *"Avez-vous venir a Miramichi?"*

Jenny broke into a smile. "Aye." She nodded. "I'm on my way there to get married." She pointed to the fourth finger of her left hand.

"Ah, mari!" The woman nodded.

"Ye ken!" Jenny cried. "Married at Miramichi." She pointed off in several directions. "Which way is it? How do I get there—to Miramichi?"

"Miramichi, c'est ça." The woman pointed to the woods across the creek. Jenny could make out a narrow gap in the bushes. That was the road?

"Thank ye." Jenny bobbed her head. She took but a

few steps toward the path when her stomach growled piteously.

She spun around again. "I've not eaten since early this morning." Rubbing her stomach, Jenny hoped the woman would understand she was hungry and not think she was pregnant. "Could ye spare me a bite of what ye've got cooking?" She inhaled appreciatively. "It smells very good."

"*Restez ici.*" The woman held up her hand.

"*Restez?* Rest." Jenny translated for herself. "Stay where ye are."

The woman and her children retreated into the cottage, but she returned in a moment, without the baby. She held out two golden brown balls that fit comfortably into Jenny's palms. They were still warm.

Jenny transferred the food all to her left hand. With the right, she fished in her apron pocket for one of her coins.

The woman eyed the money and Jenny more suspiciously than ever. She shook her head. "*Allez.*" She motioned Jenny to be on her way.

"Thank ye." Putting the money and the food into her pocket, Jenny picked up the bundle that contained her wedding dress.

"Thank ye." She called back over her shoulder. She could hardly wait to get out of sight of the cabin to devour the victuals she'd been given.

Prying off her shoes and lifting her skirts, she forded the stream with ease. Judging by the height of its banks, the water level was low after a dry summer. Jenny ducked into the woods and followed the path for a few hundred yards. Then she subsided beneath a tall maple tree and prepared to eat.

They looked something like Scotch eggs, this windfall bite. Prepared for the texture and taste of sausage meat and hard-boiled eggs, Jenny let out a faint squeak of surprise as she bit into one. Beneath the crispy fried crust was a soft layer of potato, encasing a core of salty codfish.

Jenny had never tasted anything so delicious.

Her prudent plans to save the second ball for tomorrow's breakfast evaporated. She attacked it ravenously, groaning with contentment once it was safely in her stomach.

For some time longer she sat there, listening to the children's laughter echoing from the clearing behind her. She entertained the notion of going back and asking for a night's lodging. Her unfamiliarity with the language would make that difficult, and the woman hadn't seemed impressed that she could pay her way. Better to keep going and be that much closer to Chatham by nightfall.

The hot food in her belly rekindled Jenny's strength and her spirit. Pulling on her shoes, she struggled to her feet and hoisted her bundle of belongings. Then she set off up the narrow path, which appeared to be climbing a gentle incline.

Were the only settlers in this area French? she wondered as she walked. And could she reach the next house on the road before night fell?

"Have ye seen a lady go by? Wearing a blue bonnet and carrying…" Seeing the query in the old woman's eyes, Harris switched into the rusty French his grandfather had made him learn in honor of the "Auld Alliance". *"Avez-vous vu une femme…avec un chapeau bleu…et un…"*

As he plundered his memory for a word that meant parcel or bundle, the woman pointed ahead. *"Oui. La fille, elle est allé sur le chemin."*

Thank God! *"Merci, merci!"* exclaimed Harris, in what he knew must be a dreadful accent. *"Quand?"* he asked. *When?*

The woman pondered the question for a moment. Or perhaps she was thinking how to tell him in words he'd understand.

"Peut-être, deux heures?" she said at last, holding up two fingers to drive home her meaning. *"L'àpres-midi, tard,"* she added. *Late in the afternoon.*

Harris sighed. He had closed the gap between him and Jenny to just two hours. Could he reach her before the sun set?

"Merci encore, mistress." He bobbed the woman a quick bow.

He had taken several long strides down the road before her question stopped him. *"La fille, oú va-t'elle?"*

"Miramichi," he called back, unable to keep the concern from his voice. "She's bound for the Miramichi."

"Miramichi, à pied?" Walking? The woman sounded properly horrified. *"Mais, ce n'est pas le chemin. Personne n'habite la route après Louis Vautour."*

"That's why I need to find her." Harris didn't bother to translate. He was certain the old woman would take his meaning. Judging by the way the road had narrowed, he'd already reached the conclusion it would soon disappear altogether. Whoever this Louis Vautour was, Harris hoped Jenny would have sense enough to stop there and ask for shelter before the darkness overtook her.

If only he could be certain. He'd never met a woman as determined—nay, as mule stubborn—as Jenny Lennox. Whether in crossing the ocean, surviving a shipwreck or learning to read, she went after what she wanted with a singularity of purpose that he could not help admiring. No matter how much it exasperated him at times.

As it exasperated him now.

She had set her mind on marrying Roderick Douglas and nothing would stand in her way. Least of all her heart, which had perhaps begun to yearn in another direction.

How much farther?

Jenny stopped, her light but awkward bundle falling unnoticed from her hand. The evening sun of summer waned on a horizon she could not see for the press of trees. Lengthening shadows made it harder than ever to pick out the path. Perhaps she had strayed from it already?

The salty codfish had made her thirsty, but she hadn't come across another brook or creek since she'd eaten. Which would explain the absence of settlement, Jenny reasoned, forcing down the flutter of panic within her. People needed a source of fresh water, for drinking, and washing and for their livestock.

She held herself still, eyes closed, reaching out with her other senses for any sign of human habitation. The faint pungency of wood smoke or food cooking, the bark of a dog or the bleating of sheep. All she heard above the rapid tattoo of her heart and the shallow hiss of her breath was the nearby chatter of a squirrel. All she smelled was the muted but pervading aroma of dry pine needles. For all she knew, there might not be another living soul for miles in any direction.

It suddenly struck Jenny that she was alone. Never had she felt so solitary as in these vast miles of empty forest. Never had she felt so small as in the shadow of these towering trees.

Never had she felt so alien as in this wild, rugged land.

Fighting to stifle a sob that strained to escape, she set her mouth in a resolute line, picked up her fallen parcel and pressed on. No matter how daunting, she had no choice but to move forward. Going back was not an option, though it whispered seductively in her thoughts. Somehow, she sensed that in returning to Richibucto and facing another month with Harris, she might unleash forces more frighteningly powerful than the raw might of nature presently arrayed against her.

Doggedly placing one foot in front of the other, she cursed under her breath as low-hanging branches swiped her and tree roots tripped her. On she walked, eyes straining to follow the ill-marked trail. Her spirits lifted for an instant when she spied a swatch of cloth caught on a length of bramble up ahead.

It could be a sign she was nearing another settlement. If nothing else, it meant she was still on the road.

By the day's dying light, she peered at the threads. As a noose of panic tightened around her throat, Jenny recognized the color. Seeking confirmation but praying it was a mistake, she reached down and felt along the hem of her skirt.

There it was.

A small patch of cloth torn free when she had snagged her dress on these same brambles at least a quarter of an hour ago.

The thought that she had forced herself on for that long without coming an inch closer to Chatham brought Jenny to her knees. She had walked for a whole day with little in her stomach, after an all-but-sleepless night. Now her body ached with exhaustion and her head spun with a lethal drowsiness to which she dared not surrender.

Clenching her fists, she lifted her face to the darkened sky. "Damn ye, Harris Chisholm!" she cried defiantly at the top of her lungs.

The outburst relieved her feelings somewhat.

Damn Harris Chisholm, indeed. This was all his fault. If only he'd let her alone. Kept his distance. Instead of making her entertain doubts where she needed to be most certain. Making her feel things she could not afford to feel.

What choice had he left her but to run away?

"No." Jenny corrected herself aloud, just for the momentary comfort of hearing a human voice. "I'm *not* running away from Harris. I'm going *to* Roderick Douglas."

Catching the note of uncertainty in her voice, Jenny let loose with the foulest curse she'd ever heard let alone uttered. And why not? There wasn't a soul within miles to shock with her profanity. Her father might have washed her mouth with soap, but he was thousands of miles away.

Even her dour Old Testament God seemed far distant from this primal woodland.

Jenny fought her exhaustion, trying to decide whether it was better to press on or better to spend the night where she was. Then she heard a noise.

It was a combination of sounds that made her hackles rise and her fatigue-addled wits search desperately for escape or a safe place to hide. Dry branches snapped and pine needles rustled beneath the heavy onrush of some large animal. A wolf? A bear? As it lumbered closer, Jenny could also make out the fast hiss of breath.

With a sharp squeak of terror, she dodged behind the wide trunk of an ancient pine tree. Then she turned and ran blindly into the night. She collided with another tree and fell back for an instant, stunned. A whisper of logic told her it would be safer to curl up somewhere and lie still, praying the beast might miss her in the dark.

Casting cool reason aside, Jenny picked herself up and ran on, spurred by the sounds of pursuit drawing closer. Wild predators were said to have uncanny powers of night vision, not to mention keen ears and a feral ability to scent their prey. That was not what mattered to Jenny. She simply could not bring herself to stop and face danger. Let it overtake her on the run. At least, that way she stood a chance.

At least she would die with the hope of escape in her heart.

From behind her, nearer than ever, she heard a thud and a deep grunt of pain. It gave her ragged energy a boost. Her legs pumped faster.

Then Jenny felt the ground open up beneath her right foot. She lurched forward, sprawling onto a bed of moss. Her pitiful reserves of breath rushed from her body. Her heart hammered in her chest and every particle of her flesh pulsed in vain with a craze to flee.

As she whimpered in the first painful gasps of air, the

stalker overtook her. She felt the muscular weight of it crash down upon her, driving the wind from her lungs again. Its hungry breath seared her neck. At any second its fangs would close on her throat.

And she would die.

Chapter Ten

Feeling Jenny squirm beneath him, Harris collapsed on top of her, pulling the night air into his lungs in great heaving gasps. Each intake of breath slashed into his chest like a dull razor. In his mad, blind chase through the woods, he'd been battered to a jelly. He could feel his flesh bruising and his overworked muscles throbbing in protest.

But he had found Jenny, and that was all that mattered.

As soon as he could gather the energy, he rolled off her, panting. "Don't fret. It's only me, lass."

"H-Harris?" His name retched out of her, followed by a frenzied fit of sobbing.

He groped for her in the darkness, pulling her close. "There, there. It'll be all right now, lass. Ye're safe with me."

Barely had he got the words out when she homed in on his lips. Planting her mouth on his, she stormed it with reckless abandon. Harris did not get a chance to enjoy this strange, violent kiss. For in the next galloping beat of their hearts, she wrenched free of his embrace and boxed his ears.

Reeling from the sudden turnabout, he raised his hands to fend her off. His own banked fury with her burst into open flame. Clutching her slender wrists together with one hand, he shook her until he could almost hear her teeth rattle.

"Enough of that, woman! Come to yer senses, now."

"Ye miserable blaggard!" She struggled to free herself from his grip, no doubt anxious to mount another assault. "How dare ye scare the life out of me like that? Couldn't ye have called out instead of charging through the brush like a wild beast?"

"Would ye have answered if I'd called?" he roared back at her.

"Are ye daft? Of course I would."

"Would ye? Well, I had no way of knowing it. Not after ye sneaked out of town this morning without so much as a word to me. For all I knew, ye'd keep quiet and hide, and I'd never have found ye in the dark."

She had no spiteful retort for that. Not for a moment at least. When she finally did reply, it sounded as though her wrath had abated—somewhat.

"If I'd told ye where I was going, ye'd only have tried to stop me."

"Aye. Stop ye from the folly of walking into the wilderness without a scrap of provisions."

"I brought money," Jenny flared. "And my wedding dress," she added in a less certain tone.

"Did ye expect fish to jump out of the streams and cook themselves for a penny?" Relief at finding her alive finally caught up with him. In spite of himself, he began to laugh. "Or were ye planning to eat yer dress?"

"I thought there'd be inns," she flared, as if the lack was his fault. "Houses. People. I thought I'd be walking on a road. I've seen better cow paths back home."

"Aye, so have I." A last chuckle died in his throat. "But this isn't home where ye can walk forty mile in a day or two and lay yer head down at night in a decent inn." He felt for the pack slung over his shoulder. "Would ye like a drink?"

"I would." She sounded subdued. Perhaps even contrite.

He unstopped the water jug and passed it to her. "Go easy now. I haven't much. I hope it'll last us till we get back to the wee creek by Vautour's."

The sounds of eager drinking ceased abruptly. "What do ye mean?"

"We can't start back now." After the chase they'd just been through, shouldn't that be obvious? "We'll have to stay put for now and try to retrace our route as soon as it's light."

"Retrace *yer* route, ye mean, I'm not going back to Richibucto, Harris. When that sun comes up, I'm pressing on to the Miramichi."

This stunned him more than her violent kiss had.

"Are ye daft, woman? Did ye learn nothing from what happened tonight? Ye could get lost and never walk out of these woods again. Ye could starve or die of thirst. Drown trying to ford a stream." The possibilities for disaster were so many and so obvious, Harris could not spit the words out fast enough.

"On top of everything else," muttered Jenny, interrupting him, "ye made me drop my bundle. I reckon I can find it in the morning, but it would have made a fine pillow for tonight."

His mouth kept moving, but no more words would come out.

Jenny *had* gone daft. There was no other explanation for it. Talking calmly of pillows and wedding finery. Insisting she would carry on to the Miramichi when any fool could see how dangerously absurd a notion *that* was. Their hair-raising chase through the woods had clearly addled her wits.

Fighting down his indignation, Harris tried to keep his tone neutral and soothing. The lass was likely exhausted. She'd come to her senses by morning.

"Neither of us is going anywhere tonight, Jenny." Surely she couldn't argue with that. "I'm going to rest up against the trunk of this tree. Ye can lay yer head against my shoulder if ye like. It may not be as soft a pillow as yer wedding dress, but if ye're as tired as I am, ye won't notice."

She yawned deeply. "I suppose it won't do any harm."

Harris heard her crawl toward him. She yawned again and so did he.

"For this one night," she added in a drowsy murmur.

Jenny had barely settled herself when Harris heard her breath calm into the slow, even rhythm of sleep.

He tried to relax so he could drift off, too. But something kept him awake. Perhaps it was his protective instincts that roused to every rustle of the woodland, anticipating danger. Perhaps it was the worry for Jenny that he'd carried with him all day, like a second pack. Or perhaps it was the warmth of her head resting so trustingly against his shoulder and the faint scent of her. They provoked feelings he could no longer afford to entertain.

Harris gazed up at the night sky, a small patch of it visible through the leaves overhead. Luminous and almost full, the moon stared back at him with her delicate, feminine features. He might as well yearn for the moon as for Jenny Lennox. From the very beginning she'd served him notice that she belonged to another man. A man with so much more to offer than dreams and ambition and a heart that ached to bursting with suppressed desire for her.

Suddenly Harris was tired of that ache. Tired of lurching from feverish hope to chills of doubt to the prostration of despair.

The woman was like a disease with him.

No sooner did he think himself cured than he'd suffer a relapse of lovesickness. He could conceive of only one remedy—purging Jenny from his heart completely. Harris shrank from the thought. In the past two months, she had become a part of him. Cutting her out of his life would be as difficult and painful as amputating one of his limbs.

Sometimes the dire course of amputation was the only way to save a patient's life. Reluctantly Harris conceded that the sooner Jenny got to Chatham and out of his life, the better.

It took Jenny a moment to recollect where she was when the sunrise warbling of forest birds woke her the next morning. Memories came flooding back. Her increasing unease at finding no more homesteads. The futility of realizing she'd been walking in circles. The blind panic of pursuit.

Then discovering it was only Harris and being able to surrender to her weariness. Secure in the simple fact of his presence. Not that he would fend off wild animals with his bare hands, or lead them unerringly back to civilization—though she didn't doubt he would try. Just by being there, he gave Jenny the confidence that she could face anything.

Anything, she reminded herself, but the life she would doom them both to, by marrying him. She had no doubt a man as smart and capable as Harris would make his way in the world. Not when saddled with the responsibility of a wife and family, though.

Easing away from his slumbering form, Jenny gazed around her. After the terrors of the previous night, the New World timberland looked positively benign by the first light of day. The high canopy created by this stand of tall, ancient pines kept much of the forest floor in shadow. Only the odd bed of soft green moss or swath of filmy fern relieved the carpet of dry, tawny pine needles. Unlike the dense walls of new growth she'd struggled through on the previous day, this area would afford easy walking.

Gaining her feet, she soundlessly stretched the stiffness from her limbs. It was easy to discern the trail she and Harris had blundered along last night. Follow it, and she'd soon find the parcel with her wedding dress. Then she'd take her bearings and be on her way. Or perhaps she would find a spot to hide until Harris gave up looking for her and went back to Richibucto, where he should have stayed in the first place.

For a long moment, she hesitated, staring down at him as he slept. Though his chin bristled auburn whiskers, there was something appealingly boyish about his face relaxed in slumber. How could his mother have gone away and left him, no matter how hard her lot?

Jenny's conscience pricked. After all, she was about to abandon Harris in her own way. Might he think that, like his mother, she shied away from his scars? The painful notion held Jenny there, watching Harris, yearning for him, when she knew she must go—and go quickly.

"I'm doing this as much for ye as I am for myself," she whispered. "I wish I could make ye see that."

Willing herself to turn away, she tiptoed toward the trail of broken saplings and crushed vegetation that she and Harris had hewn the night before. She tried to ignore the heartache it cost her to leave him.

"Where are ye sneaking off to now, woman?" Harris's voice rang out, sharp with vexation.

The sudden noise, combined with her own stricken conscience, made Jenny's heart lurch in her chest.

She rounded on him. "Won't be satisfied until ye scare the wits clean out of me, will ye?"

Stiffly he rose from his sleeping place and scratched his unshaven chin. "And ye won't be satisfied until ye drive me clean out of my wits with worry." He traded her glare for glare.

Then, unexpectedly, one corner of his wide, mobile mouth curved into an irresistible grin. "Since we're each bent on driving the other mad, maybe we ought to find a nice cosy lunatic asylum and settle down."

"This is nothing to joke about." The unbidden chuckle

that burst out of Jenny belied her words. "We're at each other all the time. Ye and I never would have made a happy match, even with all the money in the world."

"Don't ye believe it, lass," Harris replied in quiet earnest. A ray of rising sun pierced the foliage, burnishing his hair like new copper and lighting the rich warmth of his hazel eyes.

It cost Jenny every crumb of her self-control to keep from bolting straight into his arms.

"I ken a little good-natured tormenting is only natural between a man and a woman." He brushed away several stubborn pine needles that clung to his trousers. "When things get solemn and serious all the time, *that's* when ye can tell there's a spark gone out. If it ever was there to begin with."

"For a man who claims to know so little about women, ye sound like quite an authority on the subject all of a sudden," Jenny retorted, even as she privately acknowledged the truth of what Harris had said. There was no rancor in this give-and-take of theirs—more a gleeful sparring that added zest to the softer, warmer feelings of their companionship.

Instead of delivering a clever riposte, however, Harris reddened and averted his eyes. "Don't...don't...pay me any mind. Likely ye're right...and I don't ken what I'm talking about."

What had she said to distress him so? Jenny wondered, reviewing their conversation in her mind.

"Anyway..." He cleared his throat, an abrupt and obvious prelude to a change of subject. "There's no sense us standing around wagging our tongues when we have a long day ahead."

Jenny sighed. "I told ye last night, Harris, and I've no intention of changing my mind. I'm heading on for Chatham, and that's final." She peered back into the trees from the direction they'd come. "As soon as I can find my wedding dress."

She braced herself for a lecture or an argument. Perhaps he'd pick her up bodily and march back to Richibucto with her. Remembering how Harris had shouldered her below decks during the pirate attack on the *St. Bride,* Jenny felt her knees tremble with anticipation.

Instead, he replied with cool composure, "I've come too far with ye not to see the folly of trying to talk ye 'round once yer mind's set. If ye're bound for Chatham, so be it. I'll go, too."

"But…" *That's almost as bad as going back to Richibucto* Jenny wanted to wail. *Maybe worse, for we'll be alone together.* She clenched her lips tight, lest the words work their way out. It would never do for Harris to realize the powerfully disconcerting effect he had upon her.

"Aye?" he prompted her. A hint of that endearing, exasperating grin hovered at the corner of his mouth.

"That is…" Jenny struggled to regain her composure. "If ye mean to come with me, there's a few things we'd better get straight right now."

All traces of levity disappeared from his face. "There are, and I'm going to make them plain. I'm not coming with ye so I can press my suit along the way. Ye made yer choice when ye left Richibucto. Fool I may be in plenty of ways, but I'm a hardheaded businessman, too. I ken there's no sense throwing good money after bad. The same goes for time and energy. I'm putting my feelings for ye in the past, and I'll not speak of it again."

Jenny took an involuntary step back, as though he'd thrown a basinful of cold water on her. That was the gist of what she'd planned to say to him. Hearing it from Harris chilled her to a degree she hadn't expected. She could not think what to reply.

"And," he added with grave dignity, "I'll thank ye to do the same."

"I…I'm glad ye've decided to be…sensible, Harris."
Jenny fought to swallow the queer lump in her throat, but
it would not budge. "I'll welcome yer company…of
course. It gets tiresome walking a long ways with no one
to talk to."

"Go find yer things, and look smart about it." Harris
waved her away. "Then we'll have a quick bite and set
out. We have to find water soon and try to get our bearings."

Discovering her bundle only a few hundred yards away,
Jenny shook her head in disbelief. Last night, when she'd
thought she was running for her life, it had seemed like
miles and miles. She breathed easier knowing she would
not face that same terror tonight, even if she and Harris
failed to find shelter.

She knew she should be pleased that he'd come to his
senses and didn't mean to pine for her. Nor make a nui-
sance of himself trying to court her all the way to Chatham.
Still her pride stung at how promptly and casually he'd
written her off, like a bad debt.

Well, Harris Chisholm wasn't the only one who could
make his head rule his heart.

"I still don't ken how ye did it, Harris." Jenny cupped
the icy spring water in her hands and drank as though it
was the elixir of Eden. "Finding this place."

Having spent the day rationing the last drops of warm,
stale water from his jug, Harris was apt to agree. After
drinking all he could hold, he rinsed out the jug and refilled
it. Then he scooped a palmful over his face. Too bad he'd
been in such a hurry to leave Richibucto. Intent on fetching
Jenny back, he'd never thought to bring his shaving soap
and razor. By the time they reached Chatham, folks would
probably mistake him for a well-dressed bear. Or a giant
red squirrel.

"My grandpa always used to say, the birds and animals will lead ye to water, if ye let them."

"Oh, aye?" Jenny sounded skeptical as she eased the shoes off her feet and wet them down with a trickle of water from her hand. "How did the animals lead us here?"

"I watched for their tracks," explained Harris. "And I kept an eye on how the birds were flying. When they're going to water, they fly straight, but when they're coming away from it, they swoop from tree to tree."

"I never knew ye were such an outdoorsman, Harris."

He ignored the teasing note in her voice, but nothing could make him disregard the unfeigned light of admiration in her eyes.

"When I was a lad, my grandpa used to take me into the hills to hunt and fish."

"Speaking of food…" Jenny gazed hungrily at his pack. Several times today she had told him about the fried cod and potato delicacy she'd eaten. Now and then he had caught her sniffing the breeze—sensitive, no doubt, to even the slightest whiff of hog fat.

"I've got some oatcakes left," said Harris. "I'd like to save them for as long as they'll keep, though. In case a day comes when we can't get anything else. Now that we've found water, we can think about something to eat. I saw a place back a ways where it might be worth setting a snare."

Jenny came to rest in a small patch of sunlight. "I hope ye're as good at finding food as ye are at finding water, Harris. I could eat a whole deer."

He tossed a pinecone at her. It missed. "If ye can catch one, ye're welcome to it, lass."

They both laughed at the absurd mental image that conjured.

"For now, ye can make yerself useful by gathering wood and kindling," said Harris.

"Don't ye need something to cook, first?" Jenny quipped.

"I have to rub the snares and my hands in ash, to get the human smell off them. Otherwise the animals'll stay clear. Once the fire's going, ye can hunt for pinecones to roast the seeds."

"Aye, aye, sir." Jenny pulled a jaunty mock salute.

Several hours later, the snares yielded them supper in the shape of a good-size hare, which Harris promptly dressed and arranged on an improvised spit over the fire.

While foraging for pinecones and deadfall branches to fuel the fire, Jenny had discovered a clearing rich with plump, sweet blueberries. Valiantly resisting the urge to gorge herself, she'd gathered as many as she could carry in her apron. When she presented them to Harris as her contribution to the meal, her face radiated pride.

The succulent aroma of roast game hung temptingly in the summer air as Harris broke a dry branch across his knee and added both halves to the fire. Jenny rotated the long stick that skewered their supper, exposing another part of the meat to the flames.

"If I catch anything in my other snare tonight, we should be able to cover more ground tomorrow," said Harris. "We won't have to spend all our time scouting for food and water."

"That's good," Jenny replied, though without the enthusiasm he'd expected. "It'll put us in Chatham all the sooner."

"Aye." Despite his best effort, the word came out as a brief sigh. No matter how often he impressed upon himself the necessity of getting Jenny to her destination as quickly as possible, some stubborn streak of fancy in him yearned to prolong their journey.

For a time they sat in silence, watching the flames dance. Listening to them crackle. Inhaling the smell of the meat, as though every savory breath would nourish them. Now and then Harris refueled the fire. Now and then Jenny turned the spit. Now and then their gazes strayed to each other, met for a blushing, breathless instant, then skittered apart.

At last, Harris pulled a short-bladed knife from the sheath in his pack and stuck it into the thickest part of the carcass. When he pulled it out, a few drops of clear fluid gushed from the cut, hissing as they spattered on the fire below.

"I ken it's done." He transferred the spit to a pair of forked sticks planted away from the fire. Glancing up at Jenny, he grinned. "I don't care if it isn't. I'm too hungry to wait another minute."

He did not give the meat long to cool, but hacked off a chunk and passed it to her on the point of his knife. Though it clearly burned her hands, she took it eagerly and began to eat. Cutting a piece for himself, Harris devoured it, then licked the fat off his fingers.

"A bit fresh," he said as he cut more meat for Jenny. "If I'd known all things, I'd have brought along salt."

Between bites, Jenny assured him, "It's fine."

"If ye wanted salt," Harris continued as if he hadn't heard her, "we could take the first river we come to and follow it out to the sea. One fine day is all we'd need to draw salt from the water."

"I don't miss it—truly."

"Not yet, maybe. But a doctor in Edinburgh once told me it's bad for a body to go without salt. I'd…I'd hate to see ye get sick."

Jenny appeared to give the notion some thought as she chewed on her meat. "Aye," she agreed at last. "I wouldn't want to show up at Mr. Douglas's doorstep ailing."

"No, ye wouldn't." Harris fought to keep a note of elation from his voice. "Besides, we can't get lost if we follow the coast. Sooner or later, we'll strike the Miramichi. Inland like this, it's a sight easier to lose yer bearings.''

''There's sense in that,'' conceded Jenny. ''Let's hope we find a river tomorrow. At least if we follow the coast we'll have clear, flat beach to walk, instead of weaving through these blasted trees.''

Looking up from his supper, Harris gazed around them. ''I like the trees. They're all so different. The tall pines with their tufts of long needles—they put me in mind of big solid Highland men, with brawny arms and ginger hair. Then there's the birches. Those are elegant ladies with their fine white bark and slender branches.''

''Ye've quite a poetical streak in ye, Harris.'' She made it sound like a compliment, and a rare one at that.

Feeling a most unmanly heat flicker in his cheeks, he pretended to occupy himself with removing the last shreds of meat from the bones of their supper.

As they rounded out the meal with a few well-roasted pine seeds and Jenny's harvest of blueberries, she asked him many questions, drawing him out about his early adventures in the hills with his grandfather.

''I don't ever mind him coming into Dalbeattie, Harris. Not even to kirk.''

''That's because he was a Papist from the Highlands. My grandmother brought Pa up in the Free Kirk, but she died a good while before I was born.''

As the day waned, Harris found himself telling Jenny more and more about his grandfather, the young refugee from Culloden Moor who'd found sanctuary and a bride in the Border lands.

Above them, the narrow strip of visible sky darkened from the pale hue of cornflowers to a deep indigo and gradually to a velvet black. The fire subsided to a bed of glowing embers. When Harris looked over it at Jenny, the flickering shadows and rising heat from the coals gave her face a spectral shimmer.

He felt an uncanny chill ripple up his spine.

Chapter Eleven

Jenny's eyes flew open. Abruptly she woke to a man's firm hand pressed over her mouth. When had she gone to sleep?

"It's only me, lass," Harris whispered in her ear.

Tell that to my heart, she wanted to snap at him. The man did have a nasty habit of making her pulse race.

Often without even trying.

"We have to leave here, now." Though the words were spoken so softly Jenny could scarcely hear them, their note of urgency was unmistakable.

Pulling his hand from over her mouth, she hissed, "Why? What's going on? What's wrong?"

"Listen."

For a moment she wondered what nonsense he was talking. Then she heard it.

The beat of a drum. Voices in the distance, chanting in a strange minor key.

"Indians." Harris confirmed Jenny's own deduction. "Jardine said we'd do well to avoid them."

"For once, I agree with ye, Harris."

As soundlessly as possible, they broke camp, first feeling their way to the spring where they drank their fill and topped up Harris's jug.

"Take my hand," he whispered, and they were off.

They made achingly slow progress through the dark woods, with only the moon's pale rays to illuminate mysterious shapes in their path. On they stumbled, away from the sound of the drum, holding their breaths each time one of them snapped a dry branch with footfall. They had not gone nearly as far as Jenny would have liked, when the music finally stopped.

"We'll have to stay here till it's light." Harris pulled her down among some tall ferns. "We wouldn't want to lose our way and end up stumbling into their camp."

Though the night was warm, Jenny began to tremble. Harris wrapped her in a comforting embrace. "It's all right, lass," he murmured. "We know they're around, so we can be on our guard. We'll have to be careful from now on, though. About shouting and laughing and lighting fires."

Despite his reassurance, Jenny slept hardly a wink the rest of the night. Every call of a night bird, every rustle of the underbrush, jolted her to full alert. She tried to calm herself by diverting her thoughts elsewhere.

That was no better.

Against her will, she found herself dwelling on the perilous enjoyment of lying in Harris's arms. His lean strength cradled her. His breath danced a warm whisper in her hair. Deep inside, she ached for him.

Every time they kissed it had felt different—though always far too pleasant to suit her peace of mind. Some long-suppressed spirit of adventure within her yearned to plumb the experience to its sweetest depths. Her hands trembled to explore the spare, manly contours of his body. Her blood roused with the urge to invite him on a similar expedition. One of intimate discovery. Perhaps even conquest.

Feeling beads of sweat break out on her hairline, Jenny strove to rein in her wayward inclinations. Whatever would her father say, if he knew? His daughter and Harris Chisholm lying down together on the ground, like a pair of savages. His daughter, entertaining all manner of wanton notions. His daughter, fairly melting with the heat of her own wicked desire? He'd probably thrash her backside raw before exploding in a fit of righteous apoplexy.

The very thought of it made Jenny smile to herself in the darkness. Perhaps she'd better go back to worrying about an Indian attack.

She slipped into a brief doze only to waken sharply again when she heard strange sounds close by.

A high, excited chatter of people talking...or singing. Jenny could not make out any words to tell if it might be French, or the language of the Indians...or even—please God—the King's English.

She nudged Harris, but he was too deeply asleep to respond. Jenny didn't want to say his name aloud and risk being overheard. Gathering her courage, she rolled away from him and crept toward the source of the sound, scarcely daring to breathe. As she peered around the high stump of a fallen tree, her mouth dropped open in a slack gape of amazement.

Silver moonbeams bathed the tiny clearing before her, and the curious animals that crowded within it. Most were the size of young pigs, but closer to the ground. They were covered in coats of long spiky fur, like giant hedgehogs. What had the Glendenning children called them... porcupines?

Some walked on four legs, but some pulled themselves erect as they chattered and danced in the moonlight. After watching this extraordinary performance for some time, Jenny shook her head, wondering if she might not be dreaming it. At last, deciding the animals posed no great danger, she slipped back to her bed in the ferns and once again stretched out beside Harris.

Yawning deeply, she let the uncanny chorus of the animals lull her back to sleep. This new land was far stranger

than she'd ever expected. For all that, mused a drowsy
Jenny, it was not without its own queer charm.

"Can we stop and rest a minute, Harris?"

Without waiting for him to say yes or no, Jenny wilted
onto a large moss-covered rock and wiped her face with
the corner of her apron.

Noting the bright flush in her cheeks, Harris reluctantly
followed suit. Unstopping the water jug, he passed it to
her.

"Just a wee bit farther, lass, and we'll be able to ease
up. I ken we should be coming to a river soon. Once we
put that between us and the Indians, I'll rest a mite easier."

As Jenny took a long swig from the jug, Harris half
wished it contained something more potent than spring water.

"Aye, I'll feel better about it, too." She glanced over
her shoulder, as though expecting the forest dwellers to
materialize out of the trees.

"While we're sitting down anyhow, would ye like an
oatcake?" Harris fumbled in his pack for them. He cursed
the necessity that had made him leave his second snare
behind...along with whatever it might have caught. Having
eaten their fill the previous evening, he hadn't worried
about gathering food today. Getting safely away from the
Indians was his first priority.

Unwrapping the small canvas parcel Mrs. Jardine's hired
girl had tied up for him, Harris took out a thick wedge of
oatcake and broke it in two. He gave Jenny the larger
piece, insisting he was still full from last night's supper.
Now if only his stomach wouldn't give him away with a
hungry growl.

"How many miles do ye reckon we've come today?"
asked Jenny, gnawing on the hard, flat biscuit.

"Four or five, at least."

Jenny gave his answer a moment of silent concentration.

"Then we can't have much more than another twenty to go," she announced brightly.

Chewing on his oatcake, Harris twisted his mouth into a wan smile. Let Jenny take that for confirmation if she cared to. Privately he doubted they'd gained more than a mile in their journey to Chatham. Most of their walking had moved them south, out of range of the Indians. Once they crossed the river, though, he hoped to strike out on a more direct route.

They washed the dry stale oatcakes down with the last of the tepid water, then Harris rose from their rocky perch as unwillingly as he'd lighted on it. Flexing his tired limbs, he offered Jenny his hand.

"I could sit here and chat all day, but we won't have light too many more hours." Why must he sound apologetic? This trek through the woods had been *her* idea. "If we do find a river, I want to cross it while we can still see what we're about."

Hoisting Jenny up, he clung to her hand for an extra heartbeat or two, savoring the feel of it in his. In Dalbeattie they had a complimentary saying for a lass like Jenny. *She has hands that make light work of a chore.* Apart from everything else, he hoped that marriage to the wealthy Roderick Douglas wouldn't turn Jenny's deft, capable hands idle or weak.

"Poor Harris." She smiled as she said it, her voice lingering fondly over his name. Though he looked for it, he saw no trace of pity in her eyes. "I don't suppose ye reckoned what ye were letting yerself in for, that day on the quay at Kirkcudbright."

"Aye, that's a fact," he replied brusquely, conscious that he wasn't telling the whole truth.

Seeing a flicker of hurt shadow her expression, he amended, "Now, now. It hasn't been as bad as all that. Quite an adventure, in fact. Stories to tell our grandchildren."

Her smile twisted into an embarrassed grin and the scarlet flush of her face intensified.

"I mean…" Harris cursed himself for a dolt. "Ye'll tell yer grandchildren…and I'll…tell mine." Hastily he added, "If I ever have any, that is."

"I like the thought of that," said Jenny, evidently meaning to rescue him from his blunder. "Us still being friends when we're old and gray. Telling our grandchildren all about how we crossed the ocean and got shipwrecked, then walked all the way to Chatham overland."

"Let's get on the move then." Harris strode away, muttering under his breath, "Or we'll be telling them how we wandered in the wilderness for forty years."

Jenny must have overheard him, for she chuckled softly as she fell into step behind him.

They trudged on in silence for some time without coming upon any sign of a stream. Harris was beginning to doubt himself when suddenly a fresh breeze ruffled the leaves overhead. On that wind came the welcome gurgle of flowing water.

"Did ye hear that, Harris?" Jenny clutched his arm. "There's a river ahead, just like ye said there'd be."

Though his chest swelled at the note of respect in her voice, Harris tried to make light of it. "Robert Jardine told me there were four or five small rivers between the Richibucto and the Miramichi. Unless we were going in the wrong direction entirely, we had to come upon one sooner or later."

Picking their way down the wooded slope, they soon reached the shore. One look at the expanse of water before them and Jenny's bubble of elation promptly burst.

"How'll we ever get across it, Harris?" she wailed.

"Not over a bridge, that's for certain," he replied wryly.

With a groan of dismay, Jenny dropped to the ground. Her eyes stung with tears of fierce anger at herself. "Oh, Harris, I'm worse than daft! Take a notion into my head and I charge on after it without looking to see what's in the way.''

Easing to his haunches beside her, Harris slipped an arm around Jenny's shoulders. "Now, lass, don't be so hard on yerself. So ye take after what ye want and make light of the obstacles in yer path—what's so bad about that? It may land ye in hot water now and again, but in the end ye get where ye're going. It'd be a poor world without folk who pursue their dreams.''

Her doubts and worries lifted at his words, as though he'd taken a heavy pack from her shoulders. The very blood seemed to pulse in her veins stronger and faster. A tide of confidence and power rose within her. When a furtive voice in the back of her mind whispered that she was not pursuing her dreams but fleeing her nightmares, Jenny ignored it.

She turned on Harris with a smile that warmed her whole face. "I thought I was only joking about ye being a fairy godfather. Now I'm not so sure. Ye do work magic on me.''

No lie, that.

As their gazes locked, Jenny longed to dive into the green-brown velvet of his eyes. That was one enchantment she must resist, no matter how it compelled her.

"What are we going to do about crossing this river?'' She forced herself to look away, warding off his sorcery with practical considerations.

Harris peeled off his boots and socks. Then he rolled up his trousers to the knees and waded into the river. Shading his eyes from the glare of the bright sun on the water, he took a long look upstream and a longer look down.

"I ken it gets narrower that way.'' He pointed downstream. "Let's follow the shore and see if we come upon a ford. Either that, or we find a downed tree to float ourselves across.''

"Let's look for a ford,'' said Jenny. "Only give me a

minute first to cool my feet.'' Shedding her shoes and
stockings, she hitched up her skirts and joined him in the
river.

"Mmm!'' She wiggled her toes in the wet sand. "I can
tell ye one thing, Harris. After this, I'll never take water
for granted again.''

He chuckled. "Nor a decent bed.''

They tarried a few minutes more, enjoying the rest and
the soothing cool of the water on their tired feet, until
Harris squinted at the position of the sun and said they
really should be on their way.

Once again his prediction proved correct. They had not
hiked far when they came to a narrow neck in the river.

"Look, Harris!'' Jenny could scarcely believe the wonder. "And ye said we'd never find a bridge.''

She ran toward it.

Behind her, she heard Harris caution. "I don't ken that's
a bridge, Jenny.''

Perhaps not, she realized as she drew closer. The strange
wooden structure did range from one side of the narrows
to the other, but nothing bigger than a squirrel might walk
across it. Why on earth would anyone build a fence across
a river?

Jenny gave the notion only passing thought. At least it
would provide a handhold for them to wade to the other
side.

"Come back, lass!'' She heard Harris call softly but
urgently.

Turn back now, when they were so close? Balancing the
awkward bundle on her head, her shoes tied together and
slung around her neck, Jenny felt the swift water flow over
her knees.

She gasped as Harris clutched her arm.

Ragged with muted alarm, his warning exploded in her
ears. "It's not a bridge, Jenny. It's a fishing weir. An In-

dian fishing weee…'' The last word waxed into a cry of alarm.

Perhaps he lost his footing on the stony riverbed, or perhaps the racing current threw Harris off balance. Jenny turned just in time to see his arms thrashing wildly as he fell. His coat sleeve caught on one of the weir's pointed stakes.

Letting the bundle fall from her head, Jenny waded back to help him. At that moment, several large, bronzed men burst from the forest behind them.

One carried a musket. Two others wielded long forked spears. Spying Harris and Jenny, they moved forward with their weapons raised, shouting words Jenny could not understand.

"Come on, Harris!" She grasped his left arm, and with a strength born of desperation helped him stagger to his feet.

Caught on the weir, his coat held him fast.

"Go, lass! I'll hold them back for as long as I can!"

Jenny froze.

Time froze with her.

Or so it felt, as scores of sights, sounds and perceptions bombarded her consciousness.

The terrible beauty of the Indians as they surged toward the river—tall, bare chested, with manes of hair dark as midnight.

The hoarse urgency of Harris's voice as he bellowed at her to flee. The desperate courage in his eyes, and the fear—not for himself, but for her.

The cold, powerful tug of the river on her body.

Every nerve in her screamed to let herself go—to let the swift current carry her downriver, away from danger.

Something else, something she could not explain, pushed her forward. Past Harris she struggled, to meet the threat head-on.

Chapter Twelve

"Damn ye, lass! Go!"

With every fiber of his being, Harris willed her to get away. The Indians could only kill him. What they might do to a fetching lass like Jenny didn't bear thinking about.

Paying him no more heed than she ever did, she brushed past, putting herself between him and the armed men. Harris nearly wrenched his shoulder from its socket trying to free himself from the shackle of his coat.

Jenny seized a large deadfall branch that had caught on the weir. Clutching it in both hands, she brandished it at their attackers. "Come on, ye blaggards!" she roared. "I'll give ye a right good braining for yer trouble!"

If he could have laid hands on that stick, Harris might have brained Jenny. For a long, agonizing moment, the world stopped as he braced for disaster.

Then, like a gaggle of puppets jerked back by the strings of their master, the dark men skidded to a halt. The nearest one threw back his head and let out a whoop of wild laughter. Dropping his wickedly lethal pronged spear, he bent forward until his head nearly touched the knees of his buckskin leggings. Spasms of laughter shook him.

The others laughed, too, until the river rang with it.

"And what may I ask is so cursed comical?" Jenny demanded.

Gasping for breath, the man with the musket called out to Harris in an oddly accented French. *"Alors, Barbe-rouge…" Red-beard, you must be quite a man to handle a she-bear like her!* Once again, laughter overtook him.

Anyone who could make such a joke couldn't mean them harm. The conviction hit Harris with such a powerful clout of relief that his knees almost buckled.

"Ha-ha." His own laughter welled up, weak at first and tinged with mild hysteria. Soon, however, he caught the contagious amusement of the other men, laughing hard, until tears rolled down his face.

Jenny rounded on him with eyes that blazed amethyst fury. "Have ye gone daft, Harris? What did that savage say? What are ye all laughing about?"

"He…" Harris fought to recover a straight face. "He said he…admires a woman of spirit."

"Aye?" She sounded suspicious.

"Put yer stick down, lass. They're not going to hurt us."

Jenny looked back at the warriors, slapping their thighs, all but helpless with laughter. In their present state, she could probably have walked up to any one of them and clubbed him unconscious. Warily she lowered her weapon.

"Pardon," Harris called as he staggered a step toward Jenny and put an arm around her shoulders. He warmed to anyone prepared to mistake her for his woman. *I'm sorry we startled you. We just wanted to ford the river. I hope we haven't damaged your weir.*

"Pas de problème," replied the one with the musket. He looked to be the senior of the group. *Don't worry about it, Red-beard. It's a long time since we had such a good laugh. We've had trouble with a bear stealing fish from us. When we heard the noise, we thought it was him.*

Jenny looked at Harris expectantly. "What'd he say?"

Harris explained about the bear.

When he had finished, the Indian chief asked, "Where are you and your woman bound, Red-beard?"

"Miramichi," replied Harris. "It's easy to get lost in these woods. I want to go to the mouth of the river and follow the shore."

Laughing again, the tall Indian shook his head. "That's a bad way to travel on foot."

Passing his gun to one of the younger man, he held out his hands to help them wade ashore. "*Venez et mangez…*"

"He's inviting us to stay and eat with them," Harris told Jenny. "He says we're welcome to spend the night."

"What's the French for *thank you*, Harris?"

"*Merci.*"

"Well then—*merci* to ye." Jenny made an awkward curtsy to their host in her waterlogged dress.

The man beamed back at her and for an instant Harris was glad of the mistaken impression that Jenny belonged to him.

The other men waded into the river and began taking fish from the weir with their pronged spears. One came back bearing Jenny's bundle. Like Harris's coat, it had also snagged on the pointed stakes.

"*Merci!*" she exclaimed, hugging it to her like a lost child. "Why, it's hardly even damp."

Harris wished Jenny's wedding dress had floated down-river and out to sea.

They followed their host for some distance until they came to a clearing. There stood three tall, conical tents, each framed by several long stakes and wrapped with sheets of bark. Half-a-dozen brown children, all but naked, raced around the encampment, shrieking with laughter as dogs barked at their heels. A woman looked up from stirring something in a hollowed-out log. Giving the white visitors a curious but indulgent smile, she called to the children in their own tongue.

Harris admired the sound of it—like a verbal brook gurgling over its stony bed. It was a language for laughter, and prayer, and a hundred domestic endearments.

Their host spoke to the woman. By some unaccountable intuition, Harris knew she must be his wife. Clearly he was explaining how Harris and Jenny had come to be there, for he began to laugh. The woman soon joined in.

She said something to Jenny in her own language. Though he could not understand one word, Harris recognized a mixture of amusement and admiration in the tone. Perhaps she was commending Jenny for standing up to the men.

"Merci," replied Jenny, as if she understood. She pointed to herself. "I'm Jenny, and this is Harris."

"Aw-reez." Their host tried to repeat the name. Evidently some of the sounds did not come naturally in either his own language or French. *"Barbe-rouge."*

Harris smiled and nodded. Among these people, he was content to be known as Red-beard.

"Et vous?" Harris asked.

"Levi," the man tapped his chest. "Levi Augustine. *Bienvenu à mon feu." Welcome to my fire.*

"The honor is ours," replied Harris in French. At least he hoped that was what he'd said.

The woman clucked her tongue over Jenny's wet dress. She motioned them to the tallest of the three structures.

Levi translated her words into French. "Suzannah says come into the *wikuom* and put on dry clothes."

Before Harris could repeat it in English for Jenny, she'd already ducked through the low entry of the family's dwelling. With a self-conscious shrug to Levi, Harris followed.

His eyes had not yet accustomed themselves to the dim interior when he heard Jenny say, "Did ye do all this beautiful beadwork, yerself? It looks almost too pretty to wear. I wouldn't want to spoil it on ye."

As though she'd understood every word, Suzannah replied something that Harris guessed to mean, *"Go ahead. Clothes are to wear. When you've changed, I'll hang your dress to dry."*

From a hamper woven of long wooden splints, the woman brought out a pair of leather leggings like those worn by Levi and the other men. She handed them to Harris. With a few more words, possibly to say that she must get back to her cooking, she left them alone.

Jenny touched the garment to her cheek. "It's softer than kid leather," she breathed. Then she glanced up at Harris in some alarm. "Mind ye keep yer back turned while I'm getting into this thing."

Harris felt his Adam's apple bobbing in spasms. "I...will...if ye will."

Thankful that the flickering firelight masked her blushes, Jenny twitched the hem of her borrowed dress a bit lower on her leg. Suzannah and the other women of the family looked so natural in their skirts, which fell an inch or two below the knee. Jenny felt naked in hers.

She cast a covert glance at Harris, to see if he might be watching. His eyes were on Levi and the other men as they played a game, tossing dicelike disks of bone onto a wooden platter. He looked rather strange, wearing his own shirt with the buckskin leggings. Jenny half wished he'd emulated their hosts, by going bare chested.

With a fine meal of smoked duck and shellfish warming her belly, she wrested her concentration back to Suzannah's beading demonstration. One of the children wandered over and settled into her lap. Jenny rested her chin against his dark hair. Suzannah held the piece of buckskin she was stitching closer for Jenny to see. Tracing the outline of the design with her forefinger, she said something.

"Aye," Jenny replied. "It's a bonny pattern, and the colors so fine and bright."

They had been carrying on this queer kind of conversation for several hours, each in their own language. Though the words surely made no sense to either of them, Jenny was confident they understood each other. By contrast, Harris and Levi Augustine talked away in their common second language, French. Harris asked question after question—all about how the people lived, what they ate, their traditions.

Any answer of particular interest, he'd passed on to her.

"The young fellow there…" While they ate, Harris had pointed to one of the men.

Jenny recognized him as the first member of the party they'd encountered—the one who'd all but fallen down laughing at her.

"He's Noel Peter Paul. His people live on the Richibucto. He's staying with Levi's family for a while and working for them to prove he's a steady lad and a good provider. Then he'll get Levi's daughter, Christianne, for a wife.

Glancing up from Suzannah's beadwork, Jenny intercepted a special look that passed between the betrothed couple.

Surely Christianne couldn't harbor the kind of romantic daydreams of a European girl. She could expect a life very much like her mother's—without a proper house, wandering from the shore to the tide head to the deep woods, depending upon the season. Relying for food on what the family could hunt or gather.

In many ways, it was a much more difficult life than the one Jenny had fled. Yet, the people seemed happy. They laughed a great deal. They cared for their children with obvious affection. Even between Levi and Suzannah, who had been together many years and surely endured many hardships, Jenny recognized a strong, tender bond. Listening to the singing and the storytelling around their campfire that summer night, she felt a pang of wistful envy.

Before she could recover from it, Harris sauntered over

from his place by the fire. "I ken everyone's soon going to bed down for the night."

A powerful yawn racked Jenny. "It sounds like a fine idea to me. I know I'll sleep sound."

"Aye, well…" Harris hesitated. "Ye see, it's like this. Levi says we can sleep in the smaller *wikuom* with his son and daughter-in-law."

His tone and his look of guilty embarrassment made Jenny exclaim, "Sleep—together, ye mean? I should say not!"

"We slept together last night. And the night before."

Men! Could they understand nothing?

"That was different, Harris. We were out in the woods, and…and…it was different."

He shrugged. "We're still in the woods. And these folks won't think anything improper of it."

Something about the way he said it made Jenny inquire sharply, "And why not, may I ask?"

Even in the firelight, she could see him redden. "Well, I may have led them to assume ye're my…woman."

"Then ye can just have a wee talk with yer friend, Mr. Augustine, and set him straight on *that* score, Harris Chisholm."

"Aye, I would." He raked the long fingers of one hand through his hair. "It's just that Levi's brother, Joseph, lost his wife last year in childbed. I ken if he knew ye weren't mine, he might make me an offer for ye."

Jenny glanced over at Joseph Augustine, in earnest conversation with his brother. It was a wonder he hadn't remarried already, for he was a fine figure of a man—tall and broad shouldered with strong, handsome features. He reminded Jenny of Roderick Douglas the last time she'd seen him. Would seven years in this harsh land have changed him much?

Remembering Harris and the sleeping arrangements, she

cast him a wary glance. "I suppose there's not much help for it. But make certain ye behave yerself, mind?"

He raised his hand, as if to swear an oath. "Get it through yer head, lass, I've given up on any notion of the two of us making a match. I only want to see ye safe to Chatham so I can get on about my business with a clear conscience."

"That suits me," Jenny replied half-defiantly.

Remembering the delicious torture of the previous night lying with Harris, she knew it was her own wilful desires that truly worried her. She should rest easy in the knowledge that he'd do nothing to take advantage of her wayward inclinations. Instead, her heart contracted in a stab of disappointment.

It was going to be a long night.

It had been a long night!

Harris scratched the bristly three-day growth of whiskers on his face. Then he yawned and stretched. Despite a luxurious mattress of animal furs, his body ached worse this morning than it had the past two days.

He ached for Jenny.

All night, as she lay beside him, her body warm and oh so accessible in the brief buckskin gown, he had ached for her. Ached until he feared he would explode from the effort to contain his own yearning.

As soon as he heard the first stirrings of the Augustines preparing for a new day, he rose and joined them. When Jenny got up later, he hardened his heart against the early morning softness of her face.

"Eat and get dressed," he snapped. "We can't be dawdling here all day. We've a long way still to go."

"Aye, Harris, I won't be long."

She sounded subdued. There was a look of puzzlement and hurt in her eyes, which Harris made grim efforts to ignore. An answering echo of that pain and perplexity tugged at his own insides.

As Harris watched Jenny enter the *wikuom,* Levi Augustine clapped a hearty arm around his shoulder. "*Mon ami,* stay with us a few more days. Eat and rest for your journey. Tell me more about this land of yours far across the water."

"*Merci pour votre hospitalité.*" Harris meant it sincerely and with more than a touch of chagrin.

Here he'd been, fearful and suspicious of these native people, when they had far more cause to be wary of a foreigner like him. Yet they had made him more truly welcome than he'd ever felt. Had the need to deliver Jenny to Chatham not goaded him, Harris would have been content to linger on the banks of this river with the unpronounceable name, basking in the unexpected fellowship he'd discovered.

"I'll return this way, when my business is done in Chatham," he added, purposely neglecting to mention that Jenny wouldn't be with him. "Then I'll stay a while with you, if you'll have me."

Before continuing their journey, Harris and Jenny fed fully on berries and more shellfish, and drank deeply of the savory game broth that was the family's principal beverage. Then Suzannah Augustine packed them a woven-rush basket of smoked fish and Levi ferried them across the river in his canoe.

Jenny almost wore out her one word of French, *merci.*

"*Je regret…*" Harris said to their host. "I'm sorry I haven't a gift to give you in thanks for all your hospitality." He resolved to bring something back with him on his return trip from Chatham.

Their host waved away his apology. "You brought us the gift of laughter, Red-beard. And the gift of respect. White men, the English especially, talk to my people like we are foolish children. You talk like we are brothers. You will always be welcome in our *wikuom.*''

Harris forced his feet forward. He'd lived most of his life as an outsider, and he'd made his peace with that. He wasn't sure what to make of this instant kinship he felt with the native folk. He only knew it was a wrench to leave them.

"Encore une chose!" Levi called after them. "One more thing. Be careful with your fire. This has been the driest summer I can remember. The trees are thirsty. The creeks are low. Light one if you must, but tend it well and be sure you don't leave hot embers behind when you break camp.''

"Je comprends," replied Harris. "I hear ye." A fire raging out of control in heavily wooded country like this was a terror he preferred not to dwell on. He hoped Suzannah's smoked fish would last them the rest of the trip so they wouldn't have to cook their food.

"Now would ye mind explaining to me again," said Jenny when they were out of Levi's sight, "why we aren't walking up the coast, like ye planned.''

Though the question exasperated him a bit, implying that Jenny didn't trust his judgment, Harris welcomed the distraction of conversation—on any subject.

"It's like this." He did his best to sound patient. "According to Levi, the coast bows out quite a ways. It would likely double our journey. Besides, we have three more rivers to ford…four if we kept to the coast, and they're all wide at the mouth. We'd need a canoe to get across them. Levi gave me good directions that'll take us to Chatham almost as the crow flies, and we'll miss one of the shorter creeks altogether.''

"Aye?" Jenny sounded skeptical. "What use are directions in open country like this?''

"We'll get there fine, ye'll see. We just have to follow this ridge until we come to a big stand of birch trees. Then we look for a dry creek bed and keep to it until we reach a rock taller than a *wikuom*…''

Repeating the litany of directions over to himself, Harris experienced a twinge of doubt. If only he had a paper and pen to copy them down. Levi, whose people had no use for writing, possessed a formidable memory. He could recite the list of his ancestors back more than ten generations. He could tell many tales, of why the beavers built dams and how the porcupine got his quills. Most importantly to Harris at the moment, Levi Augustine seemed to know this trackless wilderness with astonishing intimacy.

Harris hoped his own memory was equal to the task. His survival and Jenny's depended on it.

Chapter Thirteen

"Are ye sure we're going the right way, Harris?"

The August sun beat down on Jenny. A nasty fat fly with a green tail lit on her arm and bit. She swatted and killed it, taking grim delight in her vengeance.

Yesterday they'd emerged from the cover of the forest into an area of newer growth. A few charred tree trunks bore witness that the territory had once been scourged by fire. At first Jenny had enjoyed the open country. Blueberries were plentiful. They could see much farther in any direction. Best of all, she no longer had the suffocating sense of the trees closing in on her.

As a second day passed, with stubborn barricades of alders blocking their way and the sun beaming relentlessly upon them, she had begun to crave the friendly shade of the woods.

"No, I'm not sure," Harris barked. He began to mutter the bewildering list of Levi Augustine's directions. "We passed the big rock, then skirted the shore of that wee lake, climbed the hill and forded the river."

"Aye, we did all that. What did Levi say about this bush country?"

His brows knit together in a worried frown. "He said to

head north, and half-a-day's walk would bring us back into the trees."

"But we've gone a day and a half. Blast!" Jenny slapped at another fly that had bit her. This one escaped. "We've eaten all Suzannah's smoked fish, and the last of yer oatcakes."

"Are ye hungry? We can stop and pick some more berries if ye like."

"No." Jenny sighed. "I've eaten so many the last while, I've lost my taste for them."

"Still we should take some more, if only for the moisture." Harris stooped and quickly picked a handful of the tiny, deep purple orbs. "We've only a mouthful or two of water in the jug."

Icy fear prickled in the back of Jenny's throat. She could scarcely swallow her berries. "We're lost, aren't we, Harris?"

He begrudged a curt nod. "We aren't where we're supposed to be, and we don't know where we are. I'd say that's a fair definition of *lost*."

How long could they continue to wander, Jenny asked herself, until they died of heat and thirst?

Part of her took grim comfort from the fact that she was not alone. She never would have gotten this far without Harris. Another part deeply regretted that she had dragged him into her foolhardy adventure. What had he done to deserve this? Nothing but caring for her—and making her care for him in ways she could not afford. It wasn't his fault she'd lacked the mettle to face a month of his courting in Richibucto.

"Harris, I…" She wanted him to know how sorry she was. Owing him so much, she had repaid him so badly. Even if he wanted her, or mistakenly fancied he did, he deserved better. Before she could get the words out, everything around her began to spin. Darkness enveloped her vision and her mind.

The last scrap of sensation that reached her was Harris's voice. His urgent cry of her name reached Jenny as though from a great distance. She felt herself slip into a deep, black pit.

"Jenny!" Harris lurched toward her as she melted to the ground. He barely managed to break the fall of her limp deadweight.

Anxiously he felt at her throat for a pulse. After a breath-bated moment, he was rewarded with a weak flutter beneath his fingertips.

Wiping the sweat from his own brow with the back of his hand, he gazed at Jenny. Her fair skin was flushed to a furious red and perspiration beaded along her hairline. Harris cursed himself for forcing her to walk so far in the heat of the sun's ruthless glare.

Gathering her up in his arms, he strode to the blackened trunk of a large dead tree. Gently he laid her down in the shadow of the charred stump, the only sliver of shade available. With trembling fingers he untied her blue bonnet and slid it off her damp, tousled hair. Then he fumbled in his pack for the water jug. It felt terrifyingly light.

He dribbled a few drops of the water between her lips, heartened to see her swallow it. Two of those vexing flies lighted on Jenny's face. Harris fanned them away before they had time to bite. Stubbornly he thrust back the thought of how flies were attracted to a corpse.

Another miserly splash of their precious water went into Jenny. And another.

"Come now, lass." Harris patted her cheek. "Ye've had a bit of a rest. It's time to open yer eyes now, before ye get me too anxious about ye."

He toyed with the thought of kissing her. Such an unpleasant sensation might bring her around quick enough, like the noxious stink of smelling salts. And if it didn't revive her, at least he'd go to his grave with one final stolen intimacy.

Before he could act upon the impluse, Jenny moaned softly. Her eyelids fluttered.

"Harris? Where am I? What happened?"

Relief engulfed him. "Ye swooned dead away, lass. I wish I could say I hoisted ye up and carried ye off to the shore of a cool river, but I can't. We're still in the bush."

He raised his eyes to the pale blue firmament above them, with only a wisp of cloud draped here and there like gossamer. It was a beautiful sight, but just then Harris would have preferred a bank of fat, dark thunderheads threatening a downpour.

"We're not going to stir another step until the sun gets down a ways," he remarked, as much to himself as to Jenny. "Until we get back into the shade of the woods, we're going to travel at dusk and at dawn. When the sun gets high, we'll find whatever shade we can and rest in it."

"That sounds like a fine plan, Harris." Jenny's tone was light and breathy, suggesting a tenuous grip on consciousness. "Ye'll find us a way out of here soon. There's nothing ye can't do when ye put yer mind to it."

Harris barely restrained the urge to throw back his head and laugh like a lunatic. Do anything he set his mind to? Why, he could barely get anything right. After all, he'd indulged Jenny in this perilous folly of walking to Chatham, knowing something of the danger that lay ahead. If he'd been half the man she seemed to think he was, he would have slung her over his shoulder and marched her back to Richibucto. Then he'd have mounted armed guards, day and night if necessary, to make certain she stayed.

There might be a scrap of truth in what she said, he admitted reluctantly. He did feel more able, more competent, when Jenny was around. Perhaps it was her unconditional faith in him. Perhaps it was the way he felt about her that inspired him to try harder, dig deeper within himself. Or perhaps, he concluded with an unuttered sigh, it was the desperate scrapes she landed them in, which left him no choice but to rise to the occasion.

Jenny fanned her face weakly with her hand. ''Do ye ever mind being so hot, Harris?''

Moist with sweat, the bust of her dress clung provocatively to her bosom. Harris tried to wrest his gaze away, but his eyes refused to cooperate. Suddenly his mouth felt dry as dust. He could scarcely choke out his reply.

''No. Never.''

It was the truth, though not the whole truth. What he didn't admit was that the remorseless sun wasn't entirely to blame.

''Harris, what's that, over there?''

He squinted in the direction Jenny pointed. ''It looks to be a big rock, lass. Well spotted! Let's go see.''

Sure enough, it was a tall boulder, with tufts of moss clinging to its pitted surface.

''At last!'' Sliding the pack from his back, Harris began to climb. ''A bit of height so I can get a decent look around.''

Jenny held her breath as he clambered to the top of the rock. In the past three hours, since Harris had declared the sun low enough for them to resume their journey, she had battled her dizziness. She hated to think what would happen if Harris should take a faint spell so far off the ground.

Fortunately, he gained the top of the rock without mishap. Then Harris shaded his eyes from the glare of the setting sun and scanned the horizon.

''Can ye see anything?'' Jenny called up to him.

''Just more bush that way,'' came his dispirited answer. ''Miles and miles of the cursed stuff.''

Surrendering to the weakness in her knees, Jenny let

herself drop to the ground. Tears prickled her eyelids, but she fought against giving way to them. She and Harris had shared the last few mouthfuls of water in his jug. Before much longer they would have to stop for the night. Up at dawn and a few hours' walk before they'd be forced to stop again. If they didn't find woodland or water by then…

Jenny thrust back the thought.

From his precarious perch atop the boulder, Harris surged up. Had he lost his balance?

"Trees!"

It took Jenny a moment to grasp the import of the word. A moment in which Harris scrambled down from his lookout.

"Trees, Jenny!" Clutching her arm just above the elbow, he hoisted her to her feet. With his other hand, Harris scooped up his pack. "This way. Not too far, either."

Before she could gather her thoughts or breath for a question, Jenny found herself stumbling through the bush, towed by the insistent momentum of Harris. It was all she could do to keep her feet moving so she wouldn't pitch face first onto the ground. For an instant, she feared they had abandoned her bundle of wedding clothes. A wave of relief buoyed her as she realized it was clutched tightly in her hand.

Then she saw them.

Dead ahead. A dark, uneven line of tall trees silhouetted against the dusky red sky. Until the past two days, Jenny had thought she'd be content never to lay eyes on a tree again. Now her legs found fresh vigor as they carried her closer and closer to the eaves of the forest. Once Harris let her go, Jenny fully intended to clasp the first tree trunk she encountered, and kiss its dear bark.

As one, she and Harris gasped for breath, allowing their forward rush to carry them deeper into the woods.

Then Harris stumbled.

Abruptly he released Jenny's arm, and she found herself

teetering on the lip of a steep, unstable slope. She lunged to grip some part of Harris and check his fall, but her hand closed around empty air. Loose earth and pebbles scuttled beneath her feet. Jenny threw herself back.

Harris's falling cry rent the warm stillness of twilight. It ended in a loud, emphatic splash.

Scrambling down the embankment, Jenny stopped short at the water's edge. "Oh, Harris, are ye killed?"

With a choked whoop of laughter, he rose from the river and shook himself like a rangy red setter. "If I am, then for sure I've gone to heaven, lass!"

He let himself collapse backward into the water again, with another infectious yelp of glee.

Suddenly limp with relief and the residue of worry, Jenny settled onto a fallen log and whispered a brief but profound prayer of thanks for their deliverance.

"What are ye waiting for, lass?" Harris waded toward her. "Can't ye see this is water?"

"Aye, I see. I just sat down to take my shoes off. Yer boots are going to be soaked."

Harris shrugged. "I didn't have time to think about taking them off. I don't know if I'd have bothered anyhow. After the past two days, I ken a fellow can do worse than walk in wet boots. Though now that ye mention it, I'd like to feel the sand between my toes instead of the wet wool of my stockings."

Daylight was fading fast.

Jenny could make out the shape of Harris jumping around, trying to pry off his boot. With a grunt of satisfaction from him and a deep sucking noise from the boot, it parted company with his foot at last. He pitched it onto the shore, followed by the drenched wad of his stocking. Then came their mates.

"What's keeping ye, Jenny?"

"It's these hooks. I can't get them unfastened." Or were her fumbling fingers to blame?

Harris splashed toward her. "Allow me, *mademoiselle*."

Though she tried to stop herself, Jenny glanced up. She could only make out his shape in the dying light. Tall. Lean. Shirt plastered to his wide shoulders in a way that made her heart flutter queerly in her bosom and her bosom strain against the bodice of her dress.

Kneeling before her, Harris deftly dispatched her footwear. One hand held her foot in a firm caress as the other slid her shoe off. A strange, hot current surged through Jenny's flesh, like the painless pricking of a thousand tiny bees. Radiating from her foot, it flamed at the base of her throat, the tips of her breasts and the deepest, most intimate pit of her belly.

Jenny scarcely knew what to make of it. All that fuss over a foot? Her foot, touched by a man she'd spurned. A man who'd given up any notion of winning her. Surely it was only the heat and the weariness of the journey catching up with her.

Pulling her foot out of Harris's hold, she gasped, "I can get the other one myself."

"Good." His voice had an odd, strangled tone, as though he couldn't catch his breath.

Jenny grasped for something to say that would break the awkwardness and dangerous intensity between them.

"Do ye ken the water's fit to drink?"

Sitting back on his haunches, Harris chuckled. "I swallowed a good bit of it when I landed in the river. It hasn't done me any harm so far."

Pulling off her remaining shoe, Jenny groped under her skirt to roll down her stockings. She knew Harris couldn't see much of anything with the sun down, but the thought of hiking up her dress and exposing her bare calves and thighs set that swarm of bees to work on her again.

"I could do with a drink, I'm that parched."

A warm, fickle breeze from off the river whispered up Jenny's naked legs, like the nuzzle of a man's whiskers.

Her mouth went drier than ever. It would take more than water to quench this deep, ravenous thirst.

"Ye shouldn't drink right at this spot," advised Harris. "I've churned up the riverbed too much. Go upstream a bit."

Her legs wobbled beneath her as Jenny picked her way up the shore. When a sudden chill swept through her, she tried to ignore that, as well, only to realize she had stepped in an icy spring that flowed into the river.

She drank and drank from it until her stomach felt queasy. Then Jenny splashed cold water on her face and wrists and anywhere else where it might extinguish the unwelcome excitement that blazed within her.

From downstream, she heard Harris whistling to himself as he splashed about in the river. Kilting her dress up around her knees, she waded out. Harris was right. The fine, soft silt of the riverbed oozed between her toes in the most delicious sensation imaginable.

One of the most delicious sensations, she amended privately, recalling the way Harris had touched her foot.

As if alert to her thoughts, he called out, "Come on in deeper, Jenny. What are ye doing, picking yer way along the shore like that?"

"Ye didn't have any choice about yer clothes getting wet, Harris, but I do. I've no intention of sleeping in a sodden dress tonight."

"Take it off, then."

"Get away with ye!"

"I mean it, Jenny. Who's to know? There's probably not a living soul around for ten or twenty miles, and it's too dark for me to see anything improper."

True enough on both counts. Still Jenny hesitated.

"Bathing now and again is good for a body," persisted Harris.

It was not his arguments that persuaded her, Jenny fiercely insisted to herself. It was the stifling way her sweat-soaked dress clung to her arms and back. It was the seductive sound of rippling and splashing as Harris cavorted in the water. And perhaps it was the Eden-like setting that restored in her womankind's lost innocence.

Before she had time to think better of the idea, she slipped out of her dress, leaving it draped over a fallen tree trunk. Out into the river she waded, deeper and deeper, now and then gasping as the bracing caress of the water rose to claim another part of her body. Thighs. Hips. Waist.

Heaven.

After two solid days walking in the simmering heat of August, it was heaven to drench herself this way.

"What did I tell ye?" Harris chuckled from nearby.

Jenny could just make out the vague shape of him.

"Feels good, doesn't it?" He scooped a splash of water in her direction.

"Aye. Very…refreshing." Jenny splashed him back.

Suddenly he disappeared beneath the surface of the water.

"Harris?" She waded toward the last place she'd seen his shadow. "What's the matter? Ah!"

She let out a shriek as something coiled around her ankle.

Harris bobbed to the surface, within arm's reach. "It was only me, lass," he sputtered with laughter. "The way ye jumped, ye must have mistaken me for a sea monster."

"Think it's a lark to scare a lass out of her wits, do ye?" Before he could move out of range, Jenny bobbed up and grasped a handful of his hair. "Mistake *this,* Harris Chisholm!"

With all her might she pushed him under the water.

Struggling to free himself, he brushed her thigh. Abruptly she let go of his hair. As Harris's head emerged from the water again, Jenny's hand slid down his neck to his shoulder.

His bare shoulder.

"What happened to yer clothes?" The question almost blurted itself. With all her will, Jenny wrenched her hand off Harris. It came away reluctantly.

"My clothes?" He sounded surprised. "The same as yers. I didn't care for the feel of them, so I stripped off while ye were taking a drink. I wrung them out and hung them on branches. With the warm breeze, they may be dry by the time I need them."

He ducked down low again. Fearing another assault from the depths, Jenny stepped back. Harris only filled his mouth with water and spit a stream of it at her.

"Bounder!" she squealed. "Take that!" She slapped the water with open palms, producing a satisfying splash.

"Ye missed me." Harris materialized behind her.

"Oh, did I?"

Their water frolic continued, to the accompaniment of good-natured taunting, shrieks of surprise and much gleeful laughter. Like two children.

But they were not children and their games were not entirely innocent. A touch might stray into forbidden territory, igniting a wild heat no river could quench.

Once, Jenny rose from the water only to discover she'd ventured closer to shore. In the silver light of the rising moon, her naked breasts were clearly visible. More shocking still, she did not care.

She dove underwater, meaning to grab Harris by the ankle and make him lose his balance. Instead, he reached in and grasped her by the arm, pulling her toward him.

Though she knew she should struggle and protest, the only word she could utter was his name. "Harris…"

He gathered her close—the cool, slippery contact of their wet bodies an exquisitely addictive sensation.

"I know, lass."

Know? What did he know?

"Ye're going to wed Roderick Douglas and all the howling hounds of Hades aren't going to stop ye."

Roderick Who? Jenny wanted to ask. The hard length of
Harris pressed against her belly, eloquent testimony that
he wanted her. After weeks spent fighting it, she was almost ready to admit how much she wanted him.

"I...like ye fine, lass." His tepid words belied the inferno that throbbed between them. "But I see now ye're
no more than a passing fancy to me."

A blunt pain stabbed Jenny's heart.

"There's no reason in the world for us to be doing this."
He bent forward, catching her bottom lip between his and
nuzzling it invitingly.

Just as she prepared to kiss him back, he abandoned her
mouth and went to work elsewhere. "No reason except the
moonlight," he whispered. His warm breath filled her ear,
gently ravishing it.

"And I'm a man..." Harris continued, his lips and his
new growth of beard grazing her neck until Jenny feared
she would crawl out of her own skin with searing need.

From her throat, suddenly parched again, came the
words she tried to hold back. "And I'm a woman."

"Aye." She could sense his smile in the warmth of Harris's murmur. "Ye're every inch of that, lass."

Their lips blundered over each other's faces, driven by
urges as old as humankind. As irresistible as the tug of the
tides. As inexplicable as moonlight.

Just as their searching mouths homed in on each other,
eager to devour and be devoured, Harris froze. "Listen!"

From downstream drifted the unmistakable drone of
bagpipes.

Jenny heard herself gasp, as if smitten by two centuries
of righteous prudery. This was no Eden and she was no
Eve.

Harris pushed her toward the shore. "Get dressed,
Jenny. We shouldn't be doing this."

In a daze of shame and unbearable frustration, she
waded onto the riverbank and collected her clothes.

Chapter Fourteen

Harris scarcely dared look at Jenny as they made their way downriver a few hours after daybreak.

So much for Walter Scott and all his chivalrous ideals!

He hadn't risked letting himself get close to her during the night, for fear he'd once again succumb to moon madness. It had taken every fiber of God-fearing decency in him to push her away when his whole being craved her.

This must be a sign he didn't love her. Harris entertained the wishful thought. Surely that respectable, tender emotion could have nothing to do with the feral yearning that had possessed him last night. Had he mistaken the first stirrings of that unholy desire for a pure, romantic attachment?

"Mind where ye're going, Harris!"

"What?" He looked down in time to see his boot land squarely in a pat of pungent cow dung.

He cursed under his breath, casting Jenny a black glare when she chuckled.

From nearby, an ox raised its broad, placid face and surveyed Harris with bovine indifference.

"What are ye looking so smug about?" Harris snapped at the big beast. He knew well enough. The muscle-bound gelding might be a mild, stupid plodder, but at least he was free from the tyranny of she-creatures. Completely indifferent to their charms. Unlike the fractious bull who was kept in a constant state of near-frenzy by his carnal instincts.

When Harris stole a look at Jenny, he found her watching him. Their eyes met for a single, searching instant, then she quickly diverted her attention elsewhere. He had to get this woman to Chatham, fast. Before his heart and his honor were totally compromised.

They entered an open glade, where another ox and half-a-dozen milch cows grazed. On the opposite side of the clearing a big man hacked away at the trunk of an ancient maple tree with his double-bitted ax. After four ringing strokes, he stopped to rest. By that time, Harris and Jenny had closed some of the distance between them, going slowly to avoid treading in any more manure.

The man spotted them.

Laying his ax aside, he drew out a handkerchief nearly the size of a tablecloth and began to wipe his brow. His wide, florid face radiated welcome.

"Failte!" he thundered. *A thousand welcomes!*

"Does everybody in this colony talk French, Harris?" Jenny sounded almost plaintive.

The man threw back his round, bald head and laughed.

Before Harris could answer, Jenny added, "Whatever they talk, folks here seem to take *everything* comical."

"Not *everything,* ma'am," replied the man, his chuckles subsiding.

"That wasn't French," Harris informed her. "It was Gaelic. These folks must be Highlanders."

The ruddy giant held out one huge hand. "Alec McGregor, late of Rannoch, at yer service. And who might ye be, stranger, that ye can tell the difference between a Gaelic welcome and French one?"

"Harris...Chisholm, sir." He fought to keep from wincing as McGregor wrung his hand. "Late…of Dalbeattie in Galloway."

"Chisholm, ye say? That explains it, then. But what's a good Highland name like Chisholm doing as far south as Galloway?"

"My grandfather had to make himself a bit scarce after The Forty-five." Though Harris could not fathom the resemblance, this massive man put him in mind of his wizened, wiry grandfather. Perhaps it was the sibilant Celtic cadence of his rumbling voice.

Alec McGregor nodded sagely over Harris's explanation. "I hear tell it was a hard time. Folks did what they had to and many went away. Twice a thousand welcomes, Harris Chisholm, to ye and yer bonny missus."

Harris hesitated only an instant in his reply. Letting Levi Augustine's people think Jenny belonged to him had been a show of wishful weakness.

"I'm not a married man, Mr. McGregor. This is Jenny Lennox, a neighbor of mine from Dalbeattie. We're bound for Chatham."

"We've come all the way from Richibucto—overland," said Jenny with audible pride in their accomplishment.

A pair of grizzled brows shot to attention. "Have ye now? It's not a journey I'd care to make. If ye've got this far all in one piece, though, ye can count yerselves as good as arrived. It's not but five miles from here to Chatham, and a fair road for these parts, too. Except in spring and fall, ye can bring a wagon over it."

It was as though the man had swung his ax and hacked Harris's legs off at the knees. Only five miles of good road left between Jenny and Roderick Douglas. By moonrise tonight, she'd be gone from his life forever. Though he had spent the past several hours longing for this end to his torture, its coming left him curiously bereft.

"Thank ye for the information, Mr. McGregor." Harris

almost gagged on the words. "If ye'll be kind enough to point out the road, we'll be on our way."

"Can ye not stay the day? Ye've come at such a grand time. The parson's here from Pictou. We're going to have a wedding."

"It's mighty hospitable of ye to ask." Harris charged ahead with his answer. "But we have pressing—"

"It *is* kind of ye to invite us," interrupted Jenny. "We'd love to stay, wouldn't we, Harris? Who's getting married?"

"Who isn't?" The man laughed again—a hearty, infectious sound. "Most all the young folks. My daughter, Isabel. Two of my nephews. The wife's youngest sister. They'll be getting their wee one baptized at the same time."

Evidently he intercepted the look that passed between Harris and Jenny, for he hastened to add, "It's been more than two years since we've had a Free Kirk preacher come. Betwixt times when a man and his lass want to wed, they get their folks' blessing and promise to do it proper at the next marrying day. If ye've a mind to tie the knot yerselves, I ken the preacher might wink at publishing banns."

A furious blush suffused Harris's face. "We do appreciate the offer, but Miss Lennox has a bridegroom waiting for her in Chatham. I'm just her escort."

The man shrugged, as if to say *suit yourself.* "If ye've a mind to settle in these parts, Chisholm, ye'll find some likely lasses here. Wedding day is always a fine time for courting."

Indeed. That sounded like just the physic he needed to purge Jenny Lennox from his system before he died of her fever.

Alec McGregor spit on his palms and hoisted his ax once again. "Well, this tree won't chop itself, more's the pity. I don't fancy leaving the job half-done, though. It'd be just as likely to fall and kill one of the cows. Go along and ye'll soon come to my place. It'll be humming like a beehive. Tell everyone who ye are and that ye're staying for the wedding. I'll be along by and by.''

With the crack of the ax sounding rhythmically behind them, Harris and Jenny followed the path Alec McGregor had pointed out.

Harris cleared his throat. While they were alone, there was something he needed to know.

"We could be in Chatham by tonight." He couldn't bring himself to phrase his question in plainer terms.

"Are ye that anxious to be rid of me?" asked Jenny.

"I'm only saying…we're mighty close."

"I don't reckon another day will make much difference."

Not to her, perhaps, thought Harris as a snug little house hove into view, aswarm with busy women. He, on the other hand, planned to make good use of every minute to fortify himself against the pain of their parting.

Not trusting himself to speak, he shrugged his shoulders as if to say *suit yourself.*

As they approached the homestead, a young woman came to meet them. Her sleeves were rolled up to the elbow and a few brown feathers still clung to her large, capable-looking hands. When she flashed a broad grin, the slight gap between her top teeth proclaimed her kinship to Alec McGregor.

"*Failte!*" she greeted them.

Harris replied with some unintelligible words Jenny took to be Gaelic. It must have been some ritual response to the thousand welcomes, for he quickly slipped back into English.

"We met Mr. McGregor back there and he invited us to stay for the wedding. I'm Harris Chisholm and this is

Jenny Lennox. We're on our way to Chatham where she's to be wed.''

Evidently he didn't want anyone else jumping to the conclusion that they were a married couple. Neither did Jenny, though she didn't see the need to blurt out the truth so abruptly.

''I'm Alec's daughter, Isabel McGregor. Ye've come to the right place to get ye in the wedding spirit, Miss Lennox.''

Jenny could only stare at the girl, with her bloodstained apron and dark disheveled curls. ''But…but…aren't ye the bride?''

''Aye, one of 'em.'' Isabel McGregor swept a look of wry amusement over her hands and apron. ''But if we're to have a proper feast, somebody had to kill and pluck those fool roosters. I'd make a poor lady of the manor, Miss Lennox. I leave that up to my sister, Morag.''

Though the young woman didn't seem insulted by her remark, Jenny still felt compelled to change the subject— quickly.

''Is yer sister getting married today, as well?''

All the merriment deserted Isabel McGregor's rosy face. Jenny wondered what she'd said amiss this time.

''No.'' The girl found her voice again, though it scarcely sounded like her own—flat and hollow. ''Not today.''

Like Ivanhoe at Ashby, Harris rode to Jenny's rescue. ''If we're to enjoy the fruits of yer feast, Miss McGregor, the least we can do is help ye ready it. Will ye put us to work?''

Isabel McGregor looked to welcome the diversion as much as Jenny did. She smiled again, albeit a rather shaky one.

''Aye, we'd be glad of two extra pairs of hands. Ye can stow yer gear in the house. Mr. Chisholm, if ye'll go along that path behind the barn, ye'll soon come to Ewan Menzies's place. They're roasting a sheep and the men are supposed to be catching us some fish. They'll put ye to good use, I expect. Just between ye and me, I'd like ye to keep them from getting into Ewan's brew until *after* the ceremony.''

''It'd take a braver man than I to come between a crowd of Highlanders and their usquebaugh,'' quipped Harris. ''But I'll do what I can to oblige ye, ma'am, and to make myself useful.''

''Do ye want me to go along with him?'' asked Jenny.

''Oh my, no!'' Isabel McGregor protested cheerfully. ''If my Murdock sees ye, he's likely to throw me over before the wedding. Ye're better off to stay here, Miss Lennox. Ye could help Grannie McPhee baking the oat cakes, if ye like. Her poor hands are awful crippled with the rheumatics, but nothing a body can say will keep her idle.''

The girl pointed to an outdoor oven some distance away. ''Mind, she loves to gossip, so she'll be after hearing yer whole life's story.''

Harris spoke up, ''We'll get to work then, Miss McGregor.'' He sounded anxious to be away.

''Just call me Isabel, both of ye, please. This is a small settlement and most everybody's relations some way or other, so we don't stand on ceremony.''

''Very well…Isabel. We'll get to work and let ye get back to yers.''

First, they stowed Jenny's bundle of clothes and Harris's pack.

''I reckon I'll see ye at the wedding,'' said Harris as they parted company.

''Aye.'' Try as she might, Jenny could not prevent a hint of wistfulness from creeping into her voice. Part of the reason she'd been eager to stay for the wedding was so she and Harris could have one last day together before…Chatham.

A day to make peace with their choices and their future.

A day to say goodbye. He didn't seem the least disposed to any of it. Just like a man to come over all practical and decide he'd better get on with his life. Not that she wanted him hanging about mooning over her, but...

"Mind ye don't get into trouble over at Menzies's." She tried to sound as brusque as he.

Fortunately, Jenny found herself with little time for reflection or regrets. The next several hours flew by in a whirl of preparations for the feast. Eggs to beat. Dough to roll. Great wheels of oatcake to lift from the oven. Though she hesitated to admit it, even to herself, Jenny found herself enjoying the homely rhythm of these familiar chores.

Courtesy of Grannie McPhee, a stout little woman of garrulous but kindly disposition, Jenny's tongue was soon working as busily as her hands.

"...I didn't ken what was going on, but I could hear them rolling something heavy over the deck..."

"...I can't begin to guess how many hours we stood in that cold water, waiting for dawn to come so we could see our way to shore."

"...then the Indians took to laughing like a bunch of fools. I was that cross, for two bawbees I'd have brained the lot of 'em."

When the last of the oatcakes finally came out of the oven, Jenny looked up to see that she'd gathered a large audience of girls and women.

"Ye tell a fine tale, lass!" chortled Grannie McPhee. "Puts me in mind of the stories my ma used to tell me about the Great Rising and the Bonny Prince. For all that, I'd rather listen to adventures than live them."

"I'd love to have adventures," breathed a tall girl on the verge of womanhood, "especially with a hero like yer Mr. Chisholm."

"Harris—a hero?" Even as the laughter broke from her lips, Jenny could see several nods of agreement, and more than one dreamy smile. The kind of smile with which she'd once contemplated her own hero—Roderick Douglas.

A sly little voice in the back of Jenny's mind told her to take advantage of all this feminine interest in Harris. Set a pack of admirers on him and he'd abandon any notion of her. Then she could wed Roderick happily, without a single qualm of guilt.

She opened her mouth to utter words of encouragement. Instead she heard herself saying, "The man's no hero, believe me. Why he can be the most annoying, opinionated…"

Stimulating. Understanding. Generous. Jenny could not bring herself to stoke the fires of girlish fancy with the truth.

By their far-off looks and secret smiles, she could tell her admonitions had fallen on deaf ears.

And she didn't like it a bit.

Harris frowned, looking from the well-trodden path at his feet to the fainter one veering left. The sound of masculine voices drifted from that direction, laughter and good-natured argument accompanied by the occasional splash. Which way had Isabel McGregor meant for him to take? Surely he must have the worst sense of direction in the whole New Brunswick colony.

"Either way will get ye there," came a woman's voice, soft as a summer wind in the leaves, with a rich Celtic lilt.

Harris gawked around, trying to find its source.

Then he saw her.

She knelt in a nearby clearing, her green plaid dress and dark hair blending seamlessly into the forest shadows. For a moment, Harris wondered if she was real at all, or only a spirit of the woodlands.

The young woman paid him no mind at first, going about her business of plucking wild roses. Her hands had a tapered natural elegance and her long, unbound hair fell around her like a lustrous cloak. Harris had never seen a woman quite like her. Why, then, did she seem so hauntingly familiar?

"P-pardon me?" he stammered.

Rebecca. That was it. She looked exactly as he had always imagined Ivanhoe's Rebecca.

Two wide, pale eyes raised to regard him.

"Either path will take ye to Menzies's," she repeated. "The less-traveled one is shorter, but ye'll have to wade the brook."

"Thank ye, ma'am. My name's Harris Chisholm. Alec McGregor invited us to the wedding. Are ye one of the brides?"

She didn't answer his question, or offer to introduce herself in return. "I thought ye might be the minister."

It seemed high irony to Harris that anyone should mistake him for a man of the cloth, considering where he'd been and what he'd been doing last night when the sound of the pipes had brought him back to his senses. Bitten hard by the serpent was closer to the truth.

On the run from those unwelcome memories, Harris started down the left-hand path. He had only gone a step or two when the woman called out, "Tell Murdock Menzies, from me, that he's to stay sober and not kill himself with any fool men's antics before the wedding. I'll not have him spoil Isabel's day."

Her warning rang with a tone of imperious command— like a lady of the manor, used to being heard and obliged.

Harris turned back. "Ye must be Morag McGregor, then. Isabel sent me over. On much the same errand, I suspect, though she put it a wee bit..."

As he strode toward the woman with his hand outstretched, she shrank back. A haunted look flickered in her green eyes, but Harris barely took note of it. His gaze fell to her ivory cheeks, where the fine veil of her dark hair had drawn back.

A low moan escaped his lips.

Two angry, jagged scars marred an otherwise beautiful face. They distorted the symmetry of her features, as though the porcelain head of a fashion baby had been smashed, then glued back together by inexpert hands.

It was the first time Harris had seen another scarred countenance, except in his shaving mirror. Something deep within him grieved for this woman. Did the wounds hurt her still? They looked like they must. Part of him grieved, too, for what those around her had lost. Surely hers had once been a face that eyes lingered upon with delight.

"Aye, I'm Morag." The passing mist of anguish in her gaze froze into a curtain of icy hauteur that Harris recognized all too well. "Get off to the Menzies place, stranger, and keep an eye on that dolt of a Murdock."

A rustle in the underbrush behind him made Harris glance away. When he looked back, Morag McGregor had disappeared as completely as if she'd never been there.

The brush rustled again, and this time when Harris looked, he saw a tall, rawboned woman striding toward him.

"Ye've met Morag, I see," she said, shaking her head dolefully. "What an awful thing, but ye know what the Good Book says about pride going before a fall."

Harris wasn't sure how to reply. Fortunately, the woman didn't seem disposed for a two-way conversation.

"I ken ye must be that Chisholm man who's come for the wedding. All the way from Richibucto on foot? I never heard of anything so daft! Ye must be on yer way to Menzies's, are ye? So am I—I'll just go along with ye."

Still half-lost in his contemplation of Morag McGregor, Harris fell into step beside the woman. Her hectoring chatter washed over him, little of it denting his consciousness as he thought about his curious encounter with Morag.

Pity. How he'd despised it in his youth. At the merest suggestion of pity in someone's eyes or voice, he had reacted exactly like Morag McGregor, wrapping himself in his protective armor of cold scorn. Now he had experienced it from the other side, and it was not what he'd expected. There were far worse things, he decided, than gentle pity.

Beside him, the loquacious woman continued to talk. Now and again he nodded his head in response. She'd introduced herself, but he'd only been half listening and couldn't recall the name. Somebody MacSomebody.

"They all thought it so queer—a Chisholm from the south, but I recollect being in service in Glasgow with a Chisholm woman, and she was no Highlander. A bonny wee thing, God rest her soul. Now what was her name? Bettina? Brenda? No. Oh, my memory ain't what it used to be."

By this time they had reached the Menzieses' homestead. From the sharp scent that hung in the still air, Harris guessed Isabel McGregor had been right about the men sampling Ewan Menzies's brew. After the week he'd spent, Harris was rather inclined to fortify himself with a wee nip, too.

He turned to his companion. "It's been a pleasure to meet ye...ma'am. Now, if ye'd be so kind as to point out Isabel McGregor's husband-to-be. There's a message she wanted me to deliver to him."

"Belinda!" cried the woman.

Harris glanced around to see whom she might be addressing. There looked to be no other women around.

"I beg yer pardon, ma'am?"

"Belinda Chisholm," the woman repeated, with a note of triumph in her voice. "She came from someplace in Galloway, I recollect."

Harris's legs turned to jelly beneath him. Spying a flat, sawed-off tree stump nearby, he lurched the few steps to it and sat down heavily.

"Dalbeattie?" The word squeezed its way out of his badly constricted throat. "Did she come from Dalbeattie?"

"Aye, now that ye mention it, I ken she did. But I can't be full sure. This was every day of twenty years ago, mind. Why? Ye don't mean to say she was some relation of yers? Ain't it a small world, though?"

He nodded. "My mother's name was Belinda."

Chapter Fifteen

Jenny's stomach throbbed with hunger by the time the women finally called a halt to their labors and began to deck themselves out for the wedding and the ceilidh to follow. Watching them emerge from the house in their modest finery, she wished she had something better to put on. The dress she'd worn to trek through the wilderness *looked* as if it had been worn to trek through the wilderness.

There was her own wedding gown, of course, which had come through their harrowing journey as though charmed. But she could not break faith with Roderick by wearing it, not when he and their wedding were so near at hand.

A skirl of bagpipes made Jenny start guiltily, remembering the previous night.

In a swaggering march, the bridegrooms emerged from the forest to claim their ladies. A fine-looking company they were on this late August afternoon, in their full-sleeved white sarks and their bold tartans. The other men of the settlement followed in similar array, but Jenny had eyes for only one.

Bringing up the rear of the procession with an air of self-conscious pride, strode Harris, attired in a handsome plaid of forest-green and black. The whiskers he hadn't been able to shave in over a week had grown into an attractive close-trimmed beard that hid his scars entirely. Why had he never thought of growing one before?

As she watched him, Jenny felt her innards doing a nervous little dance. There was something different about him. She sensed it with a powerful certainty. It was more than the roguishly attractive beard and the becoming Highland garb. For the first time in all the years she'd known him, Harris looked comfortable and confident in his own skin.

With mounting annoyance, Jenny realized that hers were not the only feminine eyes sizing up Harris. Every unattached lass in the settlement appeared to be watching him with the intensity of hungry she wolves stalking a majestic stag. Even the slender, dark-haired creature who lurked in the eaves of the woods, with a shawl wrapped around her head.

Worse yet, Jenny sensed that Harris was aware of their attention—even flattered by it.

In the best interests of all concerned, Jenny knew she should push Harris straight into the arms of one of these admiring Highland lasses. Instead, some dark, possessive force reared to life within her, ignoring the weak protestations of reason.

While everyone's attention was diverted elsewhere, she slipped into the McGregor's house and pried open the bundle containing her wedding gown.

Harris glanced around. Where had Jenny got to?

Could she have changed her mind after all and gone off to Chatham on her own? An even less appealing thought— what if her decision to stay for the wedding had been a ruse to get him out of the way so she could finish their journey unescorted?

Part of him almost hoped so. Another part mourned her desertion. After what he had learned this afternoon, there was so much he longed to tell her.

A movement nearby drew his eye. A pair of lassies a bit younger than Jenny blushed brightly and looked away, but not before Harris realized they'd been pointing and talking about him. No doubt he looked a fool in this Highland getup—him, who'd never set a foot farther north than Edinburgh.

Out the corner of his eye, he could see Morag McGregor skulking in the distance. Perhaps she was watching him, too. It struck Harris that she might understand the import of what he wanted to tell Jenny. If only he could break past her icy reserve.

Just then, the minister called everyone to worship. A fresh-faced lad, newly minted from the seminary, his ringing voice filled the small clearing. Five couples stepped forward. Two of the brides passed their babies off to older women. One infant began to squall in protest. The company laughed.

"Marriage," intoned the preacher, "was instituted by God…" Was the lad old enough to understand the full implication of what he was saying about love, help and comfort?

Harris flinched. Would he ever find a woman willing to be all that to him? He could imagine only one, and she was gone.

"Dost thou, Murdock Menzies, take Isabel McGregor to be thy lawful wedded wife?" the minister asked. "To live together under God's holy ordinance?"

His gaze fixed on the happy couple with jealous intensity, Harris heard a muted rustle beside him and a faint gasp from somewhere in the crowd. Grudging a sidelong glance, he froze in awestruck contemplation of Jenny.

So she hadn't deserted him after all. The realization pulsed through Harris. Though he endeavoured to stem a dizzying tide of happiness, it swamped him just the same. As it had that day on the Kirkcudbright quayside, her beauty overwhelmed him.

Though wrinkled and creased almost beyond repair, the gown she wore was like no other Harris had ever seen. The wide sash hugged her waist, emphasizing the provocative curve of her bosom and sweep of her hips. The heather-gray luster of the silk matched her eyes to perfection.

Scarcely aware of what he was doing, Harris shifted back and to the side, until Jenny's arm pressed against his. He expected her to recoil from this contact, but she didn't. Together they stood, as close as any of the bridal couples, the timeless liturgy of the marriage service twining around them.

"And forsaking all others keep ye only unto her, as long as ye both shall live."

While Murdock Menzies mumbled his response, Harris's heart cried within him, *I do. As God's my witness, I do.*

He stole another glance at Jenny, eager to horde up every memory of her for the lonely years that stretched ahead. Their eyes met and held, and it seemed to Harris that the whole world dissolved around them into a shimmering mist.

The vows of marriage reached him in a faint echo, as though whispered privately by the very voice of God.

"To have and to hold…" Plain words, but in the context of Jenny, the sweetest in the language.

"From this day forth, for better for worse. For richer for poorer…"

A deep shudder racked Jenny and her eyes widened as if she had beheld a frightening sight. Wrenching both her arm and her gaze away from Harris, she put a few inches' distance between them. The emotional gulf felt like a thousand miles.

Would he ever learn to buttress his heart against her? Harris wondered bitterly.

One of the village lasses caught his eye, smiling with

timid…admiration? Harris spread his own mouth into an answering expression, and stepped toward the girl.

Time to administer the physic.

For better for worse. For richer for poorer.

The terrible reality of those vows struck Jenny like a Highlander's claymore. Marriage was not some romantic summer idyll. It was toil and worry and making ends meet. Those grim realities took a deadly toll on fragile sentiments like love and desire. Jenny knew she was not strong enough to sustain a loving marriage under such conditions.

And yet…

This strange attachment she'd conceived for Harris had a stubborn tenacity of its own, compelling her to do the most contrary things. Like the foolish gesture of donning her wedding dress. She must look a fright, all wrinkled with a water stain at the hem and another under the arm, the feminine curves of her figure wantonly on display.

For a delicious moment, though, when Harris had first glanced at her, she had tasted his admiration. It made her heart skip giddily in her bosom and all her senses cry out to sate themselves on him. She yearned to lose herself in the warm light of his eyes and to breathe his essence. To run her hands through his hair and acquaint her lips with every nuance of his expressive face. To fill her ears with the rich timbre of his voice and taste his kisses to their most mysterious depths.

He had come to exert a potent influence upon her, which frightened Jenny to the core. Like the harmless-looking sandbars at the mouth of a river, Harris Chisholm stood to wreck her painstakingly constructed marriage plans within sight of her safe harbor. And her own wayward passion was the gale that swept her vessel into danger.

"What God hath joined," declared the minister, "let not man put asunder."

The two infants were returned to the arms of their newlywed parents for baptism, and several other youngsters were brought forward for the sacrament. When all had been properly anointed and prayed over, the women swung into action, laying out a feast on the improvised tables.

The smells of the food brought Jenny's hunger gnawing back to life. The savory aroma of roast fowl, the subtle nutty scent of freshly baked oatcakes, the briny fragrance of boiled lobsters. As she heaped her plate with a mixture of traditional Scots and native New Brunswick delicacies, Jenny did her best to ignore the bevy of lasses flocking to Harris.

And to ignore the sharp talons of jealousy that raked her heart.

A long trestle table and benches had been cobbled together for the wedding feast. With only a passing qualm that the rough-hewn seat might snag a hole in her dress, Jenny wedged herself in between big Alec McGregor and wee Granny McPhee. Harris secured a seat on the opposite side of the table, four body-widths up. Jenny could not help but notice that the last of those bodies was the giggly girl who had called Harris a hero. Another young woman, plump and rather pretty, claimed a place on his left side. The pair lost no time in competing for his attention with questions and compliments.

Their merry banter drifted down the table to Jenny, spoiling her appetite completely. Evidently the charm lessons she'd given Harris aboard the *St. Bride* had found soil as fertile as had the reading lessons he'd given her. He was driving her to distraction by flirting with other women, and *she* had taught him how to go about it!

With the offices of the Church now decently administered, no one made any objection to Ewan Menzies dispensing his brew. Hoping it might numb her heart the way it had numbed her bilious stomach on the *St. Bride,* Jenny bolted a deep draft of the raw liquor. She pulled a sour face as it scorched its way down her throat. Glancing up, she found Harris gazing upon her with a droll grin. His look seemed to say, *At least ye didn't spit it up this time.* The memory of that awful storm on their first night out from Scotland stretched between them like an invisible bond.

Flashing him an indignant glare, she tried to concentrate on worrying down more of the Menzies brew and making conversation with her neighbors. But her rebellious eyes— they would steal a glance in Harris's direction at every opportunity. And her ears would strain to catch the spritely conversation that bubbled between him and his admirers. Even her thoughts, if unguarded, would lapse into fond memories of her time with Harris.

At last, as the late summer shadows began to lengthen and the company had sated themselves with food and drink, the musicians took up their fiddles and began to play. The tunes rang wild and lively at first, calling dancers to venture with flying steps. Jenny found a spot under a spreading maple tree where she could watch the performances in fascination, without fear of being dragged into one. As the night wore on and Ewan Menzies's whisky flowed, the music gradually mellowed.

From somewhere a woman's voice rose in song. Jenny assumed the lyrics must be in Gaelic, for she could not understand the hauntingly beautiful ballad. From quite nearby, a hummed echo of the melody sounded. Jenny glanced around only to discover that Harris had stolen up behind her.

"Gave yer followers the slip, did ye?" She tried to disguise her eagerness with tart humor. "I was afraid they were going to pull-haul ye in twain, like the wishbone of a Christmas goose. How does it feel to be the object of so much feminine attention?"

"It makes a pleasant change."

The whisky's lazy warmth seeped through Jenny. Rather than numbing her conflicting and confusing feelings for

Harris, it lulled all her carefully constructed defenses to sleep.

"Every unwed lass in the village old enough to put her hair up is smitten with ye. To them, ye're as much a hero as...Rob Roy or Ivanhoe."

"Get away with ye. Ye've filled their heads with stories, is all."

"Not stories, Harris, just the truth. And for what it's worth, I reckon ye are a hero."

"I beg yer pardon?"

"Ye heard me well enough." Jenny fixed her attention on the singer and the fiddlers, not trusting herself to look at him. "So don't go fishing for more compliments—it's not gentlemanly." She seized upon the first remark she could think of to change the subject. "Do ye know what this song's about?"

"Aye, a bit. It's about a princess, and a knight who journeys from far away to ask for her hand."

"Then why does it sound so sad?"

"Because the princess refuses him."

"I see."

They stood in silence as the last poignant strain died away.

"There's something I have to tell ye," murmured Harris as the fiddles began to croon once more. "Ye were right about my mother. It wasn't on account of me that she left—at least not in the way I always thought."

His words caught her off guard. Though Jenny would scarcely have admitted it, even to herself, she'd hoped Harris would advise her against going on to Chatham in the morning.

"How did you find all this out? Here, of all places."

"There's a woman in the village, I can't recall her name just now. Before she married and came to New Brunswick, she was in service for a tobacco baron in Glasgow and..."

The whole story gushed out of him. How his mother had

also been a servant in the house, having fled her family in Dalbeattie. Later, when she became ill, she'd confided the reason for her desertion. Feeling responsible for the fire that scarred her son, Belinda Chisholm hadn't been able to live with her guilt. She had saved every penny of her wages, and when she died of a bilious fever, the money was sent south for her son's education.

"I always wondered how Pa could afford to send me to school in Edinburgh," concluded Harris. "If only he'd told me the truth about where the money came from. I ken he was just too bitter about her going, even after all those years."

So that was it. The change that had come over Harris.

Jenny clutched his hand. "Didn't I tell ye? I just knew it must be something like that. Oh, Harris, I'm so glad ye've learned the rights of it at last."

She made a halfhearted attempt to retract her hand, but he clung to it.

"This changes everything, Jenny."

"Changes?" Somehow the word got trapped in her throat and only escaped as a fluttery whisper.

She tried again. This time her voice regained its power. "What does it change? And how?"

The golden glow of the lamps and the silvery rays of moonlight played over his face, every plane and curve of which had become so dear to her. Fiercely Jenny prayed that Harris would find compelling reason for her to stay with him. Yet her heart ached with the certainty that he would not.

Was that a hopeful light that shone in Jenny's eyes? Harris wondered as he worked up the nerve to speak. He had promised her and sworn to himself that he was done with any thought of winning her. At the ceilidh, he'd thrown himself into charming every lass who so much as glanced at him. He'd relished the novelty of their esteem, but something about it felt hollow. For all they mattered to him, the lassies might have been an assembly of animated scarecrows.

Even as he coaxed Morag McGregor into a dance, he realized that the common bond of their scars was no basis for deeper feeling.

Jenny had asked how learning the truth about his mother had changed things. Harris himself was not certain. He only knew, with slightly tipsy conviction, that it did.

"I thought…" He struggled to put into words what he had not fully framed in his own mind. "I thought my ma left because of me and how I looked. Now I've come to find I was mistaken. When ye ran off from Richibucto, I thought it was a sign that ye didn't care for me. Was I mistaken in that, too, Jenny? I have to know."

She pinned her gaze to the open throat of his sark, stubbornly refusing to look him in the eye. "Oh, Harris, don't make me say it. Tomorrow I'll be out of yer life for good. There's plenty of lasses who'd be happy to have ye. Ones who'd make ye a far better wife than I ever cou—"

Perhaps it was the whisky working on him—Harris could not restrain himself. He grasped Jenny by the arms and let the force of his emotions take him.

"Get it through yer head, lass, I'm not like yer Mr. Douglas—in the market for a wife and not particular about who'll fill the post. Just starting out like I am, a wife's the last thing I need. But I want *ye*, Jenny Lennox, and not just in the way I said last night. Now if ye don't love me and never can, say so."

She turned her face away and uttered not a word. In that moment it seemed to Harris that every source of light and warmth in the world had flickered and died. Unwillingly, he withdrew his hands from the tender flesh of her arms, trying to choke out some civil words of parting.

Then, the moonlight glinted on a tiny bead of moisture rolling languidly down her cheek. A hopeful breath stirred the fading embers of everything Harris had ever wanted from life. That one tear whispered Jenny's answer more eloquently than any words.

Reaching up, he skimmed her cheek with the backs of his fingers, bringing them to rest on her chin. A gentle nudge tilted her face up to him. More teardrops clung to her dense dark lashes, like beads of dew on a cobweb at dawn.

In tones of hushed awe, he murmured, "Ye do care, don't ye, lass? And ye care too much to deny it."

"Yes!" Jenny burst out. "Yes, yes, yes! There. Are ye satisfied now, Harris Chisholm?"

"Aye, I'm satisfied." Subtly adjusting the pressure of his fingertips on her chin, he held her face still to receive his kiss.

Their lips tentatively brushed in a salute with no more substance than a wisp of smoke rising from glowing coals.

With a restraint of which he hardly believed himself capable, Harris waited. Waited, as every whisky-roused masculine urge in his body spurred him.

In all their past encounters of this nature, he'd been the active party. Thief. Supplicant. Seducer.

He'd coerced Jenny's unwilling confession that she loved him. Now he craved more positive proof.

So he waited.

Slowly, as if fighting a powerful current of resistance, Jenny raised her hand and brushed the palm against his newly grown beard.

Her lips pressed on his with mounting urgency. They parted and, with beguiling mobility, entreated him to do likewise. Her tongue fluttered in sweet, uncertain thrusts. The silk of her skirt grazed his bare calves in a provocative whisper. Harris's rigid, swollen desire exulted in the freedom afforded by his borrowed kilt.

By unspoken consent, he and Jenny melted onto the satiny carpet of grass beneath the maple tree. Lost to everything but the night.

Chapter Sixteen

"Caw!"

The crow's raucous rasp split the air—and Jenny's head. It focused the vague pain into a single, deep throb.

When she forced her eyes open, the fierce morning light stabbed them. She clenched them shut again. Not quickly enough to miss the black bird scavenging a gobbet of meat from what was left of the roast sheep. Jenny's stomach heaved to disgorge its contents, and almost succeeded.

Her mouth felt dry as straw and tasted like the innards of a haggis, gone bad. When she made a feeble effort to raise her head, the world spun and tilted.

She tried to think through the heavy ache in her head, to figure out where she was and how she'd got here.

Nearby she heard snoring, and the flap of heavy wings—more crows, no doubt. From farther off came the howl of a hungry infant and the tortured sounds of some poor soul retching.

By painful degrees, Jenny extracted memories of the previous day—and night. Father in heaven, what had she done?

Raising her eyelids to mere slits, she looked around.

Harris lay beside her, snoring as peacefully as on that morning aboard the *St. Bride,* when she'd woken to find him sleeping on her pillow. His kilt had hiked up to an almost indecent degree, baring a shameless expanse of lean-muscled thigh.

Had they...? Did she let him...?

Though admittedly green where men were concerned, Jenny suspected that if Harris had relieved her of her virginity, something else should be paining besides her head and her stomach. Perhaps she hadn't lost her senses entirely, last night, under the influence of Ewan Menzies's cursed brew.

But neither had she been in her right mind.

Swathed in seductive shadows and beguiling moonlight, McGregor's homestead had seemed a pastoral paradise. Where the warm night air hummed with fiddle music and lilting laughter, and cups overflowed with the water of life. In that enchanted place, Jenny had been able to believe that nothing mattered between a man and a woman but love.

Love?

Another spasm gripped her stomach. Jenny rolled over and vomited.

Romantic love was a temporary enchantment as potent as moonlight or moonshine. Making everything seem beautiful. Making anything seem possible.

Jenny whimpered.

In the night's sweet, dark magic, she had lost her head. She'd found it again in the bleak light of day. And how it hurt!

Aware that someone else was stirring, Jenny glanced up. Several women had begun clearing away the carnage of the ceilidh. Sluggish, uncertain movements betrayed the sorry state of their own heads and bellies, but that did not matter. There was work to do, chores to tend, children to feed.

The wedding feast had been a once-a-year respite from the drudgery of their lives. The rest of the time, a woman's lot in this frontier society must be heartbreaking, as well as backbreaking.

Steeling herself against the pain and the dizziness, Jenny lurched to her knees. Damned if she would live the life her mother had lived, or die the death her mother had died. Not even for the sake of the compelling attraction she felt for Harris Chisholm. She'd fled Scotland to escape it, and she would not be caught in its rapacious web with salvation so near at hand.

She'd adored Roderick Douglas once, with the fierce intensity of first love. When she saw him again, that feeling would surely revive. Wouldn't it?

Casting a final, regretful glance at Harris, Jenny staggered to her feet and went to recover her bundle of clothes from one of the outbuildings.

"Which way to Chatham?" she croaked to one of the women.

"Yonder," came the reply, accompanied by a weary nod toward a gap in the surrounding trees.

Weaving her way in that direction, Jenny stepped over several prone bodies, all snoring off the grim aftereffects of the ceilidh. Every step jarred her aching head and made her stomach roil menacingly, but she did not care.

Five more miles would bring her to Chatham. Five more miles would bring her to Roderick Douglas. Five more miles would bring her to a safe haven from the cruel realities of life.

Harris woke to the cruel reality that Jenny had gone. At first, he nurtured a vain hope that he might be mistaken. Perhaps she was just helping the other women clean up after the feast. As time passed, however, and he saw no sign of her, a clammy chill descended on his heart.

Finally, mastering the agonies of morning-after, he staggered to his feet and approached Morag McGregor.

Without any opening pleasantries, he demanded, "Have ye seen Jenny Lennox?"

Morag eyed him coolly. "This morning, ye mean?"

"Aye, this morning," Harris snapped. He had neither the time nor the humor for quibbles just now. "I ken well enough where she was last night."

She wrinkled her nose at the smell of his breath. "So do I, and a queer location it was for a lass promised to someone else."

His whole face flamed. "I reckon a lass has a right to change her mind until the moment she makes her vows."

The woman recoiled as though he had struck her. "I reckon so," she finally choked, in a subdued tone. "It was no business of mine, anyhow. I haven't seen Miss Lennox since last night, but I'll ask around if any of the others have."

Harris watched her approach one of the other women. After an exchange of words, the woman shook her head. Morag went to ask someone else.

Spying a whisky jar on a nearby table, Harris picked it up and tilted it from side to side. A faint splash of drink sounded from within. Bracing himself, he tipped it back for a quick swig. Though he'd always been a temperate drinker, he knew fellows who swore by the curative powers of "a hair of the dog."

When Morag returned, she cast him a reproachful look. "Nan Cameron just spoke to Miss Chisholm a few minutes ago. She's headed for Chatham, by the sound of it."

Harris lurched to his feet. "Not without explaining a thing or two, she's not."

He lumbered off in the direction Morag pointed him. His head pounded its protest of being upright. His eyes smarted from the punishing sunshine and rebelled at his insistence they function properly. His stomach threatened vomitus revenge for every step he took.

He did his best to ignore them all. Jenny Lennox had

plenty to answer for and this was his moment of reckoning. Spying a pair of her on the path ahead, he squinted until a single Jenny came into focus. As he stumbled after her, the agonies of his head and belly stoked his rage.

Fueling it almost as intensely as the pain in his heart.

She seemed unaware of his presence as he caught up with her. Wasn't that just like Jenny? Oblivious to him and his feelings, as if they counted for nothing.

Grabbing her by the arm, he spun her around to face him.

"Damn ye, Harris Chisholm!" She jerked away from his grasp. "Won't be satisfied until ye scare me out of my wits, will ye?"

"And ye won't be satisfied until ye've ripped my heart out and spat on it," Harris growled. "Where d'ye think ye're going?"

"Where does it look like? Ye're so blasted clever, ye cypher it!" She turned from him and took a few more steps toward her destination.

A couple of Harris's long strides put him squarely in her path. "Ye're not going anywhere until I've had my say. No more raising my hopes, then stealing away the minute my back's turned. How can ye be heading off to Chatham after last night? Blast it all, Jenny, ye said ye love me."

Against his will, his voice softened on those last words and he reached for her.

"Folks say all kinds of daft things when they've had too much to drink." Jenny squirmed away from him, stubbornly refusing to meet his pleading gaze. "Last night…that was the whisky talking."

"Fiddlesticks!" snapped Harris. "That's rank nonsense and I reckon ye know it. Folks don't lie when they're tipsy, they only say the things they want to say but wouldn't dare if they were sober. Ye *do* love me, Jenny. Don't deny it."

She flashed him a look then. Harris almost wished she

hadn't. Her blatant scorn flayed his budding confidence and pricked his long-suffering pride.

"There's more to getting on in this world than love, Harris. Ye said yerself, a wife and family is the last thing ye need, just starting out like ye are…"

"So it's back to the money again, is it, Jenny? Ye ken Rod Douglas's gold will buy ye happiness."

"Not happiness, Harris—security, at least, and peace of mind. A climate where love might stand a chance."

She had struck at the core of his manhood—his ability to provide for his mate and his young. Harris flared back with primal fury, spurred by his mounting nausea and the throbbing in his temples.

"Fine, then. Fine! If ye don't trust me to make a decent home for ye and do everything in my power to make ye happy, I'm well rid of ye. If ye hanker so bad after a rich husband, ye needn't run away from me. I'll tote ye on my back the rest of the way to Chatham and present ye to Rod Douglas with a red ribbon tied 'round yer neck."

"Oh, Harris. It's not that I don't—"

Save her cold consolation. Harris cut her off. "Douglas has bought and paid for ye and as far as I'm concerned, he's welcome to ye!"

"Ye won't even try to understand, will ye?" she stormed.

The gall of her casting *him* in the wrong!

"I don't know what I ever fancied I saw in ye, Harris Chisholm." She turned away. Not before he saw the tears in her eyes. They unmanned him entirely. Inflicting pain on her did nothing to soothe his own.

He reached for her. "Jenny…"

"I'm going to Chatham." She hurled the words back over her shoulder. "If ye so much as try to lay a hand on me…" Her voice thickened with every word. "Ye'll be sorry, Harris Chisholm!" came out on one great gust of a sob.

Before he could say or do anything to stop her, Jenny bolted away at a speed he could never match in his present condition. What was the use in trying?

Harris crumpled to the ground.

He wanted to crawl inside a whisky jar and never come out. He wanted to put his fist through something solid. He wanted to lay his head on Morag McGregor's shoulder and bawl like a wee babby. In spite of her admission that she cared for him, Jenny had left. This was not the first time she had led him on, only to push him away, or run from him.

Suddenly, as if conjured by his need, Morag knelt beside him. "Come back and sleep off the drink," she urged.

"Women!" Harris snarled. "I was right to steer clear of the lot of 'em for as long as I did." This was how he'd always feared a woman would treat him, if he ever let one sink her claws into his heart. "More's the pity I didn't keep on with it."

Morag did not flinch from his outburst. A look of obvious pity softened her face. Once it would have burned him like lye. Now it soothed his soul like healing ointment.

"Why did she have to go away?" he asked, not expecting an answer. Uncertain whether he was talking about Jenny, or his mother...or both.

"I ken she had her reasons. Ye said yerself—a lass has a right to change her mind. That goes for ye as much as it does for the man she's promised to."

Reluctantly Harris acknowledged the natural justice in that. He knew Jenny had been pulled in two directions at once. What did he have to offer her, after all, compared to a man like Roderick Douglas? If he truly cared for her, perhaps the kindest thing he could do was let her enjoy the affluent life she craved with the man she'd adored since girlhood.

Stirred from his melancholy musing, Harris realized Morag had asked him a question. "How's that again?"

"The man Miss Lennox is promised to—I asked ye his name. I may know him."

"I'm sure ye know *of* him." Harris heaved a gusty sigh. "Jenny is to marry none other than Mr. Roderick Douglas."

He braced himself for some brusque remark about how it was no wonder Jenny had made her choice. Instead, a strange, unnatural quiet met his announcement.

When he glanced at Morag, her ivory complexion had gone almost blue-white, as though every drop of blood had been drained from her veins. The angry scars on her cheeks flamed in livid contrast.

"What's the trouble, Miss McGregor? Are ye feeling ill? Can I fetch someone for ye?"

Before he could stir himself, she reached out, clutching his wrist. Harris winced. Her massive, ax-wielding father would have been hard-pressed to exert such force.

"Ye must go after her."

"I'm done with that. Like ye said, she made her choice."

"Ye *must* go after her!" Morag insisted.

"I'll go. I'll go." He was prepared to promise anything, if only she'd loosen the crippling grip on his arm. "If ye'll just tell me why?" Though he hadn't known her long, he sensed Morag would not make such a demand lightly.

Something haunted and hunted looked out at him from her pale green eyes. "I can't say," she whispered. "I daren't."

The sound of that word sent a shiver down his spine. What danger had Jenny fled toward this time, like a moth to a flame? A pang of guilt stabbed him in the conscience. Whatever the threat, *he* had driven her toward it.

"For my sake and yers," continued Morag with compelling force, "and especially for hers, go to Chatham and stop Miss Lennox from marrying Roderick Douglas."

It was not the words themselves as much as the dire

urgency of her tone that vaulted Harris to his feet and sent him pursuing Jenny Lennox yet again. That, and his burden of guilt, and his own vexing, daft devotion to her.

With a furtive glance over her shoulder, as if she feared pursuit, Jenny tapped on the door of Roderick Douglas's house. At least, this imposing fieldstone structure was the one to which folks had pointed her. Queer looks they'd given her, too, when she stopped them to ask directions. Likely they wondered what such an unkempt creature wanted with a prosperous pillar of their community. Perhaps they'd questioned why her eyes were all red and swollen.

Jenny tried to swallow an enormous lump in her throat. When Harris had caught up with her, she'd almost been ready to abandon her dream of marrying Roderick Douglas and risk her whole future by staying with him. Only he'd made it clear he didn't want her after all. He hadn't even tried to understand that she feared as much for his prospects as for her own. Hadn't he come to North America to make something of himself? How would he ever accomplish that with a wife and family to keep?

The door jerked inward, just then, and a tall, angular woman stared out at Jenny. She was dressed from head to toe in a shade of rusty black that matched her severely pinned hair. She had a sharp, narrow beak of a nose and dark eyebrows so dense they appeared to be one unrelieved line of bristling disapproval.

"Don't just stand there, girl." Even her voice shared a harsh quality with that of the crow who'd wakened Jenny. "State your business."

"Please." Jenny tamped down the lump in her throat and tried again. "Please. Is this the house of Mr. Douglas?"

"Yes."

"Mr. Roderick Douglas?"

"Didn't I just say so? What do you want with Mr. Douglas, girl?"

Jenny tried to still her trembling knees. If the house did belong to Roderick Douglas, this woman must be his servant. She would soon serve Jenny, as well.

"I'm afraid that's private between Mr. Douglas and myself. Is he in?"

The woman looked Jenny slowly up and down, distaste plainly written on her features. She appeared to be weighing the decision whether to vouch that information.

"No," she announced at last.

Jenny sensed the woman took pleasure in her own look of disappointment.

"No, and not likely to come home until supper—if then."

"Where might I find him in the meantime?" Though she tried not to let the woman cow her, it was hard work.

Again a pause, and a hard stare. Finally she said, "He may be down at the yard, if you've a mind to go there looking for him."

"Thank—" Before Jenny could get the word out, the massive door with its brass fittings shut in her face.

As she turned away, Jenny muttered, "Ye need charm lessons worse than Harris Chisholm, ye old crow."

It took some little while, and more queer looks before Jenny found her way to the shipyard. The place was deserted, though the pungent scents of sawdust and tar mingled in the air, imparting a vision of busier days past and those soon to come.

From his short tenure at Jardine Brothers, Harris had taught her something about the business. How it often slowed in the summer while the colony's labor force tended to their farming and haying. Come autumn there would be a short frenzy to get another ship fitted and under sail before winter ice closed in the river. Once the ground had frozen, lumbermen would take to the forests, looking for big old trees to fell for keels and masts. As March ice rotted in the tide head, shipyards up and down the coast would hum with activity, preparing their first vessels of the New Year for an Atlantic baptism.

Jenny inhaled a deep breath. This was the odor of prosperity.

Hearing men's voices, she looked up to see Roderick Douglas walking from a large warehouse, arguing with a smaller man about something written or drawn on a large sheet of paper.

"I tell you…" There was no mistaking his voice, as he gestured toward a skeleton of wooden scaffolding. His Lowland brogue had muted, though. "A barque like that will ride too low in the water for…"

As he caught sight of Jenny, his sleek dark brows drew together in an inquisitive gaze. His aquiline nose wrinkled ever so slightly. "Can I help you, miss?"

For a moment she stood, dumbstruck to see him again after five long years. If anything, he had grown handsomer in the interval. His mid-height frame had filled out most agreeably, complemented by his well-tailored clothes. The North American sun had bronzed his face to a perfect complement for his dark hair. The air of promise he'd worn as a youth had ripened into one of success and accomplishment. And the hint of his smile could still set Jenny quivering like a jelly.

Her mouth worked open and closed several times, but no sound emerged.…Lord, she must look like a walleyed codfish!

At last, in a desperate rush, she gasped, "I'm Jenny Lennox, remember? I've come from Dalbeattie to be yer bride."

The hesitation in his eyes struck her like a blow. She was not what he'd expected. She was a disappointment to him.

"Bride?" As he moved toward her, his expression

brightened and a smile of singular charm lit his fine features. "Janet—of course! But where have you come from? There haven't been any ships that docked today."

He clasped her hand warmly. To Jenny it felt as if dark clouds had parted and the sun had finally begun to shine. If anything could have crowned that blissful moment, it was Roderick's heartfelt avowal. "You were so long in coming. I was beside myself, thinking what might have happened to you."

Jenny gathered her breath to explain that something had happened, and how she had come to be in Chatham when there was no new ship in port. Before she could get the words out, she heard a commotion behind her and someone calling her name.

Not just someone—Harris.

She turned to warn him away.

Catching sight of him, Jenny cringed. She was thankful there were no more people around to see him. Bad enough she'd have to introduce him to Roderick Douglas. What would her suave, well-tailored fiancé make of Harris in his present state?

The green plaid that had looked so manly in the wedding procession now twisted and flapped around him in the most comical way. His long, bare shanks stuck out beneath the hem like double trunks of some improbable tree—a tree on fire. His rusty beard and wildly flying hair provided the flames. For all that, the sight of him stirred her heart with unwelcome intensity.

An intensity almost equal to that of his expression. Bearing down on her with the force of an Atlantic gale, Harris wrenched her hand free of Roderick's and pulled her clear.

"No, Jenny! Ye mustn't do this. Morag told me…"

She struggled to work free of him. Had he decided to wreak his revenge upon her by ruining her chance of a match with Roderick Douglas? She'd teach him to play dog in the manger.

Before she could get the words out, Roderick Douglas stepped forward. "I don't know who you are or what you want." He jabbed a forefinger at Harris's chest. "But lay hands on my bride again and you will be *very* sorry."

A look passed between the men—contempt on Roderick's side, desperation on Harris's. Jenny feared they might soon come to blows.

"It's not what ye think, Roderick." She took his arm and faced Harris, to show where her new loyalty must lie. "This is Mr. Chisholm. He's been my escort from Scotland. When our ship was wrecked on the bar at Richibucto, he brought me overland to Chatham...so ye and I could be married."

Intended to allay his hostility, her words seemed to inflame Roderick further. His dark eyes flashed and his perfectly proportioned features hardened. "Escort? You mean this fellow has been with you all the way from Dalbeattie, and day and night through the woods? What's he been up to with you along the way?"

Jenny flinched at the accusation. Roderick was right to be angry with her. She'd behaved foolishly at best, wantonly at worst. Without a thought about the consequences it might have for his reputation.

"I know it may look bad, but I assure ye Harris was a perfect gentleman, and nothing improper took place between us."

The lie burned on Jenny's tongue. Well, it was partly true, she tried to salve her conscience. She would still be a virgin bride, and that must be Roderick's chief concern. Fiercely she strove to suppress the memories of how passion had arced between her and Harris during their journey.

"I'd have thought ye'd be grateful to him," she insisted, eager to change the subject. "If it wasn't for Harris, I never would have made it to Chatham alive."

"I see." Roderick sounded contrite, but his tightly

clenched jaw did not relax. His glare did not soften. "I apologize, Chisholm."

Jenny fairly squirmed with shame. She was the one who'd behaved badly—to both these fine men. She was the one who should beg forgiveness and atone.

"I thought you meant harm to my lady," Roderick continued. "I couldn't stand for that. I'm sure you'll understand."

His lady? Jenny nearly melted into Roderick's arms. After how she'd behaved, in spite of how she must look, he was prepared to call her that? No question, here was a knight errant capable of shielding and defending her from anything that might blight their future happiness. As for Harris—he was better off without her. If only he could see it.

"I thought you meant harm to my lady. I couldn't stand for that. I'm sure you'll understand."

"Aye." Harris took a step back, more dismayed by the adoring look on Jenny's face than by Douglas's vague threats. "I mind ye well enough."

So this was why Morag had sent him tearing down the Chatham Road after Jenny. Harris had few memories of his rival from their schooldays in Dalbeattie, but he remembered Roderick's father, Gregor Douglas. Though the man had been a pillar of the kirk and community, local gossip held that all three of his wives had died of a broken spirit. Likewise, Old Douglas had dominated his children—all but Roderick.

Harris had assumed the rancor between father and son sprang from their differences. Now he knew better.

Judging by the look on Jenny's face, it was no use trying to convince her. At least not for the moment. Her fierce denial that anything improper had occurred between them was clear proof that she didn't love him as she'd claimed.

Still, in spite of himself, he cared for her. He could no

more abandon her to a future with black-hearted Roderick Douglas than he could have let her brave the dangerous journey to the Miramichi on her own.

Reaching into his vest pocket, Douglas extracted a few coins. "I owe you a debt, Chisholm, for seeing my lady safe to the Miramichi." He tossed the money at Harris in a gesture both graceful and contemptuous.

As the coins fell around him into the sawdust, Harris wanted to hurl the money back with a bloodcurdling oath. If he was to stay in town, though, and watch for a chance to apprise Jenny of her fiancé's true character, he'd need something to live on.

"Even *ye* don't have enough coin to pay me for my trouble." Harris had the bitter satisfaction of seeing Jenny flinch at his words.

"I suppose you'll be on your way, now that you've discharged your escort duties?" asked Roderick Douglas.

So that's what the money was for—to speed his departure.

"On my way? Not necessarily. I may hang about for a while. See what opportunities there are for a man with my skills."

Roderick Douglas cocked an eyebrow and half raised one corner of his mouth. "And pray, what are your *skills*, Chisholm?"

Harris strove to keep his temper in check. "I was the manager of a large granite quarry before I emigrated. I know how to keep accounts and I write a good hand."

"We don't have much call for *clerks* in Chatham."

"Aye? Then I reckon I'll have to move on. Though after all I went through to get her here, I've a mind to see Miss Lennox properly married off. That way I'll feel I've kept my word to her pa. How soon will the wedding be?"

"It could be as much as a month."

Beneath the pretended regret, Harris heard a note of barely concealed triumph. No doubt Douglas assumed he couldn't afford the money or the time to wait around until then.

"A month?" wailed Jenny. "Why so long?" She sounded as desperate to get the wedding over with as he was to prevent it.

"Banns, my dear Janet." When Douglas treated her to a proprietary smile, Harris feared he might vomit again. "They have to read them for three Sabbaths, you know."

"Aye, I know about banns," said Jenny. "Only, I reckoned a ri—, that is a well-off man like ye could afford a license."

"Of course, I can afford it," Douglas snapped. Catching his lapse of temper, he continued with exaggerated civility. "It's a question of propriety. What the community expects of a man in my position."

It was too clean a shot for Harris to resist. "And a man in yer position must always be mindful of his position."

Jenny fired him a look, half chiding, half pleading, as if to say, *Please don't do this—not now.*

Roderick Douglas did not appear to catch Harris's meaning. "Mindful of my position." He seemed to savor the words on his tongue. "Just so. You *do* understand, then, Chisholm?"

"Now that I've met ye, Mr. Douglas, I understand a great deal."

"I'm pleased to hear it. Once again, thanks to you for delivering my Janet safely. If you'll excuse us, I must see her properly installed at my house, and confer with the vicar about posting banns on Sunday."

"Vicar?" said Jenny. "We aren't getting wed in the English church, are we?"

"But of course, my sweet Janet. Only Church of England marriages are recognized by civil law. This *is* a British colony, after all."

"Then why did the McGregors and their neighbours

have a Free Kirk minister to say the words at that wedding?''

''The Highlanders are…sentimental folk about such things. I assure you, the weddings in question aren't recognized by law.''

''What about God's law?'' Harris challenged quietly.

Douglas cast him a smug look that set his blood boiling. ''I won't loll about in a shipyard debating theology with you, Chisholm, when a lady obviously needs her rest and nourishment…and a change of clothes. Come along, Janet. Cousin Binnie wrote me all about you, but I confess her letters didn't do you justice.''

He continued to talk as he escorted her away.

Jenny glance back once. Harris could not read her expression.

When they were quite out of earshot, he muttered to himself, ''Ye haven't seen the last of me, Jenny. Nor ye neither, Rod Douglas.''

''A-hem.''

At the deliberate sound of a throat clearing, Harris spun around to see a small man, holding a roll of paper—ship's plans, no doubt. Though he had not noticed the fellow during his exchange with Roderick Douglas, Harris guessed he'd been a silent witness all along.

''A word of advice, friend,'' said the man mildly. ''Do yourself a great favor. Don't tamper with Mr. Douglas. You may live to regret it.''

Turning to walk away, he added thoughtfully, ''Then again, you may not.''

Chapter Seventeen

With a sigh, Jenny put down a piece of fancywork she'd been trying to stitch. She was making a mess of it. When Roderick asked how she was getting on with it, tonight at dinner, she'd either have to tell him and brave his look of gentle reproach. Or she'd have to lie.

Why couldn't he understand? She'd never had the time to spare for such stuff. She could wade her way through a mountain of mending where stitching only needed to be quick and strong. She had no patience for this fine, precise needlework. It was tedious and of no earthly use.

Casting a hopeful glance around the parlor, she wondered if a bit of light housework might occupy her time. But the room was in its accustomed state of fastidious order, every bit of woodwork oiled and polished within an inch of its life, brass and copper fittings rubbed to a soft glow. Even the cushions on the settee were placed with unerring precision. The smug chamber seemed to mock her timid attempts to make it her own.

For sheer spite, Jenny picked up one of the cushions, flattened it unmercifully and placed it back on the settee—slightly askew.

Going over to the window, she stared out through the painstakingly buffed glass. She would like to have gone for a walk, but where was there to go? She knew no one in Chatham. Roderick said she must be careful of the company she kept, yet he never offered to introduce her to the better sort of people in town. Was he ashamed of her?

The notion stung—and not for the first time. She owed Roderick so much. Back in the old country she never could have hoped for a match like this one. Yet again, she swore to do everything in her power to be a dutiful wife so he would not regret marrying her.

Only one more reading of the banns, and they would be wed on the following Friday. Jenny wished the time would pass more quickly. Perhaps once she was Roderick's wife, she would feel less intimidated in his house. And she would have more to do, seeing to his comfort. She would lose these vague feelings of discontent and emptiness—as though something vital was missing from her life.

Such nonsense. What could possibly be missing?

The day she'd arrived in town, Roderick had installed her in his house, taking quarters at the inn for the sake of propriety. He came to dine most every evening, though, and Jenny looked forward to his visits…for the most part.

He talked a good deal about his business, and she tried her best to make sense of all the strange shipbuilding terms. He frequently complained of his difficulty in securing reliable employees. This one was shiftless, that one dishonest, the other defiant. With such workers, Jenny wondered how the company managed to produce any vessels at all.

"Of all the useless, ignorant, ham-handed…"

Faint but sharp in their invective, the words echoed Roderick's complaints about his men. They were followed by the sound of blows landing with a force that made Jenny flinch.

She flew to the parlor door and down the stairs to the kitchen.

"What's going on? Is someone hurt?"

The lanky form of Roderick's housekeeper, Mrs. Lyons, loomed between Jenny and a cringing, whimpering housemaid.

"It's nothing for you to concern yourself with, ma'am." Her words were servile enough, but the housekeeper's tone sounded dismissive, if not downright insolent.

Though she shrank from any confrontation with this imposing creature, Jenny persisted. "The well-being of Mr. Douglas's servants is very much my affair, Mrs. Lyons. If not now, then surely once we are wed. What happened?"

Mrs. Lyons prefaced her reply by drawing in a deep breath that seemed to say, *If you must know…* "Marie was acting the fool and not paying close enough mind to her ironing. She left a scorch mark on one of the master's shirts."

Jenny spied the shirt, laid out on a nearby table. The offending mark was scarcely visible to the naked eye, and besides… "It's clear up the back, between his shoulder blades. No one would see it. A word to Marie should have been enough. I fear ye're too harsh with the lassies, Mrs. Lyons. Everyone makes mistakes."

Plainly, the housekeeper thought Roderick had made a huge mistake in his choice of a bride. Her pasty complexion went even whiter, and her single brow lowered menacingly.

"Will that be all, ma'am?"

Having expected to come off rather worse from their exchange, Jenny replied, "Aye, thank ye. For now. Dry yer eyes, Marie, and get back to work. Mind ye pay attention to what ye're doing after this."

"*Oui…* I mean, yes, mistress."

Nothing more was said on the subject until that evening.

"Mrs. Lyons tells me you're meddling in her management of the house, Janet," said Roderick as they ate dinner.

Despite his temperate tone, Jenny's innards constricted

and her heart raced. The quiet formality of the dining room chilled her. The perfectly prepared dish of boiled beef turned to sawdust on her tongue. Unbidden, a wistful memory rose of one meal she and Harris had shared. Wild rabbit, charred over an open fire, eaten with their fingers. Seasoned by the spice of his company and a sense of complete freedom, it had been a feast to relish.

"I…" Jenny took a sip of ale to relieve her suddenly parched throat. "I didn't think there was any need of her boxing poor Marie's ears over such a wee mistake." Indignation overcame her unreasonable disquiet. "If ye ask me, Mrs. Lyons is far too harsh with all the hired girls. She's got them so cowed they hardly ever speak. The house is like a tomb in…"

Roderick quietly set down his fork and looked at her. Jenny's words trailed off.

"Good housekeepers are hard to come by in a place like this, Janet. I know, for I was quite a while finding Mrs. Lyons. She's been able to run this establishment in a manner befitting…"

"…a man in yer position." The words were out of Jenny's mouth before she realized it. She held her breath.

To her surprise and chagrin, Roderick replied in an even quieter voice. "I'll thank you not to take my position lightly, Janet." When she finally steeled herself to meet his eyes, however, she saw a glint of cold wrath in their dark depths.

"I had to work very hard to get where I am today." Before she could squeak out an apology, he continued, evidently more to himself than to her. "My father swore I'd never make anything of myself, but I showed him."

Was everyone in the world prompted to live their lives to please or defy parental expectations, Jenny wondered? Roderick driven to prosperity by his father's scorn. Harris driven to pursue a woman who, like his mother, was destined to desert him. Finally, herself, driven to "marry well" by her mother's dying words.

Roderick smiled suddenly. "You're a fine lady now, my dear Janet. No need to trouble yourself with domestic matters. Leave that up to Mrs. Lyons. She's been with me long enough to know how I like things done."

Trying to work up an answering smile, Jenny gave a nod of agreement—or was it submission? No question Roderick was a very handsome man. Yet, more and more, in the fortnight since she'd come to Chatham, Jenny found his good looks an impersonal fact of life. He might have been a fine painting or an expertly crafted piece of needlework. Pleasing to the eye but not necessarily engaging to the heart.

"Rum, gin or whisky?" Harris asked his customer, swiping a wet rag across the surface of the bar.

Serving drinks at a tavern was the only employment he'd been able to secure in Chatham, despite diligently making the rounds of every business in town. Even the ones that had sported Help Wanted signs seemed to have recently filled the positions. Harris didn't doubt for a minute that Roderick Douglas was behind the subtle campaign to deny him a job.

"Wha'sa cheapest?" asked the customer, leaning heavily against the bar.

"Rum, by a long ways," said Harris. "And if ye'll take a bit of friendly advice, ye'll keep drinking as ye've begun and not try to mix yer spirits."

"Rum it is." The man slapped several pieces of silver on the counter. "As long as this'll last."

His customer didn't seem disposed to talk, so Harris held his peace, refilling the glass at suitable intervals. The fellow looked to be off one of the ships presently in port. A peddler of some sort, if the well-stuffed carpetbag he carried was any indication. Harris made no attempt to coax him into conversation, as he did the Chatham natives.

His days and nights tending bar had yielded almost as little result as his job search. And perhaps for the same reason. Everyone in town lived in fear of Roderick Douglas. Harris had done his best to wring out even one tale of the man's doings, with which to confront Jenny. No one, no matter how deep in his cups, was willing to volunteer anything more incriminating than a nebulous warning or a vague imprecation on Roderick's name.

Harris had only seen Jenny twice in the past two weeks, riding to church—the English church—in Roderick's buggy. Several times, he'd gone to Roderick's house during the day, only to be turned away by that dragon of a housekeeper Douglas employed. Were they holding Jenny prisoner? Or was she content in her new life and wanted nothing more to do with him? He had to see her face-to-face one last time to find out for sure.

"Fill it again," demanded Harris's customer.

"I'd like to, friend. But yer money's given out."

The man rummaged in his pockets for several minutes to no avail. Then, bending down, he opened his carpetbag and extracted a book. "Wha'll ye gi' me fer this?"

Harris shook his head. "The proprietor says I'm only to take coin, sir." Then he noticed the title of the volume—*Ivanhoe*. He'd left his own books behind in Richibucto and he sorely missed them.

It was not of himself that Harris thought, however, as he turned the book over and over in his hands.

"I tell ye what, friend. If ye'll make me a fair price of it, I'll pay ye for the book. Then it's yer affair what ye do with the money I give ye."

The man slurred out a sum.

"I ken it's worth every penny." Harris shook his head regretfully. "But I haven't got that much."

"Wha' do ye have?"

Harris emptied his pockets of the silver Roderick Douglas had given him, along with a few pennies he'd earned here, beyond his bed and board. "That's the lot."

"Done!" said the book vendor. "Take it b'fore I sober up and think better of the idea."

The next day, Harris slipped a scrap of paper deep within the pages of the book. Then he entrusted it to a young lad he'd befriended. To be delivered to the house of Mr. Douglas for Miss Jenny Lennox, with no word of its source.

For half an hour, he paced and fretted. Would Jenny get his message, or would Rod Douglas's black dragon of a housekeeper intercept it? And even if the note should pass unmolested into her hands, would she heed it?

"Pardon, mistress."

As Jenny glanced up from her sewing, the needle went astray and jabbed her finger.

"Ow!" She brought the tiny wound to her mouth. "What is it, Marie?" Glancing at the drops of bright blood that stained her fancywork, Jenny felt her heart sink.

"Madame Lyons went to lay down with a sick headache, mistress. Lizzie told me to ask if you might like a cup of tea in the kitchen. She just took blackberry tarts from the oven."

Jenny longed to jump from her chair and race Marie to the kitchen. How she yearned for a scrap of womanly society and conversation.

What would Roderick say, though, if he came to hear about it? She knew well enough what he'd say—the wife of a man in his position shouldn't fraternize with her servants.

"Tell Lizzie, it was kind of her to ask, Marie." Jenny tendered a regretful smile, hoping it would soften her rebuff. "I'll take my tea here in the parlour. No rush to bring it though. Whenever ye lassies finish yers."

"Oui, Mistress." There was no mistaking the disappointment in Marie's voice or the look of hurt in her eyes.

The lassies would think she meant to snub them—that she was too grand for their company. Perhaps the wives of men in Roderick's position shunned the fellowship of their hired help, but she was not his wife yet. Plenty of time to put on fine airs in the future if she must.

"Marie," she called after the girl, "I believe I'll just come along and see that everything's in order, below stairs."

Perhaps recognizing that Jenny's duty warred with her personal inclination, Marie grinned at this compromise between the two. "You might wish to sample the tart, mistress, to see that the crust is not too tough."

"Aye, I wouldn't want Mr. Douglas served tough pastry tonight. Who knows but I might test the tea, to see it's not brewed too weak."

As mistress and maid passed the front door, a hesitant knock sounded upon it. If they'd been much farther away, they surely would not have heard it. Marie glanced at Jenny. Ordinarily, Mrs. Lyons answered any and all summons to the front door.

"Ye may see who it is, Marie," Jenny prompted her. "We wouldn't want to disturb Mrs. Lyons's rest."

Marie drew the door slightly ajar and exchanged a few words with the person on the other side. When she turned back to Jenny, there was a book in her hands. *A book!*

"The boy said this is for you, mistress. He wouldn't say who sent it."

Jenny reached for the volume, her hands fairly trembling with suppressed eagerness.

"I ken Mr. Douglas must have sent it, Marie." Jenny hoped her lie sounded convincing. "To give me something to do besides needlework."

Whether she believed Jenny or not, the girl nodded agreeably.

"Go along to the kitchen and have yer tea, Marie. I'll come in a little while. I'd like to look over my new book first."

The girl bobbed a little curtsy and headed for the back stairs.

"And another thing, Marie."

"*Oui,* mistress?"

"No need to mention this to Mrs. Lyons. Ye know how particular she is about answering the door. I wouldn't want ye to get in trouble about it."

"*Oui,* mistress." Marie sounded in no hurry to confide in the housekeeper.

Jenny returned to the parlor, her hands caressing the book's leather cover, her eyes lingering on the gold-stamped lettering of the title. *Ivanhoe.* The memories it brought back, simply to hold it again. Only one person could have sent her such a gift. That person, for good or ill, was not her betrothed.

"Oh, Harris, ye poor daft dreamer," Jenny mused, turning the thick pages. She fought to stifle sweet, vivid recollections that threatened to engulf her. "This must have cost every penny ye had. Did ye mean it for a parting gift?"

Her throat constricted at the thought.

A wistful revery took her, and she was back aboard the *St. Bride,* nestled in the shadow of the mainsail, with Harris by her side. So deep was Jenny lost in her remembrance that she almost missed the scrap of paper wedged between two pages.

"What's this, then?" She smoothed out the folded note.

Its spiky script was so different from book printing that Jenny could hardly decipher it. After much rereading and puzzling, she decided it said, *Will you see me to say a proper goodbye? I'll wait for you in the kirkyard. H.*

Goodbye? So he had decided to go away at last. Jenny

fought down a pang of regret. It was the best thing for both of them. Perhaps Harris was learning some sense at last.

In the kirkyard. Would he be there now? How long would he wait?

Jenny knew without asking that Roderick would never approve such a meeting, yet she sensed he wanted Harris out of town. If this would speed him on his way, and if Roderick knew nothing of it, what could it ail anyone?

Stealing up to the bedroom, Jenny hid the book at the bottom of her clothes chest. Taking up her bonnet and a light wrap, she crept back downstairs again and let herself out the front door.

"Jenny, over here!"

When he'd first seen her coming, Harris felt so light with relief and happiness that he almost lifted off the ground. It was everything he could do to keep from enfolding her in his arms. Only the certainty that it would drive her away checked the almost irresistible impulse.

Besides, it was no longer a question of having her for himself. Harris doubted that could ever be. If Jenny had to belong to another, though, it must be a man who could make her happy.

He drew her behind a tall burial monument of rust-colored sandstone. Not completely out of sight of the road, but not readily noticeable, either.

She looked as beautiful as ever, in fine new clothes with every hair in place. But there was something restive in her eyes and a fixed tightness in her smile that had never been there before. They fueled his conviction to say what he'd come to say.

"It's good to see you again, Jenny."

"Ye're leaving town, then? Where will ye go?"

He shrugged. "I haven't given it much thought. Before I go Jenny, I have to warn ye about Roderick Douglas. Ye mustn't marry him."

"Oh, Harris. We've been over and over this. I came here to wed Mr. Douglas and I'm going to. It's the only way for me."

"Do ye truly think ye can be happy with him, Jenny? There's more to life than fine clothes and a big house and plenty to eat. He's a rich man, lass, but he's not a good man."

She backed away, coming to rest against the tombstone. Harris couldn't bear the thought of her sharing the fate of Roderick Douglas's mother and stepmothers.

"How dare ye say that!" she flared, with a spirit he prayed would never be broken. "What's he done?"

Leave it to her to come straight to the heart of the matter, to expose the one gaping weakness in his whole argument.

Harris moved toward Jenny, trapping her between himself and the grave marker, so she'd have to hear him out. "I haven't been able to find that out, exactly. Folks are too scared of him to talk. But I've heard hints enough."

"Hints? Ye expect me to call off my wedding on account of hints? Roderick Douglas is a successful man. He didn't build up his business by letting shiftless, dishonest folks take advantage of him. He says they tell the most awful stories, just to stir up trouble for him."

"There's more to it than that, Jenny. I *know* there is." Abandoning the futility of this strategy, Harris groped for ammunition of any kind.

"Do ye *love* him, lass? Now that ye've seen him again, up close? Can ye look me in the eye and tell me what ye feel for him is stronger than what ye felt for me?"

"Ye can stow all this talk about *love* and *feeling,* Harris Chisholm." She squeezed past him, like an animal desperately wriggling out of a trap. "That foolishness wilts almost as fast as a bride's posies. The first breath of frost and it dies. I've seen it again and again. Maizie, my mother...your mother."

Jenny's words left Harris agape. He knew she was

wrong, though he could not put the how and the why of that wrongness immediately into words. But he would. All he needed was a few moments' reflection.

For he had seen Jenny's private devil at last. A huge beast, black as a shadow. Just as full of unreasoning terror. Just as insubstantial. He realized, now, how it had driven and stalked her. At other times, it had barred her path to happiness, hulking before her with vicious, yellow fangs bared.

Harris had fought his own beast. In unguarded moments he still fell prey to it. He knew it was not within his power to vanquish Jenny's for her. Only she could do that.

He could give her a weapon, though, and a reason to fight.

"Janet!" Roderick Douglas strode toward them, through the tall thin grass of the kirkyard. "Why are you skulking around a cemetery, my dear?"

As Jenny's mouth opened and closed without producing a sound, he appeared to catch sight of Harris for the first time.

"Ah, I see."

"Please, Roderick, it's not how it looks."

Fearing Douglas meant to strike her, Harris hurried to put himself between Jenny and her intended. "It's my fault, Douglas. Don't blame the lass. I sent her a message that I was leaving town. I asked her to meet me so we could say a civil goodbye."

Roderick Douglas shot him a venomous look. "That's as may be. Janet could have invited you to the house for supper and a proper farewell. This all looks rather furtive to me."

Jenny hung her head. "I'm sorry, Roderick. Ye're right. I should've thought of that."

Harris wanted to throttle Roderick Douglas with his bare hands for the way he'd managed to intimidate Jenny. He wanted to rage at her for surrendering to such domination.

"I'm sorely distressed by your disloyalty, Janet." Roderick put his hands behind him, like a schoolmaster scolding a troublesome pupil. "That you felt you had to go behind my back. That you'd risk damaging my reputation in this town."

"Let her be, Douglas." Harris took a step nearer, trying to provoke the fellow into taking a swing at him. "All Jenny's guilty of is a soft heart. If ye have a quarrel, it's with me. Pick on someone yer ain size."

Douglas sneered. "Don't flatter yourself, Chisholm. You'll never be my size."

He turned his attention back to Jenny. "I came by the house to see if you fancied a stroll on such a lovely day. Can you imagine my worry when I found you gone and no one knew where? I was frantic, Janet. This is too rough a town for a woman of your position to go about unescorted."

"Aye, Roderick."

Before Harris could step between them again, Jenny circled him and took her place at her fiancé's side. "I promise I'll never do such a thing again."

With a meekness that made Harris bilious, she took the arm Roderick offered her and let him lead her away.

Too late, Harris knew what he needed to tell Jenny. The words that might arm and hearten her to confront her black devil. Now if he could just get close enough to her to say them... Before Roderick Douglas whisked her to the altar.

"I'm not done with ye yet, lass," he muttered aloud. "Nor with ye neither, Douglas."

From behind him a strange voice replied, "Now that's where ye're wrong, feller-me-lad."

Harris spun around to confront two men, a pair he'd often seen shadowing Roderick Douglas. Neither one was as tall as he, but they were solidly built, with broad shoulders and thick forearms that thrust out of their rolled shirtsleeves. One had a jowly, florid face framed by ginger hair and side-whiskers. The other was dark, with a massive nose, crooked from more than one breaking.

They sauntered toward Harris, smiling too broadly.

"Wh-what…" He stifled the sense of dread that gripped him by the throat. Animals, it was said, could smell fear. "What do ye want?"

"It's like this, friend," said Jowly Ginger. "We understand ye're leaving town. Ye might say we're yer farewell committee."

Broken Nose sniggered as he ambled around Harris.

"Very obliging of ye, gentlemen." Harris took a slow step back. The last thing he wanted was to get caught between Rod Douglas's hired ruffians. "If ye'd care to escort me back to my workplace, I'd be pleased to tip a glass with ye…in honor of my going."

The pair exchanged a look.

Whatever their employer had instructed them to do, Harris's offer clearly appealed to them. If he could just get them back to the tavern, he might be able to slip away unharmed.

"I'm tempted, boyo." Jowly Ginger sighed his regret. "But orders is orders."

They moved with the synchronized precision of a well-trained ox team. Before he knew what was happening, Harris felt his arms solidly pinned behind him. His feet flailed out, connecting with something that yielded to the kick.

Ginger let out a grunt of pain. "That's gonna cost ye, boyo."

A leg hooked around his ankles and sent him sprawling onto the ground. As he fell, his head hit one of the tombstones. A soundless explosion of pain glittered inside his skull for an instant, before everything went black.

Chapter Eighteen

"Wake up, Harris Chisholm. Ye're breathing, so I ken ye must be alive."

Jenny?

Harris shrank from consciousness. He had hovered on the edge of it before, each time driven back into peaceful oblivion by the pain. But this time was different.

Jenny called him, and he could not resist the lure of her voice. Not if he had to run the gauntlet of a hundred devils with red-hot pitchforks.

He tried to open his eyes, but only one of them would cooperate. The world blurred and swam for a bilious instant before Harris let his eyelid fall shut again. A groan escaped his lips, swollen as they were. His throbbing tongue felt twice its normal size. After a quick mental inventory, he decided that his left leg had somehow escaped injury. Every other part of his body ached or stung or burned or pounded with its own unique pitch of agony.

"Who did this to ye, Harris?"

For a split, lunatic second, he forgot all his hurts. He would tell Jenny that Rod Douglas was responsible for his brutal beating, and that would be the end of their wedding plans.

He willed his mouth to form the words, but nothing intelligible emerged.

"Don't try to talk now," she said in the infuriating way of womankind, forgetting that she had urged him to speak with her question. "I'll fetch some water to bathe yer hurts. Then I'll find someone to help me carry ye home."

Home?

With his tenuous grasp on consciousness, Harris puzzled the word. Where was home? Not Roderick Douglas's house, surely. His own lean-to shanty behind the tavern?

His poor addled wits were still pondering the question when she returned with water. Harris heard a high whine of cloth tearing and his wounded lip twitched up. Wasn't it just like Jenny to rip up her petticoat in order to tend him?

The cool, sodden cloth daubed his forehead, stinging like a horde of wasps. Harris sucked a hissing breath in between his clenched teeth. One tooth wobbled at the touch of his tongue.

She began to talk again, perhaps to distract him from the necessary torture of her ministrations.

"It was Sweeney and McBean who beat ye, wasn't it?"

When he made no reply, not even a groan or a nod, she prompted, "Douglas's men? One with a crooked beak and the other with a face like a red bulldog?"

"Mmm" was all the affirmation Harris could manage, though her descriptions drove him to another painful grin.

"I knew it. I should never have sent ye after her."

Harris peered at her through the slit of his eye, forcing the shimmering image of her face into focus.

"Morag!" Her name heaved out of him.

"Aye, who did ye think it was?" Her voice took on a bitter edge. "Jenny Lennox? Sorry to disappoint, but ye're not in any shape to be fussy about who tends ye."

Harris subsided. His mangled mouth was not equal to the laborious explanation he owed Morag McGregor. He was not disappointed by her presence, but by Jenny's absence. If only Jenny could have seen the harm of which Roderick was capable, Harris would have counted his beating a blessing and taken another if need be.

"That's as much as I can do for ye here," said Morag at last. "I'll go fetch Murdock and Pa to carry ye back to our place."

He hadn't the strength to reply.

Perhaps she thought he'd lost consciousness again, for she rested her hand lightly on his brow, in something like a caress. "Did they beat her out of ye, Harris? It might be the best thing for ye in the long run."

As he slipped back into a gentle twilight, Harris almost laughed. After all Jenny had done to drive him away and all he had done to purge his feelings for her, it would take harder fists than Rod Douglas could hire to beat her out of his heart.

The sun of late September beat into Roderick Douglas's carriage as it rolled up to St. Mary's for Sunday worship. If the summer was waning, it showed no sign. The still air had already grown uncomfortably warm and the grass in the churchyard had been baked to brittle gold threads.

While pretending to concentrate on what Roderick was saying, Jenny cast surreptitious glances in every direction. On the last two Sundays she had glimpsed Harris watching her from a distance. Today there was no sign of him.

So he had been in earnest about leaving Chatham. She had…not exactly hoped, but…wondered if that had been a ruse to lure her out to the kirkyard.

Jenny assured herself that his departure relieved her mind. Now she could anticipate her wedding without fearing he might disrupt the ceremony. Perhaps with Harris gone from town, Roderick might loosen his restrictions upon her comings and goings. He protested that such measures were for her own safety, and she believed him. Still,

there were days she felt as if she was being slowly smoth-
ered.

"What do you say to that, Janet?"

"I beg yer pardon, Roderick? Something caught my eye
and I didn't hear all of what ye said."

His handsome mouth tightened into a line of disapproval
Jenny had begun to shrink from.

"I was saying that some important business acquain-
tances of mine will be in town next week—from Boston.
At least two of them will be bringing their wives along. I
mean to invite them to the wedding, of course. I also
thought we could host a party the evening before. Would
you like that?"

"Aye, I would." Jenny tried to sound enthusiastic. She
berated herself for feeling otherwise.

Wasn't this everything she'd dreamed of, back home in
Dalbeattie when the notion of her marriage to Roderick
had first been raised? A fine home, servants to do the work,
lavish parties for important guests. Confronted with the
prospect of organizing such an affair, Jenny quailed.

What did she know of entertaining such people? Where
did a body even start? Food. Music. Would she be expected
to write invitations? She didn't want to disgrace Roderick
in front of his wealthy American friends. He had such high
expectations of her, and she always seemed to be letting
him down.

Harris had never made her feel like that. The thought
popped, unbidden, into Jenny's mind. Even as she tried to
dismiss it, the idea took firm root. Somehow, Harris had
always made her feel she could do anything she set her
mind to. But Harris was gone now and the illusion of
strength and competency he'd instilled in her was fading
rapidly.

The carriage halted in front of St. Mary's. Other church-
goers hung back respectfully from the door, waiting for
Mr. Douglas and his betrothed to enter.

"You're quiet this morning, my dear," said Roderick as he helped her down from the gig. "Nothing the matter, I hope?"

Was there a hint of mocking triumph in his voice?

Of course not! Jenny rebuked herself for even entertaining such a wicked notion. Her fiancé was being solicitous of her feelings, that was all.

"Wrong?" She forced a bright smile. "Oh no. Just thinking about getting ready for the party. We can bring in the last of the garden flowers to decorate the table. Is New Brunswick always this warm the end of September, Roderick?"

"Ha! I should say not. Two years ago at this time, we had snow that stayed. This has been a freakish summer."

As they took their places in the Douglas pew, Jenny thought about the final reading of the banns. In a few short days she would be Mrs. Roderick Douglas, an honored leader of town society. Her long-cherished dream would finally become a reality. So why did she feel caught in a shifting, baffling nightmare from which she longed to waken?

Harris struggled awake from another nightmare.

His heart drummed against his bruised ribs in a frantic, aching beat. He gasped for air. A bead of sweat dribbled from his hairline, stinging the messy wound on his left temple.

For the past three nights, his sleep had been riddled with dark, disturbing dreams. They all featured Jenny in mortal peril and him trying in vain to save her. Each time he hastened to her rescue his efforts went awry. He would trip over his own feet or lose his way. Or he would reach Jenny only to discover he'd been tricked and she was nothing but a scarecrow.

The overwhelming sense of urgency and futility stayed with him long after the dream had passed.

He had to find some way to wrest Jenny from the power of Roderick Douglas—if only he could think how.

Pondering that complicated riddle, he relaxed onto his bed of straw in one of Alec McGregor's outbuildings. He had not managed much productive thought when he heard Morag's brisk step approaching and smelled the savory aroma of beef broth wafting on the still, warm air.

"How are ye feeling this morning?" she asked as soon as she'd confirmed he was awake.

"Better," Harris allowed cautiously.

For the first two days, as bruises bulged and gashed skin began to knit, he had hurt worse than just after his beating. Morag had told him it was a good sign, and a warning for him to rest and let his battered body heal.

"At least words don't sluice over my tongue so bad. I don't suppose ye've brought me anything solid to eat. Yer beef broth and egg yolk custard are tasty, but they don't stay a man's stomach for long."

"I ken a man's on the mend for certain when he can eat and talk." Wry humor warmed her tart words as she knelt beside him. "Aye, I've brought a bit of boiled beef, if ye think ye can manage it, and some new tatties mashed with cream."

Harris made quick work of the meal, taking care to spare his loose tooth. Having a good full stomach revived him further.

"Where will ye go, when ye're well enough to leave?" Morag rose abruptly and moved toward the entrance to the shed. Was that a note of longing in her voice?

"I can't leave until I get Jenny away from Rod Douglas."

She rounded on him, her eyes flashing verdant fury. "Don't be a fool, Harris. Miss Lennox has made her choice. Let her live with it. That beating Sweeney and McBean gave ye was only a warning. If ye dare to come back they'll do ye real harm."

"How do ye know so much about what those ruffians are apt to do?" he snapped.

Morag's left hand flew up to cover her cheek. The gesture answered his question more eloquently than any words.

"They did that to ye? Why?"

"It was too dark for me to see them." The confession choked out of her. "But I recognized them from their voices. It was all *his* orders, of course, but those two animals love their work. To them, a cry or the crack of a breaking bone is almost as good as pay."

Swept by a tidal wave of indignation, Harris tried to rise, only to have the world wobble and sway around him. "Did ye never go to the Justice? Swear out a complaint against them?"

"Pa tried. They claimed they were in each other's company the whole night and nowhere near the place where I was…" It sounded as if a powerful hand had tightened around her throat, squeezing off the flow of words.

She fought for composure and won.

"Roderick Douglas also gave them an alibi, and that was good enough for the Justice. He came back with a verdict that I'd been attacked by Indians."

Harris sputtered his outrage. The thought of Levi and his people accused of such a heinous crime disgusted him. The thought of what Morag had suffered sickened him. And the thought of Jenny legally bound to a man who would casually mastermind such atrocities chilled him to the bone.

One question remained unanswered, though Harris could guess. "Why did Douglas order Sweeney and McBean to do…what they did to ye?"

"Because I was a fool, Harris." With those words of confession, she moved closer to him. "A proud, vain fool. From the time I could walk, folks had told me what a beauty I was."

By the way she held her head and savored the words on her tongue, Harris knew she was remembering. "I came to think no man in the colony would do for me but Roderick Douglas. So handsome. So rich. When he came courting, I welcomed him. And when he asked for me, I said yes."

Her voice tightened. "My pa tried to talk me out of it, but I wouldn't listen any more than Miss Lennox listened to you."

Harris shook his head. "Why didn't ye wed him?"

"I said I was a fool," she snapped, recovering a measure of her composure. "Not an ass. I finally recognized Black Roderick for what he is—a self-centered, domineering bully who can't stand being or having less than the best in anything. When I called the wedding off, he went into a cold rage. I ken he decided if he couldn't have the most beautiful lass in the county—" she hesitated "—he'd make certain she wasn't the most beautiful anymore."

Fighting down his dizziness, Harris raised himself enough to reach for her hand. "I'm sorry, Morag."

She stiffened and pulled her fingers from his weak grasp. "Don't fret for me, Harris. Roderick robbed me of my looks, but not my pride. I can't abide pity, and that's all anyone feels for me anymore."

"Maybe if ye let them show their pity, they'll get past it." For all her hard-won wisdom, could she not see that? "In time, perhaps they'll see the whole woman again, not just the scars. Ye're not Morag the Fair anymore, but ye don't have to be Morag the Tragic."

"How in blazes do ye know so much about it, Harris Chisholm, that ye can presume to tell me how to live my life?" She looked ready to finish the job Sweeney and McBean had started on him.

"Fetch me a razor and some shaving soap."

She looked bewildered by his request. "What's that got to do with anything? Why do ye want a shave at a time like this?"

"Just do it, Morag—please."

She flounced off without a word, leaving Harris to wonder if he'd ever see her again. A short time later, though, he heard her step and the faint slosh of water in a basin.

Alec McGregor squeezed into the shed behind his daughter. "Morag tells me ye fancy a shave, Chisholm. She's afeared ye'll slit yer throat if ye try to do it yerself. I'm not used to barbering any but myself, so mind ye keep still."

Every daub of the lather and every stroke of the razor, stabbed Harris with regret. He'd come to like his beard, and not just for its protective cover. Oh well, he could always grow another.

Wiping the last smears of soap from his face, he called out, "Have a look, Morag."

She spared him a grudging glance. Her eyes widened, and Harris recognized a fleeting mist of pity in them. For the first time in his life, he welcomed it.

Alec McGregor looked from Harris to his daughter. "Ye've got some talking to do, I see, and I've got a hog to butcher."

When her father had gone, Morag settled herself beside Harris's pallet of straw. "From the minute I clapped eyes on ye, I felt ye were different—that ye understood, somehow."

"I didn't understand, Morag. Not until I saw ye. Nothing like seeing things from a fresh angle to make sense of them. Most folks are like me—hiding scars nobody else can see."

He thought of Jenny and how her early life had left its wounds.

"Morag, will ye do something for me?"

"Aye, if I can."

"Will ye go to Jenny and tell her what ye told me—about what Roderick had done to ye?"

Rising, with the basin in her hands, she stepped to the

entrance of the shed and tossed out the soapy water. "How can ye ask me that, Harris?" She refused to look back at him. "Did ye not hear what I told ye? Miss Lennox probably wouldn't heed me anyhow." Her voice died away to a frightened whisper. "And who knows what Roderick would do to me in return."

"Ye're right." Harris cursed himself for even suggesting it. "I'm sorry I asked. I'll have to come up with another way."

"There is no other way, Harris." She shook her head. "The banns have been read. Jenny's as good as wed to Rod Douglas."

Three months ago, if he'd been faced with the same situation, Harris would have cut his losses and admitted defeat. Not now. His ordeals with Jenny had strengthened his powers of endurance and resilience like fire-tempered steel.

"Banns!" he cried. "That's it, Morag. Hand me my shirt. I have to be on my way."

She stared at him as though he'd taken leave of his senses. "Where do ye mean to go, Harris, and how? Ye can barely sit up, let alone stand or walk. What good is it going to do Miss Lennox if ye kill yerself on some fool's errand trying to save her from her ain folly?"

Setting his teeth, Harris pulled himself erect. To his surprise, he did not immediately keel over. "My legs took the least of the beating, Morag. And ye can save yer breath, for there's nothing ye can say to keep me from going. I may well fail, but I can't let that stop me from trying."

"Well, go ahead then." She threw the shirt at him. "But I won't see ye leave here the way ye came, with nothing but the clothes on yer back."

He flashed her a smile of gratitude as he pulled on his shirt. "I'll take whatever supplies ye can round up for me, and be grateful."

Morag made to leave without a further word, but at the

door she hesitated. As she stood silhouetted against the sunlight, Harris saw a tremor go through her. On the late summer breeze he heard a catch in her breath. "I always wished a man would love me the way ye love her."

Harris lurched the few steps toward her—his legs were far sounder than his balance. He put his arms around Morag to keep from collapsing on the floor, as much as to offer her a crumb of comfort.

"One will, lass. Maybe there's one who does already. Have ye looked outside yerself long enough to see?"

She let herself surrender to his embrace for just a moment before pulling free. "Don't talk nonsense, Harris. I'll go collect ye what gear I can."

In her curt admonition, it heartened him to hear a degree of thawing.

He set off a half hour later, gamely, if not very steadily, muttering to himself a list of Alec McGregor's directions. By his reckoning, he had five days to reach the Richibucto and get back again. A tall order, but possible. Or was it?

From her expensively glazed bedroom window, Jenny stared off into the distant woods.

"Where are ye now, Harris?" she murmured. "And why did ye pick this time to heed me when I told ye to go away?"

The blame rested squarely on her own shoulders—Jenny knew that. It did not improve her humor.

She had been pushing Harris away or fleeing from him ever since she'd realized what a threat he posed to her plans and her peace of mind. Sooner or later he'd been bound to take her at her word.

Why, then, did his going feel like abandonment?
Desertion.

Apart from her mother's death, Jenny had never experienced it before. Now she understood, at least in part, how his own abandonment had shaped Harris's character. She understood, at least in part, the pain it had caused him. What she could not fathom was why he had courted a revival of that pain by pursuing her—a woman destined to desert him.

Apparently he had come to his senses, at last, and that vindicated all her cherished beliefs about romantic love. Harris had protested deep feelings for her. They'd quickly withered when it became obvious she was committed to wedding Roderick. Better to have learned that harsh lesson now than to have succumbed to the attraction between them and discovered the truth only when it was too late.

Off in the distance, a tiny figure detached itself from the forest background. It moved closer, then stopped and retreated again.

A woman. That much Jenny could make out.

A black shawl billowed up in the dry west wind. Something in that movement sparked Jenny's memory. There'd been a woman with a black shawl at the mass wedding she and Harris had attended. Perhaps he had heeded Alec McGregor's invitation and gone back there to settle.

Suddenly Jenny was possessed by an overwhelming compulsion to glean one scrap of news about Harris—to hear his name spoken and to taste it aloud again on her own tongue.

Mrs. Lyons had gone off a short while ago to do the marketing. Ever since Harris left town, her strict wardenship of the house had eased. If Jenny wanted to slip out for a breath of air, now was her chance.

As she descended the stairs, Jenny heard the hired girls sanding the parlor floor for Roderick's party. Slipping unnoticed out the kitchen door, she set off across the meadow, toward the woods where she had seen the woman lurking. Her heart sank when she found the spot deserted. Perhaps she'd only imagined that hesitant figure, out of her longing for word of Harris. Or out of her need to escape the stifling atmosphere of Roderick's house.

With a deep sigh, Jenny turned to go.

A faint rustling sound made her look back.

The black-shawled woman cowered in the shadow of a dark spruce tree, casting a feverish glance around the meadow, like a doe wary of predators. Hesitantly she beckoned.

"Who are ye and what do ye want?" The woman's behavior made her nervous. What if the creature was a lunatic?

The woman pulled back the shawl from her face. Before she could stop herself, Jenny gasped.

"I'm Morag McGregor and I've something to say that ye must hear."

Her face was more frightening in its marred beauty than plain ugliness. The intensity of the woman's voice did nothing to reassure Jenny. Slowly she began to back away.

"If ye ever cared for Harris Chisholm, ye'll hear me out, for his sake."

Every instinct in Jenny screamed at her to turn and run. Instead, she planted her feet and challenged Morag McGregor, "Speak then."

Chapter Nineteen

Harris cursed the fading light.

He had pushed on through the two previous nights, taking his bearings by the stars and stopping to snatch an hour of sleep only when exhaustion threatened. Now he feared he might have strayed off course on either of those nights. His time was running out. Even if he managed to reach Richibucto by morning and do his business immediately, how could he hope to turn around and make it back to Chatham in time to stop Jenny's wedding?

Morag had been right. This was a fool's errand. Another man might have accomplished it. A man in better condition. One with greater powers of endurance. One with a decent sense of direction.

Goaded by desperation, Harris picked up his pace. He must cover as much ground as possible while daylight lasted. His stride quickened to a trot and finally to a dead run. He'd stop and rest when he could no longer see the trees in his path.

This was perhaps the quietest hour of the day—when songbirds found a perch and folded their wings to sleep. Before owls and other night creatures began to stir. The only sounds Harris heard were the crunch of pine needles under his tread, the pounding of his pulse and the hiss of his labored breath.

His body ached from this heightened exertion when it yearned to rest. Harris pushed himself on. His weary mind teetered on the brink of sleep. He willed himself not to surrender. When the physical and mental effort grew too great for him to sustain, he began to strike bargains with himself.

Just twenty more strides. Just past that tall fir tree, up ahead. Just beyond this rise.

As Harris crested the rise, his legs continued pumping even after his mind had given them leave to stop. He lost his footing on the uneven ground. Down he fell, tumbling over and over. At last he hit bottom, catching all his weight on his left leg. A jolt of pain surged from his ankle, making him cry out.

Night and despair dropped on Harris like a giant slab of black granite.

"You look pensive tonight, Janet. Are you still fretting about arrangements for the party?"

Jenny glanced up from her supper. Roderick's deep voice sounded so solicitous. His smile looked so charming. Surely the ravings of that madwoman couldn't be true.

"I beg your pardon, Roderick. I don't mean to be such disagreeable company for ye."

"Quiet, yes. Disagreeable, never. Why, if all I did was look on you I could be contented, Janet. I'll wager you're the handsomest woman in the colony. Speaking of which, did you try on the gown I had sent over from the seamstress?"

A stinging blush rose in Jenny's cheeks. "Aye. Do ye mean me to wear it for our wedding?"

It was an exquisite creation of jonquil-yellow in the finest muslin Jenny had ever seen. So fine, in fact, that it was all but transparent. The neckline hung lower than on any dress Jenny had ever seen, let alone worn. Did Roderick really want her breasts on such brazen display?

"The wedding?" He chuckled. "Janet, you are a caution. The poor vicar's eyes would pop clean from his head. No. The seamstress is refurbishing the gown you brought from Scotland. Hard to credit it's still in one piece after your journey overland from Richibucto. The new dress is for our wedding eve party. Billings and Pruitt can stare all they like."

The thought of Roderick's business colleagues gaping at her in that immodest costume made Jenny squirm in her seat. Desperate to distract herself, she groped for a new topic of conversation. Only one readily presented itself. Roderick seemed in a very cordial humor tonight—perhaps she might dare broach the matter and set her mind at rest.

"Do ye ken a lass named Morag McGregor—bides in the Highland settlement on the way to Richibucto?"

Roderick's fork stopped halfway to his mouth. After the slightest hesitation, it continued its course. When he had chewed and swallowed that bite of food, he replied, "A sad case. How do you come to know of Mad Morag, and what made you mention her now?"

Jenny's breath shifted a little easier. So, she'd been right after all. The pathetic creature was a madwoman.

"I saw her when Har…when I came through the settlement on my way to Chatham. There was a big wedding going on then, too. Talking about our wedding must have made me think of her. Does anyone know how she came by the scars on her face?"

"Indian attack." Roderick shook his head. "A terrible thing—vicious savages. I led the militia in a retaliatory strike on their encampment at Eel River. Taught them a lesson, I hope, about molesting innocent white women. I'd still prefer you not to go out alone, my dear Janet."

Jenny tried to reconcile Roderick's explanation with her own experience of the local Mi'kmaq people. She could not imagine Levi Augustine or any of his family commit-ting such a brutal outrage. Yet, she could not afford to entertain doubts about her husband-to-be.

"The whole ordeal overset the poor woman's mind," Roderick continued. "She deluded herself into thinking she was still a great beauty and that she was going to marry me. When I declined to go along with her ridiculous fancy, she began spreading the vilest stories about me. Of course, no one with any sense believed the poor wretch."

Those dark, mysterious eyes, whose merest glance had once thrilled Jenny, now held her—an unspoken question in their disquieting depths.

Did she believe him, or did she believe Mad Morag?

"Of course," she murmured. Ducking her head to avoid his gaze, Jenny concentrated fiercely upon eating her din-ner. Each mouthful dropped into her stomach like a lump of lead.

The world still lay wrapped in darkness when Harris pulled himself to foggy consciousness. His ankle throbbed. The crushing weight of his failure oppressed him. Little by little, though, he became aware of a beckoning, hopeful sound. The sound of running water not too far distant.

Gathering all his waning strength, he tried to pull him-self erect. His injured ankle buckled under the weight with a searing burst of pain. Driven to his knees, Harris began to crawl forward. He had come too far and endured too much to give up now, no matter how futile his undertaking might seem.

By the time he reached the riverbank, the palms of his hands stung with blisters and his whole body pleaded for sleep. Songbirds had begun to serenade the rising sun. Their cheery warbling mocked Harris's anguish.

Too tired even to pry off his boots, he sat on the bank and thrust his feet into the swift-flowing water. Gradually the cold leeched his pain, allowing him to escape once again into sleep.

He woke later with a start, to the touch of a wet nose sniffing his hand. His first thought was of foxes or a wolf, seeking easy prey in a wounded creature. Then, as his exhausted mind began to clear, he realized the wet nose belonged to a dog—the kind of dog he'd seen running with shrieking brown children around Levi Augustine's encampment.

Suddenly the children were there, surrounding him, all talking at once in their own language. From their excitement, he gathered they recognized him, even without the red beard. All Harris could do was smile and tousle their dark heads, to show that he remembered them as well.

Levi Augustine edged his canoe to the riverbank.

"Barbe-rouge?" He looked Harris over, shaking his head. "Did you lose a fight with a bear, friend? A she-bear, maybe?"

Harris replied with a weak grin. "I need your help," he said in French. "Someone has stolen my woman and I must get her back. Have you heard of a man from Chatham who builds ships? Black Douglas, they call him."

He got his reply in the grim scowl that darkened Levi's face. "He is an evildoer, who blames my people for his own treachery. Tell how we can help get your woman back and we will do it."

"Can ye take me to Richibucto in your canoe?"

"Why there? Is your woman not in Chatham?"

"*Oui,* she is. But there's an important paper I must get to set her free from Douglas. I can only get it in Richibucto."

Levi paused in their conversation to call out to the younger men of his family. Then he spoke to Harris again. "I do not understand this store you white men set by bits of paper. They are not living things with spirits, like an eagle, or a river, or the wind. Yet they have strong magic for you.''

A wider, sturdier canoe beached nearby, paddled by Levi's widowed brother and the young man who wanted to marry Levi's daughter. Together, the three men helped Harris into the canoe. Levi called out to his wife on the opposite bank, perhaps to tell her where he was going and why.

As the streamlined birchbark craft swept downriver, Harris yearned to heft an oar, but he knew he'd be more hindrance than help. So he rested his injured ankle and let the reviving sun and sea air soak into him. In vain he tried to quench the foolish bubble of hope that swelled within his heart.

"Levi, do ye know what day this is?" Harris could no longer be sure.

"The third day of the new moon," came the confident but unhelpful reply.

Harris fretted. He couldn't hope to get back to Chatham in time, on foot. Not on an ankle that might well be broken. Desperate as he was, he couldn't ask Levi and the others to risk their lives by delivering him to Chatham. Once he saw to the paperwork, though, he might be able to send a messenger to deliver his announcement and fetch Jenny back to Richibucto.

Would she come with a stranger? Harris wasn't certain he'd be able to convince her face-to-face, let alone by proxy.

If only he had enough time.

Jenny glanced at the pedestal clock in the corner of the parlor. The time had gone eleven—would their guests never leave?

Her head felt like a raw egg squeezed in a man's fist—ready to shatter into a thousand brittle white shards. For all the pains taken with cleaning and decorating, for all the expensive food and drink imported, for all the affluent, socially superior company, the party had been a disaster.

Eager to return to Boston after a month's sojourn in Quebec, Mrs. Billings and Mrs. Pruitt had made not the slightest effort to be agreeable. The former had started a vicious hissing argument with her husband about the extent of his drinking. The latter gave Jenny several spiteful little digs about the immodest design of her dress.

The heavy, florid Mr. Billings complained incessantly about the stifling atmosphere, asking several times if more windows could be opened. Jenny suspected he was using the unseasonable heat as an excuse to drink great quantities of Roderick's rum punch.

For all that, Jenny preferred him to the loathsome Mr. Pruitt, who'd scarcely taken his eyes off the cleavage of her bosom all evening. She had done her best to reply politely to several lewd compliments.

Roderick appeared to be the only member of the party truly enjoying himself. There could be no question that he looked well in a new suit of clothes, complemented by a very fashionable waistcoat. He made a point to impress everyone by telling how much he had paid for each item.

He talked of his record profits for the year, told of the much larger and grander house he planned to build. And all the while, Jenny kept a covert eye on the clock, wishing the time would magically disappear.

Finally Mr. Billings stretched, yawned and said he and his wife should return to sleep on the ship that night to escape the oppressive heat. Jenny could scarcely restrain herself from throwing her arms around his stout midsection.

"I suppose we all must get our rest," Roderick replied. "I don't want my bride oversleeping and missing the ceremony tomorrow." He sent Mrs. Lyons to dispatch the carriage around for their guests.

When the Billings and the Pruitts had gone, he lounged

on the settee, patting a place for Jenny beside him. She lowered herself gingerly, fearful, as she had been all evening, that her bosom might burst clean out of her brief bodice.

Roderick heaved a self-satisfied sigh. "I thought it all went off quite well, don't you? Have a word with the cook, though. The poached pears might have been firmer and the sauce a little sweeter. I saw Mrs. Pruitt pucker up when she tasted it."

Jenny had seen the woman's sour expression, too. She thought it had more to do with Mr. Pruitt's lascivious comment on her dress than with the poached pears.

"You were very quiet this evening, I must say, Janet. In future when we entertain, I hope you'll cultivate a more vivacious humor."

"I…I'm sorry if I let ye down, R-Roderick." She could feel tears stinging the back of her eyes. "It's just so awfully hot and this is the very first time I've ever *entertained,* and with the wedding tomorrow…"

"There, there, Janet."

For the first time since she'd come to Chatham, Roderick took her in his arms. He'd been so circumspect until now, with only the odd kiss bestowed on her hand or her forehead to bid good-night. Surely a deeper intimacy between them would help quell her memories of Harris.

"I know this is a far grander life than you're used to," said Roderick. "I'm prepared to make allowances. You'll grow into your new role, I feel certain of it. Just heed me and I'll do my best to mold you into a perfect wife."

She knew he meant this for reassurance, but his words chilled her. The sensation of his embrace held none of the wonder she had once imagined. None of the wonder she'd experienced with Harris.

He kissed her then, on the lips. Slowly, deeply and with expert precision—as though he'd practiced his technique on many willing women before her. Jenny tried to relax and enjoy it. She failed.

Likewise, when Roderick raised his hand and swiped it across the exposed flesh of her breasts. His mouth released hers, kissing its way across her cheek to her ear. Instead of rousing her, it only made her hackles rise.

"Oh, Janet," he whispered, his voice hot and husky. "I've held myself back from you these past weeks, wanting everything to be right and proper. But tonight, seeing you in that gown and the way those men looked at you, I can't keep my hands off you a moment longer, my dearest."

He trailed a string of kisses down her neck and across her collarbone, veering down to the cleft between her breasts. His hands ranged over her, taking triumphant possession of his conquered territory. Did he mean to have her for the very first time, here in the parlor, where Mrs. Lyons or one of the hired girls might walk in at any moment?

"Please, Roderick." She pulled back from him, turning her face away when he tried to kiss her again. Modesty was only an excuse, Jenny realized. She didn't want him pawing at her—would she ever? "Can't we wait until…" *Until hell freezes?*

Braving a quick glance into his eyes, Jenny shrank from what she saw there. Something intense and remorseless glared back at her. His hand squeezed down on her breast so swiftly and so hard that she gasped in pain.

"Have it your own way." He spat the words at her. "Traipse around the countryside like a trollop with that oaf of a Chisholm, then act all missish and proper with the man who has an honest claim on you."

She opened her mouth to protest the injustice of his accusation, but no words would come. It was true. She'd allowed Harris far greater liberties than her fiancé had just tried to claim. *Allowed?* Why, she'd positively encouraged them.

"I'm sorry, Roderick." Would she have to spend every day of her marriage apologizing to him for something?

He rose abruptly from the settee, adjusting his clothes. "The hour is late. We both need our sleep."

"Yes, Roderick." She rose to accompany him to the door.

He took her face in his hands. Jenny nearly wilted with relief. So he meant to pardon her rebuff after all.

The force of his fingers increased, until Jenny felt as if her head was being squeezed in a vise.

He pressed his nose to hers and gazed deep into her eyes. "Tomorrow night you'll be mine, Janet. Then you'll not deny me."

As suddenly as he had taken her, he released Jenny and strode for the door. She lapsed back onto the settee until her fluttering pulse slowed and her trembling subsided. Then she took herself off to bed.

Seated before the night table, she pulled the brush through her hair again and again, long past her usual fifty strokes. Tomorrow she was going to marry Roderick Douglas. It was the dream of a lifetime finally come true. The sumptuous party fare roiled in her stomach. It was natural for a bride to be nervous on the eve of her wedding, she told herself firmly. She was merely anxious that tomorrow's ceremony should go off smoothly.

Jenny kept on brushing. If she stopped, she feared her hands would shake again. Surely it was nothing unusual for a maid to anticipate her wedding night with uneasiness…or apprehension or…stark terror?

She would become accustomed to Roderick's ways once they'd been married awhile, Jenny tried to reassure herself. She'd work hard to be a good wife. She'd keep their home quiet and serene. Gentle his fierce temper with her womanly influence. Avoid giving him cause to treat her roughly. In time, she'd grow used to his kisses and his touch, ceasing her constant and unfair comparisons with Harris.

The hairbrush dropped from Jenny's hand, clattering on the floorboards.

Hurriedly she scooped it up again, her heart hammering. What if Mrs. Lyons came to investigate the noise? Jenny anxiously inspected the silver back of the brush for dents. Roderick would not appreciate her careless handling of the fine things he bought for her.

She glanced over at the wide tester bed. She hadn't slept soundly in it since coming here. By rights, she ought to be a sensible lass and try to get some rest. When she looked at it, though, she could only contemplate the years of nights to come, when she must share it with Roderick Douglas.

Jenny could feel a dull ache in her face and arms and the soft flesh of her breast where his hands had plundered so roughly. When she recalled the hungry light in his eyes and his parting words, her supper threatened to erupt from her seething belly.

Rifling through her wardrobe, she took out the copy of *Ivanhoe* that had been Harris's parting gift to her. Perhaps the book would distract her from unwelcome thoughts and lull her to sleep. She settled in the rocking chair, opening the volume not to the first page of text, but to the last.

Softly she paraphrased Scott's prose to fit her own situation. "She lived long and happily with Roderick, for they were attached to each other by bonds of early affection and loved each other the more for recollection of obstacles which had impeded her union. Yet it would be inquiring too curiously to ask whether the recollection of Harris Chisholm's courage and magnanimity did not recur in her mind more frequently than the noble descendant of Douglas might altogether have approved."

The last words escaped in a hoarse whisper. But it was

not until she saw the first teardrops splatter on the open page that Jenny realized she was weeping.

The long shadows of that early October evening seemed so much at odds with a heat like mid-July. One final push of the paddles brought Levi's sea canoe to dock at the Richibucto wharf, astern of a strangely familiar vessel. A small clutch of curious townsfolk had gathered to meet them.

The lofty figure of Robert Jardine detached itself from the others. "Is that you, Chisholm? Did you ever make it to Chatham? We feared the worst when we didn't hear any news of you. All your gear is safely stored at my house…"

Harris cut him off. None of the rest mattered, except the one question that had been burning in his brain all day. "Robert, by all that's holy, man, can you tell me what day it is?"

"What day? Why it's Thursday, of course. The sixth of October. Why do you need to know?"

Thursday. The sixth. By noon tomorrow Jenny'd be wed to Roderick Douglas, and Harris was now powerless to stop it.

Chapter Twenty

Jenny could not remember at what early hour of the morning she'd fallen asleep in the rocking chair. She shook her head to disperse the lingering echoes of a nightmare. In it, she'd been bound to the stake, like Rebecca in *Ivanhoe*. The Templar, who looked uncomfortably like Roderick, had held a torch to the faggots. In vain, Jenny had scanned the horizon for some sign of Sir Wilfred riding to save her. Even as she choked on the rising smoke and felt the first lick of flames, he had not come.

She'd wakened, only to realize she had exchanged one nightmare for another. All her experience of Roderick Douglas from the past weeks had merged in her sleeping mind. She now believed Morag McGregor—mad or sane. The altar at St. Mary's would be her own stake, today. And no sign of a knight in armor galloping to her rescue.

"Mistress?"

Jenny started at the timid tap on the door.

"Just a moment, Marie."

She clasped the book to her in a desperate embrace, then buried it in the depths of her wardrobe. As soon as possible, she'd have to dispose of it—though it would break her heart. Mrs. Lyons would not be above snooping it out, and Jenny shrank from the prospect of Roderick's reaction.

"Come in," she called to the hired girl.

Marie entered with a kettle of steaming water. "Mrs. Lyons said I was to help you prepare for the wedding, mistress. Would you like me to wash your hair?"

Jenny nodded. Time to wash, dress and otherwise prepare this sacrificial creature for the altar. Fleetingly she considered running away. It was her speciality, after all, she reflected bitterly. Jenny knew the price Morag McGregor had paid for disappointing her bridegroom, though. And she was too great a coward to risk it.

Only one thought gave her any comfort. At least she'd done the right thing in persistently refusing Harris. He deserved so much better than a woman like her. Sooner or later, she would have brought him great suffering. Fortunately he had escaped her—relatively unscathed.

Mrs. Lyons stalked into the bedroom without bothering to knock. "Cook wants to know if you'll have a bowl of porritch to stay your stomach until the wedding luncheon. If you mean to, you'd better eat now, before you get into your gown."

"No, thank ye, Mrs. Lyons. I'm not hungry. Bride's nerves, ye know."

The housekeeper sniffed. "Nerves? What's to be nervous marrying a man in the master's position? You should be down on your knees thanking the Lord for such an opportunity."

Jenny knew it was futile, sparring with this woman. Roderick had made it clear that Mrs. Lyons would have the upper hand in their household. Still she could not hold her tongue.

"If I thought the Lord would listen, Mrs. Lyons, I *would* be down on my knees, ye may be sure."

The woman shot her a suspicious look, as though she knew what Jenny meant but could find no grounds in those words to challenge her. "You'll tempt judgment, uttering such blasphemy on your wedding morn. If you thought the Lord would listen, indeed!''

She marched off, muttering darkly to herself about Jenny's want of appetite, and what a bad breeder she would prove.

The thought of bearing and raising children by a man like Roderick Douglas took the stomach out of Jenny entirely.

''Oh, mistress!'' Marie handled the wedding gown as though it was a sacred object. *''Elle est belle. Elle est très, très belle!''*

Jenny slipped the lavender-gray silk over her head and let Marie fasten the buttons. She caught a glimpse of herself in the mirror above the night table. A pale, haunted creature stared back at her. Sackcloth or a hair shirt would be more appropriate raiment for the undertaking before her.

By the time she descended the stairs and took her seat in Roderick's carriage for the short drive to St. Mary's, Jenny could scarcely walk or speak for paralyzing fear.

The day was hot and hazy. Farmers dug potatoes. A tinker's cart drove past in the opposite direction, metalware jangling. Out in the harbor, a ship sailed in from the Northumberland. Just another ordinary day for everyone else in the world. But for Jenny, the blackest of her life. Even that mightn't have been so bad had she not envisioned worse days—years of them, to come.

From the prow of the *St. Bride,* Harris Chisholm watched the Northumberland coast pass by. Pass by far too slowly for his liking. Since the barque had cast off on the daybreak tide, he'd stood here, willing the Atlantic winds to fill the sails and speed them on to the Miramichi.

Involuntarily, his hand went up to the pocket of his waistcoat, to reassure him that the wedding license was still there. After the despair that had crushed him on reach-

ing Richibucto, and believing himself too late, Harris tried
to keep his surging hope in check this morning.

It was not easy.

Indeed, it seemed as though the hand of the Almighty
had intervened, suddenly flinging open a window where it
had firmly slammed a door. When he'd retched out his tale
of woe to Robert Jardine, the shipbuilder had replied with
impossibly hopeful news.

"You aren't too late, Harris. The *St. Bride* is seaworthy,
man. She's set to sail the day after tomorrow, but I'm certain we could persuade the master to go a day sooner."

"The ship's just part of it, Robert. I need to get a license
for Jenny and me to wed. It's the only way I can pry her
out of Douglas's foul clutches."

"I'll take you along to the magistrate. I hope he hasn't
gone to bed yet." The shipbuilder shook his head. "I'll
warn you, a wedding license doesn't come cheap."

"There should be a little money among the things I left
at yer house, Robert. There's also my books. I'll...sell
them to ye, if ye'll take them."

"Never you worry about that. Between us, I reckon
we'll come up with the fee some way or other."

Old Justice Weldon had muttered his disapproval of the
irregularity of issuing the document. "You know, young
fellow, the license is meant to be issued by me at the time
I perform the ceremony—not for some wedding to take
place in another county. How can I even be certain you
have the lady's consent?"

Harris placed his hand on the judge's Bible. "I swear
before God, sir, I have her promise."

"I have her promise," he repeated to himself twelve
hours later, drawing in a deep breath of sea air.

He hadn't lied...exactly.

On the quayside at Kirkcudbright, Jenny had vowed to
grant him any favor within her power, provided he saw her
safe to the Miramichi. He'd kept his part of the bargain.

Now he meant to hold Jenny to hers. He knew she'd intended nothing like this when she'd made the compact. And he recalled something else she'd once said. *If ye do anything to queer my marriage to Roderick, Harris Chisholm, I won't marry ye, supposing ye're the last he-creature in North America.*

Harris could only pray for wind to drive the *St. Bride,* and pray that Jenny had changed her mind.

The vicar of St. Mary's bestowed a benign smile on the bridal couple. If he noticed the stricken look on Jenny's face or the stiff way she held herself apart from Roderick, he gave no sign. Opening his Book of Common Prayer, he proceeded with the liturgy of the wedding service.

Jenny let the words wash over her. If she heeded their meaning, she might not be able to keep her distress in check. For all the bloody conflict between the Church of England and the Free Kirk over the years, their offices of marriage were not all that different.

"Dearly beloved, we are gathered together in the sight of God to join this man and this woman in holy matrimony..."

Time seemed to stop and Jenny's every sense heightened. Simultaneously she was aware of the dust motes shimmering in a shaft of sunlight, the stale air within the sanctuary, and the faint creak of door hinges from the vestibule.

"I require and charge thee both," intoned the vicar gravely, "as ye will at the dreadful day of judgment when the secrets of all hearts shall be disclosed, that if either of ye know any impediment why ye may not be lawfully joined together in matrimony, ye do now confess it."

"Likewise, if there be any man present," he continued after pausing for only a beat, "who can show just cause why these persons should not be joined in matrimony, let him now speak or else hereafter forever hold his peace."

He scarcely drew breath before moving on with the service. "Wilt thou, Rod—"

A voice rang out from the back of the sanctuary. A voice Jenny had never expected to hear again. A voice she now realized she had missed to the core of her being.

"Give a body a chance to get a word in, Reverend."

Jenny could not bring herself to turn around, in case she might be mistaken and it might not be Harris after all. The vicar wore the dumbstruck look of a flayed mackerel.

Roderick's dark visage blackened further. "Pay no mind, Vicar. Get on with the ceremony."

"But...the...this is highly irregular. Young man, do you wish to speak against this union?"

"I do."

"Come forward then, by all means and have your say."

Jenny heard footsteps making their way to the altar. Footsteps with a pronounced limp. She spun around to see Harris hobbling down the aisle.

What had happened to him?

A messy-looking wound on his forehead appeared to be healing. A black eye was fading to mottled brown and green. One side of his lower lip was slightly swollen. He was the dearest, most welcome sight Jenny had ever beheld. She could scarcely keep from bolting into his arms.

"Well?" the vicar prompted Harris.

"This wedding can't go forward." Coming to a halt beside Jenny, he cast her a furtive look that might have been an apology. "Because I have a prior claim on the bride and I've come here today to wed her, myself."

"Nonsense!" thundered Roderick. "I warn you, Chisholm, get out now before I..."

"Before ye have Sweeney and McBean beat me to a bloody pulp? They had their fun with me once. Can't ye come up with a more original threat?"

Jenny wrenched her hand from Roderick's. "Oh, Harris!" She should have known how he'd come by his injuries. Rather than have him suffer like that for her, she would have taken every blow herself.

"This is ridiculous!" insisted Roderick. "I'll be damned if I'll let you barge in and turn my wedding into a free-for-all with your baseless accusations."

"Now, now, Mr. Douglas," pleaded the vicar. "Remember your language. This is a house of God."

He looked to Harris. "Young man, you'd better be prepared to produce convincing proof of what you say. Interrupting a wedding service is not an act to be committed lightly."

"Why are you bothering with this rubbish, Vicar?" demanded Roderick. "You've read our banns here for the past three Sundays. This scoundrel can't just march in and take my bride."

Harris pulled a rolled paper from his waistcoat pocket. "I have a license for Jenny and me to wed. It's duly authorized by the magistrate in Richibucto. If ye'll give me a moment to speak to Miss Lennox, I'm sure she'll confirm that she gave me her promise long before she arrived in Chatham."

"Damned if I'll let you talk to *my* bride at *my* wedding! Take your miserable forgery of a license and get out."

A voice rose from the back of the church. "That paper's no forgery," said Captain Glendenning. "I saw Justice Weldon put his seal to it with my own two eyes."

The vicar looked positively apoplectic. "I must examine this document for authenticity. In the meantime…" he nodded to Harris "…you may speak with Miss Lennox."

"I forbid any such…" Before Roderick could complete his sentence, Harris leaned over and murmured something to him that Jenny did not catch.

Roderick's mouth fell open. Then he shut it again into a grim, intractable line. Jenny could almost see the thunderheads gathering over his brow.

"Very well," he snarled. "You have two minutes, while

I examine this license.'' Roderick motioned the Chatham magistrate up from his pew.

Harris clasped Jenny's hand and drew her to a corner of the chancel. With each step, he winced. He had suffered too much for her already.

"Why did ye come back, Harris? And what's all this about a promise and a license? Ye ken right well I never said I'd marry ye.''

"I ken. But ye did make me a promise, that day at Kirkcudbright Harbor. Ye swore if I saw ye safe to the Miramichi, ye'd grant me any boon within yer power. Well, I got ye here safe, and now I want ye to honor yer word. It's within yer power to grant me yer hand in marriage. That's what I'm asking.''

She knew then how a drowning victim must feel—to be going under for the last time and suddenly be thrown a rope. How she longed to clasp the lifeline Harris offered her. She did not dare, for fear of pulling him into the murky depths with her.

Tentatively she reached out. Her fingers grazed the healing gash on his temple. "Haven't ye been put to enough trouble on my account? I made my bed, Harris. Now I must lie in it. Ye don't have to pretend ye're one of those book heroes.''

The color drained from his face. Did he honestly think she'd *prefer* to wed Roderick Douglas than him? Better, perhaps, if he did.

"Are ye going back on yer word, lass? I know I can't give ye all the *things* he can, but if ye'll give me a chance, I know I can make ye happy.''

The plea in those dear, wounded eyes undid her. "Oh, Harris, don't ye see? It's not *ye* I'm doubting. Ye couldn't pick a worse wife than me. The first sign of trouble and I'd be gone—just like yer ma.''

He grasped her by the arms. If Roderick had done it, Jenny would have flinched, fearing what would come next.

With Harris she trusted no harm would come to her, no matter how intense his emotions.

"Ye're *not* like my ma, Jenny. Nor like yers, neither. Ye're strong, and stubborn, and loyal. Did ye run away that day in the river, when ye thought Levi Augustine and his lads were going to hack me to pieces?"

"Well, of course not, but..." The notion transfixed Jenny. She had stood her ground once—for Harris. Could she do it again? "That was different. I didn't have time to think of what I'd do. It's one thing to stand fast for a moment, but it's another thing altogether to stay when life grinds ye down day after day. Ye may trust me, Harris, but I don't trust myself. I won't see ye hurt on my account any worse than ye have been."

He glanced over at the vicar, the Chatham magistrate, and Roderick Douglas. Their argument over the marriage license was obviously winding to a close.

"Listen to me, lass. *Nothing* on this earth could hurt me worse than the thought of ye wed to a brute like Douglas. It almost drove me mad every step of the way to Richibucto. Don't turn me down because ye think ye're being noble and doing what's best for me. Trust that I know my own mind and keep yer promise."

Jenny reeled. Knowing now how she loved Harris, she only wanted what was best for him. He had twisted that concern and left her with no option. One way or another, she would hurt him.

The vicar cleared his throat. The wedding guests, who'd been whispering feverishly amongst themselves, fell silent. Jenny wasn't sure if she was still breathing.

"Mr. Chisholm, although this situation is highly irregular, your document appears genuine." The vicar cast a sheepish glance at Roderick Douglas.

"I still say it's a forgery. Where did a penniless newcomer like him get the cash for a marriage license?"

Harris replied in a voice of calm strength. "No man is

destitute if he has friends, Douglas. But I don't expect ye've much experience of that.''

''Why you troublemaking scoundrel...'' Roderick strode toward Harris, one black-gloved hand raised.

Jenny stepped between them. She shut her eyes, fully expecting to feel the full force of the blow.

She heard the vicar cry, ''Mr. Douglas, please!''

Opening her eyes again, she saw Roderick fight to regain his composure. Lowering his hand, he held it out to her.

''The license means nothing, Janet, if you tell everyone Chisholm is lying. Come, let's have this over and get on with our wedding.''

No question the man had an air of command. When he ordered, it was difficult to refuse. After the way she'd treated Harris, she deserved no better than this. Jenny drew a deep breath and blurted out her answer.

Harris waited for Jenny to speak. His innards bounded like butter in a churn. From the look on her face, he knew she'd come to recognize Roderick Douglas for what he was. Even knowing that, was it possible she would choose a life with Douglas to a life with him? And if she did—how would he bear it?

''I'm sorry,'' she began, looking deep into his eyes.

An invisible fist thrust into his chest.

''What Mr. Chisholm says is true. I did make him a promise, before we left Scotland. I didn't think he meant to hold me to it, so I went ahead with my wedding to Mr. Douglas. But, if Harris wants me after all, I must honor my first pledge.''

Had he heard aright—or did he long so deeply to hear those words that his ears had manufactured them?

''Whore!'' spat Roderick Douglas. ''Bitch! Strumpet! You were lifting your skirt for this oaf every step of the way from Dalbeattie, I'll wager.''

This outpouring of bile released Harris from his paralysis of wonder. The realization that he'd won Jenny sent him surging forward on a crest of unnatural strength. Gripping Roderick Douglas by his pristine white stock, Harris pulled him clear off the floor.

"I'll thank ye to keep a civil tongue in yer head about *my* bride. And mind the preacher about foul language in kirk."

Douglas struggled free. Looking out at the dumbstruck wedding guests, he made an effort to remuster his lost dignity. "Take her then. I wouldn't have her now, in any case. A loose little baggage like that is hardly the wife for a man in my position." With a parting glare at Jenny, he stalked out of the church.

After a moment's stunned silence, the wedding guests rose and departed, until the sanctuary was deserted but for Harris and Jenny, the vicar and Captain Glendenning.

Harris drew Jenny toward the altar.

"Will ye marry us, sir?" he asked the vicar.

"Bless my soul, why not?" The vicar adjusted his spectacles. "In for a penny, in for a pound, I suppose. You'll need another witness, though."

"I'll stand witness," said a husky, feminine voice from the back of the church.

"Morag!" Harris tried to infuse his smile with a thousand welcomes. "What are ye doing here? This is dangerous for ye."

"I had a feeling ye might need me." She glided up the aisle and took her place beside Jenny. "Ye certainly made a grand entrance, Harris. I'd have given five pounds to see Douglas's face when ye walked in the door."

Harris would have given anything to *forget* the naked threat in Black Roderick's eyes. He needed to get Jenny safely married to him so there could be no question of her returning to that man.

He flashed his bride what he hoped was a reassuring

smile. "We've got our witnesses, Vicar. Let's get this done."

The clergyman heaved a sigh so massive it vibrated his tiny frame. "Dearly beloved, we are gathered together here in the sight of God to join *this* man and this woman in holy matrimony…"

When it came to the part about marriage being ordained to prevent fornication and for the procreation of children, a stinging blush rose in Harris's cheeks. It was not enough to have the license signed and the vows read. To insure Jenny's safety from Roderick Douglas, they'd have to consummate their union, as soon as possible. Part of him roused at the prospect, but another part shrank from it. Having such pitifully little experience with women, could he make his beloved Jenny happy?

As they repeated their vows, Jenny's voice quavered with uncertainty. Harris strove to give his words enough conviction for both of them. Yet, deep in his heart, he doubted. Had Jenny wed him only because he'd forced her, and because he represented an escape from Roderick Douglas? Could a marriage thrive built on such shifting sand? He had told Jenny that seeing her wed to Roderick Douglas would hurt him even more than the possibility she might desert him. Now he was not so sure.

The mood of the wedding lifted slightly when it came time to sign the register. Jenny looked so proud of herself, being able to write her name. A lump rose in Harris's throat as he watched her. Perhaps he could not shower her with silk and diamonds, but he had given her the priceless gift of literacy.

"Where will we go now?" Jenny asked, as their subdued bridal party left the church.

"Back to the *St. Bride,*" replied Harris. "Tomorrow she casts off for Jamaica. I'm certain I can find work there, perhaps on one of the big estates. Robert Jardine wrote me a letter of introduction to some folks in Kingston."

He tried to sound enthusiastic about the prospect. True, the West Indies had long been settled and would provide a more amenable life-style than this rough-hewn frontier colony. But Harris liked New Brunswick. Its landscape had much in common with his native Galloway. The virgin territory offered men of resource and imagination a place to make their mark.

Captain Glendenning cleared his throat. ''Hold yer horses, lad. The crew passed the hat, ye might say, and came up with the price of a room at the inn for ye tonight.''

It was difficult to tell if the captain's perpetually weather-reddened face sported a blush. Harris thought it might.

''A ship's berth is no fit place for a bride to pass her wedding night,'' added the master of the *St. Bride* gruffly. ''Consider it a wedding present.''

No question that Jenny was blushing. ''That was very...thoughtful, Captain. Only...'' She looked from Harris to Morag and back. ''It might not be wise to linger in Chatham any longer than we have to.''

''She's right.'' Harris hated to admit it. Much as he longed to undertake the ordeal of their wedding night in the relative quiet and privacy of the inn, he had better reason than most to fear retaliation from Roderick Douglas.

''Don't fret yerself on that account,'' Captain Glendenning nodded to the kirkyard gate, where two members of his crew idled. ''Young Thomas and the bosun offered to keep watch at the doors so no one'll disturb ye.''

As Harris searched for adequate words of thanks, Jenny raised herself on tiptoe and planted a kiss on the master's rough cheek. He grinned self-consciously.

''Ye haven't much choice that I can tell. Who knows what kind of foolery the crew's apt to get up to if ye spend the night on board.''

Taking the hand Harris offered, he shook it warmly. ''Go along with ye, now. Ye'll want to turn in early, for we sail at sunrise tomorrow. I'll see Miss McGregor back to her home.''

Harris swallowed a massive lump in his throat. ''To the inn it is.''

He could not bring himself to look his bonny bride in the face. Had he gone through so much to win Jenny, only to lose her where it mattered most?

Chapter Twenty-One

As Harris nudged open the door of their room at the inn, a billow of hot air surged out into the hall, redolent with the fumes of lye, camphor and ammonia. With his leg still a bit lame, there was no question of him hoisting Jenny up and carrying her over the threshold. Instead, he stood back to let her enter first. Their bridal chamber was nowhere near the size of the bedrooms at Roderick Douglas's house, reflected Jenny. In fact, it was not much of an improvement over a cabin on the *St. Bride*—unless you counted the advantage of privacy.

A high tester bed occupied most of the limited space, with a three-foot-wide easement at the side and the foot. Wedged tightly into the opposite corner, a three-legged washstand was the only other piece of furniture in the room. A heavy china basin sat on top of it, a ewer of water on the shelf below, while a matching chamber pot rested on the floor beneath.

By the foot of the bed, a single narrow window looked out onto the roof of the house next door. Three wooden pegs on the wall beside the door, and a candle sconce by the head of the bed, completed the spartan amenities. Perhaps to compensate for its other deficiencies, the cramped little room looked and smelled painfully clean.

Jenny stared at the bed. "It's hot as Hades in here!"

Tossing her shawl and bonnet onto the quilt, she flew to the window. With an energetic tug, she managed to wrench it open a little way. The still, heavy air outside brought little relief, but it did give the smell someplace else to go.

The door swung closed on squealing hinges. Jenny glanced back to find Harris gingerly settling himself on the edge of the bed. They held their positions for some time without exchanging a word. The confines of the stifling little room imposed an awkward intimacy. At the moment, they were as far apart as they could get—less than ten feet.

Faint noises drifted in through the half-open window, muffled by the torpid air: the clop of horses' hooves, the rhythmic pounding of a hammer, the forlorn sound of a dog howling. Jenny could barely hear them over the loud, rapid thumping of her heart.

Abruptly Harris stood up. Keeping his back to Jenny, he took off his coat and hung it on one of the pegs by the door. Seeing the dark patches of sweat below his shirt collar and under his sleeves, she suddenly felt conscious of the beads of moisture trickling down between her own shoulder blades.

Harris cleared his throat. "Ye might as well know, straight off…" He did not turn to look at her. "I've only a vague idea of what's supposed to go on between us now."

His voice sounded so lost and anxious, it eased Jenny's own apprehension. She sidled along the perimeter of the bed until she was standing beside him—close, but not quite touching.

"Ye mean, ye've never…?" she asked in disbelief.

He shook his head, eyes firmly fixed on the floor.

"Not even…?" Jenny tried to phrase her inquiry as delicately as possible.

Harris seemed to catch the drift of her half-asked question. Head still hung, he glanced over at her. An embarrassed grin rippled across his lips.

"Do ye think a fellow who's too backward to court a proper lass would have the nerve to pay a call on a Glasgow whorehouse?"

Her bridegroom's blunt admission prompted a hiccup of nervous laughter from Jenny.

"I'm sorry," he said.

It made no sense to feel shy of each other now, Jenny thought, not after all they'd been through together. Harris had made no secret of his desire for her. She'd assumed he knew exactly what it was he desired. Heaven knows, she had! One of them would have to make the first move, Jenny decided, or this would be a very awkward marriage. At the altar of St. Mary's, she'd sworn in her heart never to give Harris the slightest cause to regret making her his bride.

Summoning all her nerve, she reached out and took his hand. "What is it ye're sorry for?" she whispered. "Sorry ye had to go to all the trouble of wedding a daft, heedless, stubborn wench, just to save her from the likes of Roderick Douglas?"

Harris looked her in the face then, pulling his spare frame to its full dignified height. "I'll never be sorry for that, if ye're not. I've wanted ye long, Jenny. I haven't much to offer a wife. Not compared to a man like Rod Douglas."

A bright blush spread up from his collar. He looked down at his hand clasped in hers. "It seemed the least I could do—knowing enough to make it easy for ye…the first time."

She gave his hand a reassuring squeeze. "Ye needn't talk so daft, Harris Chisholm. Ye're a fine catch for any lass. Ye're the cleverest man I know, and not just book-learning, either. Ye're honorable, and brave, and kind-hearted. Whenever I see yer face I want to smile. Whenever ye're near, I want ye nearer still. And when ye're not around, it's like the sun's gone behind a cloud and the birds have stopped singing.''

She hesitated. ''As for the other…I ken we're clever enough to puzzle it out between us. I'm willing to try, if ye are?''

''Oh, aye.'' A tender, hopeful smile spread up from Harris's mouth, igniting an amber glow in his hazel eyes. It transformed his battered face into the handsomest Jenny had ever seen. She raised her free hand, brushing her fingers against his auburn whiskers in a gesture of affection and trust.

Far less to fear from the gentle, clumsy ardor of Harris Chisholm than from the practiced seduction and lurking violence of Roderick Douglas. So Jenny thought, as her new husband bent forward to deliver a kiss. She tilted her head to meet it. Tentatively their lips brushed. Then, perhaps recalling that he had kissed her before—kissed her well enough to make her want more—he let his tongue dart between her slightly parted lips. Jenny gave a little gurgle of surprise deep in her throat, which subsided into a purr of enjoyment.

When Harris finally drew back to catch his breath, she reached up, twining her arms tightly around his neck. ''Ye've made a fine start, Mr. Chisholm,'' she whispered, her own breath coming fast. ''Don't stop now.''

Harris pulled the pins from her hair, catching his fingers in her unbound curls. He dropped a kiss on her earlobe. ''Ah, Mrs. Chisholm…'' His voice lingering with proprietary warmth on the word *Mrs.* ''I couldn't stop now if I wanted to.''

They kissed again, their lips quivering with anticipation. Harris's left hand remained in Jenny's hair, massaging the back of her head, maintaining the gentle pressure of her face toward his. Slowly his right hand fell to her shoulder in a fluttering caress. It trailed down her arm halfway to the elbow before making a daring detour inward to the soft swell of her bosom. There it came to rest, with a feather-light touch that demanded nothing, *asked* everything. Jenny strained forward, offering herself to his hand while she reached back, tugging impatiently at the buttons of her bodice.

Pulling away from her, Harris dropped back to his seat on the bed. He appeared to be making a determined, though not entirely successful, effort to master his eagerness. "Hold a minute there, lassie."

Jenny fought back a hoot of laughter. Harris sounded as though he was trying to rein in a runaway mare.

"Until we get to yer trunk on the *St. Bride,* ye've only got the gown ye're wearing," he explained in a husky, breathless tone. "Ye ought to have a care of it."

"Aye, ye're right," she agreed, promptly twirling about and presenting her back to him. "Will ye do the honors?"

She could feel his fingers, usually so deft, fumble over the close row of tiny buttons.

"Just try to stop me," she heard him murmur as the dress fell open.

When the last button had broken free, Jenny took a step back toward the bed. She could feel Harris's knees part to accommodate her full skirts. He drew the sleeves of her wedding dress off her shoulders and down her arms, his hands acquainting themselves with her bare skin. In spite of the heat, Jenny felt her flesh ripple into goose bumps. Her nipples stiffened, pushing out against the lace of her chemise. If Harris's hands found their way to the front of her shift, Jenny suspected his concern for her dress might be in vain. Skipping just out of his reach, she let the heather-colored silk fall in rustling folds around her ankles.

She gathered the garment up and hung it carefully beside Harris's coat. Bending forward, she pulled off her shoes and began to roll down her stockings. The sound of a sharp inhalation made her glance up. She saw Harris pulling distractedly at his neck linen, his gaze firmly fixed on the scoop neckline of her shift and the cleft between her breasts that showed above it. He finally managed to pull his stock loose, disengaging the top several buttons of his shirt in the process. The open collar and flying fillets of his stock gave him an endearingly raffish air.

"Have I ever told ye what a bonny lass ye are, Jenny?"

"Ye're not so bad yerself," she replied, looking up at him through her lashes in a deliberately flirtatious manner. "But I feel as though there's a party and I'm the only one going. Do ye plan to take off any more of yer clothes, or are ye waiting for me to help ye?"

Harris's smile grew broader, if possible. "That sound's a right inviting prospect, m'dear."

Straightening up, Jenny reached back to untie her petticoats. "Well, in the meantime ye can make yerself useful by hanging up my shawl and bonnet and turning down the bed."

The layers of starched cotton and lace slid over Jenny's hips, followed by Harris's wondering stare. "If ye can stop yer gawking long enough, that is," she added with an exasperated chuckle.

Harris managed to wrest his gaze away from Jenny long enough to see her shawl and bonnet safely hung up, and the bedding pulled down. Before he had a chance to turn back from the latter task, Jenny kicked her crinolines aside and stepped up behind him. Pressing lightly against Harris, she reached for the buttons of his trousers.

"There's one thing ye needn't be shy about," she teased. "I've seven brothers, ye ken? Ye've nothing I haven't seen a time or two before."

That wasn't quite accurate, she decided a few minutes later, after she'd helped Harris shed the last of his clothes. None of the boys had been quite so generously endowed as her husband. Certainly none of them had boasted such tantalizing thatches of golden-brown body hair, glowing softly in the dim light of an overcast afternoon. Fascinated, Jenny couldn't resist running her hand over the silky mat on his chest, letting it stray to the firm, smooth plane of his belly.

Harris sank back onto the pillows. "Oh," he groaned. "Go easy on me, lass. It's been a rough week."

Jenny chuckled. Humor had helped to ease the strain of this first awkward encounter. It would go a long way toward compensating for their mutual lack of experience.

"Do ye not want me to touch ye again, then?" she asked with feigned innocence as her index finger delicately traced a line from Harris's knee up his inner thigh. Not quite touching the skin, it skimmed over the fine hairs on his leg.

"I didn't say that." Emboldened by her shameless interest in his body, he loosed the top button of her shift. "I'm just trying to tell ye, a man can only exercise so much restraint when a beautiful woman sets to rouse him like that."

"Do ye think I'm beautiful?" Jenny asked, searching the warm depths of his eyes for the truth. She wasn't teasing now. He'd called her a bonny lass and she knew he meant it. As she'd always heard it used, *bonny* meant little more than rosy and healthy. The English word *beautiful* carried connotations of delicacy and distinction.

With a look that took in every nuance of her face, Harris replied solemnly, "Indeed ye are, lass. Beautiful as an angel in a painting."

As he tugged open several more buttons on Jenny's shift, her breasts suddenly tumbled free of the restraining undergarment. Full and firm, moist with a fine dew of perspiration, one fell blatantly into the palm of his hand. His smile quirked into a roguish grin.

"Or maybe a goddess," he amended.

Jenny's reply stuck in her throat. The sensation of his

hand cupping her bare breast made her feel faint with pleasure.

In a gesture of reverent homage to his goddess, Harris bent forward, brushing the tawny pink nipple with his lips.

Jenny gasped. "Is that how it feels when I touch ye? As though all yer bones had melted like a crock of butter in the sun, and yer body's gone all warm and limp and yielding?"

"Nay," mumbled Harris as he took the outthrust nub of her breast into his mouth. He ran his tongue over it, in a series of delicate swipes that made Jenny respond with convulsive gasps of delight. Then, nuzzling his way up her breast, throat and chin, he assailed her mouth with a kiss that left her dizzily imploring for another.

"When ye touch me, lass…" He kissed her cheeks and her brow. "I feel like I've pitch in my veins instead of blood, and ye've just set it on fire." He kissed her hair and the exquisitely sensitive spot on her neck, just below her ear. "I feel like I'm swelling up with pleasure, aching from the effort to contain it."

Jenny understood what Harris meant about the ache of pleasure. Her breasts ached with it, and the hot, secret place between her thighs. With every beat of her pulse it throbbed a plea, growing more urgent by the second. *Touch me. Kiss me. Take me. Fill me.*

She arched her hips high off the bed as Harris eased her pantelettes down. As much as she was capable of thought at that moment, Jenny wondered that a cloud of steam was not rising off her sultry lower limbs. Responding to her body's urgent demands, she twisted her hips to nudge against his hand.

"Do ye think ye're ready, lass?" he whispered.

"How should I know?" Jenny asked impatiently. "Never done this before, have I?" She pressed herself against Harris and kissed him hard. "I just know I want ye now, whether I'm ready or not."

Harris rolled onto his back. "I ken it hurts a lass some the first time. Why don't ye lie on top of me. That way ye can take it as slow as ye like."

Accepting that generous invitation, Jenny straddled his belly, using her hand to guide his entry into the warm, wet crevice between her legs. She felt a pang of resistance within her, but the powerful urges that ruled her body would not be denied. With a hard, purposeful thrust of her hips, she impaled her virginity on the shaft of his desire. Biting back an exclamation of pain, she heard Harris gasp a Gaelic oath.

She brought her head down to rest on his chest. He wrapped his arms around her, rubbing her shoulders and back with one hand, running the other over the round, firm flesh of her rump.

"That wasn't so bad," Jenny mused softly. Not so good, either, she confessed to herself with a twinge of disappointment. Whetted by the feel and the taste of Harris, her ravenous appetite hungered for so much more.

"We're not done yet," he murmured, planting a kiss on the top of her head.

"Not done?" She looked up at him in surprise. "What do ye mean? We've coupled, haven't we?"

"We've made a brave start. But I've still to sow my seed in ye. It's how babies are bred, ye ken."

"How do ye go about that?" Jenny's hips gave a slight reflexive twitch, sending the most delicious sensations skittering through her.

Harris writhed beneath her and she could feel his taut, lean muscles contract. "Keep that up, lass, and it won't take very long." He seemed to hiss the words on a breath drawn in through his clenched teeth.

"I...see." Concentrating, she lifted her hips and eased them down again. Oh, yes. This was what her body craved so desperately.

"That's the way, lass." Harris brought his hands down

to cup her buttocks, helping to lift her nearly free of him before letting her slide back on.

Eight strokes. Nine. The sweet sense of yearning mounted to an almost unbearable pitch. With a convulsive shudder, her body became a nexus of pleasure so intense it bordered on pain. Jenny pressed her face into Harris's chest, greedily inhaling the briny musk of his sweat, trying to muffle her cries. She heard him utter a deep, wild growl as his hips plowed up hard, burying himself deep within her. Then he subsided, limp and spent.

For a time they lay still, their throbbing hearts and panting breath gradually slowing. At last Harris raised a hand to Jenny's hair. With infinite gentleness, he fondled her moist, tousled curls.

"Is my heart beating still?" he asked in a hoarse whisper.

Jenny looked up at him, propping her chin on his breastbone. "Aye. Did ye think it wouldn't be?"

Raising his eyebrows, Harris pursed his lips in a droll grimace. "For a while there, I didn't ken whether my heart would burst in my chest, or just stop dead altogether."

"Did I hurt ye that much?" Jenny asked with a pang of remorse.

"Nay. What makes ye think ye hurt me, lass?"

"Well, the noises ye were making, for a start." She cast an embarrassed glance back at the barely open window. "If anyone heard ye, they likely thought I was hacking yer bowels out with a dull knife!"

Harris laughed until his body shook with it, bouncing Jenny crazily atop him. The sound and the movement proved an infectious combination. Soon Jenny was laughing, too—laughing with relief and gratitude and happiness. It took them a while to master this mirth. But in time they laughed themselves out, surrendering to a contented exhaustion.

Jenny rested her head in the hollow of Harris's shoulder,

vaguely wondering if he might be squashed by the dead weight of her body on his for so long. For her part, she felt as light as thistledown. Why, a warm breeze might blow in at any moment and waft her up to the ceiling. Seared in the crucible of passion, she no longer even noticed the heat of the room.

"Harris?" she murmured, not looking up. "Did ye ken it would be like that?"

He raised a hand, sliding the backs of his fingers over her cheek. "Nay, lass. Not in my wildest dreams. Did ye?"

Jenny shook her head. "Do ye suppose it's like that for everyone?"

"I don't reckon so," Harris mused. "If it was, folks'd never get anything else done."

Jenny smiled to herself. "Do ye ken it'll always be like that for us?"

Harris chuckled quietly. "Ye are full of questions tonight, aren't ye? I'll tell ye one thing, lass. If it's never that good between us again, I'll be plenty grateful to have felt like that just once in my life."

Nuzzling his chest, Jenny planted a light kiss over his heart. It pleased her to know she had given Harris the same brush with ecstacy he'd given her. A sense of ease and deep satisfaction stole over her. Hovering on the brink of sleep, she roused herself slightly.

"Harris?" she whispered.

"Aye," he murmured drowsily. "What now?"

"I love ye, Harris." With all her heart she prayed it would be enough. That she could find the strength within herself to keep on loving him through good times and bad, as she'd vowed.

He slipped one arm around her waist. With his other hand Harris cradled her head against him, as though he wanted his body to open and take her into himself, as she had taken him.

"And I love ye, lass. It'll be all right—ye'll see. We belong to each other, you and I. That's all that matters."

As Jenny surrendered to the sweet peace of sleep, she prayed that Harris was right.

Outside on the streets of Chatham, the air was unbearably close and hot. No breeze blew from the river or the sea to bring a breath of relief. From the surrounding forest there rumbled a faint sound like far-off thunder or the report of distant artillery. Thick dark clouds shrouded the sky, their undersides glowing an eerie, lurid yellow.

Chapter Twenty-Two

Harris woke later, with no idea what time it might be. His stomach growled piteously, reminding him that he hadn't eaten since early morning. It must be evening, he decided, though a queer amber light filtered in the narrow window, gilding the outline of objects in the room and casting unnatural shadows. It must have been every minute of eight o'clock, yet he could see Jenny quite clearly. That was all that mattered.

If he lived to be a hundred, he would never take for granted the daily miracle of waking next to her. His body roused anew at the sight of her stretched out beside him, splendidly naked. He could happily spend an eternity exploring the lush landscape of her body with his eyes. Followed by another eternity questing with his hands. And another roving with his lips...

He remembered the hot, ravenous way she had gripped him at the height of their lovemaking. Tugging him over the brink of desire into the sweet, churning cascade of release. She had plunged over the waterfall with him and drunk deeply from the well of pleasure. That knowledge warmed Harris and lightened him in a way he'd never known before.

Unable to resist the urge to lose himself in Jenny once

again, he slid down until he could press his face into the dewy fullness of her bosom. She stirred lazily, causing one daintily arched nipple to brush his lower lip. Harris did not stop to wonder if it was a deliberate invitation. His lips parted in a reflex as old as time, shaping themselves to envelop her with a smooth, wet grip—a delicious reversal of how she had recently favored him.

A sound bubbled from her throat, halfway between an infectious chuckle and mellow purr of enjoyment. "Ye know what, Harris?" She didn't give him time to reply—perhaps she could not bear to distract his lips from their present occupation. "I ken this may be like reading or playing the fiddle. We'll get better at it the more we practice."

Reluctantly he released his intoxicating hold, with a lingering caress from his tongue. "I'm willing to drill for hours on end, until we get it right." His words slurred, as though his mouth resented being pressed into service for speech when it had found much more exciting occupations.

"Drill?" She ran a playful hand over his shoulder and down his chest. "Ye make it sound like soldiers marching up and down the square. I think we ought to *wander* a bit. Ye know…explore?"

"Experiment?" Harris teased, licking his way down her belly, parting her thighs with gentle but eager hands.

"Aye." She sighed. "Experiment."

That word hung urgingly in the air when the door suddenly crashed open.

Jenny screamed and grasped for the bedclothes to cover herself. Harris scrambled to come between his bride and whatever danger might be upon them.

"Now what mischief are ye getting up to, boyo?" a sickeningly familiar voice mocked him. "I thought yer tumble in the graveyard would take all the starch outta yer trousers. But there's no teaching a tomcat, I guess."

They lunged for him.

An enormous fist caught Harris a glancing blow to the jaw. A hand pinned one of his flailing arms. He struck blindly with the other, exulting in the solid contact and the ensuing roar of pain.

He lashed out with his feet, as well. This was no time for finesse. One landed against something solid but yielding. Following the sound of a breathless grunt, Harris dove at the shifting shadow. He brawled like a madman—fists, elbows, knees and feet thrashing at once with all the force he could put behind them. The bulky phantom—Sweeney, he presumed—raised his arms to fend off the delirious rain of blows.

Take that for Morag! And that for the lies against Levi Augustine's people! Take this one for tossing me into the bush, half-dead! And this one for not letting a man make love to his wife in peace!

"Leave off, Chisholm! I've got yer woman."

Harris checked a blow of righteous vengeance to Sweeney's ample midsection. In the unearthly light from the window, he could make out the muscular figure of McBean holding a knife to Jenny's face.

"Leave her be," Harris cried as visions of Morag McGregor haunted him. "What do ye want with me?"

"Just come to take ye for a little walk, is all."

"Yer boss wanted me to see the Miramichi by moonlight before I leave, is that it?" Harris infused the question with scorn.

"Aye, ye might say so."

"Let me dress, and get ye clear of my wife. Then I'll come peaceably."

Even as her eyes homed in on McBean's knife in widened terror, Jenny cried, "No, Harris, ye mustn't!"

"Don't fret yerself, lass. I'll be fine." Groping for his shirt and trousers, Harris tried to charge his words with an assurance he did not feel. "Once we get clear of here, I want ye to go board the *St. Bride*. Stick close to Captain

Glendenning. I'll find my way back to ye, come what may—I promise.''

''Oh, leave off, Chisholm,'' growled McBean, ''before ye set me bawling.''

''Or puking,'' grunted Sweeney.

Ignoring the stares of their uninvited guests, Jenny dove to grab Harris's hand. Pulling him back onto the bed, she kissed him with all the pent-up ardor of a lifetime. Much as his body yearned to linger, he could not take the chance of Roderick's ruffians getting unseemly ideas. He doubted either of them would scruple defiling Jenny and making him watch.

With bitter reluctance, he tore himself free of her. ''Do as I say, lass. To the *St. Bride!*''

From one of the other rooms, someone shouted a complaint about the noise.

Sweeney jerked him toward the door. ''Enough of this billin' and cooin'. Let's go.''

Though he found his injured ankle much improved, Harris exaggerated his limp, groaning softly with each step. Once out of the inn, they paused long enough for McBean to tie his hands behind him. Seeing a figure huddled beside an empty rain barrel, Harris wondered if it might be the bosun of the *St. Bride*. He prayed the man was only unconscious.

They herded him down toward the river, where a rowboat waited. One of them pushed Harris in. He barely escaped braining himself on the oarlock. As the small craft approached the opposite bank of the Miramichi, he let himself exhale a breath of relief, knowing the width of the river lay between Jenny and the men who had attacked them. Now that she was safe, he could think about himself.

''What are ye meaning to do with me?'' he asked, as they manhandled him ashore.

Sweeney snickered. ''Not a thing in the world, boyo. It's them Indians—the savages. They're going to slit yer throat and peel the scalp off ye and who knows what all else.''

His hackles rose to hear the man discuss such atrocities in morbid jest. ''Then Roderick Douglas will lead a raid on the Mi'kmaq to avenge my untimely death?'' Harris's tone dripped acid sarcasm.

''Ye're right quick on the uptake, Scotty-lad. I'll give ye that. Yeah, the boss'll put the boots to them Indians all right. Says they got control of too bloody much land and they don't do nothing with it. He's got big plans for it, though. Plans for comforting yer fair widow, too.''

Harris could picture the leering grin on Sweeney's broad face. His fists ached to erase it—permanently.

A faint breeze stirred the trees beside the road. Harris gulped a deep breath, then coughed and spat.

''Ash! The air's full of ash. It must be a fire in the woods that's casting that queer light and making the noise.''

''Fire?'' McBean barked a derisive laugh. ''Something's always burning around here this time of year. Don't fret yer head about it, Chisholm. Ye got worse things to worry about.''

He didn't intend to hang about and find out what they might be, Harris reflected. If only something would distract this pair for a moment, he'd seize the opportunity to give them the slip.

The idea had scarcely formed in his mind when a deafening noise, like a clap of nearby thunder, roared from the woods. The earth trembled. Then came another great crash and another.

In the midst of his own shock and vivid images of Judgment Day, Harris realized he would get no better distraction. Pretending to stagger on this wounded ankle, he hooked his leg around McBean's at the knee. McBean lurched forward into his partner. Harris did not pause to watch them fall.

He bolted into the undergrowth, ran a few steps, dropped

to the ground and rolled. Then he froze. In the time it would take his pursuers to grope around for him, he might work his hands free.

Thundering clamor continued to issue from the forest in waves, and with each report the earth shook. Thankful that the din masked his panting breath, Harris heard Sweeney and McBean blundering through the dry brush, cursing him and each other. With fingers numb and clumsy, he tugged at the rope knotted around his wrists. They'd be on him soon.

"Fire!" Muted by the general tumult, the cry and the frantic tattoo of horses' hooves sounded on the road. "The whole Miramichi's ablaze! Get to the river while you can!"

A fresh volley of thunder discharged from the woods, pushing in its path a rain of glowing cinders. Abandoning their search, Sweeney and McBean turned tail and ran.

With a final desperate tug, Harris managed to free his hands. He hissed in pain as the blood surged back into them.

One of the falling cinders lit on a parchment-dry fern, which burst into flame. Harris stamped the tiny blaze out, only to see others lighting all around him.

The whole Miramichi ablaze? The notion struck terror deep in his bowels and fanned long-smoldering memories into open flame. He must get back to Chatham and make sure Jenny had boarded the *St. Bride*.

Roderick Douglas was the least of their problems now.

As the footsteps of Harris and his captors retreated down the hallway, Jenny fumbled for her clothes. Under her breath, she cursed the fancy silk gown. What she wouldn't give just now for serviceable cotton and a sturdy apron.

"Don't get dressed too quickly, Janet."

Jenny stifled the scream that rose in her throat. "Damn

ye to the devil, Roderick Douglas! Ye're behind this, aren't ye? Where have those men taken Harris?''

From out of the shadows, a hand slammed into Jenny's cheek, sending her reeling with tiny lights flickering before her eyes.

''Shut up, you deceitful slut! Do you have any notion of how you shamed me at that church? In front of people like Pruitt and Billings. I'll be the laughingstock of Halifax and Boston, as well as the Miramichi.''

He shut the door behind him and his voice changed suddenly. Quiet—almost wistful. ''We could have had a fine life together, Janet. Why did you throw it all away for that gangling buffoon? You betrayed my love.''

Her cheek smarted from the force of his blow, urging Jenny to hold her tongue lest he deal her another—or worse. But the white-hot flame of indignant rage consumed her caution like so much dry tinder.

''Love? Do ye ken what the word means, Roderick Douglas? I wounded yer pride, and I don't regret it. That kind of pride's a sin.''

She gasped as his hard hand snaked into her hair, coiling itself around and pulling her face close to his.

''I like you this way, Janet,'' he whispered. ''All fiery and defiant. You were such a meek mouse before, there was no *sport* in breaking you.''

Where had this defiant spirit come from? Jenny wondered. Was it her freedom from dependence on Roderick Douglas? Was it payback for the way he'd bossed and bullied her these past weeks? Or could it be a strength born of her love for Harris, the security of his love for her.

She spat in Roderick's face.

Bracing herself for a blow that would make her ears ring, she hardly knew what to make of it when he only laughed.

''I fear you're going to be a widow very soon, my dear Janet. This is an unforgiving land for a woman on her own. I couldn't possibly marry you now, of course. But you'll do well enough for my whore, while I look for a suitable wife.''

He released her hair then, assaulting her mouth in an act of brutal possession that defiled the notion of a kiss.

In a fit of desperate fury, Jenny jerked her knee into the lap of his trousers. As he reeled back with a bellow of pain and rage, she plowed her fist squarely into his Adam's apple. Grabbing the water jug from the nightstand, Jenny brought it down on the back of his head in an explosion of water and shattered crockery.

She heard Roderick hit the floor. A low moan assured her she hadn't killed him, and that was good. She had something to say that she wanted him to hear.

''Mind me well, Roderick Douglas. If any harm comes to my husband, I won't rest until I make ye pay for it.''

With that brave, foolish threat hanging in the torpid air, Jenny hurried away. The bosun of the *St. Bride* met her at the back door of the inn.

''They snuck up on me, ma'am.'' He rubbed a spot on the back of his head. ''I just came to when I heard them hustling yer husband off. They must have got Thomas, too. I'll see ye both safe onto the *St. Bride,* then call out the crew to search for Mr. Chisholm.''

The notion was most inviting. The promise of safety lured Jenny even as Harris's final behest pushed her toward it.

''No,'' she said, after a brief but intense struggle within herself. ''I can't go with ye, bosun. Find Thomas and see *him* back to the barque. I know Chatham better than any of the *St. Bride*'s crew and I can't afford to lose the time finding Harris. Did ye see which way they went?''

The bosun pointed down toward the river. Hoisting her cumbersome skirts, Jenny set off at a run.

After reaching the wharf, she hunted for someone to give her information.

"Have ye seen three men about?" she called to a fer-ryman lolling on his barge.

"I seen lotsa men." He spat into the river. "Ships are full of 'em. Who ya lookin' for, missy?"

"Two of them work for Mr. Douglas. One's stout and the other one has a broken—"

"Sweeney and McBean? I seen 'em cross the river not a quarter of an hour ago. Now I recollect there might have been another bloke with 'em. Staggering like he was drunk."

Jenny scrambled onto the barge. "Can ye take me across, please? I have to find them."

The man stretched and scratched his head. "Nobody in their right wits wants to find them two, missy. Scouting for trouble, that is. But if ya got a penny, I'll pole ya across."

"I haven't got any money." Jenny had never felt so helpless. Only a penny stood in the way of her finding Harris, and she didn't have that paltry sum. Not even a piece of jewelry she could barter.

"Please, sir. I promise I'll pay ye as soon as I can. I *have* to get across the river. That third man wasn't drunk. He's my husband, and Sweeny and McBean have been ordered to kill him. Perhaps ye know him—he's been around town for the past few weeks. Harris Chisholm?"

The ferryman hoisted his pole. "Sit down, missy. I seen Chisholm around town. Seemed a good sort. Many's the pint been hoisted in his honor today, for having the gall to steal Black Roderick's bride right from the chapel."

As Jenny settled herself for the crossing, her eyes stung. As much from suppressed tears as from the dust in the night air. Or was it soot?

She remembered the defiant words Harris had hurled at Roderick Douglas that morning. *No man is destitute if he has friends.* Harris had won many friends and admirers in this town for his willingness to stand up to their local tyrant. That admiration had become her currency.

The ferry had barely touched the opposite shore of the Miramichi when a loud, ominous roar broke from the forest. Above the treetops flickered a strange orange glow, not unlike a sunset. But the October sun had set over two hours ago.

And no sun had ever set in the north.

Harris lurched down the road, trying to keep his rising panic in check. He could hear the crackling of flames in the distance. Smoke hung thick in the air. Now and then a faint breeze would stir, sending down a hail of sparks.

Every instinct in him cried out to leave the road and make for the river. Harris resisted. Sweeny and McBean had run for the river. He didn't dare go there.

Behind him, he heard the pounding of horse's hooves. Harris turned to see a Clyde mare galloping toward him, tossing her great head in a frenzy. Behind her, the horse pulled a small cart.

It was on fire.

"Whoa, girl." He leapt out of the way of those massive hooves, then threw himself onto the cart. By some kind providence of the Almighty, he was able to unhook the traces without scorching his backside or having his arms torn clean from their sockets.

"Whoa, big girl!" Harris stumbled along, clinging to the reins.

With flames no longer snapping at her hocks and a man's soothing voice filling her ears, the mare slowed to a nervous walk. Crooning every blandishment he could think of, Harris threw himself across the Clyde's broad back and urged her to a jog.

At the shore, he found the rowboat Sweeney and McBean had used to bring him across the river.

"No way you'll fit in here, ye big sowdy lass." Harris

lost no time in stripping the harness from her. He stowed it in the rowboat, hoping against hope that he might eventually be able to return it to its owner.

"Thank ye for the ride, lass." He petted the big beast's nose. "Ye can probably swim better than me." With a firm swat on the rump, he urged her to wade deeper into the river.

Slowly and awkwardly, he plied the oars, coaxing the little boat across the Miramichi to the relative safety of the far bank.

A good stiff wind, Harris reflected with a chill, and that safety would disappear. On the northern horizon, all down the river, the ruddy glare of flames streaked the night sky, punctuated only by columns of dense black smoke raging heavenward.

Thank God, he and Jenny would soon be reunited aboard the *St. Bride,* fleeing this terrible inferno.

Pity swelled within his heart for the people of the Miramichi. Their hard-won independence, and the promise of future prosperity, swallowed up in the blink of an eye. Where would they go? If they had enough stubborn courage to stay, how would they survive with winter almost at hand?

Harris tried to put the thoughts from his mind, as he came alongside the *St. Bride.* It wasn't any of his concern. He had to think of Jenny and himself first. Still, after years as an outsider in Dalbeattie, he relished the easy, unconditional acceptance he'd found in this boisterous young colony.

He would miss it.

One of the crewmen recognized him and called out to the captain.

"Thank God, ye're safe and sound, Chisholm." Captain Glendenning clapped him on the back as they hoisted him aboard. "When the bosun and Thomas staggered back to us with their heads bashed, we feared the worst."

Harris clutched the master by the breast of his coat. "What about Jenny? She came with them, didn't she?"

The captain shook his head, as though reluctant to impart bad news. "Was she not with ye? Thomas didn't know what had become of either of ye and the poor bosun barely knew his own name. He passed out again shortly after they came aboard. Mumbled something about yer missus and Roderick Douglas, but I couldn't make any sense of it. What happened?"

"Douglas sent two of his men after me. They must have sneaked up and brained Thomas and the bosun first. They took me across the river to do away with me, but I gave them the slip. I told Jenny to come here."

"We've seen no sign of her." The master glanced up to the forecastle, where a falling cinder had ignited a coil of tar soaked rope. "We were just about to set sail, Harris. It's too dangerous for us to linger here."

"I have to get back to the inn to see if I can find out what's become of Jenny."

A plume of flame from the town drew Harris's eye. If these spot fires could not be contained and the blaze gained a foothold on this side of the wide Miramichi, what would stop it from sweeping down the coast to ravage Levi Augustine's hunting ground and lay waste to the Richibucto?

"Can ye give me half an hour, Angus, and will ye take a load of passengers? After I find Jenny, we'll bring aboard as many women and children as the *St. Bride* will hold. We can take them out to the safety of the strait until this is over."

"Go." The master nodded curtly. "I'm ashamed I didn't think of that myself. We'll jettison what we can to make more room."

A smaller vessel weighed anchor just then, heading for safety downriver. As it glided past the *St. Bride*, Harris recognized Roderick Douglas's private sloop. Among the crew scurrying to hoist sail, he detected the figure of a woman.

Was it only his tortured imagination—or was it Jenny?

Chapter Twenty-Three

Jenny struggled along the path, praying she was headed in the right direction. Hearing horses' hooves pounding toward her, she scooted for the safety of the underbrush, as she had several times before. Perhaps there was nothing to fear. After seeing firsthand the power Roderick Douglas wielded on the Miramichi, however, she was not about to take chances.

Another volley of thunder rolled. But where was the rain?

As the sound of the galloping horse faded, Jenny emerged from her hiding place and hurried farther down the road. She wasn't certain what she could do if she managed to catch up with Harris and his captors. Hopefully, the ferryman would deliver her message to the *St. Bride* promptly, and she'd soon have reinforcements.

No need to remind herself that Harris wouldn't be in danger now but for her. By wedding her, he had pitted himself against a powerful and ruthless man. By granting her the chivalrous luxury of a wedding night at the inn, he had left himself vulnerable to treachery. When Douglas's foul minions had burst in on them, Harris had fought like a man possessed to defend her. She had been his weakness and his downfall. Now Jenny swore she would make it up to him if it meant attacking those loathsome ruffians with her bare hands.

Another great crash cleaved the air. The earth beneath Jenny's feet trembled. This was no ordinary storm, she realized, as panic tightened around her throat.

Suddenly the forest around her erupted with animals. Jenny screamed as a large hare darted past her. A pair of foxes followed hard on its heels, but she sensed they were not in pursuit. A doe and two fawns bounded across the road in a single stride, making for the river.

Then Jenny saw the flames.

Joining the race of terror-driven wildlife, she bolted for the sanctuary of the Miramichi.

Even as she fled for her life, a small voice in the back of her mind taunted. *On the run again, Jenny. Will you never stop?*

"Come along, ma'am. Ye bring the baby and I'll carry the wee lad." Harris stooped to pick up the child.

The boy promptly kicked him in the shin. "I ain't a wee lad! I'm a big boy an' I can walk just as well as you can. Let me alone!"

Even with the urgency that goaded him, Harris had to work at stifling a smile. He glanced doubtfully at the small bare feet poking out from under the child's nightshirt.

"Aye, no doubt ye can," he gave a wry chuckle, even as his ankle twinged. "But it's a fool who walks when he can ride. Will ye let me be yer horsey?"

The boy looked to his mother, who was struggling to quiet her squalling infant.

"Do as the man says, Willy! We've got to get on that ship."

"I s'pose."

Hoping he wouldn't get a chubby knee in his kidney, Harris hoisted the lad onto his back and strode for the wharf. His ankle protested the added weight with every step. That pain was nothing to the sharp talons of dread tearing at his heart.

It hadn't come as any great surprise to find Jenny gone from the inn and no one willing to admit they'd seen her. Harris feared what the shards of a smashed pitcher on the floor might mean.

Had Roderick Douglas come and kidnapped Jenny before she could flee to the safety of the *St. Bride?* Or had she given her bridegroom up for dead and decided to take her chances with the brutal but prosperous Roderick rather than try to fend for herself? Harris wasn't certain which alternative distressed him more. The familiar desolation of being deserted threatened to engulf him again.

He fought it.

Time enough to mourn and fret about himself in the days to come. For now he must take some crumb of comfort in knowing Jenny was safe—from the fire at least—and do all he could to secure the safety of other men's families.

Tottering up the rickety gangplank, he handed the child off to an older woman who held out her arms to him. Then he steadied the boy's mother, who was having trouble boarding with the baby in her arms.

"This'll have to be the last, Harris!" called Captain Glendenning. "We can't risk staying any longer."

As if to bolster his claim, something exploded on the foredeck of a ship nearby. In seconds, the whole vessel was bathed in flames, her crew diving into the water to escape.

"Cast off!" roared the captain. As the crew made to haul the gangplank aboard, he held his hand out to Harris.

Shaking his head, Harris scrambled back onto the wharf. "I'm going to stay and do what I can to help contain the fire," he called. "Keep an eye peeled for Jenny, will ye?"

He lingered a moment watching the *St. Bride* ease into the channel.

"Chisholm," someone called. "What'll we do with these other folks?"

Harris turned to find the vicar shepherding two women, half-a-dozen children and an old man who looked ready to faint at any second.

After a moment's deliberation, he said, "Take them to Roderick Douglas's house. It's made of stone with a copper-clad roof. If any building in town survives the fire, it will."

"But, but," the vicar sputtered. "Surely we cannot... commandeer the place in his absence."

Harris offered the old man his arm and an encouraging smile. Starting off up the street, he called back to the vicar. "Commandeer—that's exactly what we must do. As ye say, Mr. Douglas is absent. He'll have no use for his house. Once he comes back, I'll answer to him if he objects."

The group picked up several more strays on the way to Roderick Douglas's house. They were within sight of it when a soot-blackened man caught up with them.

"Chisholm, can ye come? Loban's place is afire. We've had a bucket brigade going from the river, but I doubt we can save it."

"Concentrate on keeping the surrounding houses from catching, then. Wet down the roofs. Pull them down if ye have to. I'll come as soon as I get these folks to safety."

He wondered fleetingly why everyone kept coming to him for directions and advice. Perhaps they'd grown so used to living under the dictates of Roderick Douglas that initiative no longer came easily to them. He had challenged Douglas's authority and bested him—if only temporarily. Did that make him a leader in their eyes?

Harris didn't feel like a leader. He felt like a rudderless ship, far from land, blown by capricious winds, uncertain if he would ever make safe harbor again.

"Oh, Jenny," he whispered to himself. "Where have ye gone, lass? And will ye ever come back to me?"

* * *

Would she ever see Harris again? Jenny asked herself as she huddled in the shoals of the Miramichi. She did not know how long she had been there. Day and night had lost all meaning. The river had begun to boil and churn ominously, mirroring the fiery apocalypse on land. A scene from the Book of Revelations.

"Ahh!" Jenny screamed as a glowing ember landed on her shoulder.

She ducked under water, relishing the cool stillness below the surface. If only it had been possible to breathe down there...

Sputtering for air, she lifted her head again, pushing the sodden mass of hair back from her face.

The flames had marched almost to the water's edge, consuming the parched trees with swift rapacity. Harris and his captors had been some distance ahead when the fire overtook her. With disaster at hand, had Sweeney and McBean done away with Harris and let the fire hide their crime? Or had the flames taken them all by surprise?

Either way, the situation did not bode well for his survival.

A tall spruce at the very edge of the river burst into flame and pitched into the water. Swallowing a gulp of air, Jenny dove. She heard a strange, muted noise as the tree crashed. A hiss of steam, as water consumed the flames. When she lifted her head again, she shuddered to see how close the tree had come to landing on top of her.

A powerful undertow of despair threatened to swallow her. Her body reeled with fatigue and hunger and the strain of her fears for Harris. All her life she had dreaded experiencing the death of love in the face of adversity. Now she faced an unforeseen hardship—being robbed of newborn love just when it had begun to flourish.

What would become of her, supposing she did survive the fire? Could she bear to face so bleak a future? Of all the deprivations it was sure to hold, none grieved her as sorely as the loss of Harris.

How much easier it would be simply to abandon the struggle. Surrender to the seductive lure of sleep. Let the waves close over her. Pray for the mercy of a reunion with her husband on the other side of death's wide chasm.

Harris bent double, hacking the smoke from his lungs. Through this harrowing night he had somehow managed to transcend most of the dictates of his body. He was beyond hunger now, and beyond exhaustion. He still needed to breathe, though.

There wouldn't be much of Chatham uncharred after tonight. From what Harris could see, however, they had managed to stop the fire from spreading past town into another stretch of dense forest. That knowledge lifted his spirits.

In the distance, he heard a frantic cry that the church had caught fire. With one last rasping cough, he hefted his bucket and ran toward St. Mary's. His heart sank as he caught sight of it. They'd never save it now. The fire had too deep a foothold. Once the flames climbed that spire, there was nothing to do but let it burn. Except cut down the surrounding trees so they would not catch and spread the fire.

"Have ye got an ax?" he called to the two men coming out the vestry door.

As they turned toward him, he recognized the brawny build of one and the broken nose of the other.

"Well, if it ain't Scotty. Ye got more lives than a cat, boyo. I was countin' on ye gettin' well roasted on t'other side of the river."

"I could say the same. What are ye doing here?" Catching sight of the sack McBean had hoisted over one shoulder, Harris deduced the answer to his own question.

"I ain't got time to chat, Scotty-boy. And I ain't got

time to deal with ye now, so use yer head for once and stand aside.''

Rage exploded in Harris, like a cache of resin in a burning pine. He and the other men of the settlement had battled for hours to stem the tide of destruction, while these two rogues looted the town of its few valuables. Sense told him not to risk another confrontation with this pair, but he paid it no heed.

''Have ye no shame at all, looting a church?'' He took a deep breath and planted his feet wide. ''If ye mean to make away with those things, ye're going to have to get through me first.''

Sweeney took a menacing step forward. ''Have it yer own way, boyo. Guess I'll have to finish ye off, like I should've done the first time we had a go-round in this here graveyard.''

He sent one meaty fist hurling toward Harris's face, but at the last second Harris ducked under it. The force of the blow towed Sweeney along. Harris thrust out a foot, tripping him into the dust.

A jangle of silver plate hitting the ground warned Harris that McBean had joined the fray. In the orange flicker of the burning church, he caught the flash of a knife. He raised his only shield—the bucket, heavy with all the water it had soaked up.

It seemed to take him forever to hoist the pail, which grew ten times heavier for each inch he lifted it. By some miracle, though, when McBean's knife came to rest, it had embedded itself in the tight, wet wood. Harris brought the bucket up over his head and sent it hurtling down on McBean.

His momentary flash of triumph died when Sweeney grabbed his arms from behind, pinning them back with a force that nearly wrenched them from their sockets. As he tried in vain to break free, he saw McBean struggle up from the ground with a murderous light in his eyes.

"Let him go!"

Harris fought to turn toward the source of that command, but Sweeney held him tight. He prepared to use his feet, should McBean lunge at him, but McBean held his ground.

"Are ye deaf, Alf Sweeney?" demanded a second, different voice. "Let Chisholm go."

"This ain't yer fight, Tom Loban," Sweeny spat, his voice heavy with belligerence. "Now git, the lot of ye, else I'll deal with ye one at a time, later."

Harris heard a musket cock.

"We've had about all we can stomach of you two terrorizing folks around here. Now take your hands off Chisholm or I'll blow you clean to hell."

Sweeney thrust him away like a hot coal.

Harris spun around to see a crowd of Chatham men standing shoulder to shoulder. He recognized some from his weeks tending bar. Others he had met for the first time tonight, fighting fires by their side, helping to evacuate their families on the *St. Bride*.

Some carried firearms. Most wielded pitchforks. Faces blackened with soot and wet hair tufted wildly, with the Miramichi burning behind them, they looked like the very legions of hell.

Harris had never beheld a sweeter sight.

After years of submitting to the tyranny of Roderick Douglas and his hired bullies, what had it cost these men to stand up for him? More than he could ever hope to repay.

McBean made the grave mistake of trying to run for his life. A hail of shot blew apart the turf at his heels. He threw himself to the ground, quivering like a jelly.

"Don't shoot! For God's sake, don't shoot again!"

One of the other armed men looked to Harris. "Can I save us all a lot of bother and finish him off?"

Though he was sorely tempted to nod, Harris shook his head. "Let's not sink to their level. If ye can find a bit of rope, tie the pair of them up good and tight. Once the fire's over, we'll see they get justice for what they've done.''

A few of the crowd grumbled over his judgment, but most seemed willing to follow his lead.

"Somebody stow that sack of valuables at Douglas's place. Bring the axes. We'll be in trouble if those elms take fire.''

As the men dispersed to do his biding, a young lad shouldered his way toward Harris.

"Can you come, Mr. Chisholm? There's a poor creature we pulled from the river. More dead than alive he is and burned bad. Keeps calling for the master of the *St. Bride*—real agitated like. We've tried to tell him that the *St. Bride* sailed hours ago, but he don't pay no mind.''

It was on the tip for his tongue to ask why he should be the one to deal with it. But something in the boy's eyes silenced Harris.

Glancing around to make certain the elms were being felled, he called out, "I'll be back directly. Mind ye be careful when those trees drop.''

As he followed the lad back through town, toward the river, Harris began to shiver. Was it just a symptom of exhaustion, he wondered, or had the air turned colder?

They entered a warehouse near the dock, which had so far escaped the blaze. It had been converted into a make-shift infirmary for the injured, though most of the people who'd been brought in looked far past any human aid. The smell made Harris's gorge rise and the scars on his lower face itch beneath his new growth of beard.

The boy stopped at the foot of a crude pallet, where one of the fire's victims lay. From the boots protruding beneath a blanket of sailcloth, Harris guessed it must be a man. Nothing in the ravaged face suggested it was even human. The poor creature twitched and muttered in obvious agitation.

Harris winced. "Can they give him nothing for the pain?"

"Oh, he ain't in pain, sir," replied the boy. "Leastways not in his body. A light burn'll hurt like hell, but the deep ones deaden the flesh—a mercy it is, too. He's troubled in his mind. Keeps raving about the *St. Bride*."

"Let's see if we can give the poor fellow a little peace, then." Harris knelt beside the body, trying to contain his exasperation that no one here had considered the obvious.

"I'm Angus Glendenning, master of the *St. Bride*," he murmured into the contorted remains of an ear. "Ye have a message for me?"

The man instantly quieted. Then his voice wheezed out—the words blunted by his mangled vocal organs. "Went to the wrong boat. Could'n' find *St. Bride*. Got a message for ya from the lady…" A cough racked him.

"Take it easy, man. I'm not going anywhere. Ye can tell me in yer own good time."

"Can't wait. Must send men. She crossed the river after Chisholm. Never should have took her. She'll be caught in the fire."

"She?" Harris could scarcely get his own breath. "She who?" Not Jenny. Not Jenny. Not Jenny.

"Chisholm's bride. Send men to help her get him back."

A gaping pit seemed to open in the floor and swallow Harris. His heart cried out for Jenny in a high keening wail that echoed through the emptiness of his being. How could he endure such pain and still live?

Then he remembered the man on the pallet, who had struggled to deliver Jenny's message when it surely would have been easier to slip away quietly.

"Thank ye for telling me." He pushed the words out of a constricted throat. "I'll send the men she needs and it'll be fine. Ye try and rest now, mind."

The burned man drew an easy breath. Before Harris

could rise, the death rattle sounded and he was gone—mercifully. With gentle hands, Harris drew the sailcloth up over the dead man's face. This poor creature's suffering was over.

His own had just begun.

Chapter Twenty-Four

Against all odds, the sun rose that morning over the Miramichi. Few had expected to see it. The charred remains of the forest steamed in the frigid air. Snowflakes fluttered to the ground, ominous out of all proportion to their size.

Pulling his well-singed coat tightly around him, Harris cupped his hands over his mouth and breathed out to warm his fingers. He wandered down to the wharf, shaking his head at the sight of several vessels gutted by the fire. Their scorched hulls bobbed in the choppy water like blackened corpses. How many human remains they would pull from the river in the days ahead, Harris could not bear to think.

A joyous shout went up behind him. It sounded completely out of place amid such desolation. Only when the men of Chatham surged past him onto the dock did Harris notice the *St. Bride* sailing in on the morning tide, hull riding low with her precious cargo of life.

Melting back to the fringe of the crowd, he watched passively as families reunited—laughing, embracing, weeping. He wanted to rejoice for them, to mourn with them, to share and allay their fears for the future. But some unseen force had excised his heart and left in its place a chunk of stone. As with burns, the earlier hurts he'd suffered on Jenny's account had smarted and stung. This final, deepest one had cauterized his emotions.

Captain Glendenning disembarked and shouldered his way through the press of townspeople. "I've bad news for ye, Harris." He stared at the ground and swallowed hard, as if working up the nerve to say his piece.

Harris waited for the master to speak, without dread or even much curiosity.

"'Twas rough seas last night," said the captain at last. "More times than I care to recall, I thought my wee barque would end up at the bottom of the strait. But the Almighty held us in his hand and we rode it out. That's more than I can say for some."

He drew a deep breath. "Douglas's sloop floundered at the mouth of the river. Went down with all hands. I'm sorry."

In answer to Harris's questioning look, he added, "About Miss Len…that is, about yer wife."

Harris shook his head. "She wasn't with Douglas, after all."

"Oh, Thank God! The crew'll be beside themselves to hear it. Where is she?"

Nodding toward the opposite bank of the river, Harris could scarcely find his voice. "Over there somewhere. She didn't run away. She came after me. I'll need a boat to go look for her."

He did not say, *whatever the fire has left of her body*. That was what he meant, though. His face remained impassive and his words emerged calm though rather wooden. But deep inside, the rock that had once been his heart wept tears of blood.

Jenny swallowed her tears.

Thinking she heard the slap of oars against the water, she'd roused herself and tried to call out. The sound would not push past her tightly clamped lips. She threw every ounce of her remaining strength and will into it, but all that came out was a strangled peep.

It woke her.

She longed to turn and flee back into blessed unconsciousness, but that way lay death. At some time during the endless night, while the world burned around her, Jenny had made the hard decision to live. She owed it to Harris.

He had never given up on her, no matter how often she pushed him away. If by some miracle he was alive now, he would cling to life for her sake. Difficult as it might prove, she could do no less for him.

"Ye can't stay here any longer." She spoke the words aloud. Hearing a human voice, even her own, heartened her. "At least the fire's stopped burning."

She gazed at the seared tree trunks, stabbing the air like row upon row of ebony lances. A bitter wind whipped the last wisps of smoke heavenward.

"It's no use waiting for someone to come along and rescue ye," she scolded herself, "like Harris did at the wedding. Grow a backbone, lass!"

Steeling herself against the cold, she wallowed ashore. She gasped as the raw wind blasted her drenched clothes.

"D-d-don't just stand here and f-f-freeze, ye dolt. Move!"

She lurched up the gentle incline of the riverbank. Perhaps she could find a patch of charred moss to cower under while her clothes dried. Or a pocket of glowing embers by which to warm herself.

To her vast surprise, Jenny heard herself laugh. "T-to think I'd be longing for a fire so s-soon again."

Hearing the edge of hysteria in her laughter, she clamped a hand over her mouth to stifle it. To survive, she would need all her wits about her and they were already badly dulled from hunger and exhaustion.

She heard the slap of oars against the water, just like in

her dream. Oh, no—had she begun to hear imaginary noises? At first she tried to ignore the sound, convinced it could not be real. Only when it began to recede in the distance did Jenny believe her ears.

Scrambling over fallen timber and the ash that had once been underbrush, she cried out, "Stop! Help! I'm alive!"

She reached the water's edge just in time to see a small boat making its way upriver. Back into the Miramichi she waded up to her knees. Hands cupped around her mouth, she threw the dregs of her strength into cries for help.

"Turn 'round and come back, damn ye! Don't leave me to die here!"

It appeared the boatmen meant to do just that.

Jenny's voice faltered. Sobs shuddered through her.

What now? taunted a wee voice in the back of her mind. The same one that had asked her if she would ever quit running.

Roderick Douglas's voice. If she gave up now, who would ever make him pay for what he'd done to Harris?

"I don't know *what now,*" she growled, dashing the tears from her face. "But I'll think of something."

As she looked up again, squaring her shoulders to meet the next crisis, Jenny saw that the boat had turned and was rowing back toward her.

"Did ye hear that?"

Harris scanned the shore, desperately searching for some pocket of unscathed forest where survivors might huddle. Though he could see none, he was certain he'd heard a voice calling for help. Where had it come from?

"Still yer oars and let me listen!" he ordered the men Captain Glendenning had loaned him.

They rested as Harris strained to catch any sound from the shore. All he heard were the gulls wheeling overhead, their shrill cries mocking him. If only he could throw a net over a hundred or so of the creatures, like the hero of a

Jack-tale his grandfather had once told him. They would bear him aloft for a bird's eye view of...

Of whatever there was left to see.

Could his numbed heart withstand it—gathering up Jenny's burned body? Or would it thaw, showing him that he had depths of pain yet to plumb?

For years he had sheathed his heart in a protective mantle of ice, fearing the hurt only love could inflict. The greater the love, the sharper the weapon, the deeper the wound. Though a thick-enough coating of ice could blunt the sharpest sword, it was still vulnerable to the gentle warmth of the sun. Jenny had come into his life like sunshine, melting all his defenses, laying him bare to the unbearable.

Did he regret it?

Not for a minute.

Harris nodded to the oarsmen. "Go ahead and row, lads. My ears must've been playing tricks on me."

The boat began to move.

"What's that, back there?" One of the men pointed downriver.

Harris squinted in that direction. "The fallen tree, ye mean?"

"Near that. Whatever it is, it's moving."

"A deer, most likely."

"Never saw a deer that color."

The young fellow's eyes must be better than his own, for Harris could not properly make out any color. "Take us back for a look then."

As they rowed closer, it became evident that the figure was human. And he or she was wading out to meet them. The oarsmen put their backs into each stroke, shooting the small craft along, with a welcome push from the river's current.

It was a woman.

She raised one arm out of the water, waving. Her sleeve—what color was it? The lavender-gray of heather?

At first Harris refused to let himself believe it, for hope only opened the door to despair. At last, there came a moment when he could no longer deny it was Jenny.

Alive. Whole. His.

Harris threw himself into the Miramichi.

He half expected rapture to buoy him up and let him walk over the water.

"Harris!"

Seeing his own wonder mirrored in her face, it dawned on him that she'd despaired of his life, just as he had despaired of hers.

"Jenny! Oh, Jenny, lass!"

They grappled each other and all the power of hell could not have torn them apart. They kissed and time stood still. As if from a great distance, Harris heard the oarsmen cheering. Then, for an instant, a ray of sunlight broke through the clouds and the lingering pall of smoke.

Suffocated with panic, Jenny struggled to pull herself awake. She felt warm, and that was wrong.

The warmth of dry blankets. The warmth of hot food in her belly. Sweetest of all, the warmth of the man she loved pressed close against her. Surely it must be some trick of her mind beguiling her to surrender to sleep and death.

She woke gasping in Harris's arms.

"Wist, Jenny. Ye're with me, lass. It's over."

"Harris?" All was dark. "Where are we?"

"Aboard the *St. Bride*. Don't ye recognize yer ain berth? It's a mite snug, but that's all to the good. Ye were so cold when we brought ye here, I feared ye might never warm up."

She kissed him then, to further convince herself it was real. Kissed him deeply, possessively, longingly.

He responded in kind.

The tight confines of the berth gave them little room to maneuver, but that didn't matter. Their bodies blended together. Flesh rubbed against flesh, kindling an elemental heat. The barque rocked them in a seductive echo of the mating rhythm. They breathed the musk of each other's desire. She imbibed his intoxicating kisses and he hers— potent and delicious as Highland usquebaugh.

Their hands roamed, reassuring themselves that they were truly together again. Each drawing the other closer, as if it could be done.

Ah, but it could…

Jenny tugged Harris on top of her. A gurgle of pleasure and fulfillment gushed from her throat as he entered her.

A reunion in the sweetest, most personal sense.

The time had come for Harris and Jenny to sail away, leaving the devastation of the Miramichi behind them, like a bad dream. The prospect gnawed at Harris as he paced the dock, poisoning even the fresh joy of his *happily ever after* with Jenny.

There was so much here that needed doing, to meet the early winter. Otherwise the fire would claim more victims in its aftermath. For now, survivors were digging roasted potatoes out of the blackened fields to sustain them until help could arrive. They needed to build temporary shelters. They needed to distribute clothing and other essentials to those who had lost everything. They needed to tend the injured and to dig graves.

Knowing they'd need the kind of leadership Harris had provided during the fire, they had asked him to stay.

Harris pulled his coat tighter against the bitter wind.

Stay—how could he?

Jenny loved him. She had said it, she had shown it, and at last he believed it. But he also knew what Jenny believed about love—that adversity would kill it as surely as an autumn frost withered summer's choicest rose. Harris had no illusions that this wouldn't be a winter of painful adversity for the Miramichi. One followed by years of struggle and hardship to rebuild their settlement.

Could he bear to watch Jenny's love for him wither and die in such a harsh climate, turning to resentment…even hatred? Could he bear to watch it blight their children's upbringing as his and Jenny's had been blighted?

Yet how could he turn his back on people who needed him? People who had welcomed him into their community. People who had faced *their* fears to come to *his* aid.

So lost was he in perplexity that he scarcely noticed Jenny steal up beside him, until she rested her head against his arm.

"If I'd a penny, I'd offer it to ye for yer thoughts, Harris."

"Ye'd make a bad bargain then." He smiled down at her to soften the rueful tenor of his words.

"I doubt it." She clasped his hand and glanced up at him through her lashes. "Maybe there's something else I could exchange ye?"

That suggestion, together with her look of winsome mischief made his knees go weak. The wind wafted her unbound hair around her like a mantle of chestnut silk. The day's chill had nipped her cheeks to a vibrant pink. A man would be a fool not to follow her to the ends of the earth, if she lured him.

"I ken these folks'll have a hard winter ahead." He didn't mean to sound so gruff. But he continued, gruffer still. "They've asked me to stay, Jenny. They need someone to lead them, and I know I can do it."

She opened her mouth to speak.

Resisting the urge to hush her with a kiss, Harris hurried on. "I know how ye feel—that love can't last in hard times, but I ken ye're wrong, Jenny. We didn't fall in love at some fancy party or courting in a fine parlor. It was a storm that brought us together. Since then we've been through fire and flood and the wrath of Roderick Douglas. I *will* love ye for better or worse, Jenny. For richer for poorer. Can ye not love me that way, too? I'll go away from here, if ye ask me to, for ye mean everything in the world to me. But…''

He couldn't bring himself to say the rest. If Jenny chose to go, to run from adversity as she had so often in the past, what did it bode for their future together? He could not promise her a life of perfect happiness, no matter how much he wanted to. If trouble did find them one day, as was all too likely, would Jenny run from it again—and from him?

''Oh, Harris…''

He braced himself to hear her out.

''Of course we'll stay, if that's what ye want. As long as I have ye, nothing else matters. I know I used to reckon love was like a greenhouse flower, and maybe that's the way of it for some folks, poor souls. Ye've shown me another kind of love, though. It's strong and hardy as the heather. For all that, it's beautiful and sweet…and wild. Do ye mind what it says in the Good Book—'Whither thou goest, I will go'?''

Harris gathered her into his arms, too overcome to say anything more than ''Jenny. My ain Jenny.''

Epilogue

Chatham Gleaner, Oct. 1, 1850.

The Honorable Harris Chisholm and Mrs. Chisholm will be at home to their friends on the afternoon of Sunday, the seventh, to receive congratulations and good wishes upon the occasion of their silver wedding anniversary. Our Honorable Member wishes to thank constituents for returning him to office in the Legislative Assembly for a second term.

The family will also be celebrating a reunion of their happy circle as the Reverend Mr. Levi Chisholm, their second son, is now at home, having recently graduated from his seminary studies in Edinburgh. Eldest son, Mr. Angus, is the able manager of Cunard's local operation, while Miss Belinda and Miss Morag will be attending Mount Allison Academy next year. Mrs. Chisholm reports that a recent parlor concert to raise funds for a public library was a great financial success.

Readers of mature years may recollect that the happy couple were wed on the very eve of the Great Miramichi Fire, a conflagration not soon forgotten in our region. Despite such an inauspicious beginning to their union, they persevered through numerous hardships in those early years, to see their deep affection and mutual constancy amply fulfilled.

"Love is not love,
Which alters when it alteration finds,
Or bends with the remover to remove.
O, no! it is an ever-fixed mark,
That looks on tempests, and is never shaken.
It is the star to every wandering barque,
Whose worth's unknown, although his height be taken..."

Sonnet CXVI

* * * * *